PRAISE FOR CONNIE MANN

Deadly Melody

"Mann's book will take you on a wild ride. The main character is intriguing, well drawn, and brave. The romance is sizzling and the danger is palpable. A must-read for fans of romantic suspense!"
—Christy Barritt, bestselling romantic suspense author

"Mann is an exciting storyteller. *Deadly Melody* is the perfect combination of romance and suspense. I loved Cat and Nick. You will, too. Not to be missed."
—Rachel Hauck, *New York Times* bestselling author

"An engaging story that has it all—mystery, suspense, and a nice dose of sweet romance!"
—Cindy Kirk, bestselling author of the Good Hope series

Hidden Threat

"Once you start reading *Hidden Threat*, you'll find it nearly impossible to put down."
—Susan Sleeman, bestselling author and host of The Suspense Zone

"Connie Mann is my go-to suspense author. I read her books when I'm looking for escape and adventure, and when I feel like treating myself to a page-turner . . . Eve Jackson in *Hidden Threat* digs into an environmental issue we all face today. She will take you on a journey you'll never forget!"
—Sara Goff, author of *I Always Cry at Weddings*

"Connie Mann does it again. Her beautiful storytelling is fast-paced and exciting, but when she slows down and develops a star-crossed romance, she really shows off her skills. This is a great sequel to *Tangled Lies* and I can't wait to see what happens in the next installment of the Safe Harbor series."

—Lindsey P. Brackett, author of *Still Waters*

Tangled Lies

"Action and danger bring coastal Florida to life as compelling characters seek to unravel long-held secrets before time runs out. In *Tangled Lies*, Mann does it again . . . A surefire must-read."

—Lisa Carter, award-winning romantic-suspense author

"Connie Mann has penned a romantic suspense that captures the reader on the first page with a deadly secret and refuses to let go until the last word—masterful pacing."

—DiAnn Mills, bestselling author and Christy Award winner

"Connie Mann has crafted a unique suspense with the sea as a backdrop for hidden danger and exciting romantic interludes. Prepare to be swept away!"

—Katy Lee, RITA Award–nominated author

Angel Falls

"This heart-pounding novel doesn't stint on its characters . . . masterful."

—*RT Book Reviews*, four stars

"If you're looking for nonstop action and heart-pounding excitement, then *Angel Falls* is just the read you've been looking to find. Connie Mann deftly weaves danger and suspense into a story that left me sitting on the edge of my seat, flipping the pages."

—Debbie Macomber, #1 *New York Times* bestselling author

"A perfect blend of fast-paced thriller, inspiration, and romance."

—Fresh Fiction

"In *Angel Falls*, Connie Mann has penned an edgy, gritty book that pushes the boundaries of Christian romance fiction while giving readers a hero and heroine to root for."

—Irene Hannon, bestselling author of the Guardians of Justice series

"A riveting read starting with the first page all the way through the book."

—The Suspense Zone

"Dark, intense, and breathlessly paced, Connie Mann's edgy novel, *Angel Falls*, is exciting, romantic suspense that kept me guessing. With tight writing and fast-paced action, Connie does a fantastic job of grabbing the reader from the first page and never turning loose until the last. *Angel Falls* is not your usual Christian suspense. Filled with intrigue, murder, and sensuality, and set in Brazil's steamy underbelly, Connie's debut is riveting."

—Linda Goodnight, author of *A Snowglobe Christmas* and *Rancher's Refuge* and contributing author of the Prairie Romance Collection

"*Angel Falls* is a powerful read from the beginning with a hero and heroine who emotionally grip you and won't let go. The chemistry between Regina and Brooks along with the suspense keeps you riveted to the story."

—Margaret Daley, author of the Men of the Texas Rangers series

"Connie Mann takes her readers on the heart-stopping journey of a woman who puts her life on the line for an orphaned baby boy and her heart in the hands of the man who came to save them. It was a remarkable story I won't soon forget."

—Sharon Sala, author of the Rebel Ridge trilogy

Trapped!

"Romance, intrigue, and suspense with a Florida twist. Great read!"
—Captain Shelia Kerney, United States Coast Guard–licensed captain

"In *Trapped!* the author lets the reader feel the heat and sweat and smell the fear from unknown dangers along the river. Her fast pace and stunning conclusion will give the reader a fascinating ride."
—Martha Powers, award-winning author of *Death Angel, Bleeding Heart,* and *Sunflower*

DEADLY
MELODY

ALSO BY CONNIE MANN

The Safe Harbor Series

Tangled Lies
Hidden Threat

Other Titles

Angel Falls
Trapped!

DEADLY
MELODY
CONNIE MANN

Waterfall
PRESS

Text copyright © 2018 by Connie Neumann
All rights reserved.

No part of this book may be reproduced, or stored in a retrieval system, or transmitted in any form or by any means, electronic, mechanical, photocopying, recording, or otherwise, without express written permission of the publisher.

Published by Waterfall Press, Grand Haven, MI
www.brilliancepublishing.com

Amazon, the Amazon logo, and Waterfall Press are trademarks of Amazon.com, Inc., or its affiliates.

ISBN-13: 9781503901483
ISBN-10: 1503901483

Cover design by Faceout Studio, Lindy Martin

Printed in the United States of America

For my beautiful daughter, Michele Klopfenstein, whose eye for capturing moments with her camera is pure art and who fiercely champions those she cares about.
Go get 'em, love!

Chapter 1

Miami, Florida—Fourteen Years Ago

"We're going to do this right, Catharine," he insisted, smile confident as he took her hand.

Was she dreaming? Daniel Habersham was tall, blond, and charming, and Catharine Wang still couldn't quite believe the most popular boy at school even knew her name, let alone held her hand in public.

She ducked her head, hiding behind her straight dark hair. She couldn't meet his eyes, afraid he would see too much. "I think it would be better if I just, um, snuck out and met you at the dance." Anxiety fluttered beneath her skin, her palm sweaty against his. "It'll be easier."

He stopped, right there on the crowded sidewalk in front of the school. Students flowed around them and hurried to waiting luxury cars and limos to escape the sweltering Miami humidity. More than one girl sent a flirty smile Daniel's way and then scowled at Catharine immediately after.

"Are you ashamed to be seen with me, Catharine?"

"No, of course not!" How could she explain her uncle and the way she lived under his constant scrutiny? Or the late-night comings and goings at the penthouse, the hushed voices and snatches of conversation that made her terrified of what her uncle was doing just beyond her rigidly monitored life. She settled for, "My uncle doesn't like strangers. And he doesn't want me, um, dating anyone."

Daniel grinned, flashing his infectious smile and looking at her with those twinkling eyes that had first met hers across the aisle in math class months ago. "Ah, but we're going as just friends, right?"

She nodded, relieved. She had insisted. She could never tell him how much she wished it could be more, that they could be more. She could never hope for such a thing, never dare to reach that far and risk him turning away from her. Or risk her uncle's anger.

Daniel shrugged his broad shoulders. "Then it should be fine. I want to meet him. I want him to know I think you're awesome."

Catharine felt the blood rush to her face and ducked her head again. Confident, rich Daniel, loved by everyone, couldn't possibly know what his words meant to her. No one had ever called her awesome. Even her parents had only ever described her as merely adequate in her schooling, somewhat proficient in her violin playing—though not nearly as good as they thought she could be—and awkward socially. It was not the ringing endorsement a fourteen-year-old girl needed. But that had been the best she'd ever heard from them.

Eight months ago, the train they'd all been on en route to a performance with the Indianapolis Symphony had crashed. Her parents had both been killed; Catharine, who had been wandering another section of the train, had survived. She squeezed her eyes shut against the images of the crash and instead focused on the dramatic changes in her life since then. Her father's brother, Richard Wang, whom she'd never met before, had swept her out of her ordinary Midwestern life and plunked her down in a luxurious Miami high-rise filled with secrets. She'd felt invisible with her parents. Now she tried to stay invisible in order to navigate this frightening new world.

They reached the black Mercedes where a driver waited to take Catharine home. Phillip straightened from where he lounged against the car and eyed Daniel from behind his dark sunglasses.

"Daniel is coming home with me today to meet Uncle." She was proud that her voice didn't shake.

Phillip gave a short nod and held the back door open. Catharine slid into the car and Daniel followed. She watched Phillip, sure he would call her uncle to warn him, but he didn't.

Inside the car, Daniel sent her a confident look and took her hand, giving it a quick squeeze before he let go. She wanted to snatch back his hand, try to absorb some of his confidence, but one glance in the mirror at the grim expression on Phillip's face, and she curled her hand into a fist instead.

Daniel leaned closer. "Does your uncle not want you to bring friends home?"

"He wants me to focus on my music and my studies." It wasn't really an answer, and Daniel's raised eyebrow said as much.

She shrugged, like an idiot. What was there to say? Her uncle had made it clear that her focus in life was to be on her music and her schooling, in that order. He did not want her to waste time socializing. And she was much too young to date. In that way, he was very much like his brother, her late father, devoted to the traditional Chinese cultural ideals of family and accomplishment, to the exclusion of emotional complications.

From her parents, Catharine had learned to hide her feelings, to keep them from ever showing on her face. Her classmates called her cold and distant. Little did they know she felt too much, had to work to hide the hurt and the loneliness.

Then four months ago, she'd met Daniel, with his bright, sunny personality. Somehow, he'd sought her out. She would never tell him this, but he was her very first real friend. She'd tried to befriend girls over the years, but whenever she'd started getting close, they pulled away. She wondered if her parents had somehow intervened but then felt guilty for thinking that. It was probably her shyness and social awkwardness that drove them away. She knew she was either too needy or too distant and had never learned to strike the right balance. What came naturally to those around her seemed awkward for her.

Now here was Daniel, steamrolling his way into her life with his kindness and confidence and a family who loved him. She didn't understand why he wanted to be her friend, and she lived in fear of doing something to make him turn away in disgust or disappointment, as her parents had so often done with her.

The closer they got to the condo, the faster Catharine's heart beat. Dread grew inside her like a living thing. Why had she let him talk her into this?

All too soon, they slid up to the curb, and the doorman hurried over to open the door. Catharine sent him a weak smile and followed Phillip to the elevator, where he held the door for them to precede him, then followed them inside.

When the elevator doors opened at the penthouse, Catharine let out a relieved breath. There was no sign of her uncle, though crossing the threshold, she could hear his voice, angry but controlled, coming from his study just off the foyer. The other voice seemed familiar, but she couldn't place it immediately.

"Wait here," Phillip said to Daniel and then went to the partially open study door and knocked. He slipped inside, and moments later, the door opened wide and her uncle stepped out, gray suit impeccable, a smile on his face. "Catharine, come in. And bring your friend."

Daniel gave her an I-told-you-so smile, but she wasn't fooled. Her uncle's rigid posture gave his anger away. Though she hoped it had to do with the interrupted argument, and not with her. Or Daniel.

"Hello, Catharine." Her uncle leaned over and kissed her cheek, then extended his hand to Daniel. "I am Richard Wang, Catharine's uncle. And you are?"

Daniel shook hands. "Daniel Habersham, sir. Very nice to meet you."

Her uncle led them into the study, where a heavyset man with a swarthy complexion sat smoking a Cuban cigar. He rose and also extended a hand.

"This is Carlos Garcia, my associate."

More hand shaking, then her uncle waved them to seats on the sofa. Behind them, a wall of windows overlooked the ocean, where departing ships made Catharine long for an escape from her narrow life here.

The housekeeper appeared in the doorway, and her uncle gestured to her. "Mrs. Chen, would you fetch us some refreshment, please, while we get acquainted?" Then he turned to Daniel. "Catharine has not brought a friend home with her before." He shot her a look. "She is usually too busy with her studies and her music lessons." He made a point of checking his Rolex. "You have a lesson this afternoon, yes?"

"Yes, Uncle. In a little while." She took a deep breath, unsure of what else to say. They made small talk until the housekeeper returned with a tray of drinks, which she set on the credenza before leaving the room.

Mr. Garcia went to the tray and picked up the pitcher. He looked over his shoulder and smiled as he poured them each a glass. "Virgin mojitos for the youngsters." Catharine hid her surprise at how relaxed he seemed in her uncle's space.

"Your father is in real estate, isn't he, Daniel?" Uncle asked.

Catharine marveled at the casual way Daniel answered her uncle's questions, completely comfortable in his own skin. Then she switched her attention to her uncle and the hard look in his eyes. The fact that he knew all about Daniel's family made her hands want to shake. How did he even know she and Daniel were friends?

Mr. Garcia carried the tray over and set it on the coffee table in front of the sofa she and Daniel were sitting on, then took a seat in the armchair next to her uncle, facing them. He raised his glass. "To new friends!"

They all raised their glasses and drank. Catharine wasn't a big fan of the lime-and-mint cocktail, but here in Miami, it seemed to be the drink of choice.

"So, Daniel. What exactly is your relationship with our Catharine?" her uncle asked.

Catharine choked on her drink, and nobody spoke while she coughed. Daniel winked at her before he turned back to her uncle.

"Catharine is a beautiful, immensely talented young lady, and I am proud to call her my friend. I came by to ask if I could escort her to the upcoming dance, with your permission, of course."

Her uncle glanced from one to the other, expression carefully bland. "Is she your girlfriend?"

"No, sir. Catharine says her focus is on her music and her studies."

"But you would like to be more than friends."

He sent her uncle that lopsided grin that always made Catharine's stomach flip. "If she'd have me, I'd be honored. But I respect her. And her wishes."

Catharine had never been more proud of Daniel—or felt more cared for in her life. Had he really meant all those things he'd said, or were they strictly for her uncle's benefit?

Her uncle pierced her with a hard stare. "Catharine, please go upstairs and work on your studies while the men continue our conversation."

She wanted to refuse, because something about the look that passed between Garcia and her uncle tightened the knot in her stomach. She tried to protest, but no words came out. Daniel smiled encouragement, and she slowly rose from the couch, nodded to her uncle, and left the room.

Phillip stood outside and closed the door behind her.

Catharine started up the stairs, then stopped on the landing and waited. She heard Phillip's shoes on the tile, then a slight squeak when he sat down in a chair opposite the study door. Fortunately, it was just out of view of the stairs.

Heart pounding, she slipped off her shoes and tiptoed back down, then crossed the hall and went into the library next door to her uncle's study. She left the door slightly ajar so she could hear if anyone approached, then eased over the tile floor to just below the air-conditioning vent in the ceiling, right by the study wall. She'd discovered when she first came here that if she stood flat against the wall, she could hear what was being said in the study.

As a rule, she felt guilty for eavesdropping but not guilty enough to stop doing it. How else would she know what both Phillip and the housekeeper reported to her uncle about her?

Now, though, she had to know what he was saying to Daniel.

She took several deep breaths to slow her rapid breathing. Then she waited.

"No, sir. I respect Catharine. I told you that. She just wants to be friends. So that's what we are."

"Are you trying to tell me you've never touched her? A young buck like you? She's a good-looking girl."

She heard movement and pictured Daniel leaping to his feet. "That's what I'm saying. Just because she's beautiful doesn't mean I would take advantage."

"So you've never kissed her?"

Silence. Catharine's palms started to sweat. Would he admit to that one awkward moment when he'd stolen a quick kiss and she'd been so surprised she smacked her head into his? They'd laughed about it then, but the memory mortified her now.

"I did give her a quick kiss on the lips, once. She was horrified and said we should just be friends, so that was the end of it."

"What if I don't believe you?" her uncle asked smoothly.

"I'm sorry if you don't, but it's the truth. You can ask Catharine."

"Oh, I plan to. Make no mistake about that."

Catharine tensed, ready to rush back upstairs in case they came looking for her. But then she heard an awful choking noise.

"Daniel? Are you all right?" She heard pounding, as though her uncle was thumping Daniel on his back.

She waited for Daniel to say something, but he just kept coughing and choking while her uncle pounded his back.

"Get me some water," her uncle barked.

Catharine had turned to race into the other room when the choking abruptly stopped. She froze. Her heart raced as the silence lengthened. What was happening?

Her uncle muttered a curse. "How much Devil's Breath did you give him, Garcia?"

"Not too much. Just enough to be sure he told the truth."

A pause. "It was too much. He's not breathing."

Catharine shook her head, trying to make sense of the words. *Not breathing? Well, then do something! Help him.*

She clamped her jaw to keep from crying out as indecision swamped her. Listen? Or run to help?

"He's dead." Garcia's voice was flat.

Catharine reared back as though she'd been struck. This couldn't be happening. She had to see for herself, to help, but some sixth sense kept her frozen in place. Her feet felt nailed to the floor.

"Get out of here, Garcia. Now. I'll deal with this." Her uncle's voice was brisk, businesslike.

"Calm down and get me a duffel bag. I'll take care of the body."

Nausea climbed into Catharine's throat. A duffel bag?

Garcia's voice hardened. "You just deal with Catharine. I want her delivered as agreed. I won't wait any longer."

Catharine shivered, trying to make sense of his words. What did he mean exactly?

"This changes things," her uncle said evenly.

"It changes nothing. I believe the boy. Her virginity is intact. I'll expect you to keep your end of the bargain. I'll make the body disappear. You get Catharine ready."

"Look, Garcia, I'll get you the money. I told you that. I just need a little more time—"

"You are out of time. I want the girl. And I will have her. Today."

A long pause followed. Catharine held her breath as she waited for her uncle to shout a protest, to express his indignation. Instead, his casual words shattered her world. "All right. Fine. You will have her."

Had she heard right? Was her uncle really giving her to Garcia, with his lecherous eyes and grabby hands? Surely she was dreaming and would wake up in her sterile twin bed, covers tangled around her, and realize it was nothing but a nightmare.

But when she heard footsteps on the tiles in the hallway, urgency propelled her into motion. She peeked around the door, checked to be sure Phillip wasn't there, then leaped across the hall and raced up the stairs to her room. She ran right into her bathroom and threw up. Then she leaned against the locked door, hands shaking. Had she really heard what she thought she had? Or had the words been distorted by the air vent?

But in her heart, she knew it was true. Scary-looking people came to the condo at odd hours with bodyguards in tow. She'd overheard enough to know it had something to do with drugs. Tears ran down her cheeks, and she let them fall. How could this be? Had they really given Daniel something called Devil's Breath? Just because he wanted to take her to the dance? *Oh, Daniel!*

Nausea churned as she replayed the rest of the conversation. They'd been talking about her virginity like it was a commodity. Deliver her? She twisted her hands together to stop their shaking. Without batting an eye, her uncle had promised her to Garcia. She had led a pretty sheltered life, but she understood what that meant, and it terrified her. Had they really killed Daniel over it?

She turned and threw up again, heaving until there was nothing left in her system.

Maybe Daniel wasn't really dead; maybe they'd been wrong. Maybe he was just unconscious. She had to try to save him. Somehow. She had to. She could call 911. The paramedics would know what to do. She had her hand on the doorknob, ready to run down the stairs and prove it was all some crazy mistake or get to a phone and call for help, when she heard footsteps coming up toward her room. She wiped her eyes and splashed water on her face. Her uncle. Or Phillip. *Oh God.*

Her heart raced like a runaway train, but her head suddenly cleared. She had to think. If this nightmare was all actually true, she had to pretend she knew nothing. Otherwise, who knew what her uncle might do?

Somehow, she had to find out where they were taking Daniel. Try to save him. She didn't think for a second that Garcia would take Daniel to his house, so letting them bring her there wouldn't help. She'd have to bide her time, then escape. But for now, she'd hide behind the invisible, passive persona she'd adopted for most of her life.

When her uncle knocked on the bedroom door, she stayed where she was. "I'll be right out." She made her voice sound weak and shaky, which wasn't hard to do at that moment.

"Are you all right, Catharine?"

She leaned over the toilet and pretended to heave some more. Then she flushed and ran water in the sink, swished mouthwash. "I am not sure what it was, but I think today's school lunch did not agree with me," she said wanly as she opened the door. She gripped the knob like a lifeline, all the accusations crowding her tongue begging to escape, but she wouldn't let them loose. Daniel's life might depend on her acting ability right now. She kept her head down, as was her custom, and didn't look her uncle in the eye. But she could only carry the charade so far. If he looked too closely, he'd see her fury. She couldn't allow that.

"I am sorry to hear it." In a surprising move, he touched her shoulder, then quickly pulled his hand away. She didn't think he'd ever offered comfort before. She nodded and kept her eyes averted.

"I will have Mrs. Chen send up a tray with tea and toast."

"Thank you, Uncle." She looked past his shoulder. "Where's Daniel?"

"That is what I was coming to tell you. He said to give you his regrets. He had to leave, but he will see you at the dance tomorrow night."

Hope sprang up in Catharine's heart. He was all right. She'd misunderstood, somehow. He'd just been unconscious. Everything would be OK.

"Phillip will drive you to your music lesson in"—he checked his watch—"one hour. Kindly be ready."

After her uncle left, she collapsed on the bed, shaking. It was what he hadn't said that terrified her. Phillip would take her to Garcia, though whether before her lesson or after, she didn't know. She prayed with every fiber of her being that Daniel really was OK, but the two men's casual dismissal of him, their indifference, filled her with doubt.

She swallowed hard and tears slid down her face as she pictured his smile and easy manner.

Curling into a ball as grief overwhelmed her, she let the tears fall until there were no more. Gradually, through her grief, a stone-cold determination grew. She sat up and wiped her cheeks. No more tears. They solved nothing.

If Daniel really was dead, somehow, some way, she would figure out how to make her uncle and Garcia pay. Her uncle might not have given him the drug, but he was there. He'd allowed it to happen and he didn't care. That part was the worst of it. Daniel's life didn't matter to them. Who were these people? Her parents had been distant, but not without hearts, without souls.

First, though, she had to get out of here. Then she'd find Daniel. Until she knew for sure that he was dead, she wouldn't give up hope.

Glancing at her watch, she realized she didn't have much time until they came for her. She made her way downstairs to the kitchen. "Hello, Mrs. Chen." She nodded to the tray with tea and toast waiting on the counter. "Is that for me?"

"I was just about to bring it to you."

Catharine forced a smile. "I'll just eat it here, if that's all right." She looked around the stark, utilitarian room with its wall of windows. "I like it here."

Mrs. Chen eyed her with suspicion but then waved a hand and went about her business, checking the roast in the oven. The smell made Catharine's stomach roil, but she swallowed hard and pretended this was just another day. When the intercom sounded and her uncle requested a drink, Catharine saw her opportunity.

The minute the door closed behind the housekeeper, she hurried to the kitchen desk and pulled open the drawer where the household cash was kept. She'd stumbled upon Mrs. Chen putting bills in her apron one day, so she knew where to look. Worried she'd get caught, she quickly counted out ten hundred-dollar bills and stuffed them in the pocket of her school uniform.

She made it back to the table and picked up her tea just as Mrs. Chen hurried into the room.

Catharine finished her toast, thanked Mrs. Chen, and slowly walked upstairs, feigning weakness.

Once in her room, she stashed the money in her violin case. Then she changed out of her school uniform and into a blue blouse, dark slacks, and comfortable shoes, so she could run. She tucked Daniel's school picture and a photo of her parents into her violin case alongside the cash, then looked around the room. There was nothing else here she needed or wanted.

With a deep breath for courage, she picked up her mother's violin and walked calmly downstairs just as Phillip rose from his chair. "Are you ready, Miss Catharine?"

"Yes. Thank you." She glanced at the closed door to her uncle's study, but it didn't open. She let out a sigh of relief.

She tried to stay calm as they drove through the city, but desperation clawed at her. How was she going to get away from Phillip? Would he take her straight to Garcia?

When Catharine realized he was taking her to Mrs. Wu's second-floor apartment in a less-affluent part of the city, relief and hope shot through her. She had an idea.

The elderly lady shuffled to the door, nodded to Phillip, and then led Catharine inside with a tight grip of her bony fingers, as always. "Have you been practicing?"

"Yes, Mrs. Wu. Every day."

The older woman eyed her with the same disdain she'd sometimes seen in her mother's eyes. "Let us hope it will finally make a difference."

Catharine nodded, eyes downcast as expected. Then she gripped her stomach with one hand, violin still in the other, and made a moaning sound. "Bathroom, sorry," she gasped and ran down the hall to the small bathroom at the end. Once inside, she locked the door and spun to the small window. She unlocked it and tried to open it, but it was stuck.

"Miss Wang? What is going on?"

Catharine made a retching sound, then flushed the toilet to cover her grunt as she shoved the window open. It finally eased up enough for her to squeeze through. She pushed her violin case out onto the fire escape, then stepped up on the toilet seat and climbed out. She looked down. Phillip stood by the car, but unless he looked over his shoulder and up to the corner of the building, he wouldn't see her. She had to hurry.

She tiptoed down the metal stairs and stopped when she reached the ladder. If she lowered it to reach the ground, the noise would alert him.

She glanced at the sidewalk below, then at the hedge that separated Mrs. Wu's building from the next one. It would have to do.

Clutching her violin, she climbed down as far as she could, then leaped out and into the hedge, making sure she didn't utter a sound when she crashed. Twigs and branches poked her, and she was scratched all over, but she lay perfectly still, panting, hoping Phillip hadn't heard.

When he didn't burst around the corner, she carefully climbed out of the hedge, relieved she hadn't broken anything. She brushed the leaves from her clothes, picked up her violin case, and eased down the alley between the buildings. Once she was out of sight, she picked up her pace, racing from one alley to the next, her only thought to escape before they realized she was gone.

By the time Mrs. Wu stumbled downstairs and told Phillip that Catharine had climbed out the window, she was on a bus headed across town, wearing a baseball cap and dark sunglasses.

With nothing but her mother's violin and some stolen cash, Catharine Wang disappeared.

Chapter 2

Present Day—Nashville, Tennessee

The No Name Café was crowded, as always on Thursdays. To those who came every week to hear the band, tonight was no different from any other. But the woman known as Cat Johnson knew something was off. She couldn't settle, couldn't shake the dread that rolled through the smoke-filled room like an approaching storm. As she did before every show, she peeked through the curtain and studied the crowd, making sure there were no familiar faces. Just in case.

Everything looked as it should. Yet the nagging worry that had been expanding in her belly had grown fur and fangs and dug deep. Fear clawed at her heart with every minute that passed without a word from Joellen. There could be a simple, logical explanation. Maybe the sixteen-year-old runaway was sick, had lost her phone—but Cat's gut wasn't buying it. Something was wrong. She'd go track her down, Cat decided. The minute the show ended.

She scanned the crowd through her light-blue-tinted sunglasses once more. Reassured she was safe, for now, she smiled as she stepped onto the stage, her wide performer's grin as much a part of her getup as the short-shorts and boots. She bowed at the hearty applause, careful of her braided blonde wig, and willed the worry away, at least until her set was over.

She grinned at her bandmates and slipped into the persona she'd perfected over the years. The band started the Charlie Daniels Band's "The Devil Went Down to Georgia," and her eyes twinkled behind the tinted sunglasses and colored contacts. The crowd cheered. With a silent apology to her late mother and her classical training, she lifted her mother's priceless violin and let herself get lost in the music.

"Great job tonight, Cat," Walt Simms said later, sliding a big glass of water her way. The balding club owner smiled, showing the gap in his front teeth. "The crowd loves you."

Cat gulped half the water before she set the glass down and shrugged. "I enjoy playing."

"That's obvious. Just as it's always been obvious you're way too talented—and too well trained—to be playing in a little dive like this one."

"Come on, Walt. Nobody's beating a path to my door. Besides, I like it here." She leaned closer. "I didn't see Joellen come in. Did she show up tonight?"

Walt had hired her to wash dishes, at Cat's pleading, even though he didn't need additional help. His eyes filled with pity and he looked away, busied himself drying a glass.

An icy chill slid down her spine. She leaned closer. "Walt? What do you know? You're scaring me."

Instead of answering, he reached under the bar and pulled out a copy of the *Tennessean*. "I didn't want to tell you before you went onstage. Bottom of page six. Sorry, kiddo."

Cat's hands shook as she flipped pages until she found the right one. Her heart slammed into her chest as she recognized the face in the crime scene photo. "I have to go."

Cat cracked one eye open and glared at the sunlight streaming through the tiny window in her studio apartment. Her heart pounded as she tried to orient herself, get her bearings, remember what had happened, but the sick feeling of dread sloshing in her belly told her she didn't really want to. Not yet.

Something crinkled under her face, and she slowly rolled over and pulled the newspaper free. Swallowing the nausea, she waited for the room to stop spinning before she eased both eyes open and attempted to focus.

LOCAL PROSTITUTE FOUND BEATEN TO DEATH

The careless headline at the bottom of page six acted like a bucket of cold water. Cat's mind cleared, and the anger came rushing back. She snapped her eyes shut and slammed a fist on the sagging mattress. The article said the girl, known as Star to those who frequented her corner of Nashville, had no identification and had been listed as a Jane Doe by the coroner. "Her name is Joellen," Cat shouted. The sound slammed against her aching head and brought her surging to her feet.

Getting up proved a mistake, as Cat found herself on the bathroom floor a little while later, shivering, hatred and anger still churning in her gut. Worse, self-recrimination beat down on her like a cat-o'-nine-tails.

She leaned her head against the bilious green tile. She should have saved Joellen, gotten her away from her pimp and put her on a bus back to her family in Oklahoma, no matter how often Joellen claimed she was fine, that she had everything under control. She hadn't been fine, and she hadn't been safe, and Cat had known that with every fiber of her being. She'd tried to teach her capoeira, Brazilian self-defense, but she knew it wasn't enough to protect her from the monster she worked for. Cat should have forced her onto a bus, anyway. Sent her somewhere far from here, somewhere safe.

But Joellen wouldn't go. Even after Cat had begged her.

Two days ago, she'd disappeared. And now she was dead.

It was Cat's fault, and that knowledge made it hard to breathe. She staggered to her feet and swiped at the frustrated tears running down her cheeks. "Why wouldn't you listen, Joellen?" she whispered. "You crazy girl. You knew he'd never let you go." She gripped the sink. "Why wouldn't you let me help you?"

The words hovered in the air as Cat splashed water on her face. She accidentally glanced at the mirror and froze when she saw her reflection. She was a mess—a scrawny, hungover, worthless mess.

Her cell phone buzzed from the other room, and Cat held on to the wall as she made her way to the rickety end table. She scooped up her cheap burner phone as she sank onto the musty sofa. She eyed the empty tequila bottle, and her stomach threatened another revolt.

The text was from Eve. Was this text number forty-two? Or maybe forty-three? If this kept up, she'd have to get another phone. Again.

Please, Cat. Come home. My wedding won't be right without you there. Will you play your violin? For me? Please? Let me know.

Cat tossed the phone on the sofa and leaned her head back. Something niggled in the corners of her mind as she realized how much sunlight hit the threadbare carpet. She sat up, fought a wave of dizziness, and tried to think. What day was it? There was something she was supposed to do . . .

"Mrs. Fletcher! Oh no." One look at the clock, and she knew she was really, really late.

She leaped to her feet and staggered to the kitchen alcove where she swallowed several ibuprofen while she heated instant coffee in the microwave and choked down a piece of dry toast.

Ten minutes and one quick shower later, she left her apartment and crossed the hall, the tap of her cowboy boots on the wood floor making her wince. At the last second, she'd stopped to tuck her hair under her blonde wig and pull on her usual jeans, Western shirt, and horn-rimmed glasses. Now was not the time to get sloppy.

"Mrs. Fletcher? It's Cat." She knocked on the door and waited, but no sound came from inside. Usually, her elderly neighbor was waiting by the door for her. But usually Cat wasn't—she checked her phone—three hours late, either. "Mrs. Fletcher?"

Footsteps sounded from inside just before the door was wrenched open. Cat found herself face-to-face with two hundred pounds of annoyed male. "What do you want?"

"Um, hi. I'm Cat. Mrs. Fletcher's neighbor. Who are you?"

He crossed flabby arms over a sagging gut and regarded her from under a dirty ball cap. "I'm her son."

Cat narrowed her eyes. "I didn't know she had any family nearby."

"I live over near Knoxville. I got called when they took her to the hospital."

"The hospital?" Cat waited for more, but some deep part of her already knew. "When?"

"This morning. Dang fool old woman tried to go down the stairs by herself and fell. Tripped over her walker and broke her hip."

Cat gripped the doorframe and swallowed hard. "I'm so sorry. Can you tell me which hospital they took her to?"

"Nashville General. Wait. She said someone was supposed to take her to the doctor this morning. Was that you?"

She felt the color drain from her face. "I have to go. Thank you."

"It *was* you! Stay away from my mother, you hear? You've done enough."

After he slammed the door in her face, Cat slumped against the wall. She was a horrible person. Every instinct urged her to return to her apartment, pull the covers over her head, and hide. No matter what she did, she failed the people she cared about. It was hopeless, so why even bother?

But then she remembered Mrs. Fletcher's kindness and decided she wasn't that much of a coward. Not yet.

She headed for the hospital and found the birdlike white-haired lady tucked in a curtained alcove in the emergency department. Despite her obvious pain, her eyes lit up when she saw Cat, which stopped Cat in her tracks.

"Oh, Cat. How lovely of you to come to see me. Come here and let me hug you, child."

Cat carefully leaned down and gave her a gentle hug. Then she pulled a chair over and took the older lady's hand. "Mrs. Fletcher, I can't tell you how sorry I am that I wasn't there this morning. I let you down and now you're here. I'm so sorry. You should have banged on my door."

Mrs. Fletcher patted her hand. "I did, my dear, but you didn't hear me. You were sobbing too loudly to hear anyone. Are you all right?"

Shame flooded Cat's face. "I should be asking you that, not the other way around. And I should have been there to help you down the stairs and get you to the doctor. This is all my fault."

Mrs. Fletcher snorted. "Your fault? Not on your life, dear girl. Despite what my son thinks, I'm fully capable of making my own decisions—and taking responsibility for them. I could have cancelled my appointment and gone with you another day, but I didn't want to. I decided to go alone. That is not your fault—and I won't let you steal my independence by taking responsibility for it and for me."

They stared into each other's eyes until the caring in Mrs. Fletcher's gaze forced Cat to look away. "Yes, you are fully capable of making your own decisions. But I let you down, and I'll have to live with that."

Mrs. Fletcher gripped Cat's hand, forcing her to look at her again. "Let it go, Cat. This is not your fault." She paused. "Can you tell me what had you crying your heart out all through the night?"

Cat swallowed, her throat raw. "A friend of mine . . . was killed. She was beaten to death."

The older woman's eyes filled with tears. "Oh, that poor girl. How terrible. For her. And for you."

"She wouldn't let me help her," Cat whispered. Her phone chirped, and she glanced at it to see yet another text from Eve.

"Who is looking for you? Are you in trouble?"

If you only knew. Cat met the woman's kind eyes and decided to tell her, at least a little bit of the truth, which was more than she usually did. "It's my foster sister Eve. She's getting married and wants me to come home for the wedding."

"Then go home, Cat. Maybe it's time to stop running, to stop hiding who you really are." Mrs. Fletcher glanced at the blonde wig, and Cat resisted the urge to make sure it was still in place. "Family is what matters."

The words tempted Cat, like snatches of a melody that drifted on the night breeze. But then reality slapped her, hard. She couldn't go home. Even if she belonged in Safe Harbor—which she most definitely did not—she couldn't go back permanently, not without putting those she loved in danger. The idea was crazy.

But maybe, just maybe, she could pop in for the wedding and sneak out again before her uncle or Garcia found her.

Cat stood and kissed the woman's papery cheek. "I'll miss you." She hadn't realized she'd decided to leave until the words popped out of her mouth. She'd gone home for Mama Rosa's birthday party several months ago, and nothing bad had happened, so maybe she could do it again. Just in and out. Maybe she could do the right thing for once.

After that, she'd decide where to go next.

"I'll be praying you find your way home, Cat. Godspeed."

Cat knew she'd never truly have a home, not the way Mrs. Fletcher meant, because she'd never be able to stop running. But as she climbed into the nondescript little car Walt had loaned her, she pulled out her phone and texted Eve: Stop hounding me. I'll be there tomorrow.

Several hours later, Cat had collected her last paycheck, apologized to Walt, and thanked him again for the use of his car. One of the waitresses had been happy to move into her apartment. Cat packed her duffel bag and violin and headed south. The day Sal Martinelli had found fourteen-year-old Cat hiding behind the Safe Harbor Marina, the Martinellis had taken her in and made her part of their family. She only hoped she wasn't bringing danger to their doorstep.

———

Two days later, Safe Harbor police officer Nick Stanton pulled up at Sutton Ranch and climbed out of his personal pickup. Every instinct urged him to hightail it out of there. He ran his finger under the collar of his starched white shirt and his brand-new tie and wished he had the courage to walk away. But he couldn't. He'd given Eve his word. And after the childhood he'd had, and the lies his adoptive parents had told, he'd sworn his word would mean something. But he didn't want to be there.

No, that wasn't right. He didn't know how to be here, surrounded by all the Martinellis. His family, but not really. Not yet. Maybe never. He was still trying to wrap his brain around the fact that he'd been born Tony Martinelli, Sal and Rosa's biological son. The people he'd thought were his parents, the Stantons, had been friends of the Martinellis and had kidnapped him when he was three and raised him as their own. Who did something like that? His adoptive parents were both dead now, so he couldn't even question them about it. Everything he'd believed about his childhood had been yanked away when the truth had come out a few months ago, and now he stood at the fringes of the Martinelli clan, awkward and unsure. How were you supposed to act around people you were related to but barely knew?

He approached the ranch house and was intercepted by sixteen-year-old Blaze, the newest Martinelli foster child. Her hair had a green stripe in it for the occasion, and if he was not mistaken, she had her combat boots on under her long dress. She took his arm and glanced at his face as they marched along. "You look like you're gonna puke, Nick. It's a wedding, not a firing squad. Sheesh. Besides, you're not the guy getting hitched."

That surprised a laugh out of him. "Thank you, Dr. Phil. You're right." He patted her hand and followed her into the house. After an awkward almost-hug with his biological father, Sal Martinelli, and a too-tight hug from his mother, Rosa Martinelli, he spotted Eve and some of his trepidation fell away.

Eve leaned over and kissed his cheek. "Thanks for doing this, Nick. Being around us will get less weird over time, I promise."

"I hope you're right. You ready?"

When she nodded, they headed toward the barn that had been decked out for the wedding at the groom's family ranch. Hay bales covered in canvas created rows of seating to one side while a dance floor and long tables lined the other side of the huge building, awaiting the reception. The smooth strains of a violin played as Nick and Sal walked Eve down the makeshift aisle. After they'd handed the bride off to a grinning Cole Sutton, Nick took his seat in the second row, but he couldn't take his eyes off the woman tucked in the corner playing the violin.

This must be Cat, the Martinelli foster sister he'd never met. She was more than beautiful. Chin-length straight dark hair, porcelain skin, and almond-shaped brown eyes. She was too thin, though, and he wondered about the shadows under her eyes, eyes she mostly kept closed as she played. The music, haunting and beautiful, drew him in like nothing he'd ever heard before. It didn't sound familiar, and he wondered if she'd written it herself.

As Mama Rosa sniffled into her handkerchief in the row in front of him and the preacher's words floated over a grinning Eve and Cole, Nick's gaze kept straying to Cat. Their eyes met for one split second, and a jolt of awareness pricked him like a sharp stick. He glanced away, unsettled by the unexpected connection.

As the preacher droned on, he kept his eyes focused squarely on Eve and Cole. That was why he was here. When he accidently glanced Cat's way again, he caught her eyeing him, too.

Annoyed with himself, he looked anywhere but where she stood until the ceremony ended. Once he made it outside, he loosened his tie and chatted with the other guests.

He didn't see her come out of the barn, but then, he reminded himself, he wasn't looking for her.

———

Cat knew the minute he walked back into the barn during the reception. Tall and powerfully built, he had that special something people noticed. She certainly did. She might have faltered as she played, but years of practice kept the music flowing effortlessly, despite her hyper-awareness of him. She forced herself to focus on the music for several minutes before she allowed herself to look up again. But she knew he'd been watching her the whole time, propped against the wall, his arms folded as if he had nothing more important to do all day than watch her.

She met his gaze, and this time, she did miss a note. She corrected and kept playing, eyes locked with his. Something shimmered in the depths of his brown eyes, a familiar sadness and bone-deep weariness she knew too well. She saw the same thing in the mirror whenever she dared to look. That kinship pulled her in like a powerful piece of music, drawing her ever closer.

Who was he? From his gaze, she knew he felt the same connection, the same recognition of a kindred spirit. Then he smiled, a slow, easy grin, and Cat felt it all the way to her toes. How long had it been since a man had looked at her that way? Had looked at her at all? She couldn't say, especially since she took great pains to be invisible.

She shifted in the unfamiliar flowing dress, feeling exposed without her usual disguise. In her Western clothes and wig, she knew how to blend in. But here, like this? She felt naked and vulnerable.

She finished the piece and bent to put her violin away. She'd just go get an appetizer, sneak out the back door. The DJ was getting ready to take over the music, anyway. Nobody would miss her.

But as she stood, she turned and almost ran into him. She hadn't heard him move, and that alarmed her. Staying aware of her surroundings kept her alive.

He reached out a hand to steady her, and Cat jerked at the shock of his touch. How long had it been since a man had touched her?

"Sorry, didn't mean to startle you. Just wanted to tell you how much I enjoyed your playing. At the ceremony and just now."

"Thank you. Now if you'll—"

"Have you played long?" He had to know she was trying to get away, but his grin said he wasn't giving up that easily.

Cat shook her head. "All my life, I think. I started when I was three."

"Seriously? Wow."

"My parents were musicians. My mother played the violin. My father, the cello."

"That must have been really cool growing up, all that music in the house."

His words touched a spot she kept hidden and made her wish she hadn't said anything. "It might have been, if they had shared it. They died when I was fourteen."

She turned away, but again, he put a light hand on her arm to stop her. "I'm sorry. That must have been horrible."

Cat shrugged, uncomfortable with his caring. "You get used to it."

He met her eyes and shook his head. "You never get used to it. You learn to live around it."

While Cat tried to figure out what to say, the DJ started a slow ballad. The man held out his hand. "May I have this dance?"

———

He thought she'd refuse, but she surprised him when she nodded and let him lead her out onto the dance floor. Nick couldn't remember the last time he'd danced, but right then it didn't matter. She fit into his arms like she belonged there, though he made sure to keep a nice respectable distance between them. Instinct told him that if he got too close, physically or emotionally, she'd bolt. And right now, he just wanted to hold her in his arms and move with her to the music. He could feel the bones through her skin, and he had the urge to feed her, well and often, to soften those sharp angles. But for now, he simply let himself enjoy the company of a beautiful woman whose eyes told him she had seen too much.

The song ended way too soon, and as they stepped apart, he spotted Sasha heading their way, looking surprisingly feminine in her loose dress, baby bump just barely visible.

When Cat spotted Sasha, he felt her stiffen, so he reached over and took her hand. She slipped hers away and wrapped her arms around her middle instead. He'd heard there was tension between the sisters, but he didn't know the details. None of his business anyway.

Sasha's smile was tentative. "I'm so glad you came, Cat. Your playing was amazing, as always. It meant so much that you were here."

Cat's chin came up. "I came for Eve." She glanced away. "And Mama."

Sasha nodded. "I know. Thank you." She turned to include Nick. "I'm so glad you got to meet Nick Stanton, aka Tony Martinelli. He works for the Safe Harbor Police Department."

Nick saw the color drain from Cat's face before she narrowed her eyes at him, giving him a quick once-over and obviously finding him sorely lacking.

She eyed his outstretched hand. She shook it briefly, then shot him an annoyed glance when he held on a little too long. He couldn't seem to help it. He wanted to know why she was suddenly freezing him out.

"Nice to meet you, Nick. Or do you go by Tony?"

"Nick is fine, thanks. So, how long are you in town?"

"Not long. If you'll excuse me."

She turned and walked away, leaving him thoroughly at sea. When Sasha looked over at him and shrugged, he said, "I guess she doesn't like cops."

"No idea. But we think she's in some kind of trouble. I'm glad you're here, Nick." Sasha patted his arm and walked over to her husband, Jesse. Nick searched the room, but Cat had disappeared. Not surprising, he supposed.

He knew all about secrets. And in her gorgeous dark eyes, he'd seen plenty. He'd also seen the shutters slam shut when Sasha had said he was a cop. That could mean she'd had a bad experience with cops, or that she was hiding something.

As he strolled over to the buffet, he decided he'd best keep an eye on her.

Just in case.

Chapter 3

Cat snuck out the back door and leaned against the barn's rough siding, trying to slow her galloping heart rate. The man with the gorgeous bod, kind eyes, and gentle touch was a freaking cop. Unbelievable. And worse, he was Pop and Mama Rosa's biological son, so he was family. Kind of. Well, in the loosest sense of the word, since there was never any official paperwork filed on her, at her request. None on Sasha, Eve, or Blaze, either, as far as she knew. But they were her family, doggone it, and she had to protect them.

Coming here was a bad idea. She'd known that.

But a cop? Really? Cat had no use for cops, good or bad ones, and she'd met both. The good ones made her worry she'd end up in jail because of her past. And the bad ones made her furious. She'd seen too many turn a blind eye to sex trafficking and drugs.

She turned to leave, but then Blaze burst out the door and spotted her. "There you are. Eve is getting all bossy because she couldn't find you, and she wants you to play something while they cut the cake."

Cat rolled her eyes and followed Blaze inside. She picked up her violin and played her heart out, knowing it'd be the last time she played for them. She should never have come.

Through every piece, she knew Nick Stanton watched her from his spot against the back wall. Those eyes tracked her every move, as though trying to ferret out her secrets.

Cat tried to ignore him, but every few minutes, she'd look up to find him watching her, smiling like a panther who had neatly trapped his prey. But he didn't know who she was, why she was on the run, so he couldn't hurt her.

Just when she thought she'd go crazy if he didn't stop watching her, Cat saw him reach into his coat pocket and pull out a cell phone. As he listened, his expression grew grimmer and grimmer.

He hung up the phone, then said his goodbyes to Eve and Cole. As he turned to leave, he looked over his shoulder and sent her a two-fingered salute.

Then he was gone.

Cat let out the breath she hadn't realized she'd been holding and packed her violin in its case. No more. She had to get out of here before they tried to keep her any longer. Some sixth sense told her it was time to go—past time, actually. She hadn't ignored that warning yet, which was why she was still alive.

She'd just turned to say goodbye to Eve and Cole when she spotted Blaze across the room talking on her cell phone, despite Eve's edict that there be no cell phones at her wedding. Suddenly, Blaze stiffened and her eyes widened in panic. She hung up and raced from the room.

Cat hesitated for only a second before she grabbed her violin and followed. The sultry evening air dropped over her like a blanket when she reached the parking lot. Blaze had disappeared.

Cat started walking around the building, concerned. She might not know her well, but she knew panic when she saw it on someone's face.

"Come on, come on."

She followed the voice to see Blaze fumbling with the keys to Mama Rosa's big boat of a Buick.

"What are you doing, Blaze?" Cat asked, coming up behind her.

Blaze froze, then looked over at her, all teenage attitude. But Cat didn't miss the desperation in her eyes. "Geez, you scared the bejebees out of me." She fumbled some more and finally got the door open.

"Do you have a driver's license?"

Blaze turned, one leg already in the car. "I don't answer to you. I have to go."

Cat put a hand on her arm, felt the teen stiffen and jerk away. She knew that feeling, too. "What's wrong, Blaze? Maybe I can help."

"I have to go. Teddy needs me."

"Teddy, the young man you were dancing with earlier?"

She nodded miserably. "He said he had to go, that he had a meeting and I couldn't talk him out of it. And then he-he—"

"Take a breath. Then tell me. He what?"

"He called me just now, said he was in trouble."

"What kind of trouble?"

Blaze shoved Cat aside and climbed all the way into the car. "I don't know. He didn't say. But he was scared and said to come get him. I have to get over there."

"It could be dangerous. Let me get some help first."

"There isn't time." She tried to close the door, but Cat gripped the frame.

"Scoot over. I'm driving." Without giving Blaze a chance to protest, Cat slid into the car and used her hip to nudge Blaze across the wide bench seat. She kicked off her heels and yanked her dress up over her knees so she could drive.

"Get out. I don't need you. I don't even know you."

"I realize that, but right now, I'm all you've got, especially if things are as bad as they seem." Cat put the car in gear and swung out of the parking space in a wide turn, nearly swiping a pretty convertible. "Dang, wide turning radius," she muttered. "Tell me where I'm going."

Blaze glared at her, but something about Cat's tone must have registered, because the teen blew out a frustrated breath and said, "The old quarry outside town." Then she tucked her dress up just like Cat's, showing off her black combat boots.

Cat spun out of the parking lot and hit the two-lane road going way too fast. She righted the car and sped toward the local teen hangout. "Do you know which entrance he's near?"

Blaze stopped drumming her fingers on her leg. "You've been there?"

"I grew up here, too, remember." She raised an eyebrow.

"I heard you couldn't wait to leave."

"Something like that." Cat let the silence lengthen.

"We usually go in the south entrance."

Cat headed in that direction, hoping Officer Stanton wasn't lying in wait somewhere to give her a speeding ticket, or he'd realize that her license didn't match her name. Or any of her names, for that matter.

"Did he give you any clue what's going on?"

Blaze shook her head, arms wrapped tight around herself. "No," she whispered. "But he sounded really scared."

"Let's find out what's going on before we panic, OK?"

"I'm not a little kid, and I don't cry wolf."

Cat glanced at her in the waning light. "I believe you."

At the words, Blaze raised her chin and nodded, pulling further into herself.

Several minutes later, Cat pulled through an old metal gate, and they bumped along a gravel track through what had once been a farmer's field but now stood fallow. They passed a thick stand of pines, and the area suddenly gave way to big piles of limestone and sand, and deep water-filled craters that were the remnants of the property's past as a limestone quarry.

"That's his car."

Cat figured as much, since it was the only one in the makeshift parking area. Before she'd gotten the car in park, Blaze swung the door open.

Cat reached out and grabbed her arm. "Wait. Let me go first." She hiked up her long skirt and pulled out the dagger she had strapped to her thigh.

Blaze gaped at the knife, and her eyes flicked from Cat to the blade and back. "Do you know how to use that?" she demanded.

Despite herself, Cat smiled. "I do. And since I figure you won't stay in the car, at least stay behind me, OK? We need to find him, but since he said he was in trouble, we have to be quiet and careful. I don't want us to go crashing right into danger."

"Are you, like, a cop or something?"

Another time, she might have found that funny. "Or something. Let's go."

Blaze nodded and slipped out. She followed Cat's lead and closed the car door with a quiet click. Cat motioned with her head, and Blaze followed her down the narrow path that led to one of the most popular make-out spots in Safe Harbor, both of them clutching the hems of their long dresses in one hand. Cat kept her knife in her right, her dress and tiny key-ring flashlight in the other.

As they hurried into the deepening shadows along the path, Cat kept her breathing slow and steady, just like when she played her violin, so she could focus on everything around them. She heard Blaze's rapid breathing behind her and her feet shuffling through the thick grass.

Around them, the twilight was alive with sounds. Cat had never been one for tromping around in the woods at night. Certainly not in Florida, where the creepy crawlies could kill you. She was more comfortable around two-legged creeps. And what did that say about her? she thought wryly.

She focused on the sounds, trying to listen for anything that wasn't an animal. She had no idea what they were going to find. Hopefully, just some teenage angst, maybe that Teddy had gotten into a fight with someone. But as she'd learned in the school of hard knocks, often the worst thing you could think of really was what happened.

She glanced at Blaze, who gamely kept up with Cat's rapid pace, eyes darting around just as Cat's were.

They reached the clearing that served as a makeshift beach, complete with a fire ring. Several yards away, the ground fell away into the quarry where the kids would dare each other to dive into the blackness below.

"Teddy? Are you here?" Blaze called quietly.

Nothing.

"Teddy? Where are you?"

Cat glanced up at the sky. They didn't have more than a few minutes before it was full dark. She didn't want to turn on a flashlight unless she had no choice. It would put them at a distinct disadvantage if anyone was watching.

Blaze turned and headed toward the edge of the drop-off. Cat caught up to her and grabbed her arm. Blaze shrugged it off and spun to face her. Before she could say whatever had her eyes narrowing, Cat said, "We stay together, got it?"

Blaze rolled her eyes and whispered, "Geez, you haven't been back a whole day and already you're as bossy as Eve and Sasha."

Cat flashed a quick grin, though the knot in her stomach was growing by the minute. "Safety first and all that." She turned, and they walked along the ledge, peering over the steep drop-off. Cat breathed a sigh of relief when there was no sign of Teddy's body anywhere below. Nothing floated in the water, either.

She turned and led them in an ever-widening circle, hoping against hope to find Teddy sleeping off alcohol or pot and not something worse. Every instinct urged her to hurry, but she didn't want to make a lot of noise. She didn't have that twitchy feeling that someone was watching, but she wouldn't risk Blaze's life on it.

As they went farther into the wooded area, something on the ground caught Cat's eye. She flicked on her flashlight, saw it was just a button, and kept going. Another glance showed evidence that someone had walked through the tall grass into the trees from this spot. And recently, judging by the way the grass was bent. She nodded in grim satisfaction. Her obsession with cop shows and the ways criminals gave themselves away might just come in handy.

She nodded her head at Blaze, and they followed the trail into the woods. Once under the cover of trees, it was too dark to see, so she reluctantly aimed the flashlight right at her feet to minimize the light.

But with every step—and every minute they hadn't located Teddy—Cat's worry inched up another notch.

She picked up the pace and would have missed seeing the boy if she hadn't stubbed her toe on a tree root and stumbled off the path. Trying to regain her balance, she almost fell over his still shape, and she threw herself sideways, hands skidding across grass and rocks to keep from landing right on top of him.

"Teddy!" Blaze gasped, rushing over.

Cat rolled away from Teddy and onto her knees, shaking her stinging hands. She didn't have time to worry about pain now.

Teddy lay on his stomach, still in the same clothes he'd worn to the wedding, his head turned away from a frantic Blaze, who shook his shoulder. "Teddy. Are you OK?"

Cat winced as she grabbed her flashlight with her torn-up hand and aimed the light at Teddy's face. She froze.

Oh, dear God.

Chapter 4

Cat crouched down and put her fingers by Teddy's neck, hoping against hope for a pulse. But there was nothing. And unfortunately, she'd seen death too many times not to recognize it. Joellen wasn't the first runaway she'd tried to help. Sadly, she wasn't the first who'd died a violent death, despite Cat's best efforts, either. And of course, Daniel.

She closed her eyes and whispered a prayer while she blinked back tears, snapping them open again when she felt Blaze try to roll him over. "We have to help him. Come on, Cat. Help me. I can't tell where he's hurt."

Cat put a gentle hand over hers. "Stop, Blaze. We can't help him. I'm sorry."

"What? What are you talking about?" Blaze's eyes were wide and glassy in the faint beam of light, but Cat knew the second her words registered. "No. Oh God, no. He can't be dead. Is that what you're saying? That he's dead? No, you're wrong. You're not a doctor." With surprising strength, she pushed Cat aside and rolled Teddy over, crying out when she focused on his unseeing eyes. "No, no. Wake up, Teddy." She turned to Cat, desperate. "You have to do something. Like CPR or something."

Cat nudged her aside and started doing compressions, but she knew it wouldn't help. After several minutes, Blaze realized it, too, and she slowly collapsed and slumped over Teddy's still form, sobbing.

"We need to call the police, Blaze," Cat said quietly, sitting back on her heels.

Blaze swiped tears from her cheeks and rubbed her hands on her long dress. "Call Nick. Not the chief. Monroe's a total jerk."

"Do you have Nick's cell number?"

"I left my phone in the car." She turned to run back for it.

"Hang on." Cat pulled her phone out of her meager cleavage where she'd stashed it as they left the car. At Blaze's snort, she said, "What? It's not like I have pockets. Give me his number."

Cat punched in Nick's number as Blaze dictated it, relieved to see she had cell service. She turned her back on Blaze and walked a few steps away while she waited for the call to go through. Her stomach flipped and rolled at the thought of a cop having her cell number, but she couldn't worry about that right now. Teddy and Blaze were what mattered. She'd just get another burner phone.

"Stanton." He sounded tired and annoyed.

She took a deep breath, pushed her emotions aside. Blaze needed her to be strong. "This is, ah, Cat Johnson. You need to come out to the old quarry right away."

She could almost hear him snap to attention. "What's wrong?"

"Blaze and I are at the quarry, and it looks like Teddy—" She covered the phone and asked Blaze, "What's his last name?" Then she told Nick, "Unfortunately, it looks like Teddy Winston is dead."

"What? How do you know?"

Cat rubbed her forehead. "No pulse. Sightless, unseeing eyes. No apparent sign of a struggle."

"Don't be flip, for crying out loud."

Cat stiffened. "I meant no disrespect. I was trying to be precise."

"Are you and Blaze safe there?"

Cat looked around. Glanced at the knife she still held. "Yes. I think so."

"I'm on my way. Don't touch anything."

He hung up before she could say anything else. Cat turned to Blaze, who sat beside her friend, stroking his arm as silent tears poured down her face. Cat swallowed and looked away. She couldn't let her emotions get the best of her now. She had to stay clearheaded so she could think. "Nick's on his way. Why don't we go wait by the car?"

Blaze swiped her arm under her nose. "I'm not leaving him."

"I need to go back to the car for a minute."

"What? Why?" She scrambled to her feet. "Don't leave me."

"I won't be gone more than five minutes. You can come with me or wait here."

Blaze looked from Teddy to Cat and back. "I don't want him to be alone."

"I understand. We'll make it quick."

They hurried to Mama's Buick, where Cat stashed the knife in her tote bag. She locked the car, and they returned to Teddy and sat on either side of him while the mosquitos chewed on their skin and they waited for the sound of sirens.

———

Nick climbed into his official Safe Harbor police SUV and backed out of his driveway way too fast. He spun the tires of the Ford Explorer as he headed for the old quarry, shaking his head. A dead teenager. In Safe Harbor. Cat had said there was no sign of a struggle. Dollars to donuts that meant drugs. Probably an overdose. But why? Teddy was a good kid from a good family. He'd been at the wedding reception, had gazed at Blaze like she was a dream come true. He didn't think it was suicide.

So it was probably drugs. He banged a fist on the steering wheel. Several months ago, when local boat captain Roy Winchester had died while trying to kill Sasha during a drug transfer and Nick arrested another boat captain, Demetri Markos, he'd thought that was finally the end of the drug trade in Safe Harbor. But then, Demetri got shanked in jail, and he knew that was nothing more than wishful thinking. Whoever had been running drugs through this little town since even before Nick's childhood kidnapping hadn't gone away, and they hadn't given up. And he still didn't know who was behind it.

He'd thought—OK, he'd hoped—he'd left senseless teenage deaths and drug trafficking behind when he resigned from the Tampa Police Department and took the job in Safe Harbor. Somehow, he'd let himself get lulled into a false sense of security. He shook his head at his own stupidity. He was a cop. He knew better. Evil didn't confine itself to cities.

Still, he couldn't help noticing that less than twenty-four hours after the Martinellis' long-estranged daughter showed up in town again, they suddenly had a dead teenager.

OK, it was a total leap, and an unfair one at that, which made him realize he truly had become part of the town. Because he didn't want one of the locals, anyone he saw at the Blue Dolphin or at church, to be responsible for a teen's death.

Not that he wanted Cat responsible, either. She'd gotten to him, somehow, with her talent and the passion he saw lurking just below the surface. Her calm, serene expression obviously covered a backbone of steel, if her phone call was any indication.

"Get your head in the game, Stanton," he muttered. Once he left the downtown area, he flipped on his official lights and flew down the two-lane highway. He wanted to get there before Monroe or anyone else did. He wanted to make sure Blaze was OK. And yes, he wanted to be the one to question Cat.

When he pulled in next to Mama Rosa's Buick, he kept his headlights on as he climbed out of his truck. "Cat? Blaze?"

"Over here!" Cat called.

He turned and saw a beam of light signaling from inside the woods. One hand on his gun and his Maglite in the other, he headed that way, shocked when Blaze leaped up and wrapped her arms around his waist.

Nick hugged her back, tightening his grip when he felt her tears soak his shirt. Gently, he eased her away, pulled his handkerchief from his pocket, and handed it to her. She sent him a watery smile and mopped her face.

"Can you tell me what happened?" He stepped around her, then crouched over Teddy's body and exchanged a quick glance with Cat.

"Teddy was lying on his stomach when we found him. But we rolled him over and tried to do CPR."

"We had to try," Blaze added, chin in the air just like Eve and Sasha.

Unfortunately, they'd probably destroyed evidence in the process, but he let it go. He leaned closer, trying to get a whiff of anything unusual. Poison. Drugs. "How did you know he was here?"

When he glanced up at Cat, she stood slightly in front of Blaze, as though protecting her from the sight of Teddy's body.

"He called me," Blaze said. "While we were at the reception. He-he said he was in trouble and told me to come right away."

Nick stood so fast Blaze backed up a step. "Why didn't you call me right then?"

At his shout, Blaze covered her head with her hands. "I don't know! I wasn't thinking. I just wanted to get here, to try to help him!"

Nick turned to Cat. "You drove?"

At her nod, he repeated his question, louder. "Why didn't *you* call me, then?"

Cat fisted her hands on her hips at his tone. "I wasn't sure what we were getting into, and Blaze was desperate, so I came along."

"You both could have been walking into a dangerous situation!" As Blaze seemed to shrink into herself at his tone, he lowered his voice. All the things that could have happened raced through his mind, but he pushed them aside. Right now, he had a job to do. "What time did you girls get here?"

Blaze wiped her tears with her arm. "I don't know."

"Probably about seven thirty," Cat said. "It wasn't full dark yet when we arrived."

Nick scanned the area. "How did you know to check back here?"

Again, Blaze glanced at Cat before she answered. "We didn't, not at first. We saw his car and started calling his name, but h-he didn't answer. Cat used her keychain flashlight, and we started walking farther and farther from the car. Cat tripped and almost fell on him."

A nod from Cat confirmed Blaze's version of events.

"Was he alive when you arrived?" He directed the question to Cat, who gave a quick negative shake of her head. So she'd done CPR for Blaze's sake. But had she intentionally destroyed evidence in the process? He'd check on that. Later. "He was on his stomach, you said?"

Cat described the position of the body in the same straightforward terms she'd used on the phone. "I take it this isn't your first dead"—he caught himself at a cry from Blaze—"person."

Again, the quick negative shake of Cat's head. She had her arms tightly crossed over her chest, but then she stepped over to Blaze and simply put a hand on the girl's shoulder. Blaze flinched but didn't step away, a testament to how shook up she must be. The teen was seriously averse to being touched. He studied their long gowns and Cat's bare feet, then pulled out his little notebook. "What time did Teddy leave the reception?"

"Right after we danced. They were just starting to serve dinner, but he got a text and said he had to go."

All things that would be easily checked, but Nick would start a timeline now. "Did you see him talking with anyone at the reception?"

Blaze shrugged. "There weren't a lot of people our age. His mom is friends with Cole's mom, so I think that's why Cole invited his family."

Nick looked the teen right in the eye. "Was he involved with drugs?"

Blaze's already-pale face whitened even more, and she looked away, a flash of guilt in her eyes that immediately disappeared. "What? No. Never. Teddy wasn't—"

"What aren't you telling me, Blaze?" he demanded as he stepped closer.

Her head snapped around to him. "Nothing. I don't know anything." She blinked back sudden tears. "How can he be dead? It doesn't make any sense."

"That's what I'm going to find out. You guys were pretty close, right? Did he have any health issues that you knew of? A heart condition, diabetes, epilepsy?" Things he would check, of course, but he wanted her take. He'd find out what she was hiding, too.

A blush stole over her cheeks at the mention of their relationship. "He was my friend. I liked him. A lot. I don't think he was sick."

Without warning, Blaze buried her head in her hands and burst into loud sobbing.

This time, Cat slid her arm around the girl's shoulders and held tight. "Can I take her home now?"

He nodded. "I'll let you know if I have any more questions. And, Blaze, let's keep this off social media for now, OK?"

"Like I would ever," she muttered and then followed Cat back to Mama Rosa's car.

Nick watched them go, trying to get a handle on Cat. She was obviously protective of Blaze, and based on her demeanor, she'd seen a dead body before. Her utter calm and aloof attitude intrigued him, though he figured she hoped it would keep him at arm's length. "Not a chance, lady." Not when he had a dead teenager on his hands.

He returned his attention to Teddy, scanning the body as he called dispatch to get some extra hands out there, then asked them to call the county coroner, too. He didn't bother to call the chief. He'd show up soon enough, no doubt right after he'd called the press.

Monroe's love of the spotlight got under Nick's skin, no question, but he shrugged it off. While he waited, he studied the body, took a few pics with his cell phone. He'd make sure the coroner ran a battery of drug tests to try to figure out *why* an apparently healthy teenager was dead.

In the meantime, his job was to gather as much evidence at the scene as he could. Then he'd try to figure out who had wanted the boy dead.

———

Cat started the Buick with hands that badly wanted to shake. When she'd first seen Teddy's body, for one insane second she'd thought it was Daniel, and her heart had taken a direct hit. Even after all these years, she still missed him, still wondered what would have become of them if her uncle and Garcia—she didn't even want to think his name—hadn't poisoned him. And now seeing Teddy like that, hair the same blond as Daniel's, same shape and build. When she'd seen Blaze dancing with him at the wedding reception, her first glimpse had given her a jolt, and just like that, she was fifteen again, in love with the most beautiful boy she'd ever seen. And then she'd seen the longing on Blaze's face and known exactly what the other girl was thinking and feeling.

When she'd found a frantic Blaze in the parking lot, fumbling with the keys to the Buick, of course she'd gone along. How could she have turned away?

Beside her, Blaze stared out the window, arms wrapped tight around herself, silent tears pouring down her face. Cat understood, more than the girl would ever know. She'd been frantic, too, that long-ago day. She still woke in the night, hearing that awful choking sound echoing in her mind as she desperately tried to find Daniel, to save him.

After she'd escaped from her uncle's, she'd tried to find Daniel's house, to see if he'd somehow made it home, but his number was unlisted and she hadn't known where he lived. She'd hopped on a bus, and then, days later, when she was far away from the Miami high-rise, she'd seen Daniel's smiling face plastered all over the news. His body had been found deep in the Everglades, and he'd been identified by his dental records. Cat brushed at her cheeks, surprised to find them streaked with tears, even now. *Oh, Daniel.* The gators had gotten to him.

Fury flashed through her. They'd killed him, and they'd never been punished. She'd wanted to go to the police, to tell them what she knew, but it wouldn't have made any difference. Both Garcia and her uncle had been questioned and released. Then her uncle had gone on television, all sadness and concern, asking people to help find her. He'd been very convincing. She knew the police were looking for her, too, had labeled her a person of interest. If they found her, they'd never believe her. Not then. Not now.

She couldn't take the risk.

Even if by some miracle the authorities believed her story, she had no proof. Once she came out of hiding, her life wouldn't be worth spit. Her uncle would either have her killed, if he didn't do it himself, or he'd turn her over to Garcia. To welch on his deal with Garcia by not delivering her as promised meant his reputation was on the line. That could never be tolerated.

Once Garcia had her, he'd either kill her outright or use her first and then kill her. Of that, she had absolutely no doubt.

Because she ran away, both men's pride had taken a hit, and that was unpardonable. According to the newspaper articles she'd read using public library computers, people associated with her uncle and Garcia had died for far less.

Both of them had been arrested but never charged with a variety of crimes over the years, including murder, which told her they had friends in high places. Coming forward wouldn't get justice for Daniel. But it would get her dead. She knew she had to keep moving, stay under the radar. Always.

"You have to help me figure out what happened."

Cat blinked, pulled back from the past to find Blaze aiming an accusing glare her way. "What?"

"You have to help me figure out why Teddy is dead."

Cat glanced at her, then looked back at the road. "Nick will figure it out. He's a good cop, right?"

"The best."

"Then let him do his job and get to the bottom of it."

"I can't just wait around and do nothing."

"Look, Blaze—" she began.

"Don't you dare pat me on the head and treat me like I'm a little kid. I'm tough. I can help."

Cat sent her a quick smile. "No doubt. I heard you kicked some serious butt the day Leon Daughtry went after Eve and Cole about the poisoned well." Then she sobered. "And you protected Mama Rosa, too. Way to go, Blaze. That took some serious guts."

"So you'll help me?"

"No. Look, Blaze, I'm not a cop or an investigator. Let Nick do his job."

"You carry a sweet knife."

"I do. For protection. I work in some, shall we say, rough neighborhoods."

"Doing what?"

"I play the fiddle in a club." Or at least she had, but Cat didn't want to get into all that with the too-smart teen.

"That's way cool." She sighed. "I guess you probably have to get back to work soon." Then her expression turned pleading. "But could you just help me until you have to go?"

Cat felt trapped. "What do you really think happened, Blaze? And don't give me the same answer you gave Nick."

Blaze shook her head, eyes filled with both sadness and confusion. And a touch of wariness that tripped Cat's well-honed lie detector. "I don't know. That's what's making me crazy."

"Don't know. Or won't say?"

"I told you I don't know." Blaze looked out the window, then back at Cat, scowling.

Cat sighed. Changed gears. "Is it possible he had some kind of health condition or something, like Nick said?"

"I don't think so. He was a total health nut, always eating fruits and veggies and stuff."

"Was he an athlete?"

"Not really, but he jogged a lot. He said it cleared his head. If he had some kind of disease, he wouldn't have done that, right?"

"I don't know."

"His mom is just going to die when she finds out." More tears fell as she gazed out the window. "This is all so wrong."

Cat couldn't agree more, but since Blaze wouldn't confide in her, they spent the rest of the trip to the marina in silence.

As she climbed out of the Buick, Blaze turned to her once more. "Please, Cat—"

Cat shook her head. "I'm sorry. I need to leave tomorrow. I had planned to leave today. I have to get back."

Blaze nodded and hung her head, then disappeared into the house. Cat put her head on the steering wheel. The expression on the girl's face would haunt her for a long time. She understood exactly what it was like to be all alone with a problem you couldn't solve.

But Cat couldn't help her. She'd always known her uncle and Garcia would never stop looking for her. She'd never risk them finding her here and bringing danger to the Martinellis. Sal and Mama Rosa, Sasha, Eve, and Blaze—they'd all been there for her. She wouldn't repay them this way. She'd probably already stayed too long.

Besides, if she stayed, Officer Stanton would want to talk to her again. She couldn't risk him digging into her past, either. Never mind the sense of safety she'd felt in his arms and the way his sad eyes tugged at her heart. She had to go.

But as she lay in the narrow twin bed under the eaves later that night, it wasn't Nick's face she saw. Her mind kept flashing back and forth between Daniel's face and Teddy's. Both sweet boys, both dead for no reason. She slapped a palm against the faded quilt and squeezed her eyes shut. But that didn't help, because then Blaze's desperate face called out to her and accused her of being a coward. She wished there was a way to help, something she could do that wouldn't bring danger to her family's door.

But there wasn't. There never had been. And the sooner she packed and left, the safer they would be.

Just like always. She only hoped it wasn't too late.

Chapter 5

As if on cue, Chief Monroe showed up with lights flashing and sirens blaring, the press right on his tail. He swaggered out of his police car and walked over to Nick as though he were glad-handing at an election rally. "What have we got here, Officer Stanton?"

Nick raised a brow at the formal greeting while, behind him, Avery Ames from the *Gazette* stood poised with a recorder in her hand, her inquisitive eyes bright despite the late hour.

Nick glanced from Monroe to Avery and back again. "Why don't we step over here?" He turned to the reporter. "You'll have to wait behind the yellow line, ma'am." He nodded to their newest officer, John Dempsey—JD—who was cordoning off the area with bright crime scene tape. The kid looked about twelve, and though his eyes held the excitement of an important case, his skin had a decidedly greenish cast to it.

Monroe looked like he wanted to argue, but he stepped farther away, out of the reporter's hearing. "What in blazes happened here, Stanton?"

Nick had told him they had a dead teen but hadn't said his name over the radio. No way would he let that out before his parents were notified. He inclined his head, led the chief over to the body, and then watched the color drain out of the other man's face. Just like Dempsey had, Monroe turned a sickly shade of green under the work lights that had been set up to illuminate the scene.

"That's Theodore Winston." Monroe wiped a shaky hand over his face. "Oh, my sweet Lord, this is going to kill his mama." He turned to Nick. "Walk me through it."

"I got a call from Cat Johnson that she—"

"Who is Cat Johnson?"

"One of the Martinelli girls. She's in town for Eve's wedding."

Monroe frowned. "They used to call her Cathy. And she's been nothing but trouble from day one."

"How so?" After Eve and her well-intentioned crusading for various causes over the years, how much worse could this sister be?

"She went to high school here, but she always seemed to be looking over her shoulder, or looking right past you, like you didn't exist. Kept to herself, didn't talk much, but seemed to watch everything and everyone. Which would have been OK, except she started hanging out with the Miller girl. That one was nothing but trouble, took drugs, eventually ended up in rehab. Figured Cathy would end up the same way, except she disappeared one night while she was still in high school, and nobody knew where she went for a long time."

Interesting. He'd have to look into all that, Nick thought. "Where did you finally find her?"

"We didn't. One day a couple weeks later, Sal Martinelli came into the station and said they'd talked with Cathy and she was fine, living with a family out West somewhere. Asked us to stop looking."

Nick stiffened at the mention of Sal's name. In recent months, Sal had tried to make up for the past, but Nick wasn't ready to let bygones be bygones. Not when the man had essentially sanctioned Nick's kidnapping. He wasn't sure he'd ever understand how a father could keep silent about what happened to his child—even if he believed his silence was protecting his wife and the rest of his family. Nick shook off the lingering anger and kept his face blank as he asked, "Was Sal telling the truth?"

"He had no reason to lie." Monroe turned to the body and crouched down with clear effort, his sagging belly getting in the way. "No obvious signs of a struggle." He looked up at Nick. "You find any needle marks, signs of drug use?"

Nick had checked. Arms, legs, between fingers and toes. He hadn't found anything. "Do you know if Theodore had any medical issues?"

Monroe's head snapped up. "Not that I know of. But that would explain a lot. Wouldn't it?"

Dr. Alfred Henry, a retired doctor who still served as the county coroner, arrived, and they exchanged greetings while he examined the body. "He hasn't been dead long. No obvious signs of trauma or asphyxiation, but I'll run a tox screen, check for any undiagnosed conditions. I'll also check the body and under his nails for any signs of a struggle." He bagged Teddy's hands before he zipped his body into a body bag. Nick followed the stretcher to a waiting vehicle. "Doc, would you run a full drug panel? Since I couldn't find any needle marks, I'm especially looking for drugs or poisons that could be either ingested or inhaled."

"Of course. I'll get you a preliminary report as soon as I can."

Nick turned and saw Monroe standing off to the side, cell phone to his ear, obviously deep in a heated discussion. He couldn't make out the words, but by the looks of it, the chief wasn't happy.

Once the body was gone and photographs taken and any potential evidence tagged and bagged, he instructed Officer Dempsey to keep the scene secure while he headed to the Winston home to notify the family. He hated this part of the job. Kids were the absolute worst.

As he drove, he shuffled the pieces of the puzzle around in his mind. He didn't think this was a suicide. Not after what Blaze had said. So who in Safe Harbor wanted this well-liked kid dead?

He didn't know, yet, but he wouldn't stop until he had answers.

Chapter 6

When the nightmare woke Cat for the third time, the first glimmers of light were just edging over the horizon and slipping through the aging metal blinds. She bolted upright in the narrow bed under the eaves, heart pounding like a runaway train. She was drenched in sweat, and not surprisingly, her cheeks were wet with tears. The nightmare of Daniel's death always reappeared when she was stressed. Or scared.

She tossed back the light blanket and headed for the tiny bathroom, splashing water on her face, meeting her guilty eyes in the mirror. She hadn't sounded a cry, hadn't raised the alarm, hadn't called the police to demand they investigate. Her lack of action was a shame she would carry to her grave. She'd been scared, worried for her own safety, and instead of doing right by Daniel, she'd run like the coward she was.

Was still running, because she knew if she ever stopped, her uncle—or Garcia—would find her and kill her. Men like them didn't just shrug it off when someone double-crossed them or ruined their plans. Her uncle had owed Garcia money, and she'd been the payment. Neither one would ever forgive her for ruining that.

To escape the guilt, at least for a while, she pulled on workout clothes, grabbed her violin, and slipped outside. It was barely light enough to see, but she knew the path from memory more than by sight.

She headed into the woods, trying to ignore the rustling in the underbrush as she walked. She'd never liked that aspect of the woods. Instead, it was the quiet she craved. She inhaled the smell of the tall pines overhead, the quiet shuffle of the pine needles that carpeted the ground.

The sky was just beginning to lighten when she found the clearing she'd considered hers while she lived there. She spent several minutes breathing deeply and stretching before she slid her mother's violin from the case and started playing.

Here she could play the classics she'd been taught, one after another. She had learned to enjoy fiddling at honky-tonks, where she played to put food on the table, but classical music—that was what fed her soul.

She lost all track of time as the familiar melodies flowed from her fingers, *Panis Angelicus*, Pachelbel's Canon in D. The soothing strains set her free and let her soar far above the worries and cares that dogged her heels the rest of the time. This was what she loved. Here was where peace lived.

She'd just finished a more modern piece called "Somewhere Only We Know" when Blaze said, "That's pretty cool. Where'd you learn to play like that?"

Cat spun around so fast she nearly lost her balance on the slippery needles. "You startled me. How long have you been here?"

Blaze sat on a fallen log, wearing a hoodie and a pair of jeans, black boots on her feet, watching her. How had she not heard her approach? Cat was always alert to her surroundings. Being here was messing with her usual hypervigilance, and that scared her.

"A few minutes. You were pretty into the music." She looked around. "This is usually my spot. Guess you used to come here, too, huh?"

"I did." Cat studied the dark circles under the teen's eyes. "Did you get any sleep?"

Blaze blinked back tears and shook her head. "Every time I close my eyes, I see him lying there, you know?"

Oh yes. She knew. "I'm so sorry, Blaze. Truly."

The teen hopped up from the log and stopped right in front of her. "You need to help me figure out what happened."

Cat read the fear in the girl's eyes and chose her words with care. "Nick and the coroner are going to figure out why he died, Blaze. They'll run all kinds of tests. Maybe he had some condition nobody knew about until—"

Clearly in denial, Blaze was shaking her head. "What if he didn't?"

A chill climbed up Cat's neck. "What do you mean? Did he do drugs and you're worried he overdosed?"

Blaze spun away, arms wrapped around her middle as she paced the small clearing. "I don't know. Maybe." She paced some more. "But what if it's even worse? What if, like, I don't know . . . what if someone hurt him on purpose?" The last words echoed in the clearing, bounced off the trees.

Cat studied the girl. "If you know something, Blaze, you have to tell Nick."

"Why are you pushing me to tell him? You don't even like him."

"I don't know him well enough to like him or not. But I've heard he's a good guy. And a good cop."

"Are you in some kind of trouble?"

"What do you mean?"

Blaze shrugged. "I heard Sasha and Eve talking. They're worried you're on drugs or something." She studied Cat a moment. "I don't think you are."

"What makes you so sure? What do you know about it, Blaze?"

"Chill. Don't go all parental on me. I don't smoke weed or anything else. That stuff is stupid. But I know people who do, and they're messed up. You're not like that."

"Was Teddy messed up?"

Blaze started shaking her head again. "I don't think so. I mean, I don't know. I mean, no. He didn't do drugs. But he was saving up for a car and . . ."

Cat kept her tone casual. "Somebody wanted him to sell some drugs, make a little extra cash, maybe?"

Blaze nodded miserably. "I tried to tell him it was a bad idea."

"Did he listen?"

"I don't know."

"What kind of drugs were they?"

"It wasn't a big deal. Just some weed. A few pills. Oxy."

It was a big deal, but Cat didn't react, she had to keep her talking. "To sell to kids at the high school?"

Again, the shrug.

"If you were with him, you could get busted, too." Cat studied the misery written across Blaze's face. "What aren't you telling me? Even if Teddy was dealing drugs for them, why would they have a reason to, ah, hurt him?"

Blaze flung her arms wide, fury and guilt all over her face. "Because I made him promise that he would tell them no, that he wouldn't do it anymore. What if he's dead because of me?" The last words burst out with a sob, and Cat's heart clenched. Blaze spun out of the clearing, and Cat grabbed her before she'd gone twenty feet, wrapped her in her arms, and hugged her while she cried.

It didn't take long before Blaze shrugged out of her grasp, swiped at her eyes, and glared at Cat. "You have to help me."

"Why won't you let Nick handle this? This is his job, Blaze. Besides, if somebody hurt Teddy, they need to pay. Don't you want that?"

"I promised, OK? I promised I'd never tell the cops if he promised to quit."

"That's what he was doing at the quarry last night?"

"I don't know. He didn't say. Just that he had a meeting."

The utter heartbreak etched in the girl's face made Cat's decision for her. "I'll stay one more day, but that's the best I can do. Who was Teddy working for? Was it someone local?"

"I don't know his name. I've never met him, but I've seen him around."

"Do you have a picture, anything?"

Blaze pulled a sketch pad from the front pocket of her hoodie. "I'll show you." She plopped down on the log, pulled out a pencil, and starting sketching. It only took five minutes before she stood and handed Cat a drawing.

Cat glanced down and bit back a curse. "That's Eddie Varga. I went to high school with him. He was trouble even then. You're sure he's the guy Teddy was working for?"

"Positive."

Cat took the sketch. "I'll go say hi to Mama and Pop and then see what I can find out."

"Thank you, Cat."

"Why me? Why not Sasha or Eve?"

"Because Eve's on her honeymoon and Sasha's pregnant. I couldn't ask them." She paused. "Your eyes say you know about stuff like this. More than they do."

Cat nodded. She did know. So did Blaze. "Stick close to the house today, OK? I'll see what I can find out. Do you know where Eddie hangs out?"

"No idea. Sorry."

"I'll be back later."

At the house, Cat found Mama and Sasha sitting at the kitchen table, drinking coffee. Which meant Pop and Jesse were already down at the marina.

Guilt tugged at Cat when Mama's eyes lit up as she walked in. "Cathy, you are still here. I thought you were going to leave at dawn?"

"Trying to get rid of me, huh?" Cat wouldn't meet Sasha's eyes as she leaned over and kissed the top of Mama's head.

Mama laughed. "Of course not. It's a pleasant surprise. Come, sit."

Sasha took her mug to the sink. "I need to get to the marina, too. I'll drop by before I leave, OK?" She placed a kiss on Mama's cheek before she left without another word.

Mama eyed Cat sternly. "You need to make up with your sister."

"Me? What did I do? She's the one who egged the police station and made me miss my big audition. If she hadn't—"

"Enough. It was long ago, and you are not children anymore. Family is family."

Cat sighed. Mama was right. What was it about coming home that made her revert to her teenage self? She'd never be able to tell them the terror she'd felt and the real reason she'd left that night, but she could apologize for her behavior since.

"I'm only going to stay for one more day. I have a few things I need to check on in town."

"How is Blaze? She found you in the woods this morning, no?"

"She's hurting and confused. I can't blame her."

"I am glad you went with her last night."

"I'm not sure why she wanted my help to begin with. She doesn't know me."

Mama took her hand. "Neither one of you has ever talked about your lives before you came here, and that's fine." She held up her hand when Cat looked like she wanted to interrupt. "But you both have that same haunted look in your eyes."

She studied the woman who had been more of a mother to her than her own in the short time she'd lived here. "Sasha and Eve didn't come from ideal situations, either."

"No, but their pasts were more about tragedy and heartache. You and Blaze ran for some reason." She eyed her. "I think you felt a connection with her, too."

This was exactly why she couldn't stay. Mama read her too easily, inspired her to speak too freely. If she weren't careful, she'd say things that had to stay hidden for everyone's safety.

"Does Nick know yet how that sweet boy died?"

"I don't think so. Not yet." She cocked her head. "You call him Nick."

Mama nodded and her eyes filled with sadness. "The little boy who disappeared will always be my Tony. But this big, strong man, he is Nick. He saved Sal when Leon Daughtry tried to kill him." Her eyes filled. "He is a good man."

Cat wasn't getting into that, so she stood and kissed Mama's cheek. "I'll be back later, OK? Are you good here?"

Mama smiled, pointed to her knitting basket. "I will sit on the porch and start knitting booties for my coming grandbaby."

A ray of hope filled Cat as she left. Mama was getting stronger. Sasha was going to be a mother.

She just had to get out of town before they found her. Again.

———

Nick sat at his desk in the tiny Safe Harbor police station and studied the crime scene photos. Again. Across the room, JD entered information into his computer, logging evidence, trying to keep everything organized. Wanda, the dispatcher, was scrolling through various social media sites, making a list of Teddy's friends for Nick to interview. In a small department like theirs, everyone pitched in. Except Chief Monroe, who had yet to make an appearance this morning.

Nick leaned back in his chair, folded his arms, and considered what they knew so far. It wasn't much. No trauma to the body. No needle marks or signs of drug abuse. According to Teddy's parents, he'd been declared in perfect health at his last checkup. He'd need the autopsy report to be sure, but it didn't look like the results of an illness. So why was a seventeen-year-old kid dead? Poison was always a possibility. Or drug overdose, which the tox screen would show.

Suicide? From what Blaze and Teddy's parents said and what he'd seen himself at the wedding reception, it didn't seem likely. He looked like your average teenager. But you never knew.

Wanda walked over to his desk and handed him the list. Tall and blonde, Wanda became the dispatcher last year after her third child went off to college and she couldn't handle the quiet at home anymore. She'd been a volunteer at the hospital for many years and had a calm voice and demeanor Nick had come to appreciate. "Teddy had a lot of friends, at least on social media, so I put the ones he interacted with most at the top."

Nick looked over at JD. "Have we gotten Teddy's cell phone records yet?"

"Still waiting. I'll get them to you as soon as they come in."

Wanda took a deep breath. "Pastor Barnes called earlier. The funeral will be Wednesday. The church ladies are organizing a luncheon afterward." She shook her head. "It just doesn't make any sense. Figure out what happened to him, Nick. His parents deserve that."

Nick nodded. "Yes, ma'am. I plan to." He stood, scanned the list, and headed out. He recognized some of the names. If he timed it right, he should be able to catch several of them just as church let out.

———

Cat climbed into her beige sedan and headed toward the outskirts of Safe Harbor. When they were in high school, Eddie Varga's big Hungarian family had lived in a rusting mobile home off a dirt road about five miles out of town. There were always cars up on blocks and chickens and children and dogs running around the unkempt yard, but Mrs. Varga always sat in the third row at church looking as prim and proper as an English lady, complete with a straw hat. Mr. Varga worked at the fish market, when he worked, which wasn't often.

Cat drove past their place, not really surprised to see it hadn't changed a bit in ten years. The house had more rust and looked more tired, but the rest looked the same. Only, this time, there was nobody outside, chickens or kids. The whole place had a deserted feel.

She parked her car and carefully picked her way up a few small wooden steps and knocked on the weathered front door. She didn't hear any sounds from inside, so she knocked again. After a few minutes, she gave up and headed back to town.

About a mile from the high school, she swung by Wally's Gas-n-Go, the convenience store where Eddie and his buddies used to hang out. Sure enough, there he was, sitting on a picnic table in the shade of a huge oak tree, smoking and shooting the breeze with his buddies. She climbed out of her car and started toward them. They stopped talking and watched her progress. Eddie slowly unfolded himself and looked her up and down. "Well if it isn't Miss Hoity-Toity Cathy Johnson. Long time no see, princess."

"I want a word with you, Eddie."

He waved a hand at his cronies. "Go ahead, ain't nothing my boys can't hear."

She scanned the three other men. Two she recognized. One had played football and had packed on some pounds since his linebacker days. The other was wiry—and sneaky—if she remembered right. He always did Varga's bidding. The third one she didn't recognize, but the tats on both arms and on his neck would make him easy to spot.

"What do you know about Teddy Winston's death?"

Varga put a hand on his bony chest as though wounded. "How would I know anything? It's a shame. He was a good kid."

She watched his face as she said, "I heard he was working for you."

Eddie laughed, and his buddies joined in. "Not *working*, princess. *Learning*. He wanted to learn how to fish." He shrugged a bony shoulder. "I took him out on my boat a few times, taught him a thing or two."

She shook her head. "I don't think so. Try again."

"Are you doubting me?" He moved closer, and Cat held her ground. "Because that's not cool."

The other three moved closer, and she decided this hadn't been such a good idea. But it was too late to back down now. "What happened between you and Teddy Winston last night?"

Surprise flashed through his eyes, then all emotion vanished and they turned flat, like a snake's. "You got a lotta nerve, princess, showing up here making accusations."

"I'm not accusing, Eddie. I'm asking. What went down?"

He had his hands around her neck faster than Cat could respond. Two of the others grabbed her feet and slammed her down on the picnic table. Eddie's hands tightened around her throat. "I don't like people making up stories about me, you understand?"

Cat let herself go limp, eyes wide and pleading. Let him think he had the upper hand. Then in one smooth move, she kicked out with her legs, and the guy holding them went flying. The other tried to grab her, and she sent him after his friend. Varga's grip on her throat tightened, so she reached into the sheath at her back, yanked out her knife, and jabbed it into his upper arm. He screamed and let her go, cursing a blue streak as he saw the blood welling from the wound. "You'll pay for that!" he shouted. "Get her," he growled at his henchmen.

Cat spun off the table and turned, knife in hand, shifting her weight from leg to leg in the lateral dodge stance. Billy, the ponytailed forger who'd become her friend, had taught her Brazilian capoeira years ago, and she'd immediately responded to the way it combined music with self-defense.

She glanced over her shoulder when a young family in a minivan pulled up next to her. She refused to put the children at risk, so with a hard look at Varga, she slipped into her car, backed out, and turned onto the two-lane road toward town.

Her hands tightened on the wheel when a Safe Harbor police car pulled into the parking lot just as she left, the car sliding between Varga's goons and the family. She hoped it wasn't Stanton. She kept one eye on the rearview mirror, relieved when none of Varga's posse followed her and she didn't see any sign of the cop car.

By the time she reached Main Street, the adrenaline had worn off and her throat throbbed. She pulled into one of the angled parking spaces and flipped down her visor, scowling. Dang that idiot. The red marks around her neck were already bruising.

She didn't want Mama to worry, so she got out and rooted around in her trunk until she came up with a lightweight scarf tied around the handle of her tote bag. She tied it around her neck, instead, and grabbed the tote. As she closed the lid, she eyed the meager pile in her trunk. It was pathetic that everything she owned in the world was in here and the trunk wasn't even full.

She looked around Safe Harbor. No one seemed to be paying any attention to her, which made her feel only marginally better. She had to get out of town before she drew attention to herself.

Strangely, as much as she'd hated this town when she was a teenager, it was the only place that had ever felt like home. As an adult, she knew that was because of the people, but as a teenager, she'd dismissed it as provincial and uncultured. What a snobby little brat she'd been.

She crossed to the corner pharmacy and bought another burner phone, paid cash. No way did she want the cops to have her number or be able to trace her via GPS. On impulse, she walked across the street to a flower stand and bought a bouquet for Mama and one for Blaze. At the last second, she grabbed one for Sasha, too. She couldn't really afford it, but she was leaving again and had no idea if or when she'd be back.

As she headed toward the marina, she mentally kicked herself. What had she been thinking, confronting Varga in front of his friends?

She hadn't accomplished a thing, except letting him know somebody suspected him. That wouldn't help Blaze a bit. She had no idea what else to do, and she couldn't stick around long enough to do it, anyway.

Cat was less than a mile from the marina when a Safe Harbor police car came around a bend and raced up behind her, lights flashing and siren blaring.

She pulled onto the grassy shoulder to let it pass, shocked when it pulled in behind her.

Her shock turned to worry when the door opened and the officer stepped out.

Chapter 7

Cat took a deep breath to ease the panic banging around in her chest. "Stay calm and be friendly," she muttered, but she worried nonetheless. This looked like the same cop car that had pulled into Wally's. Varga wouldn't have been dumb enough to get the cops involved, would he?

"License and registration, ma'am," a young male voice said as he walked up to the passenger side and stopped. Cat started in surprise. She'd expected it to be Nick. She leaned down for a better look. The young man looked like an eager Boy Scout, barely old enough to shave, let alone wear a uniform and carry a gun. But his intent expression and erect posture said he meant business. She had to play this right.

Cat reached into the glove compartment and spent several minutes rooting around, pulling out papers, replacing them, pretending to search for the registration.

The young man leaned toward the passenger window. "Ma'am?"

She raised pleading eyes to his. "I know. I'm sorry. I just can't seem to find it. I know it was in here." She flipped through more papers, making a show of checking each one.

"License, ma'am."

"Oh yes. Of course." She grabbed her tote off the floorboard and started the charade all over again. She scooped things out of the bag, smiled sheepishly at him, scooped some more. Finally she sat back in defeat. "I'm sorry. I can't seem to put my hands on it. Oh! Wait. I know where it is. It's in my other purse. I was at a wedding, you see, and I had to change purses and . . . If you could wait just a few minutes, I'll run home and get it and bring it down to the station."

He narrowed his eyes, pen poised over his pad. "What's your name, ma'am?"

She smiled. "I'm Cat. One of the Martinelli girls. My sister Eve just got married—"

"Step out of the car, ma'am."

"What? Why? What's going on?"

"Keep your hands where I can see them."

"I-I don't understand." She kept up the bewildered bimbo act, but panic raced through her veins. She stepped out of the car as he came around the hood, his hand far too close to his gun, in her opinion. The other hovered near a Taser, which didn't make her feel any better.

"Were you just at Wally's Gas-n-Go?"

"I . . . yes." She smiled. "Was that you pulling in just as I left? I was going to get some ice cream for Mama, but then I realized it would melt by the time I got home."

He settled back on his heels. "Eddie Varga says you assaulted him."

"What? Why would he say that?" She didn't think he wanted the cops digging around in his business any more than she did.

Just then, a Safe Harbor SUV pulled in, and Cat squeezed her eyes shut for a moment as Nick Stanton's long length climbed out. Her day just kept getting better and better.

He walked over and looked from one to the other, his stance the same as the young cop's, only Nick carried an air of authority the kid was still years away from achieving. "What's going on here, JD?"

The younger officer cleared his throat. "Well, sir, I stopped at Wally's a little while ago and saw Ms. Martinelli here leaving. Eddie

Varga and a couple of his friends were there, and he said Ms. Martinelli assaulted him."

Cat snorted in disbelief, then wished she hadn't when two pairs of eyes speared her. Nick raised an eyebrow. "Is that true, Ms. Johnson?"

"I thought you said your name was Martinelli?" JD asked. Nick shot him a look and turned back to Cat.

"He came at me first. I was merely protecting myself."

"Walk me through what happened. Why did he come at you?"

Cat studied his eyes a moment, glad he'd removed his dark sunglasses. Blaze and the whole Martinelli family believed he was a good cop, so she decided to give him the truth. At least part of it. "I went there to see if he knew anything about Teddy's death."

His gaze sharpened. "And did he?"

"He said he didn't."

"Did you believe him?"

"No."

"What made you think he might have information on a police investigation?"

Cat studied him, debated how much to say. "He was a known drug user when I was in high school. I'd heard he was still involved, thought maybe he knew something."

"You've been back in town for less than two days and you heard that, did you?"

Cat decided it was a rhetorical question and didn't respond.

"What made you think drugs were involved in Teddy's death?"

She crossed her arms to keep from fiddling with the scarf, uncomfortable under his intense gaze. She didn't figure much got past the brown-eyed cop. "Blaze didn't think Teddy had any health conditions, so drugs seemed the next logical choice."

He looked like he was about to say something, then changed his mind and asked, "What happened then?"

Oh, she so did not want the police involved in this. *You should have thought of that before you stabbed Varga,* a little voice chirped, but she ignored it. She leveled her gaze at Nick and said, "He got a little too close, and I asked him to leave me alone. Then I left."

JD stiffened. "She's lying, Nick. Varga was bleeding."

"Or maybe she's omitting a few things." His eyes flew to her neck and back again. "Do you want to file a report?"

Cat shook her head, no. *God, no.* That was the last thing she needed.

A car slowed on the road beside them, and Cat glanced up just in time to see Avery Ames, owner of the *Gazette*, lower her camera and drive away. Panic spiked. If her picture appeared in the paper . . .

She had to get away from Nick and his piercing gaze and his too-many questions, away from Safe Harbor altogether. She should have left last night. Except for Blaze's pleading, she would have. *Easy, girl. You can do this.* She kept her voice calm, with just the right amount of deference. "May I go now?"

"She couldn't provide her license or registration when I asked for them," JD said, staring her down while talking to Nick. He held up his pad. "I'm going to have to issue you a citation for that. And one for not having your license with you."

Cat found her best smile. "I know. I'm sorry. I'll bring them by the station in a little while, OK?"

JD settled his hands on his utility belt, pushed his Stetson back on his head. "You can't drive without a license."

Cat indicated the two-lane road. "You know the marina is right there."

"It's against policy to—"

Nick interrupted with a jerk of his chin toward her car. "Go on. I'll follow you."

Cat stifled an instinctive cry of alarm. If he followed her, she'd have to produce her license, which she could do, but if he started digging around . . . She nodded and climbed into her car, scrambling for the best way to handle this.

———

Nick watched as Cat eased her car onto the road and headed toward the marina.

JD looked thoughtful. "She was there last night, with the girl, Blaze, when they found Teddy."

"Yes, she was."

"You think she really went to Varga to get information?"

"I'm about to find out."

"Varga was bleeding from his shoulder. He said she assaulted him, but he didn't want to press charges."

"Good work, JD." He handed him a list of names. "Start in the middle and work your way down, talk to Teddy's friends. I'll catch up with you."

"Sure thing, boss."

Nick wanted to correct him, since he wasn't officially anyone's boss, but with only a three-man department, plus Wanda, and Chief Monroe increasingly absent, Nick found himself in charge by default. JD would make a good cop someday, but right now, he was still green as summer grass.

He climbed into his SUV, but before he followed Cat, he ran her plate. It came back with the name and address of a man named Walt Simms of Nashville. He made a mental note to call Mr. Simms, then put the SUV in gear and headed to the marina.

———

Cat raced back to the marina, then sat in her car and unpacked her new phone. She forced herself to stay calm and carefully set up the phone step by step, desperate to get it done before Nick showed up. She hopped out of her car and tucked the phone under her ear as it went through the automated process while she hurried over to Pop's workshop. She set her current phone on the workbench and smashed it with a hammer, then scooped the pieces into a trash bag and deposited them in the dumpster at the far end of the parking area.

Relieved when it finally finished the setup, she dialed Walt's number with hands that wanted to shake. He didn't pick up. She waited for the recording, then said, "Hey, Walt. It's Cat. I'm sorry to bother you. There's a cop who will probably call you about the car. Don't tell him much, OK, just that you're letting me use it. Thanks."

She reached into the car for the three bunches of flowers and turned as Nick pulled into the parking area and climbed out of his SUV, looked around. Tall, well built, he had that universal cop confidence, coupled with a terrifyingly sharp mind. How was it, she wondered, that a man who scared her so much could simultaneously make her want to curl up against all that hard muscle?

———

Nick watched Cat glance his way, wariness clear in every line of her body. He wasn't sure what had gone on with Varga, exactly, but if the punk was bleeding and she wasn't, there was more to her toned body than met the eye.

Arms full of flowers, she turned to face him as he approached. "Can I help?" he asked.

She flashed a quick smile. "I've got them, thanks."

"Nicky, what a surprise. Come have some sweet tea," Mama called from the porch. The house sat up behind the marina and let Mama keep an eye on the comings and goings. Nick was glad to see her up and about. Her voice sounded stronger, too.

Before he could respond, Cat said, "We'll be up in a minute, Mama." She turned to him with a fierce look. "I don't want to give her a minute's worry. Stay here while I put these in water and grab my license. Act friendly."

He grinned at her tone. "Yes, ma'am." He knew the Martinellis were fiercely protective of each other. He just hadn't expected it from Cat, who, by all accounts, hadn't wanted a thing to do with them for a decade. Now she was back, and within hours, a teen was dead. It put him on alert.

He stepped through the screen door to where Mama Rosa sat in a rocker, knitting, and leaned over to kiss her cheek. Overhead, a ceiling fan spun the humid air in lazy circles.

"Looks good," he said, pointing to whatever she held, though he had no idea what it was.

She held up what appeared to be a Christmas stocking. "I started making booties for Sasha's baby, but I think I got a little carried away." He saw the twinkle in her eye, and it warmed him all the way to his toes. She looked better, stronger, than she had in months.

Cat rushed onto the porch from inside the house, and Nick forced himself to look away from the long, shapely legs on display in her denim shorts. She was too thin, but she still had the firm, toned look of someone who worked out regularly. Yoga, maybe?

She thrust her license at him, and he glanced down at the name. "Catharine Walsh of Nashville, Tennessee." He looked up, saw the worry in her eyes. What would he find when he ran it through the system? He smiled at Mama. "I'll have to take a rain check on the tea." His eyes met Cat's. "Walk me to my car?"

Cat nodded, and he held the screen door open for her. When they reached his SUV, he said, "What will I find when I check on this license, Cat?"

Her eyes snapped up to his, her expression hard. "Nothing."

"And when I call Walt Simms?" He watched her reaction to the name, but she didn't give anything away.

"He'll tell you I'm borrowing his car, which is the truth."

He pointed at her scarf. "Let me see the bruises."

That got her attention. Her hand instantly covered the scarf before she let it drop, smoothed her features. "I don't know what you mean."

He played a hunch. "We can do this here, where you can give me the whole story, just the two of us, or I can take you in for questioning and start doing all kinds of checking into your background."

Her chin came up, and he saw the internal debate before she slowly untied the scarf and pulled it from around her slender neck. Ugly red marks, already turning purple, circled her throat. His jaw hardened.

"He tried to strangle you. Why?"

"I told you. He didn't like me asking questions about Teddy."

"Why Varga?" He narrowed his gaze. "What did Blaze tell you? And why didn't she tell me, instead?"

He watched her think it through, decide how much to say. When she finally spoke, her tone made it clear she thought him an idiot. "She was trying to protect Teddy. And his parents. She thought he had gotten involved with Varga, and I wanted to see what he knew, get a reaction when I questioned him."

"Oh, you got a reaction." He propped his hands on his hips. "This is an official investigation, Cat. You have no business getting in the middle of it."

"I know. And I don't want to have anything to do with it. But Blaze . . . I told her I would go talk to him, see if he knew anything."

"What does Blaze know?" Another hesitation. "Do I have to arrest you for impeding an investigation?" It was a stretch, but the way she doled out pieces of info like they were diamonds made him want to push, and push hard.

"She's just trying to find out what happened."

"Which is my job!"

"She said his parents would be devastated if he was involved with drugs."

"Was he?"

"Anything I say right now would be considered hearsay. You'll have to ask Blaze."

"You seem to know a lot about the law."

"I watch a lot of television."

He nodded to her neck. "Do you want to press charges for assault?"

He wasn't surprised when she shook her head, retied the scarf. Part of the bruising still showed on one side, so he reached over and gently covered it. She flinched, and a blush stole up her pale skin.

He pulled his hand away, worried he'd hurt her. "Sorry. Wanted to make sure Mama Rosa wouldn't see anything."

She looked up in surprise, and he wondered what kinds of cops—or men in general—she'd dealt with in the past. None of his business, he told himself. *Stay focused.*

He turned to go. "Don't leave town for the next couple of days."

"What? *Why?*" This time, there was no mistaking the panic in her eyes.

"I may have some more questions about Teddy's death."

"That's ridiculous. I've told you everything I know."

He studied her. "Maybe. Stick around anyway."

She met his gaze, eyes sparking with anger—and a touch of fear—but didn't say a word. As he pulled away, she was still watching him. He realized she hadn't protested that she had a job she had to get back to. He'd have to ask Walt Simms in Nashville about that, too.

Chapter 8

Nick pulled up in front of Wally's Gas-n-Go, climbed out of his SUV, and scanned the area from behind his shades. Varga and his cronies lounged in their usual spot around the picnic table. Nobody showed any reaction to his presence, but he could feel the change in the air. He had to play this just right. Part of him wanted to lock Varga's sorry butt up for the bruises around Cat's neck, but since she wouldn't press charges, he couldn't really force the issue. Besides, he wanted to get Varga on more than that. All his cop instincts screamed that he'd been involved with Demetri and Roy and their drug business in Safe Harbor. He just hadn't been able to make the connection yet. At least, he had no hard evidence and certainly nothing that would stand up in court.

He walked over, hands resting on the front of his utility belt within easy reach of his weapon. "How're things, Eddie? Guys?" He nodded to the other men.

Varga blew out a stream of cigarette smoke, shrugged, and winced. "Can't complain. What brings you out here?"

Nick hitched his chin toward the gauze on Eddie's upper arm. "Officer Dempsey says you accused Cat Johnson of stabbing you in the shoulder this morning." He used the name the locals knew her by and watched for a reaction, waiting to see if Varga repeated his earlier accusation. Nick itched to put a few bruises on Eddie's scrawny neck to match those on Cat's, but that wouldn't get him what he needed.

"I think Dempsey misunderstood. Cat and I had a friendly conversation. When she almost fell, I tried to help and scraped my shoulder against the picnic table." He met Nick's eyes, challenge in them. "I'm a klutz. What can I say?"

Nick glanced at the other men, who eyed Nick with distain. "From what I hear, you spent some time hanging out with Teddy Winston before he died."

Varga shook his head. "Such a shame what happened to the kid. Do you know what killed him yet? Very sad. I feel for his parents."

"Was he buying drugs from you, Eddie?"

"Now you're insulting me, Officer. You know I don't do drugs, or sell them. Especially not to kids." He paused, leaned a fraction closer. "That's just speculation. If you had one shred of proof, you'd have arrested me a long time ago." His expression had turned smug, daring Nick to disagree. Knowing he couldn't chafed Nick like too-tight jeans. "But I did spend a bit of time with Teddy. He was a good kid. Wanted to learn to fish, so I took him out a time or two. You can ask around at the marina."

"Your uncle still doing fishing charters?" Nick asked, and Varga nodded. "You go out with him?"

"When he needs help. Tourists book everything through the Internet these days. Hard for my uncle to compete with the big flashy outfits in Tampa." Varga pierced him with a look. "If you're worried Teddy was involved in drugs, you should ask Joey Bard what he keeps in his storage room at the Blue Dolphin. Now you didn't hear it from me, but there are rumors that certain items pass from there on out the back door at the Dolphin."

Nick kept his tone casual. "What kind of items?"

Eddie shrugged. "I dunno. Just what I heard, is all." He stood. "Don't let us keep you, Officer."

At the arrogant, dismissive tone, Nick grabbed him by the front of his tank top and yanked him close. "You ever lay another hand on Cat Johnson—or any other woman—and I'll come down on you like the wrath of God. We clear?"

Varga sneered. "Careful, Officer. This feels a lot like police brutality. I think Chief Monroe—or the mayor—wouldn't be too happy about that."

"Don't push me, Eddie." Nick released him and stepped back.

"Hope you figure out what killed that kid."

Nick climbed into his SUV and pulled out of the parking lot. He glanced in his rearview mirror and saw Varga salute him with his cigarette. He couldn't blame Cat for stabbing him. He was tempted to shoot him just on general principle. He sighed, rubbed the back of his neck.

He'd bet every last dollar Varga was involved in Safe Harbor's drug trade, and he wouldn't stop until he proved it. In the meantime, nobody manhandled women. Not on his watch. He'd be keeping an eye on Varga.

———

Cat went out onto the porch after Nick left. Mama looked up from her knitting. "He is a good man."

"If you say so," Cat said, then smiled to take the sting out of her words.

Mama eyed her shrewdly. "There are good policemen and bad ones. Nick is a good one."

Which was part of what she was afraid of. If he was as good a cop as everyone seemed to think, there was no way he wouldn't dig around in her background, try to figure her out. Especially since she was driving someone else's car and had shown up about the same time a local teen turned up dead. She was sure he'd already run her license and talked to Walt by now. She only hoped Safe Harbor hadn't suddenly gone high tech. Billy's forgery was good, but she wasn't sure how good.

A chill passed over her. That wasn't her biggest concern, of course. She couldn't still be here when someone in town said something to someone else, or posted something online or . . . the *Gazette.*

"Mama, where is the paper?" She tried to keep her voice calm as anxiety churned in her gut.

Mama nodded to a basket in the living room, and Cat grabbed the paper, flipping pages. Several minutes later, she let out a small sigh of relief when she found no mention of her name or, worse, any pictures of her.

Blaze walked into the room wearing a black T-shirt and jeans and saw Cat sitting on the couch. "The online version is better. There are always more pictures."

Cat's relief vanished. "Do you have a computer?"

Blaze nodded. "Laptop, why?"

"I need to borrow it for a few minutes."

To keep from wringing her hands while she waited, Cat went into the kitchen and rooted around in a lower cabinet until she found three vases. She put the flowers for Mama on the kitchen table, then put the other two bunches into separate vases. She was carrying the second one out to the living room when she heard Blaze clump down the hall.

She set them down on the coffee table in front of the teen. Blaze looked up. "Nice."

"They're for you."

Her head snapped up. "What? Why?"

Cat shrugged. "I have no idea what kind of flowers most of them are, but the gerbera daisies at least looked bright and cheery. Thought they might make you smile."

Blaze buried her head in the blooms, and when she looked up, her eyes were wet. She swiped the tears away. "Thanks." She shrugged indifferently. "Nobody ever bought me flowers before."

Something clenched in Cat's heart. She understood. Truly. But she'd also learned Blaze wasn't outwardly emotional. She smiled. "They're frivolous and beautiful just by being there. Enjoy."

Blaze turned the laptop her way. "You want me to do a search for something?"

"I just wanted to see the latest issue of the *Gazette*."

Blaze's fingers flew over the keys. "Since Avery Ames took over, they have a Facebook page, and they're on Twitter, too."

The knot in Cat's stomach grew. Blaze set the laptop on the coffee table, and the two of them scanned the paper, along with the *Gazette*'s social media sites. It figured that this little town would move into the next century now.

Cat looked up when she felt Blaze staring at her. "You have bruises on your neck."

She reached for the scarf, then dropped her hand. "No big deal."

Blaze looked horrified. "Did Eddie do that? What did he say?"

"He said he was sorry Teddy was dead but he didn't have anything to do with it."

Blaze narrowed her eyes. "Why do you have bruises, then?"

Cat made a mental note never to underestimate this girl's smarts. She was quick, too. "Let's just say I told him I doubted his story."

"I hope you gave as good as you got."

Cat's grin was quick, then she sobered. "He probably won't be pitching today, that's for sure."

Blaze's cell phone signaled an incoming text. While her thumbs flew, Cat scanned the rest of the sites, relieved that, at least for the moment, there was no mention of her anywhere. But she had to be long gone before that changed. The idea that someone would hurt any of her family on her account was enough to make her want to throw up. Or leave town right this second.

She stood, ready to run upstairs and grab her stuff. Let Nick dig around in her past. He wouldn't find anything. She had to disappear again.

"We need to go talk to Bryan," Blaze said.

Cat saw the fear in her face. "Who's Bryan?"

"He was Teddy's best friend since, like, kindergarten. He just texted that he needs to see me. It's important, he said. He sounded scared."

Cat glanced at the stairs, then at Blaze, torn. The worry that disaster would strike her family if she didn't leave right now rumbled like an impending storm.

Blaze must have seen something in her eyes, because an air of resignation slumped her shoulders. "Never mind. I'll go myself."

Cat squeezed her eyes shut. She couldn't just leave. But if she stayed too long?

She swallowed her unease. "Let me grab my keys."

Just a couple more hours. Then she'd be gone.

Chapter 9

Nick returned to the station, surprised to find Chief Monroe in residence. Lately, the man spent more time out of the station than in. He'd been making more and more noise about retiring and dropping hints that he wanted Nick to take over, which was fine by Nick. He wanted to be the next chief of police. He just had to be sure he didn't tell his boss off before he got the job. He didn't like Monroe's politicking and good-old-boy police work, but he figured there were still things to learn about the people who lived here from a guy who'd held the job for so many years.

Monroe and JD had their heads together when Nick came in the door.

"Hey, Nick," Wanda said as she handed him a stack of little pink slips. "Messages."

He'd been trying to get Wanda to send him texts instead, but she said she wasn't comfortable with all that high-tech stuff. He hid his sigh behind a smile. "Thanks, Wanda."

"Nick, I was just checking in with JD on where we are with Teddy Winston's sad death," Monroe said. "Teddy's father just called me again, asking for news. Do we know how the poor boy died yet?"

"Still waiting on the coroner, Chief," Nick replied as he approached.

"What's this I hear about you roughing up Eddie Varga?" Monroe asked.

Nick shook his head, amazed—and a little jealous—of how far and fast Monroe's network reached. "I didn't rough him up. I simply got close enough to be sure he got my point. Who is saying different?"

Monroe brushed it aside. "Don't get riled, just wondered on your take is all."

"Who told you?"

Before Monroe said anything, Nick's cell phone rang. "Stanton."

"This is Eloise from Blue Sky Cellular in Tampa. I just wanted to let you know I emailed you Theodore Winston's call log."

Nick's phone chirped with an incoming email as he was thanking her. He pulled the phone away and checked. "Yes, I just got it. Thank you for responding so quickly."

Nick hung up, then opened the email and scrolled down to the bottom of the list first, checking to see who Teddy had called right before he died.

"Who was that?" Monroe asked.

"I asked for Teddy's cell phone log. I want to know who he called the other night."

"And?"

"Two names. Blaze Martinelli and Bryan Hendricks. Both within minutes of each other."

———

Bryan Hendricks's family didn't have a lot of money, judging by the age of the single-wide mobile home set back in the trees. But where Eddie Varga's home showed both age and neglect, the Hendricks obviously took care of what was theirs. The yard was neatly mowed, there was a vegetable garden planted in neat rows behind a sturdy fence, and clothes flapped in the breeze from a line that hung between the house and an equally aging carport.

As soon as Cat parked, Bryan hurried out of the house toward them, grief and worry etched in every line of his thin face. He was tall and lanky, very similar to Teddy in build, from what she remembered, but his hair was dark while Teddy's had been blond.

He pulled Blaze into a bear hug, his eyes red-rimmed and haunted. Interesting that Blaze didn't pull away from him, like she did everyone else.

Blaze finally stepped back, eyed him carefully. "Tell me what's going on."

"I don't know what to do." He looked from Cat to Blaze and back again.

Blaze nodded at her. "She's cool. You can talk in front of her."

"So the other night, Teddy was really freaked out, you know?"

"Which night? Saturday?" Cat asked.

"No, Friday night. He brought his PlayStation over, and we were playing video games, but he was really jumpy, and scared and, like, he couldn't sit still. He kept jumping up and looking out the window, like he was looking for someone. When I asked him what was going on, he wouldn't say. We kept playing, but after a while, he said he was tired and was going to go." He took a deep breath before he reached into his back pocket and pulled out a folded piece of paper, held it out to Blaze. "He gave me this note and said if anything ever happened to him, I should give it to you."

Blaze's hand shook as she took the envelope and read the short note. Her eyes filled, and she handed the note to Cat, who read it aloud.

"Blaze, I'm so sorry. You deserved better. I never meant for any of this to happen, but it's too late. You were the best thing that ever happened to me. I hope you'll think good thoughts when you remember me. Be happy. I love you. Teddy."

Blaze leaned against the car, hands over her face, crying silent tears. Her shoulders shook, but she didn't make a sound.

When she looked up at Cat, her eyes were filled with anguish. "Does that mean he killed himself? Is that what it means?"

Cat shook her head, her heart aching. "I don't know, Blaze. It sounds like it. Or it could mean he was in some kind of trouble he didn't know how to get out of."

"But then that means somebody killed him!" Blaze shouted.

"We still don't know that," Cat said. "But I think you need to show the note to Nick." She turned to Bryan. "And he should know about Friday night." She didn't understand why she kept pushing them toward the police, when normally she ran as far and as fast as she could away from the cops, but there was something intrinsically honest and decent about Nick that made her trust him. Which also scared her enough to cause heart palpitations, since she knew that also meant he'd never stop until he got answers. About Teddy. Or about her, if he started digging.

Bryan was clearly still agonizing over something. "What else, Bryan?" Cat asked.

His head snapped toward her, and indecision warred inside him, Cat could tell. "He, uh, he left something else." He picked up a worn black backpack from where he'd set it beside the car, and Cat was surprised she hadn't noticed it before.

He slid the zipper open and showed them a gallon-size zippered freezer bag that had dozens of small bags inside it, all filled with marijuana. Blaze cursed. Cat sucked in a breath.

"I-I don't know what to do."

"You have to give it to Nick," Blaze said immediately.

"But what if he thinks it's mine?"

"He won't. Nick will believe you," Blaze insisted.

Cat wished she could be as certain. Alarm bells clanged in her head. As much as she felt she could trust Nick, when drugs were involved, things could get dicey. But before she could figure out what to do, the man himself pulled in next to her car.

As he climbed out of his SUV, Cat had to remind herself not to stare. Despite the scary uniform, he had the kind of male magnetism that made some primitive part of her want to reach up and wrap her arms around his neck, pull him close, and never let go. Since she hadn't had a reaction like that to a man in, well, forever, the thought brought her up short and yanked up all her defensive shields, quick. He was a cop. He was the very last man on the planet she should want to get close to, in any sense of the word.

She backed up several steps, and her chin rose as he glanced her way, a question in his eyes.

———

Nick was surprised to see Blaze and Cat already there. Blaze looked completely devastated. Cat looked wary. And worried.

He approached the skinny teenage boy. Dark hair. Red-rimmed eyes. "Are you Bryan? I'm Officer Stanton, with the Safe Harbor police. I'd like to ask you a few questions about your friend Teddy." When Bryan's chin quivered, he added, "I'm very sorry for your loss."

"Thank you. He was my best friend, since kindergarten."

The boy spoke well, looked Nick in the eye, lived in a well-kept house with a tidy yard. Good family, financially strapped as many were, but hardworking, from what Monroe had said. "Are your folks home, Bryan?"

"No, sir. They're both at work."

"You talked to Teddy on Saturday night?"

Bryan stiffened in surprise. "How did you know that?"

"We pulled Teddy's phone records." He watched the boy's face. "What did you two talk about?"

"Not a lot," Bryan said, frustration evident. "When he called, he was upset, scared. He wouldn't tell me what it was about, just said, 'Loose lips sink ships.'"

Nick stilled inside. "Do you know why he said that? Was he keeping a secret of some kind?"

Bryan looked from Blaze to Cat and back to Nick, pleading. "He's never been in any trouble. He never did any drugs, nothing, you've got to believe that, but . . ."

Nick waited while Bryan tried to get the words out, to say whatever so obviously troubled him. Finally the boy took the backpack and handed it to Nick. "He left this here Friday night, along with a note for Blaze. Said if anything happened to him, I should give her the note."

"Did you tell anyone about it? Let anyone know you were worried?"

At this, Bryan looked sick. "No, I thought he was exaggerating or something. When I talked to him on Saturday morning, he tried to laugh it off. Said just to hang on to the backpack and he'd be back for it."

"Did you believe him?"

"I didn't know what to believe. He was acting really weird."

Nick kept his gaze on the boy. "Weird scared? Or weird like he might hurt himself?"

"No! Weird scared. He'd never hurt himself. Things were going good for him." He glanced at Blaze. "He and Blaze were good. He was working up the courage to tell her he loved her."

Nick took the backpack and opened the zipper. He swallowed a curse but showed no outward reaction as he walked to his SUV, pulled out a pair of gloves, and put them on, then looked through the rest of the bag. "Did you touch the bag with the weed? Anything inside the backpack?"

Bryan shook his head. "I-I don't think so. I didn't even open it until after . . . I peeked in and zipped it shut again."

"Was he selling drugs?" Nick directed the question to Bryan and Blaze, who both instantly denied it.

"Do you know where he got these bags, then?"

Again, fierce denials.

"Who else did Teddy hang out with?" He included Blaze in the question as he held up the backpack. "Where would he have gotten the drugs?"

Blaze just kept shaking her head. "I don't know." She speared him with a hard glance. "I would tell you if I did."

He held out his gloved hand. "May I see the note?"

Blaze handed it over and leaned against the car, trembling. Cat moved over and stood next to her, not close enough to touch, just enough to let her know she was there.

Nick took out an evidence bag, carefully placed the note inside. "I'm afraid I need to hold on to this for a while. But you'll get it back, OK?"

Blaze swallowed, hard. "Do you think he killed himself?"

"We'll know more once we get the coroner's report. What about the phone call Saturday night? Does the saying he quoted mean anything to either of you? Was it a signal or code of some kind?"

Both teens shook their heads.

"If I hadn't shown up, what were you going to do with the bag?"

Cat shoved away from the car, marched toward him. "They were just talking about how they were going to call you and give it to you when you showed up. They're good kids."

"I know they're good kids. I'm just asking questions."

Her eyes spit fire under her cool outward demeanor. "Don't jump to conclusions."

Now she was being insulting. "I am trying to figure out what happened to their friend. Jumping to conclusions is not, nor has it ever been, part of my police strategy."

She met his gaze head-on, nodded once, as if to say, "OK, then."

He eyed both teens. "If you think of anything else, even if it doesn't seem important, call me, OK?"

Nick pulled away from the house, jaw clenched. Drugs. He muttered a stream of curses and thought through the conversation. Blaze looked ready to collapse, poor girl, so he was glad Cat was there.

Maybe.

As a cop, he'd learned long ago never to believe in coincidences. Cat's arrival at the same time as Teddy's death and more drugs showing up in Safe Harbor gave him that itchy feeling he was missing something.

It was time to check out the lady's background. See what popped.

Chapter 10

Cat breathed a sigh of relief when Nick left. Whenever he was around, Cat felt like she couldn't quite get enough air. Between his size and intensity—and those piercing brown eyes that seemed to see too much—he made her feel naked and exposed.

Blaze nodded her head toward Bryan. "I told you Nick would believe you."

He shrugged. "I hope so. What if he turns around and then says it was me. That I'm dealing drugs." He turned pleading eyes to Cat. "I'm trying to get scholarships to go to the University of Florida. I'd never do anything to mess that up."

Part of Cat shared his concern, but she wouldn't say that out loud. Bryan was worried enough. She hoped, for his sake, that they'd all been right about Nick.

She looked around, her anxiety rising now that Nick was gone. She glanced at the woods surrounding the property, and the sense that someone was watching her made her stiffen. She forced herself to act normally, but she knew with sick certainty that her time was up. She had to leave Safe Harbor. Now. She just hoped it wasn't too late.

"You ready, Blaze? Nice to meet you, Bryan. I'm sorry you lost your friend."

She climbed into the car and waited for Blaze to join her, then headed toward the marina.

"Teddy wasn't a drug dealer."

"That's what you've been saying. So maybe, like you said, he was tempted and then changed his mind. And someone, ah, didn't want him to do that."

Blaze took a deep, shuddering breath. "So he tried to do the right thing and get out of it, and they killed him."

"Maybe. We don't know."

"We have to find out. What's our next step?"

Cat glanced at her, then back at the road. "There really is no next step, Blaze. Nick has the backpack. I get the idea he won't stop until he figures out what really happened."

Blaze eyed her shrewdly. "You're leaving, aren't you?"

Cat kept her eyes on the road. "I told you I couldn't stay. I should have left already."

"You're going to make Mama cry."

Cat swallowed, hard. "I don't want to, but yeah. Probably."

"Why did you come back if you weren't staying?" The accusation reminded Cat how young Blaze really was.

She raised an eyebrow. "Have you tried telling Eve no?"

A quick smile flashed across Blaze's features. "Yeah, she's a total bulldozer."

"I've missed everyone," Cat admitted.

"Then why can't you stay, get a job here?"

"I can't, Blaze. It just isn't possible."

"Is someone after you?"

They pulled up in front of the marina. "I just need to get back to work is all."

"Fine, don't tell me. Whatever." She slammed the door and marched onto the porch.

Cat sighed as she followed. She greeted Mama, then went upstairs and packed her few belongings. A tug of nostalgia gripped her as she glanced around the bedroom, then picked up her small bag and left. If she was smart, she'd never be back.

Sasha was in the kitchen making a sandwich when Cat stepped in. The sight of her baby bump firmed Cat's resolve.

Sasha turned, sandwich in hand, and sat down at the table. She eyed the vase. "Nice flowers."

"They're for you. I got a bunch for Mama and one for Blaze, too," she added, and Sasha's mouth dropped open in shock.

"Why?"

Cat looked away and shrugged. "Why not? Thought you might like them."

The silence lengthened. Sasha looked at her bag. "You're leaving?"

"Yes, it's time. I should have left already."

Sasha studied her. "Have they found out what Teddy died from yet?"

"No. Nick is looking into it. I'm sure he'll figure it out. He seems like a nice guy, decent. For a cop."

"He's a nice guy, period. He's been there for us in some really tough situations lately."

Cat heard the unspoken criticism that she hadn't been there for her family. She couldn't explain, even if she wanted to.

The silence lengthened. So much stood between them, and Cat had no idea how to bridge the gap, or even if it was possible. Maybe the distance was for the best. Safer. But in that moment, it made her sad.

Sasha bit her lip, which was very unlike her. "Look, Cat, about what happened in high school, the night of your symphony audition—"

Cat didn't let her finish. "That was a long time ago. I don't want to go there. But it's OK, Sash. Really." On impulse, she leaned over and gave her sister a quick hug. "Be safe and take good care of everyone, especially that new baby."

She hurried out before Sasha could say anything else. On the porch, she steeled herself as Mama spotted her bag, her eyes filling with tears. Cat hated, *hated*, making Mama cry. She crouched down in front of Mama's rocker, took both her hands. "You knew I couldn't stay. I'm sorry, Mama. Don't cry."

Reaching out, Mama cupped her cheeks in both palms. "Whatever you are running from, let us help."

Cat shook her head sadly. "You can't help, Mama. But I'm fine. Please don't worry." She leaned in and gave her a quick kiss, then stood. "I'll say goodbye to Pop before I go."

"Will you let us know you're safe?"

Cat looked over her shoulder, throat thick as she memorized the picture of Mama on the porch, looking so strong and yet small in her rocker. "I will do my best. I love you."

She dropped her bag and violin in her trunk, then walked into the marina and found Pop behind the counter. He met her eyes and nodded. "You are leaving."

"Yes, it's time."

He came around the counter, gathered her in for a hug. He smelled like seawater and Old Spice and home. She hugged him back, alarmed at how thin he'd gotten. "I am glad you came for the wedding, Cathy. It was good to see you. We've missed you."

"I've missed you, too. Take good care of Mama and Blaze."

Behind the sadness and worry, a bit of his usual twinkle emerged. "That is a full-time job."

"But you do it well," Cat quipped, leaning in for a kiss. He froze at her words, and Cat realized what she'd said. All those years ago, when Nick, aka Tony, was kidnapped, he hadn't done such a good job taking care of his family, not to her mind. She still couldn't believe he'd known—or at least suspected—who'd taken Nick and had said nothing for so many years.

"Love you, Pop. Gotta go."

She hurried to her car and bumped down the drive and out to the main road before she had the chance to change her mind. She couldn't let the pull of family, the desire to be here with them, let her lose sight of the truth.

If she loved them, she had to get far, far away from here. And stay away.

———

As Nick left the Hendricks place and drove back to town, he eyed the backpack on the floorboard beside him. He didn't doubt what Bryan had said. He'd found no evidence anywhere in the boy's background that tied him to drugs. But he hadn't found anything linking Teddy, either, yet he obviously had been. The question was, who had supplied them? And with that much in the backpack, were other kids from the high school involved?

He pulled into a spot right in front of the Blue Dolphin, since he'd shown up between the lunch and dinner rush. He climbed out of his SUV and scanned the street, but nothing seemed out of place. Still, he could feel something pulsing just beneath the smooth surface of his little town, and he wouldn't stop until he'd dug up whatever it was and rooted it out.

Logic said that after Demetri and Roy had smuggled drugs through town for twenty-plus years, whoever was behind it wouldn't just pack up and leave. No, they'd restart the network. Looked like they already had. He just didn't know where or by whom. But he'd find out.

He walked into the Dolphin and waited a minute for his eyes to adjust to the gloom. LuAn was behind the old wooden bar, polishing glasses. She looked up when he entered, but before she could start asking question, the phone rang.

Nick looked around, nodded to an older couple by the window, who were obviously tourists, given their crisp new Safe Harbor T-shirts.

He spotted Alice Sutton, Cole's mother, and Buzz Casey, the Sutton Ranch foreman, sitting at a booth in the back, looking very cozy. They were holding hands, if he was not mistaken. As he watched, Alice snatched her hand away. He noted Alice's blush and Buzz's scowl and hid a smile. Well, good for them. Buzz raised a hand and motioned him over.

"Any news on what happened to Teddy?" Alice asked. Her eyes filled. "My heart just aches for his parents. I've gotten to know his mother at the quilt shop. They just seem like the loveliest people." She shook her head. "I can't imagine losing a child."

Nick shifted uncomfortably, aware suddenly that these were the same kinds of conversations that must have gone on all over Safe Harbor after he disappeared from the marina as a three-year-old. He patted Alice's hand. "It's still early days in the investigation, but we should have some answers soon."

"You thinking suicide?" This from Buzz.

"Right now, I'm waiting for the coroner's report and gathering information." He touched the brim of his hat. "You all enjoy the rest of your day."

Everyone knew he couldn't divulge the details of an investigation, but that never stopped anyone from asking.

He walked over to LuAn. "Is Joey in the back?"

Her gaze grew wary. "Yeah. Why?"

"I need to have a word with him."

She hitched a thumb over her shoulder, then raised the walk-through panel so he could pass through to the kitchen.

He found Joey Bard with his head in the bowels of the dishwasher, banging a wrench. "Joey?"

The man smacked his head, yelled, "Ouch," then climbed up from the floor, hitching up his britches as he did. His belly still slid over his belt. "Help you? I need to get this thing fixed before the supper rush." He wiped his hands on a rag looped to his belt.

"You've heard about Teddy Winston?"

"Who hasn't? Shame, though. Everyone says he was a good kid. You find out why he died?"

Nick figured he'd be asked this question at least a dozen more times today. "Not yet. Waiting on the coroner's report." He paused. "How well did you know Teddy?"

Bard's whole body went still. "Not too well. He worked for us every now and again, when we needed extra help with dishes. Mostly weekends, holidays, times like that. He was quiet, kept to himself."

"He have many friends? People he came and left with?"

"The Martinelli girl, mostly"—he circled a hand near his head—"the one with the crazy hair colors. Sometimes another kid. Don't know his name."

As he was talking, Nick was prowling the room, gradually coming to a padlocked door. "What's in here?"

Joey straightened, folded his arms over his chest. "Supplies."

"Why is it locked?"

"Because too many things have mysteriously walked out of there over the years."

"Who has a key?"

"Me. LuAn. The staff."

"Teddy have a key?"

"What's this about, Stanton?"

"Just asking questions. Trying to get a feel for Teddy's life."

"His life had nothing to do with my storage room."

"Mind if I have a look?"

"Actually, yes, I do mind. Now, if you've brought a search warrant . . . ?"

"Why would you mind if I peek at your supplies?"

"I mind nosy cops in general." Gone was the jovial restaurant owner. "I need to get back to work."

"You hear anything about drugs in Safe Harbor? Somebody moving weed, or maybe something worse? Cocaine? Heroin?"

Bard stiffened, folded his arms over his chest. "Only name that comes to mind is Eddie Varga. But I'm sure you already know that."

"Funny, Eddie said the same thing about you."

"Then he's a lying piece of trash and ought to know better." Bard straightened. "You need to leave."

Nick turned toward the door, then stopped. "Thanks for your time. By the way, where were you on Saturday night, about seven?"

Bard narrowed his eyes. "You've lived here long enough to know exactly where I was. Line clear out the door and down the sidewalk that time of night. I was here, and half the town can vouch for me."

"Good to know. You have a nice day."

Nick walked out to his SUV, thinking about their conversation. In a town where most people didn't lock their front doors and break-ins were rare, why would Joey padlock his storage room?

———

Cat refused to look back as she headed toward the interstate, hands gripping the wheel. She had to look forward, always forward. It was the only way she'd stayed alive all these years. Keep moving. Never stay in one place.

She eyed the bottle of tequila that rolled around the floorboard, tempted to pull over and lose herself in it for a while. She knew the relief never lasted long, not even through the hangover, but still, her fingers itched to grab the bottle, just hold it.

The urge was always strongest when she was sad. But she wouldn't give in. She hadn't touched a drop in years, not until Joellen's death, and look what that caused? Mrs. Fletcher had a broken hip, thanks to her.

Joellen had asked her once why she always kept a full bottle with her. Cat had said it was a reminder, that if she didn't pay attention, she could fall back down.

Today, her courage wasn't what it might have been.

Ten miles out of town, her hands were shaking and she almost ran head-on into an oncoming car trying to reach the bottle. She just wanted to wrap her hands around it.

Maybe have one sip.

No. She had to be strong. She wouldn't give in. She'd keep driving until she was somewhere over the Florida state line. Alabama, maybe.

She glanced down at the speedometer, realized she was going way too fast, and started easing up on the accelerator.

A white pickup truck suddenly appeared in her rearview mirror, coming up quick. Cat hugged the shoulder, giving him room to pass, but he stayed right on her tail.

She eyed the shoulder, looking for a place to pull off so he could go around, but there were deep culverts on either side. They were empty now, but would fill up later during the usual afternoon rain.

Suddenly, she heard a loud pop, and her car started fishtailing. She grabbed the wheel, tried to keep it on the road. Heart pounding, she was trying to straighten the tires when there was another loud pop.

Her sweaty palms slid on the steering wheel, and the car veered onto the embankment, down toward the culvert. The angle was steep, and next thing Cat knew, the car rolled over.

The seat belt jerked against her, and she heard glass shatter and felt wetness on her leg. Her head hit the side window as the car bounced once more.

Her world went black.

Chapter 11

"Ma'am, can you hear me? Ma'am? Are you OK?"

Cat fought against the banging in her head, tried to squeeze her eyes shut tighter, but she couldn't make it stop. Someone shook her shoulder, and she tried to jerk away, but she couldn't move. Something held her fast.

"Ma'am? EMS is on the way. Just hang on."

She pried her eyes open and saw a worried young face. He looked vaguely familiar, but she couldn't be sure. Her eyes slid closed, and he poked her shoulder again.

"Stay awake, ma'am. You need to stay awake. Can you tell me your name?"

The fog started to clear, and she glanced around. She looked at the boy again, realized he was wearing a uniform. Cop. Officer . . . somebody. "Cat. Um." It was hard to form words, to think. Her head pounded like somebody was beating her with a big stick. Which name? "Johnson."

She reached over, unclipped her seat belt, and almost fell forward. The cop reached in to steady her, and she winced. No airbags in Walt's car. She must have hit the steering wheel.

She looked past the cop, tried to get her bearings, but everything felt fuzzy.

"What happened?"

"How much have you had to drink today, ma'am?"

She squinted at him. She'd wanted a drink. Badly. Was going to pull over and take just one tiny sip. Just one.

But then why was she in the ditch? Something didn't make sense, but she couldn't reason it out.

Another vehicle arrived with screaming sirens, and Cat put her hands over her ears. Once they turned it off, she lowered her hands again, saw several cuts on her leg.

"Ma'am, do you remember what happened? Were you drinking before you got in the car?"

She tried to think. She'd been at the marina, saying goodbye. Sad. "I'm not sure."

The cop disappeared, and another person took his place, swung the door open with gloved hands. He wrapped a brace around her neck. Then he reached in and brushed away some broken glass, crouched down so she could see him. "Can you climb out of the car?"

Her vision became clearer with every passing minute. She took in his blue shirt, his gloved hands, the pity in his eyes.

She nodded and he helped her out, a hand on her arm. Another EMT appeared beside him, and together they walked her up the embankment. She swayed a bit, and they steadied her.

"Let's get you checked out," the tall one said and motioned to a gurney.

Cat shook her head, which made her dizzy, and she clutched his hand. "I'm OK." She didn't want to go to a hospital. Couldn't afford a hospital. She took off the brace, batted the hands away that tried to stop her.

There was something she had to do. Somewhere she had to go.

Go. Yes, she had to go. Details flitted just out of reach. She had to leave Safe Harbor, but she couldn't quite remember why.

The officer reappeared in front of her, motioning to the yellow line. "Ma'am, could you walk along this line for me, please?"

She eyed him, and the line. What was that about? Nodding, she tried to do as he asked, but the dizziness didn't let up, and she wobbled all over the place. After she'd gone a little way, he said, "Thank you. Let's get you checked out."

He led her to the EMTs, who insisted she sit on the gurney. They shone a light in her eyes and checked her head. "Ouch."

"Sorry. You must have one very hard head, because even with glass in your hair and a good-size bump, the impact didn't break the skin."

Once they stopped poking and prodding, Cat leaned back, just for a moment, and let her eyes slide closed, their words swirling around her. "No signs of a concussion . . . pupils normal . . . broken tequila bottle . . . smells like a distillery . . ."

"Ma'am, let's get you to the hospital, OK?"

Cat's eyes opened as his words sunk in. "No, no hospital. Please." She felt like she was shouting the words, but he leaned closer, as though he could barely hear her. "I'm fine." She tried to sit up, but everything spun. She gripped the sides of the gurney. "Need to leave town."

"Not just yet, ma'am. We need to take a ride to the station."

"Why?"

"We have to do some paperwork. And you're in no condition to get behind the wheel."

"OK." She let him lead her away and into the back seat of his patrol car. Something wasn't right, but she couldn't figure out what.

She dozed until the door opened again. She had a vague memory of being escorted out of the car, into a building, and down a hallway. Finally, finally, they let her sit down. She realized there was a bed and sank down onto it and fell asleep.

She didn't hear the door swing shut or the lock click into place.

———

Nick walked into the station a couple of hours later to find JD talking animatedly to Wanda. "There was tequila all over the car and all over her. She must have been drinking while she drove."

"Who was drinking?" Nick asked.

"Cat Johnson. Rolled her car into the culvert. Impact shattered the bottle and dented the driver's side door."

"How long ago was this?" Nick hadn't left Cat more than two hours or so ago, and she hadn't struck him as someone with an upcoming bender on her mind.

JD hitched his thumb toward the two cells in the back, down the hall. "Brought her in a while ago. She's sleeping it off."

"Why isn't she in the hospital getting checked out?"

"She refused to go. Kept saying, 'No hospital.'" He looked at Nick. "I tried to convince her."

"What did the paramedics say when they checked her out?"

"That she was lucky. Some bruises from where she hit the steering wheel. The car doesn't have airbags. No signs of a concussion."

Something was off about this picture. "Run me through what happened, JD."

"I was driving down CR 310 and saw a car down in the ditch, the roof a little dented but not too bad. When I got there, I saw her in the driver's seat, wearing her seat belt, out cold. The driver's side window was shattered, and there was a broken tequila bottle in the car. Glass and tequila everywhere. I tried to wake her up and called EMS to come check her out."

"Did she say what happened?"

"She was pretty out of it."

"Anything to indicate how she ended up there?"

He shrugged. "Seemed pretty obvious to me. She'd been drinking, lost control."

"What about the car? Did you have it towed?"

"Not yet. But I'm about to."

"Did you administer a Breathalyzer test? How far was she over the limit?" Maybe what happened to Teddy had gotten the best of her. But she didn't strike him as the type to drink and drive. He shook his head.

He really didn't know what type she was, barely knew her at all, but drunk driving didn't ring true to what little he knew.

JD fidgeted but didn't say anything. Nick pierced him with a look. "JD?"

"I, ah, forgot." When Nick started to protest, he held up his hand. "But I did a field sobriety test. I had her walk the yellow line, and she couldn't do it, not even close." He shrugged. "Because she refused to go to the hospital, and the EMTs didn't think there was anything wrong with her besides being stinking drunk, I brought her here to sober up."

Nick eyed the younger man. "Have the car towed to Cliff's Garage and call me when it gets there."

He didn't wait for a response, just walked down the hallway to the cells. He found Cat curled up on the narrow bed, a thin blanket over her, dark hair covering her face. She was out like a light.

———

Cat woke with a start when she heard a door slam. Her eyes opened, and panic raced through her as she tried to figure out where she was. She slowly sat up, winced at the pain in her head, and looked around.

She was in a cell.

She shook her head to clear it, but that proved a mistake, as the room spun and made her stomach churn. *Think.* A cell? How did she get here?

Slowly, the pieces started falling into place. She'd said goodbye to Mama and Pop and driven out of town. She remembered eyeing the tequila bottle, yearning for a drink, but she couldn't summon a memory of taking a sip. She sniffed her shirt. She smelled like tequila, so maybe she wasn't remembering right.

She leaned against the concrete block wall, shivered, then pulled the thin blanket around her shoulders. No, she couldn't remember opening the bottle. Something wasn't right. But it hurt to breathe.

A flash of white. Yes, a truck. It'd come up behind her. There was a loud pop, then the terrifying sensation of being upside down as the car rolled over and down into the drainage ditch.

She pulled her T-shirt away and looked down at her chest where ugly bruises were already forming. She must have hit the steering wheel.

She felt around her head for the source of the throbbing and winced when she touched a knot on the left side. Another flash of memory. Her head had hit the window as the car bounced.

Her brain still wasn't working as fast as it should, but under the confusion was panic. She forced herself to calm down, let the pieces swirl before they settled. She knew logic would come if she waited just a bit.

If she'd been in a car accident, why wasn't she in the hospital? Why was she in a cell?

A cell. *Oh, dear Jesus.* The panic returned, spurred by desperation. She had to get out of this cell. Out of Safe Harbor.

She stood up, swayed, then rushed to the bars at the front of the cell, gripping them with shaking fingers. "Hey, let me out. Is anybody there?" Her voice came out more of a squeak than a demand, so she cleared her throat and tried again. "Hello? Is anybody there? Let me out!"

———

Nick sat at his desk, drinking coffee that had gone cold long ago, the unease in his chest growing with every passing minute. He'd entered Cat's driver's license number into the computer and come up with an address in Tennessee. When he'd checked the address, it turned out to be an abandoned house.

He picked up the phone and called Walt Simms.

"Yeah? What?" he said when he answered.

"This is Officer Nick Stanton of the Safe Harbor Police Department. I need to ask you a couple of questions about Cat Johnson, aka Cat Walsh."

There was a pause. "Where the heck is Safe Harbor?"

"It's in Florida, a bit north of Tampa. Do you know Ms. Johnson, sir?"

"Sure. She's a nice kid. Hard worker."

"She says you lent her your car."

This time the response was instant. "She says right. Happy to let her drive it awhile. I didn't need it. Why are you calling? Is she OK?"

Instead of answering, Nick asked, "You said she's a hard worker. Does she work for you?"

"She plays in a band with a couple guys. They have a regular gig here at the No Name Café. What's wrong?"

"Ms. Johnson was in an accident this morning, but she's fine. Is she a heavy drinker?"

"Glad to hear she's OK." Walt heaved out a sigh. "Cat hasn't had a drop of alcohol in a long time. But she got some bad news the other day. Might have caused her to fall off the wagon."

"What kind of news?"

"You'd have to ask her about that. I don't tell tales out of school."

"Have you known her a long time?"

"Long enough. She's good people, Officer. The best. I know she'd give her last nickel to help a runaway get home."

"Thanks for your time, Mr. Simms."

"Give my best to Cat, will you?"

"I will. Have a nice day."

Nick hung up and sat back in his chair. She hadn't lied about the car, and chances were good she got paid under the table. And she had a drinking problem. Or she'd had one. He understood hiding in a bottle for a while when life completely sucker punched you in the gut. But had she been drinking today?

He decided to do a full background check. There were hundreds of Catharine Walshes, so he narrowed the search by age and area. He didn't find anything under Catharine Johnson, so he figured she made that up when she first arrived in Safe Harbor. With the help of several official databases, he determined that she had no criminal record, at least none that he could find. He ran her social security number and found out she had no bank accounts, had filed no tax returns, had no property or loans or credit cards. On paper, Cat Walsh didn't exist.

What was she hiding?

He heard her shouting from the cell area and pushed to his feet. He was about to find out.

———

When Nick walked through the door separating the cells from the rest of the police station, Cat was struck again by his air of command, his easy confidence. Tall and solidly built, Nick was not someone you wanted to mess with. But she'd seen the way he was with Blaze. He was also a protector. If he was on your side, the odds were in your favor.

Right now, she had to convince him to let her go. She had to leave town—preferably before he ran a background check on her and found out there wasn't much.

She crossed her arms and leaned against the bars, annoyed that the room still had a tendency to spin. "You need to let me out of here. I haven't done anything wrong."

"Officer Dempsey says you failed the field sobriety test."

"I wasn't drinking. I hit my head and was a little dizzy."

"Then why didn't you let the EMTs take you to the hospital?"

"I don't like hospitals. Besides, I'm fine now." She indicated the lock. "So if you'd just let me go . . ."

"There was a broken tequila bottle in the car."

She studied his dark eyes, decided to give him part of the truth. "Yes, I had a bottle with me—unopened. But I wasn't drinking. I'd never drink and drive."

"I spoke to Walt. He confirmed he lent you his car."

"Didn't believe me?"

"Let's just call it being thorough. Walt said something happened recently that might have caused you to fall off the wagon—his words. Care to tell me about that?"

Cat shook her head. She was tempted. But . . . no. "That's really none of your business, is it?"

"I'm making it my business." His tone hardened.

Cat knew his type. He'd be like a bulldog. If she stalled on the small stuff, he'd go digging around, sure there was more. She couldn't risk that. "A friend of mine died the other day. It hit me hard."

"What did she die of?"

"A beating . . . and a drug overdose."

"I'm sorry." Nick leaned against the bars, facing her, his expression intent. "I did a background check on you, Ms. Walsh, and by all accounts, you're a ghost. Or should I call you Ms. Johnson? There is no paper trail that I could find under either name. So either you live off the grid for some reason, or one of the names you gave me is fake. Which is it?"

The knot of panic in Cat's belly grew. This is what she'd been afraid of. She couldn't go back in time, so what now? "Look, Officer—"

"Just Nick is fine."

She shrugged, gave him what she hoped was an endearing smile. "When I came to Safe Harbor years ago, I wanted a fresh start, so I said my name was Cathy Johnson. It seemed easier to just keep using it when I came back for the wedding, since that's what people know me as. As for the other, I've moved around a lot. The music industry isn't what you'd call nine to five, so it's always just been easier to live on a cash basis. No paperwork to worry about, especially when I get to the next town or city." She widened her smile. "No big mystery."

When he raised an eyebrow, Cat wondered if that meant he believed her or if she'd laid it on too thick. But before she could respond, his cell phone rang.

He pulled it out of the holster on his belt, checked the display. "I'll be right back."

He walked into the police station but didn't shut the door all the way. Cat strained to hear his side of the conversation.

"Hey, Doc. I appreciate you putting a rush on this . . . Heart attack? You're sure? . . . What about the toxicology report? . . . Interesting . . . Yes, definitely run the additional drug tests . . . I agree . . . Without an underlying cause, this still doesn't give us the answers we need . . . Thanks, Doc. I appreciate it."

When he returned, Cat tried to read his expression. "Teddy died of a heart attack?" She hadn't meant to blurt out the question.

Nick looked from her to the door and back again. "You know I can't discuss an ongoing investigation."

"But that was the coroner, right? Did he find any evidence of a prior heart condition?"

"I am not discussing this with you."

"You need to let me go. You have no reason to hold me here. I haven't done anything wrong."

"I still have more questions."

"I don't need to be in here for you to ask them. Come on, this is crazy."

He shoved a copy of the *Gazette* through the bars. "Nice picture of you playing at Eve's wedding on page three. Don't go anywhere."

Cat almost dropped the paper at his words. *No, oh no.*

She sank onto the cot and flipped to the third page. Not only was the picture there, it was blown up so it easily took up a third of the page, with *Cathy Johnson* in bold type.

If her uncle hadn't known she was in town before, he'd surely find out now. She'd always known he would keep tabs on Safe Harbor, since this was where Phillip had found her the night of her audition years ago. It was why she'd run.

Her heart pounded, and she leaned against the wall, trying to keep from hyperventilating. They'd find her and she'd die.

She'd accepted that. But she wouldn't let them hurt her family.

Chapter 12

Cat was still shouting to let her out when Nick left the station and headed for Cliff's Garage. He wanted a look at her car before he made any decisions.

He pulled into an empty parking space outside the two-story block building just past the downtown area of Safe Harbor. Two bay doors stood open, a car on each lift. Cat's beige sedan—or Walt's sedan, actually—sat alongside the building.

He walked into the first bay and over to a guy wearing gray coveralls, covered in grease. "Hey, Cliff. How's it going?"

Cliff stood, wiped his hands on a filthy rag. "Nick. Good to see you. They just brought the car in." He pointed to the side of the building.

"I saw it, thanks. Just wanted to let you know I was here." He glanced at the older man. "Anything unusual strike you when you picked it up?"

"Only that whoever was driving it was dang lucky. The roof is a little dented, but it didn't cave in when the car rolled down into the culvert. This could have been a lot worse. At least she was alone when it happened." He shook his head in disgust. "People should know better than to drink and drive."

"I'll go have a look," Nick said and then walked around the building.

Cliff was right. It was a wonder Cat had walked away without serious injury. The car wasn't pretty. Walt would not be getting it back in the same condition as when he'd lent it.

He studied it as he walked around it. The passenger side was dented, and the glass on the driver's side door was missing. He ducked into the opening. The smell of tequila permeated the interior. The broken bottle was on the floorboard. He pulled on gloves and leaned halfway over the console to reach the piece of the bottle he was looking for, then held it up. The seal on the bottle was unbroken. If Cat had been drinking, it wasn't from this bottle. He'd have to check where she had gone when she'd left the marina.

He bagged the top of the bottle, just in case, and then circled the car again. He crouched by the rear tire. It was flat, but it hadn't separated. A nail would more likely cause a slow leak than a catastrophic failure. He pulled out his flashlight for a closer look, trying to find whatever had caused her to lose control.

It took a few minutes, but he finally found it. He took a picture with his cell phone, then borrowed a pair of pliers from Cliff and dug out the bullet lodged in the tire. He bagged it, then crouched down and found another bullet hole near the trunk. He popped the trunk and eyed the mess inside. The clasps on a small suitcase had popped open, and her clothes were strewn about. He eyed the clothes, surprised to find both a blonde wig and a red one among the T-shirts and jeans. The violin case was still closed. He lifted the lid, relieved to see the beautiful instrument appeared intact.

Cat not only wore disguises, and used multiple names, which tripped all sorts of alarm bells in his head, but she had been leaving town—after he'd told her not to. He put his annoyance on ice as he searched the black interior with his flashlight, pushing clothes aside so he could see. He found the bullet lodged in the trunk's interior wall.

He dug that one out, as well, bagged it, and held it up to the light. When he compared the two, it was obvious they came from the same gun.

He slammed the trunk, then scanned the interior of the car again, looking for anything he might have missed, but the car was immaculate. No trash or food wrappers or any of the detritus usually found in cars.

He slowly circled the car one more time, just in case, thinking. Teddy Winston died of a heart attack for no apparent reason, Cat had gotten into it with known druggie Eddie Varga, and now Cat Johnson's car had been shot at. What was the connection?

Why was she in such a hurry to leave town?

Was someone trying to keep her here—or shut her up for good?

———

Cat couldn't settle. She paced the small cell, trying to figure out how to get Nick to release her. She wouldn't lie, but she couldn't explain, either.

She glared at the *Gazette*. Her picture taunted her, making her heart race and her palms sweat. Over the years, she'd tried to talk herself out of her caution, to tell herself that her worry was unfounded, that after so many years, her uncle would be over it and Garcia would have forgotten her name.

Then she'd go to a public library and do an online search on Garcia, and inevitably, there would be another article about some law enforcement agency trying to build a case against him and the witness mysteriously dying. Once, the woman even died while in protective custody. No, she wasn't exaggerating. By running off, she'd thwarted her uncle's plan, which meant Garcia hadn't gotten what he wanted—namely, her. No way would he just let that slide.

In today's technological age, did he already know where she was? She knew if he didn't yet, he would soon. Any other assumption was just stupid, and Cat wasn't stupid.

The door to the station opened, and she heard voices from the main office area. She pushed closer to the bars, desperate to hear.

"I am Rosa Martinelli. I want to see my daughter. She was in an accident."

Cat leaned her head against the bars, surprised by her sudden tears. Mama Rosa was still protecting her cubs, never mind how sick she was after months of cancer treatments.

"She's fine, Mrs. Martinelli." This from Wanda, the dispatcher.

"Then where is she?" Mama demanded. "I want to see her right now."

"She's, ah, in the back. Nick, Officer Stanton, said he may have more questions for her."

"Then he can ask them at our home. Where is she? Through here?"

Cat heard Mama's voice getting closer and Wanda's attempt to stop her. "Mrs. Martinelli, you can't go back there. Only official personnel allowed."

Mama marched through the partially opened door and stopped, stunned. Blaze was right on her heels. Mama walked up to the cell and reached her hands through to squeeze Cat's hands. "Oh, my girl. Are you all right?" She patted Cat's cheek. "I will take care of this." Mama turned on Wanda. "How dare you put my baby in a cage. Unlock this door right now."

Just then, Nick walked into the police station and, at a nod from Wanda, headed in their direction. Cat's heart skipped an involuntary beat when she caught sight of him across the room. How could his mere presence ease her anxiety at the same time his cop instincts scared her to death?

Mama turned on him. "Why did you put Cat in this cell? You let her out right this minute."

Nick walked over, leaned down, and gave her a quick peck on the cheek. "Hello, Mrs.—Mama Rosa," he corrected and then took her arm to turn her toward his desk, but she was having none of it. She planted her feet, leaned heavily on her cane.

"It's good to see you up and around." He smiled at Blaze. "Good to see you, too, Blaze. Why don't we talk over here?" He indicated a chair in front of his desk.

Mama glanced at her, and Cat smiled. "It's OK, Mama. I can hear from here."

Nick scowled at that, but Mama slowly followed him. She set her cane next to the chair, folded her hands over a black leather purse the size of a laundry basket, and then speared him with a hard glance. "Do not talk around me, Nick. If she was in an accident, why is she locked up? Let her go."

Cat strained to hear his response. "Mama Rosa, she was apparently on her way out of town when she lost control of her car. Did you know she was leaving?"

"Of course I did. She'd just said goodbye to all of us."

"Had she been drinking?"

"What? No, not my Cathy. Why do you ask?"

"There was alcohol everywhere in the car, including on her."

"She had a bottle of tequila in the car. Maybe it broke," Blaze said.

Mama's eyes flew to Cat, then to Blaze. "Why did she have tequila?" Mama asked, surprised.

"I don't know. But she wasn't drinking. You know that, Nick. You just saw her a little while ago."

"Maybe she stopped somewhere after she left."

"I didn't," Cat called from her cell.

Nick turned an annoyed glance her way. He blew out a breath, then stood. "Wait here."

When he walked toward her, brown eyes steady on hers, Cat had to look away, afraid he would see too much, would somehow know what was going on in her head. He stopped in front of the cell.

"I wasn't drinking. The bottle broke when I crashed."

He looked away, then back at her. Nodded once. "I found the top of the bottle. The seal was intact."

"Then you know I'm telling the truth."

His steady gaze made her want to squirm. "I think you've told me select pieces of the truth. But I don't think you've told me nearly the whole story." He folded his arms over that impressive chest and settled in as though waiting for her to fill him in. He'd have a very long wait.

"You're making more of this than there is. The other officer drew some wrong conclusions, that's all."

"Someone shot out your rear tire. And into your trunk."

Cat felt the color drain from her face and carefully masked any further reaction, but she could see his gaze sharpen. She had to tread lightly here. "Shot at my car? Why would someone do that?"

"That's what I'm trying to find out. What kind of trouble are you in, Cat—and did it follow you to Safe Harbor?"

Cat gripped the bars. Hearing him put her greatest fear into words almost buckled her knees. She went on the offensive instead. "What kind of a question is that? I came home to play for Eve's wedding. That's all. If somebody took potshots at my car, you should be looking at which local teens get off on stuff like that." Her chin came up. "Now please let me out of here. You have no grounds to hold me, and you know it. Do I need to get a lawyer involved?" It was a total bluff, since she'd never risk such a thing—never mind not having the money to afford one—but it had the desired effect.

He narrowed his eyes, then took a key ring from his pocket and unlocked the cell door, holding it open. "Your car is at Cliff's Garage." He reached into his pocket again and held up her car keys. "If I give these back, are you going to stay put for a couple more days?"

Cat snatched the keys from his hand, then looked him right in the eye. "You have no legitimate reason to make such a demand. You're fishing, and I am not obligated to hang around while you do. Have a nice day, Officer."

She marched out of the cell with a show of confidence she didn't feel and went over to where Mama Rosa and Blaze waited. "Thanks for coming to spring me," she said, then kissed Mama's cheek and helped her to her feet.

Mama swayed slightly, her pace slowing with every step. Cat hated that she'd spent her energy having to come down here. "Why don't I drive us home," she said. At Mama's nod, Cat tucked her into the passenger seat while Blaze climbed in back. Mama was asleep before they left the outskirts of town.

———

Chief Monroe walked into the station not long after Cat and her family left. Nick sat in his chair, trying to figure out who would have shot out her tires. He studied the bullets, took pictures, and used a search engine to try to match the gun they came from.

"Nick, what's this I hear from Cliff that somebody plugged a couple shots into the Martinelli girl's car?"

Nick stood, eyed the chief, wondering how the man always knew what was going on in town without actually spending more than a few minutes at the station every day. "That's what it looks like."

"Now why would somebody do that?" Monroe crossed his arms. "That girl's always been trouble. Where's she living these days?"

"Nashville."

"I'd check around, see if anyone has seen any strangers in town, someone who doesn't belong. Chances are some lowlife from up that way followed her here." He glanced toward the cell. "Hopefully, she's on her way out of town."

Nick decided not to mention that he'd told her to stay. He clenched his jaw. Though he'd bet his pension she was already headed for the county line.

He couldn't decide if that made him mad or glad, which only annoyed him further.

He went back to the search engine, looking for connections.

Chapter 13

Once they got Mama Rosa settled in her favorite rocker on the porch, Cat steeled herself and walked down to the marina to talk to Sasha and Jesse.

Cat found Sasha sitting on a stool behind the counter, updating the books. She looked up in surprise. "What are you doing here? I thought you left."

Cat wasn't sure if that was a good surprise or not, but Sasha's face gave nothing away.

While she debated what to say, Sasha looked closer, frowned. "What happened to you? You look rough."

"I had an accident, but I'm fine. Just banged up a little." She decided to skip the part about someone shooting at her. Her sister didn't need that kind of worry. "But, my car is, ah, at Cliff's. I was wondering if you could give me a ride over. I need a new tire."

Without hesitation, Sasha stood, then rubbed her lower back. "Do you have a spare?"

Cat eyed Sasha's growing belly, and another pang of fear gripped her. Nothing must ever happen to this baby because of her.

She focused on the question, tried to remember. "I think so. I'm borrowing the car from a friend, so honestly I never checked." She shrugged.

"Seriously? You drove all the way from Nashville without knowing if you have a spare?"

Cat narrowed her eyes at Sasha. "Like you would have checked?"

They stared each other down, then Sasha huffed out a breath. "You're right. Not usually. Just this pregnancy thing has made me a lot more cautious." She eyed Cat. "Let me get Pop or Jesse. You'll need help with the lug nuts."

Within a few minutes, Jesse pulled into Cliff's parking lot and helped Sasha climb out of the cab of his pickup. Cat followed, happy to let Jesse do the male bonding thing with Cliff.

Once they had the old tire in the bed of the truck, they headed over to Barry's Quality Cars to buy a new tire from Captain Barry.

He walked out of the bays and into the office, a smile of greeting on his face. It was replaced by a scowl when he saw them. "Don't tell me someone's been slashing your tires again, Claybourne."

Cat had heard about someone doing that, right after Jesse showed up in town.

Jesse's expression didn't change. "Nope. But we do need a new tire for Cat's car." He rattled off a series of numbers.

Captain Barry narrowed his eyes, shrugged. "Those are not standard-size tires. It's going to cost you."

Cat's anxiety went up another notch. "How much?"

Captain Barry chewed the inside of his lip, then named a figure.

"That's way too much," Jesse protested. "Come on, Barry. What are you doing?"

Cat looked from one to the other, trying to decipher the undercurrents in the room. She knew about Captain Roy dying in the explosion when Jesse saved Sasha's life, so maybe Barry blamed Jesse. All the marina captains were longtime friends. But she'd also heard the captains were pretty riled up that Jesse planned to start a boat racing team in Safe Harbor.

"That's fine. I'll take it." Cat did not want to stir up any bad blood or make things hard for Sasha and Jesse after she left. She just needed a new tire so she could get out of town.

She pulled out her wallet, counted. Then recounted. She didn't have enough. She squeezed her eyes shut, trying to figure out what to do.

Jesse stepped up beside her, handed a wad of cash to Barry. "Go ahead and mount and balance it, too."

Barry didn't say anything, just rang up the sale and disappeared into the back. A young man in coveralls took the old tire from Jesse's pickup and went into the bay.

"Thank you, Jesse," she said quietly. "I'm so sorry. I'll pay you back right away."

Jesse smiled, and Cat understood why Sasha had fallen for him. He had a great smile, but it was his heart that made you love him. "No hurry. Whenever you get to it is fine."

"I need to find a restroom," Sasha said and hurried away.

As soon as she disappeared, Jesse speared Cat with a look. "Cliff said a bullet put that hole in the tire."

Cat met his eyes, saw the worry there. "That's what I hear."

"What kind of trouble are you in, Cat? Sasha doesn't need—"

Cat interrupted before he could finish. "I know. The minute the tire is on the car, I'm out of here. And I won't be back."

"You don't have to do that." He looked at her. "Whatever it is, stay. We can help."

Cat's eyes filled at his easy offer. If he only knew how much she wanted to be part of a family like that, with people who would jump in to help at a moment's notice. But she couldn't let herself get that close. She cared too much to put them at risk. "Thank you, Jesse. You're a good man, and your offer means the world. But I can't stay. I wish I could."

He reached into his wallet again, pulled out some more cash, and pushed it into her hands. "Pay me back next time you're in town, OK?"

Cat wanted to protest, but she couldn't. She nodded, tucked the cash into her pocket. "Thank you. Sasha is lucky to have you."

He grinned, and Cat saw the love in his eyes. "I'm lucky to have her."

At that moment, Sasha walked in, came over, and kissed his cheek. "And don't you forget it," she said with a smile.

Seeing them, their easy way with each other, the way Jesse put a protective arm around her and the baby, hit Cat with a longing that burned like fire. Not only to be part of a big extended family but to have a man of her own who loved her enough to have a baby with her.

Nick's face popped into her head, but she shoved it away. He was the very last person she'd ever risk getting involved with.

Within a few minutes, the young man put the new tire in the pickup, and Jesse drove them back to Cliff's Garage. "Let me go talk to Cliff," Jesse said, and Cat watched in astonishment as the older man offered to put the tire on for her.

She and Sasha stood by the truck. The silence stretched. It didn't have the open hostility of the past, but it was still . . . awkward. And Cat had absolutely no idea how to bridge it. How did she make things right, explain and apologize about all those years ago, without saying too much? Sasha and Jesse had been through enough. With the baby, she didn't want to give her anything else to worry about.

Still.

Before she could change her mind, Cat pulled out her tote bag and rooted around until she found a pen and a scrap of paper. She wrote down the number of her new burner phone and handed it to Sasha. "This is my new number. I'd rather you didn't, ah, share it with anyone."

Sasha's eyes narrowed. "Define anyone. The family in general? Just Eve?"

Cat bit back a retort. "Just family. And only if they ask for it."

"Why would they ask for it? How would they even know I have it?"

With no answer to give, Cat just shrugged. "Look, Sasha, would you let me know if anyone starts asking questions about me?"

Sasha cocked her head. "You mean like Nick? People in town?" Then she straightened. "Or do you mean someone from out of town?" She leaned closer. "You're in some kind of trouble. But you better not have brought it here." She jabbed a finger at Cat's chest, and Cat winced. That's where she'd hit the steering wheel. But Sasha was on a roll and didn't seem to notice. "Mama Rosa has been through enough. First the trouble with captains Demetri and Roy, then Leon Daughtry going after Eve. Don't you dare cause trouble here."

"Hello. Are you listening? I said I was leaving. I have no intention of causing trouble for anyone, especially Mama Rosa. I love her."

"Well you have a funny way of showing it, disappearing for years on end without a word."

The barb hit home, and Cat swallowed the lump in her throat. "Look out for them for me, will you? And let me know, OK?" She spotted Jesse headed their way. "I have to go." On impulse, she leaned over, kissed Sasha's cheek.

"That's it? Just like that, you're gone again? When are you coming back?"

"I don't know." Cat gave Jesse a quick hug, then climbed into her car and left before she lost her will. This was the right thing to do.

It had to be. There was no other way to keep her family safe.

But before she'd gone two miles, an imported black sedan showed up in her rearview mirror, two cars back on the two-lane road. She kept an eye on it, trying to get a look at the driver, but she couldn't see past the tinted windows.

In a land of pickup trucks and sensible sedans, the sleek, expensive car stuck out like a turtle in a snow bank. Cat kept her hands tight around the wheel, trying to convince herself it was just a random car. Her uncle hadn't found her. Had he?

———

Nick sat at his desk, drumming his fingers on the scarred surface. Everyone else had called it a day long ago, but he still sat in front of his computer, staring at the screen. Cat's DMV photo looked back at him. What was it about the woman that got under his skin?

Behind that soft pale skin and slender body there lurked a will of iron. That much he'd seen already. But it was her eyes that called to him. Dark and wide and vulnerable, she brought out every protective instinct he had, though he knew she'd hate it if she knew.

The woman had secrets, clearly. But were those secrets tied to Safe Harbor? Was she involved in the drug running through town?

It seemed a bit far-fetched, but he couldn't discount it. Not yet.

He picked up his phone, looked at the report, and dialed her cell phone number. He wasn't sure what he planned to ask when he reached her, but he'd figure it out as he went along.

The phone rang three times, then a recorded voice said, "We're sorry. The number you have reached is unavailable or no longer in service."

He hung up and tossed his phone on his desk. Why did that not surprise him? He grabbed his phone and dialed again. "Hey, Cliff, sorry to bother you at home. Did Cat Martinelli pick up her car today?"

"She did. You said I could release it to her, right?"

"Yes. There's no problem. Do you know if she went back to the marina?"

"I don't think so. I got the feeling from all the hugs that she was leaving, but I don't know that for sure. You might want to call Jesse."

"Thanks, Cliff. Have a nice evening."

She had left town. Again.

He decided he needed some air. He walked down to the Blue Dolphin and grabbed dinner to go, then went back to the station.

He opened the file on his long-ago kidnapping and read every word again, even though he could quote most of it from memory. Then he read the report on Roy's death and also, recently, Demetri's death the day he was to give his deposition on the smuggling operation. Someone had clearly not wanted that information made public.

Was Teddy's death tied to this in some way? He set up a whiteboard and started writing information on it: names, motives, possible connections.

Then he opened his desk drawer and took out an evidence bag from Teddy's death scene. In particular, he studied a small metallic button from every angle. Where did it come from? It was found near Teddy's body, but it could have been left there at any time by anyone. It didn't necessarily have a thing to do with the teen's death. Or maybe it did. His gut said Teddy's death was somehow connected to the drug operation in town.

He took a picture of the button with his phone, then did a search for similar ones. The list of images went on for pages and pages. He kept narrowing the search terms but didn't feel like he was making any headway.

After a while, he gave up in frustration and ran a search for illegal drugs that could cause a heart attack. He came across one in particular that made his blood run cold: scopolamine, also called "Devil's Breath" or "the zombie drug," from South America. Ingested or breathed in, the drug could cause a person to lose their ability to act of their own free will. There were reports of people who'd handed over all their money, cleaned out bank accounts, given away their electronics, all while under the influence of the drug. In cases of overdose, the person died of a heart attack, but the drug was usually not found in their system.

Nick picked up his cell phone and dialed, then winced when he realized how late it was. He wasn't surprised it went right to voice mail. "Hey, Doc, Nick Stanton in Safe Harbor. Do me a favor, would you? Run an HPLC, high-performance liquid chromatography, test for scopolamine on Teddy Winston. Just in case. And if you can run it sooner rather than later, I'd be very grateful. Thanks."

The black sedan turned off I-75 just before the I-10 interchange. Cat kept an eye out for it as she headed west toward Tallahassee but saw no sign of it. Maybe she'd just been imagining someone behind her.

It was full dark by the time she pulled off the interstate to look for a fast-food joint and a cheap motel. She pulled into the parking lot of the Shady Rest Motel and winced. Cracked asphalt, faded paint, a neon sign out front missing most of the letters. She'd stayed in too many of these places over the years. But if you wanted to go unnoticed, this was the kind of place to do it. The clerk was a bored teenager with purple hair who reminded her of Blaze, and why this was necessary.

"How's it going?"

The girl just grunted, fingers flying over her phone. "You staying all night, or just a couple hours?"

"One night, thanks." She handed over the money, grateful all over again for the extra twenties Jesse had slipped her earlier, but determined she'd pay him back right away.

The girl reached behind the counter, handed her a plastic key ring with the number twelve on it. "Last room on the end. Should be a little quieter than some of the others." She looked up briefly, shrugged. "But I'd use the safety chain, if I were you."

Cat thanked her and pulled around behind room twelve, glad it wasn't visible from the road. She opened the door, and the smell of urine, stale air, and cheap air fresheners assaulted her. She almost turned around and left, but she didn't want to sleep in her car out in the open.

Resigned, she turned on the air conditioner, relieved when it finally clanged on with a wheeze, and looked around. Brown and orange drapes, brown shag carpet worn bare in spots, a bed that sagged in the middle. No way would she climb between those sheets.

She heard a woman's laughter and a male voice coming from next door, then rhythmic banging against the wall. Cat walked over to the television, not surprised there was no remote, and turned it on to block the noise from the next room.

She sat on the one hard chair, pulled out her soggy French fries and burger, and tried to choke it past the lump in her throat. Soda helped, but the sense of desperation that washed over her settled in and stayed. How many seedy motels just like this one had she slept in during her life? She'd lost count. But they were all the same and all reminded her of one thing: hopelessness. There was no way out, no way to be a normal person. She could never truly be part of the Martinelli family, never have a family of her own. For many years, she had accepted that as her lot in life. But lately . . . Unbidden, Nick's smile popped into her head, the gentle way he dealt with Blaze. She thought of the teenager's grief over her friend. "I wish I could have helped you, Blaze. I'm sorry."

The looks on Mama Rosa's and Pop's faces as she kissed them good-bye would haunt her forever. What if Mama didn't get better? What if Cat never saw her again? And what about Pop? And Eve and Blaze, Sasha and Jesse? It had been all she could do today not to blurt out the whole story to Sasha. She wanted forgiveness, to remove the wall that stood between them. But in the end, she'd been a coward. Just like always. And she ran. Always had.

For one moment, she wished she had the strength to stand and fight for the people she loved.

She crumpled the food wrappers and stuffed them in the bag. Then she washed her hands and splashed water on her tear-stained face in the dirty bathroom with its rusting sink.

She pulled on her hoodie, grabbed her violin, and after checking the parking lot to make sure no one was watching, slipped around the corner of the building and headed deep into the woods.

Once she was far enough away no one could hear the music, she pulled out her violin and quickly tuned it, then warmed up with a series of scales and finger exercises. She launched into her parents' favorite piece, *Panis Angelicus*, and then moved into their other favorites, playing with all the sorrow and anger in her soul. Her fingers flew, the bow slid across the strings, sweat dripped down her back and the sides of her face.

By the time she started the pieces she'd played for Eve's wedding, tears also ran down her cheeks, though she was unaware of them. As the music flowed out of her, in her mind's eye, she saw her parents—the stern, passionate musicians who were so involved in their music they generally forgot they had a daughter. Then she saw Mama Rosa storming the police station, demanding Nick release her. She saw Blaze, eyes wide and scared, begging for help. Sasha's accusations hit like slaps with an open hand. Didn't Sasha understand that she wanted to be part of the family with every fiber of her being?

No, because Cat had never told her. And she couldn't now, either.

And then there was Nick, with his strength and compassion and the sense that she could be safe in his arms, if only she told him the truth.

Around and around, like a dizzying carousel, the images flashed through her mind, over and over. They haunted her, giving her tempting glimpses of what could never be.

Finally she dropped her arms, sweat soaking her hoodie, completely spent. She swatted at the mosquitos chewing on her skin. The moon was high in the sky, lighting a path through the woods as she returned to the motel. She scanned the parking lot again before she went into her room, but didn't see the black sedan anywhere.

After one more look out the window, she got ready for bed, then spread her bath towel over the bedspread. Exhausted and heartsick, she lay down on it, curled into a ball, and tried to sleep.

This was her life. And even though she hated the loneliness, she'd live this way forever if it kept her loved ones safe.

She never saw the black sedan slide to a stop across the street.

———

Blaze couldn't sleep. She was angry and scared, and she didn't know what to do about it. Those drugs that Teddy had given Bryan freaked her out. That meant that, even though he promised her he wouldn't,

Teddy had agreed to sell them for that guy, Eddie Varga. So why was Teddy dead? Had Varga killed him? But why?

Her brain felt like it was going to explode. She pulled on her gray hoodie and snuck out of the house. She didn't want to wake Mama Rosa or Pop, but the walls felt like they were closing in on her. She had to think. And the best way to do that was out in the woods.

Once she was away from the house, Blaze clicked on her flashlight. She probably didn't need it, the moon was so bright, but she felt safer with it. She walked quickly to her favorite clearing, the same place she'd seen Cat, and sank down on a fallen log. Just like she had that day.

She'd hoped Cat would stay. They'd connected somehow. Even though Cat didn't say much, Blaze figured she'd been on the run a long time. She didn't know from what, but Cat's eyes said she had seen a lot. Too much, maybe.

Why didn't she stay and help? Fine, then. Blaze didn't need her anyway. She'd figure it out on her own. Cat had suggested she let Nick handle it, but she wasn't sure she wanted Nick involved. Teddy's parents were super sweet, and the idea that their son was selling drugs would really, really devastate them. Even worse, everyone would remember Teddy as a druggie loser, which wasn't true.

Blaze pulled out her phone. She'd been blown away by Cat's musical talent the other day. She should be playing concerts and stuff, maybe on television, not in some honky-tonk in Nashville. That didn't even make sense.

The music had called to her, so she'd written down the names of the pieces Cat said she'd been playing. She found them online and added them to her phone. Now, she set the phone on the log, turned on one of the pieces, and pretended she had a violin. She copied the stance she'd seen Cat assume and followed the music as though she were playing, right arm moving an imaginary bow, left hand holding the violin.

She got lost in the beauty and closed her eyes, swaying to the music of Pachelbel's Canon in D.

By the time she heard the noise in the woods behind her, it was too late.

A gloved hand closed over her mouth from behind, and she was yanked back against a hard chest.

"Don't make a sound," a male voice said in her ear.

Blaze struggled for all she was worth. She tried to wrench out of his hold and kicked backward as hard as she could, gratified when he groaned, but he was a lot stronger than she expected. No matter how fiercely she struggled, he didn't loosen his grip at all. He just held her tighter.

"Guess we'll do this the hard way," he grumbled.

Pain exploded in her head and spots danced before her eyes right before everything went black.

Chapter 14

Cat woke to an annoying buzz in her ear. She opened her eyes, studied the water-stained ceiling above her, and tried to figure out where she was. She looked around the gloom, lit by the slice of light that seeped in around the curtains.

Right. The Shady Rest Motel. It was shady, all right. The couple next door hadn't quit all night long.

The buzz sounded again, and Cat glanced over and realized it was her cell phone.

She scooped it up. "Hello?"

"Tell me you weren't irresponsible enough to take Blaze with you, wherever you're going." Sasha's voice was clipped, angry.

Cat's blood ran cold, and she turned on the bedside light. "What's going on, Sasha?"

There was a long pause. Sasha's voice became much more subdued. "Blaze isn't with you?"

Cat's heart pounded. *No, oh no.* She kept her voice calm. "No. Why would she be? You and Jesse were with me right before I left town."

"You didn't come back to get her?"

Cat was already pulling on her clothes. If she broke all kinds of speed limits, she could get back to Safe Harbor in three hours or so. "When was the last time anybody saw her?"

"Mama says she went to her room about nine p.m. She and Pop turned in shortly after that. She's not here, and her bed hasn't been slept in."

"So you assumed I took her?" Cat couldn't keep the accusation from her voice.

"It was the only explanation that didn't make me break out in hives."

"I'm on my way. I'll be there as quick as I can."

"This *is* connected to you somehow, then."

"I don't know yet. Maybe. Or maybe we're all jumping to conclusions and she's off trying to figure out what happened to Teddy."

"I hope you're right."

"I'll see you in a few hours." Cat hung up and rubbed her hands over her face. *Oh, dear Jesus. Please don't let my uncle or Garcia have her.*

She finished getting dressed, threw her stuff in a bag, and was on the road within ten minutes.

About an hour into the trip, she glanced in her rearview and saw a black car that looked like the one she'd seen before, but she ignored it. Fine. If somebody wanted a piece of her, they could have it. But in the meantime, she was going to find Blaze. And heaven help anyone who got in her way.

Cat thought it was a wonder she wasn't stopped as she practically flew back to Safe Harbor. She didn't even look at the speedometer as she sped toward home.

All she could think about was finding Blaze. She was still hoping and praying that the teen had merely decided to play detective and was looking into whatever trouble Teddy had gotten himself into. The alternative, that her uncle had tracked Cat and taken Blaze as leverage, was too scary to contemplate.

She raced into the marina parking lot and skidded to a stop. Sasha paced the front porch. "Finally," she said by way of greeting.

On the porch behind her sat Mama Rosa, while Pop hovered beside her chair. Cat leaned down and kissed her cheek.

Mama gripped her hand. "I was hoping she was with you."

"Unfortunately, no, Mama. But we'll find her, don't worry." She looked at Sasha. "Have you called her cell phone?"

Sasha rolled her eyes. "Of course. First thing we tried. It goes right to voice mail."

"Have you checked her computer?"

Sasha shook her head. "I tried, but I'm not very good with that stuff. I couldn't get past the password."

"Let me start there." Cat hurried down to Blaze's room, surprised at how neat everything was. She spied the laptop on the desk and opened the lid. Sure enough, it asked for a password. What would a teenage girl use? She typed in *Blaze*. No. Then she tried *lame* and *Teddy*. Still nothing. She tried *MamaRosa*, and bingo, that worked. She went first to Blaze's social media pages, started looking up her friends. It made her sad to realize there weren't that many. She went to the messages feature and started contacting her friends, asking if anyone had seen her. She IM'd Bryan immediately, but he wasn't online, so she left him a message asking if he knew where Blaze was and to let her know right away if he saw or heard from her. She struggled over whether to include her new phone number, but finally did. She could always get another phone later. But in the meantime, she wanted Bryan to be able to reach her.

She sent a few more messages, then returned to the porch.

"Has anyone heard from her?" Sasha asked.

"I contacted a bunch of people, but no one has responded yet." She looked from Sasha to Mama Rosa to Pop. "I'm going to go check with some people. I'll let you know what I find out."

"I'm going with you."

Cat eyed Sasha and her growing belly and shook her head. "No, I need to go alone. You keep an eye on things here, in case Blaze comes home."

Sasha folded her arms, tilted her head. "What are you hiding, Cat? Is this connected to you in some way?"

Cat matched her sister's stance, determined to keep her feelings from showing on her face. She hoped not—oh, she hoped not. But right now, she couldn't be sure, and that terrified her. She kept her voice matter-of-fact. "That's what I intend to find out. I'll be back later."

Before Sasha could ask more questions, Cat hopped in her car and took off.

She'd start at Bryan's, see if he was home, and maybe, please God, Blaze was with him and didn't want anyone to know.

At least that's what she was praying for when she took off in that direction.

But when she arrived at the tidy mobile home where Bryan lived with his parents, it was obvious no one was there. Cat climbed the steps and knocked on the door anyway, just in case, but no one stirred.

"Blaze? Bryan? If you guys are here, let me know, OK? Everyone is worried about you, Blaze."

She waited, watched the windows for any signs of movement behind the curtains, but the place had an empty feel.

Cat walked back to her car. If Blaze wasn't here, then the possibilities got a lot more scary.

She drove out to Eddie Varga's hangout by the Gas-n-Go and found him huddled with the same guys as last time. Eddie still sported a white bandage on his upper arm, the blinding white a stark contrast to his olive skin. When he spotted her, he stood and sauntered over, a new arrogance in his stance that set off her radar. *Never let them see you sweat.*

She climbed out of her car with a confidence she was far from feeling. "Hey, Eddie, how's it going?"

He crossed his arms over his skinny chest, white undershirt hanging off his thin frame. "What d'you want? You want another piece of me? I'll take you down."

Cat flicked a glance at the bandage and raised an eyebrow. "Don't think that worked out so well for you last time, did it?"

He spewed a string of curses, and Cat wanted to take the words back. Never smart to pull the tiger's tail. Especially if you wanted him to give you information.

She made a placating gesture. "Look, Eddie. No hard feelings, OK? Let's just call it a misunderstanding."

He straightened and started toward her. "I'll give you mis—"

Her words came out in a rush. "I could use your help."

He stopped, eyed her. "What are you flappin' about?"

"Have you seen Blaze Martinelli?"

"Who?"

"The Martinellis' newest foster child. Sixteen, dark hair with a green streak in it?"

"Why would I?"

Cat shrugged, kept her tone deferential. "You keep an ear to the ground, seem to know everyone. Thought maybe you'd heard something."

He narrowed his gaze. "If I did?" He eyed her up and down, and Cat hid her revulsion. "What's it to ya?"

Before she could tell him what she thought of his slimy suggestions, Eddie stiffened as he spotted something behind her. Cat looked over her shoulder and saw Nick Stanton explode out of his Safe Harbor police SUV.

Fury rolled off him in waves as he stalked over to them. Cat froze and anxiety coiled in her gut. He looked ready to inflict serious damage on someone. He couldn't have found out about her past, could he?

But instead of reaching out for her, Nick grabbed Eddie by the shirtfront and pulled him up to his toes.

His jaw was clenched tight as he growled, "You are going to tell me what's going on in this town, Varga. Right. This. Minute."

Chapter 15

Nick couldn't remember the last time he'd been this angry. He shook Eddie like the rat he was, hoping the truth would fall out of the man's lying mouth. Eddie didn't say a word, just went deathly pale and still, frantic eyes darting around. Behind him, his minions got to their feet, but one glare from Nick, and they all sat back down.

"I don't know what you mean, Copper," Eddie squeaked.

"Do. Not. Play. Games. With. Me. Varga. Not today."

"Easy, man. I'll tell you whatever you want to know," Eddie said, tone cajoling. "Just tell me what you're talking about."

"Scopolamine." Nick tossed out the word and watched Varga's eyes widen in confusion. Behind him, Cat let out a gasp.

Nick took his eyes off Eddie just long enough to glance over at her, but her expression had gone carefully blank. She obviously had heard of the deadly drug before. He'd deal with her next.

He focused on Varga. "What do you know about it?"

"I-I've never even heard of it, man. What is it?"

"Devil's Breath. The zombie drug."

That got a response. Varga paled and his eyes went wild. "Oh no, man. I don't do that stuff. It'll kill you. That is some scary, crazy drug."

"So you have heard of it."

Varga nodded. "Everybody's heard of it. But I ain't never done it, though. Uh-uh. That's bad stuff."

"Who else here in town has it?"

"Here? In Safe Harbor? Nobody, man."

Nick waited, eyes narrowed.

"You gotta believe me. If somebody has Devil's Breath here, I ain't never heard about it. Anybody knows me, knows I wouldn't do that stuff."

"What about selling it?"

Varga would have reared back in shock if Nick hadn't still been holding him. "I don't even want to touch that stuff. It can mess you up just getting near it. I don't want no part of that. You got the wrong guy, man. If some of that's here, it ain't me."

Nick loosened his grip enough to set Eddie back on his feet. "If not you, then who?"

Varga started shaking his head before Nick finished speaking. "I don't know, man." He glanced at Nick's face. "I'm telling you. It ain't me."

Nick studied Varga's face for another long minute before he abruptly let go. Varga stumbled back a few steps, then straightened.

"If you hear anything about Devil's Breath. Any mention, anyone say it in passing, I expect to hear from you, Varga. Because if I don't—or I find out you lied to me—your life won't be worth spit. We clear?"

Varga nodded. Nick looked past him to the others, who also nodded.

He speared Varga with a look. "Are you right-handed or left-handed, Eddie?"

"Right-handed. Why? What's that got to do with anything?"

Whoever shot at Cat's car would have had to do so with their left hand. He studied Varga's cronies, circling the tables. "What about you?"

Every single one professed to be right-handed. He didn't think they had any reason to lie, so he simply nodded. "Do not leave town. Any of you."

Then he turned, took Cat's arm, and propelled her toward her car. Once they were out of earshot, he said, "You are going to get back in your car and drive to the county park just down the road and wait for me." When she bristled, he added, "Do not make me chase you down, Cat. You won't be happy."

She nodded once. He released her and watched as she pulled out of the parking lot, and then he got in his SUV and followed.

He wouldn't stop until he learned everything she knew about scopolamine.

———

Cat's knuckles were white where she gripped the steering wheel. She knew why Nick wanted to talk to her, and it made her stomach churn with anxiety. She wanted to bang her head against the steering wheel in frustration at her own stupidity. She hadn't been able to hide her reaction to the name of the drug. And Nick, of course, had heard her gasp. He'd want to know the whole story, and his demeanor said he wasn't in a very patient mood.

So, how much to tell him, without making him suspicious and sending him chasing down her past?

It was possible that Nick's mention of scopolamine had nothing to do with either her uncle or Garcia. It was also possible it would snow on Christmas Eve in south Florida. But neither scenario was probable.

The question she didn't want to think about—but honestly couldn't ignore—was what if Teddy died of scopolamine? Was that what had Nick so upset? And if that was true, then she couldn't ignore the fact that her uncle or Garcia were likely in Safe Harbor.

But did that mean they had Blaze? That wouldn't make sense.

Cat turned into the small roadside park and pulled into a spot at the farthest end of the lot. She'd have to get Nick talking, see if she could get more information. She walked past several trails leading off into the woods to a smattering of picnic tables and grills, where she climbed onto a table under a huge live oak tree.

She didn't have to wait long. Nick pulled in next to her, slammed the door, and marched over to where she sat, clearly still furious. With his dark sunglasses and rigid demeanor, along with the uniform stretching over his broad shoulders, he was an imposing sight. Good thing she wasn't easily intimidated. And had had a bit of time to school her features.

He rested one booted foot on the bench and leaned toward her. "Spill."

Cat eyed his stance, crossed her arms. "Take off the shades."

He looked up as though surprised. Then he slowly removed his sunglasses and tucked them into his shirt pocket. Cat met his gaze, expecting the fury she saw in their dark depths. What she didn't expect was the worry she glimpsed behind it.

"What do you know about scopolamine, Cat?"

She could at least tell him some of the truth. "When I was young, a friend of mine, ah, overdosed on it." A chill passed over her as she relived the horror of Daniel's death. "I did some research on it after that."

She watched his face, and her own drained of color as she read the truth there. She'd hoped against hope she was wrong. Her hands wanted to shake, and she gripped her arms, tight. Her heart pounded so hard she wasn't sure she could get the words out. "That's what Teddy died from, isn't it?" Her words were a mere whisper.

Nick wouldn't release her gaze. "That's what it looks like."

"Sweet Jesus. His poor parents." Cat scanned the woods as she thought of Daniel's parents on the news so long ago, begging for anyone with information on their son's whereabouts to come forward. Then several days later, their absolute devastation when Daniel's body was found.

"What else do you know about Devil's Breath?"

Cat snapped her eyes back to his. She had to be careful. "Why would I know anything else? From everything I've read, it's a horrible drug." She paused. "It can cause a heart attack."

"Right. So where did Teddy get it?" Nick's anger crackled in the air like a whip.

"How would I know? I've only been here a few days."

"And yet, we have a teen die of a nasty drug right after you arrive."

"Are you saying I brought the drug here?" Her horror was not exaggerated. "No. Not on your life. I told you a friend died from it. Why on earth would I bring it here?"

"That's what I'm trying to figure out."

"You are searching in the wrong place."

"Or maybe I'm in exactly the right place." When she didn't say anything else, just glared at him, he asked, "Where's Blaze?"

Cat looked away, shrugged, trying to hide her worry. "I'm not sure right now. Why? What do you want with her?"

"I want to ask her about scopolamine, too. I stopped by the marina, but Sasha said they can't find her and you'd gone to look for her. Where would she go? From what I know about her, she doesn't normally disappear on a regular basis, does she?"

"I don't know her that well. I'm trying to find her, make sure it's just teenage stuff."

He studied her. "But you don't believe that."

Cat met his gaze. "Frankly, I don't know what to believe."

"Is she in trouble? Maybe she's involved in all this somehow."

"No. She wouldn't have any part of a drug like that. I know that much." She eyed him sternly. "And you don't believe she's involved, either. Blaze is a good kid."

"Yet she's missing all of a sudden, and you're worried enough to come back to town to try to find her."

A chill shimmied down her spine. The man didn't miss a thing. "I just want to be sure she's OK." She met his eyes again. "I think maybe she's trying to find out what happened to Teddy."

"She should let me handle it," he spat.

"Which is exactly what I told her."

His eyes widened in surprise.

"Look, Nick, if what you say is true, and somebody has brought scopolamine here, she could be in serious danger. Especially if she's asking the wrong questions of the wrong people."

He straightened to full cop stance again, hands on his utility belt. "Which is why you should *both* let me handle this." He paused. "Do I need to get an Amber Alert set up?"

Cat froze. Unsure. If her uncle or Garcia were in town, and if they had Blaze for some reason, then yes, a hundred times yes, they needed to find Blaze, fast. Her life would definitely be in danger. But what if she was wrong? That would put a target on Blaze's back and announce Cat's presence in neon lights. She had to dig around a bit more first.

"I don't think so. Not yet."

They stared each other down.

"Who are you running from, Cat?"

"Me? We're talking about Blaze. Why would you ask me that?"

"Because you live off the grid. Use multiple names and keep disguises in your suitcase."

She waved that off. "I'm a performer. Wigs and costumes are part of the deal. And I told you, I move around a lot—"

"Do not insult me by lying again."

Her chin came up. She might not always be able to tell the whole truth. But she wasn't a liar. "I haven't lied to you."

"Then tell me who or what you're running from. I can help."

Oh, she was tempted. Cat studied him, at the pure masculine strength radiating from him, the concern in his rich, dark eyes and the strength of character she sensed in him. She almost launched herself into his arms, desperate to tell him the whole story, let him fight her battles for her.

But like the last time such insanity had crossed her mind when she was around him, she stopped herself in time. She couldn't think like that. No one could fight her battles for her. And if Nick got involved, he wouldn't stop until her entire past was revealed. If that happened, she had no doubt her uncle and Garcia wouldn't be far behind. If they weren't in Safe Harbor already.

That thought made her heart beat faster. She had to go, find Blaze, fast. Once Blaze was home, safe and sound, Cat could figure out if her uncle was behind this. And if he wasn't, she could still disappear before he found her.

Nick's steady gaze made her squirm. She wanted to assure him she wasn't running from anything, but she couldn't do it. She settled for, "I appreciate the concern, but it's misplaced. I'm fine. Now if you'll excuse me, I need to go."

She had one hand on her car door handle when he said, "Do not mention the scopolamine to anyone."

"I have no reason to," she assured him.

He didn't look as though he quite believed her. "Let me handle this, Cat. Do not get in my way," he warned. "And if you haven't heard from Blaze by tonight, I expect to hear from you. I'll find her."

Cat had no doubt he would, too. She just wasn't sure if getting him involved would help or make things worse in the end. Unsure what to say, she climbed into her car and drove away. She felt his eyes on her car until she disappeared from view.

She had to figure out if Blaze had gone off on her own, or had been kidnapped. Fast.

———

Blaze woke suddenly, startled by a loud bang, followed by the screech of metal on metal. She tried to sit up and realized several things at once. Her hands were tied. So were her feet. And there was some kind of black cloth over her face.

In a second, memories of last night whooshed in, bringing the same desperate panic with them. Someone had grabbed her!

Despite her galloping heartbeat, she forced herself to lie perfectly still, pretending she was asleep as she heard footsteps approach. Where was she? No light penetrated whatever was over her head, so she had no sense whether it was day or night. She strained to pick up any background noises, anything that would give her an idea of where she was, but there was nothing.

Something hard jabbed her in the side. "Wake up, girlie. The boss wants a photo."

He pulled her to a sitting position and then yanked the cloth up over her head. The blinding sunlight coming through the open door made her squeeze her eyes shut. She ducked her head, then slowly looked up, trying to memorize the man's face through the hair hanging in front of her eyes. He had a baseball cap pulled low over his forehead and a bandana wrapped over the lower half of his face, so she couldn't see much.

He lifted her chin with one hand and held a cell phone with the other. "Smile for the camera, Catharine."

Catharine? Who is—wait. They thought she was Cat. Blaze opened her mouth to correct him but then snapped her jaw shut. She'd better not say anything just yet. What if they decided to kill her if she told them the truth? Best to stay quiet until she could figure things out.

From outside the partially open door, another voice said, "Hurry up already. Let's get out of here."

Blaze heard what sounded like air brakes. The smell of diesel fuel permeated the air. She looked around without moving her head. She was inside what appeared to be a metal box. There were cardboard boxes stacked up along the walls. Was she in a trailer?

The man in front of her put his cell phone away, then reached into his pocket and pulled out a syringe. Blaze's heart sped up at the size of the needle and the look on his face. What would he do while she was unconscious?

He jabbed the needle into her arm, and she cried out. Before she could say anything else, she felt her eyes slide closed.

"Sleep tight, Catharine. I'll be back."

He laughed, and revulsion crawled along Blaze's nerve endings. But she couldn't find words, couldn't protest, couldn't fight the drug that made her whole body feel heavy and drift into sleep.

Chapter 16

One of the worst things about small-town police work, Nick reminded himself, was also one of the best things about small-town police work. He hadn't driven two miles before he got a call from Wanda telling him that Miss Ellen, who was ninety-six and still lived alone, had called about a big scary snake curled up on her veranda. Would that nice young Officer Stanton come by and shoo that awful critter away?

Wanda was still snickering as Nick said he was en route. Miss Ellen called at least once a week, mostly because she was lonely. He dutifully shooed the pygmy rattler off the veranda with the help of his snake stick. He put it in a sealed bucket in the back of his SUV, then ate a few cookies and chatted with Miss Ellen before he drove out to a wooded area and released the snake.

He arrived at the Safe Harbor police station later than he'd planned. Monroe and JD were deep in conversation when he arrived. JD sprang to attention as though he'd been caught doing something wrong, which made Nick wonder what they were talking about.

Monroe walked over and perched on the corner of Nick's desk. "Where are we with the investigation into Teddy's death? His parents keep calling."

For a second, Nick wondered why the Winstons weren't calling him, but he was still considered a newcomer in town, despite being born here. He figured he'd be somewhat suspect until about twenty years from now.

He stayed standing, not wanting to have to look up at his boss. He opened his email program and checked to be sure the coroner had sent the follow-up report. "We have a cause of death."

Monroe's and JD's gazes sharpened.

"I had the coroner run some extra tests, found enough scopolamine in Teddy's system to cause a heart attack."

JD stepped over. "What's scopolamine? I've never heard of it."

"It's from South America. Also called Devil's Breath or the zombie drug. In small doses, people lose their free will and the power to make decisions. In the case of an overdose, it can cause a heart attack."

"How would a drug like that get to Safe Harbor?"

Nick looked from JD to Monroe and back. "That is exactly what I plan to find out."

"How can I help?" JD asked eagerly.

Monroe turned to him. "JD, keep working on that report I need by—" His cell phone buzzed and he checked it. "Excuse me. I need to take this. Keep working," he told JD and then walked into his office and shut the door.

JD sagged in disappointment. Nick patted him on the shoulder as he walked past. "You're doing fine, JD."

"Where are you going?"

"Back to the death scene. I'll be in touch."

"Could it have been suicide?" JD asked. "What with the note and all?"

Nick stopped. "It's highly unlikely, given the nature of this drug, but I'm not ruling anything out yet."

He'd go have another look around the quarry. In case they missed something the first time.

And maybe, he'd find some clue that connected Cat and Blaze to all of this.

———

Cat drove to the marina, making sure she hid her worry before she arrived. As usual, Mama was dozing on the porch. Sasha was rocking next to her. Both heads snapped up when she stepped onto the porch.

"Did you find her?" Sasha demanded.

"Not yet."

"What do her friends say?"

"I've talked with several, but no one has seen her."

"I called the hospital, and she wasn't brought in," Sasha said. "And Jesse drove to town and back, but there's no sign of her along the road." She cradled her belly, made soothing motions. "He even went to the old barn where I was held captive by Demetri and Roy, to be sure she wasn't there."

"Good thinking. No sign of her?"

"None. Where could she be?"

Mama's eyes opened, and Cat realized she'd heard every word. "You will find her and bring her safely home."

Cat met her eyes. "I will, Mama. Don't worry." She patted Mama's hand and went back to Blaze's room and checked everything again. Her backpack was on the floor with earbuds, a paperback of *To Kill a Mockingbird*, and a sketch pad inside. Her cell phone wasn't there. She checked the closet. An overnight bag sat on the floor, along with a neat row of shoes, one pair missing. Cat rifled through her drawers and found a sock tucked in the back full of singles, fives, and a few tens. Cat figured it was safe to assume she hadn't packed up and run away, unless she'd gone without taking any of her possessions. And Cat knew that Blaze wouldn't have left without the money or her sketch pad.

The sketch pad triggered an idea, and she hurried across the porch and outside. She circled the property and ran to the clearing in the woods where she'd found Blaze the morning after Teddy's death. The same place Cat used to hide when she'd lived here.

She stopped at the edge of the clearing and looked at it with fresh eyes. Did anything seem different? She slowly walked closer, keeping an eye on the sandy soil.

Something was sticking out from beneath a clump of Spanish moss, and she reached over to pick it up. A flashlight. The beam of light was so dim she didn't see it at first. A chill of foreboding slid down Cat's spine. It had been on when it was dropped.

She squatted down and studied the soil. She wasn't a trained tracker by any means, but there were obviously two sets of footprints here. One was from a pair of tennis shoes, and the other looked like the heel and toe of a cowboy boot. Much larger than the sneaker.

Heart pounding, she scanned the clearing. She saw some leaves on the ground and bent closer. Yes, there. What looked like several bent and broken branches. As though someone had been dragged through there.

She got on her hands and knees, and sure enough, there were the boot prints again. But no tennis shoes.

Blaze had been kidnapped.

But was it her uncle? Or Garcia—or his men—who had her?

Why would they take her? Cat straightened and looked around, chilled to the bone. The only thing that made sense would be if they were trying to get Cat to show herself.

Which meant she was out of options.

She took a deep breath, realizing there was only one thing to do. She couldn't let anything happen to Blaze. She was terrified, but she didn't have a choice, not really.

Wait. What if she was wrong? She had to think it through. What if it wasn't her uncle or Garcia? What if it had to do with Teddy somehow?

If she was wrong, she'd bring all sorts of trouble to Safe Harbor and make things infinitely worse.

But she didn't think she was wrong. The instincts that had kept her alive for fourteen years were screaming that this was ultimately about her, not Blaze.

She hurried back to the marina, made sure her violin was safely in the trunk, and then headed toward town.

She would trade her life for Blaze, if that's what it took.

God, give me courage.

———

Nick pulled his Safe Harbor police SUV into the parking area at the quarry and got out. There was one other car there.

He walked over and saw that the two teens had the windows down and were wrapped in each other's arms, missing most of their clothes, oblivious to his approach. He rapped on the doorframe and hid a grin as they yelped and scrambled for their clothes.

He turned his back, gave them a few minutes to get organized, then said, "Come on out here."

They stepped out of either side of the car, the girl's face beet red as she stared at her feet and hid behind her blonde hair. The boy stepped out, and Nick didn't try to hide his surprise.

"Bryan? What are you doing out here?"

His face was almost as red as the girl's. "Hello, Officer Stanton. Nicole and I came out to, uh, pay our respects to Teddy." He indicated the wilting bunch of flowers on the dashboard.

Beside him, the girl nodded vigorously.

"Have either of you spoken to Blaze recently?"

Bryan's head snapped up. "I tried to call her a couple of times this morning, because she was supposed to come with us, but it went right to voice mail. Is something wrong?"

"We're not sure yet, but nobody has seen or talked to her since last night. Would she have taken off for some reason?"

Bryan shook his head. "No. She talked about trying to figure out why Teddy died. I said I wanted to help, and she promised she'd let me know. I don't think she'd lie about that. Is she OK?"

Nick turned to Nicole. "How well do you know Blaze?"

The girl shrugged, clearly still beyond embarrassed. "Not that well. We say hi at school sometimes, eat lunch together. But she spent most of her time with Teddy. They're both wicked smart brainiacs."

"You'll let me know if you hear from her?"

Both promised they would. Then Bryan asked, "Why are you here?"

Nick eyed both teens. "Still looking for evidence, trying to put all the pieces together on Teddy's death." He hitched his chin toward Bryan's car. "Y'all go on now."

They scrambled to climb into the car and escape. Nick waited for the dust to settle and then turned in a slow circle, trying to see everything from a new perspective.

He pulled out his cell phone and dialed the coroner again. "Listen, Doc, I'm real sorry to bother you again, but have you finished the autopsy report? Is there anything else you can tell me?"

"I know you wants answers, Nick, but yours isn't my only case."

Nick waited while the silence lengthened. He heard papers shuffling.

"Actually, I did find something. I was just about to call you. I found bruising under both sides of his jaw consistent with someone forcing his mouth open. It was slight, though, so I didn't notice it right away. Whoever did it was very careful. They wore gloves. There were no prints or DNA in that area other than the victim's. And before you ask, once I found the bruising, I checked the whole body for any DNA that didn't belong to the victim. There isn't any."

"So he was forced to ingest the scopolamine."

"Looks like it. You'll have my final report in a couple of hours."

"Thank you, Doc. I owe you a steak dinner."

"I'll hold you to it. With a nice bottle of bourbon."

"You got it."

Nick hung up and considered. He'd suspected as much, but the confirmation left him cold. Who wanted the teen dead? Why? From what Blaze and Bryan had said, and the bag of weed Teddy had, it made sense that it was drug related. But marijuana and Devil's Breath were two very different kinds of drugs. What was the connection?

He scanned the area again. Was Teddy poisoned here? Or was he drugged elsewhere and his body dumped here?

With the cars that came and went on a regular basis, he wouldn't find any distinct tire tracks. They had found a button, which may or may not have anything to do with Teddy's death, but he still hadn't had any luck tracing it to a manufacturer. It was a long shot, at best.

He needed some hard evidence. Something that linked someone to the crime. After he walked the perimeter of the area, he headed back to where the body was found. The crushed underbrush had perked up since the body had been moved. There were several bent and broken branches, but nothing out of the ordinary.

He walked farther into the surrounding woods and bagged a recent-looking cigarette butt and an empty beer bottle. He kept walking, tracking back and forth with his eyes, searching for something the killer might have left behind.

He came upon an almost empty water bottle, far off the path. It didn't show signs of being out here for any length of time, so it must have been tossed into the bushes recently. He bagged that, as well. He'd have JD check all three for prints. Maybe they'd get lucky.

He went back to his SUV, stored the evidence, and was getting ready to leave when the chief pulled up.

"You find any more evidence out here, Stanton?"

"Not sure, sir. Got a few things to check for fingerprints, nothing concrete, though. But the coroner says he found bruising under Teddy's jaw, consistent with someone forcing him to swallow the drug."

The chief shook his head as he climbed out of his car. "I don't know which is worse for that poor boy's parents. Suicide or murder." He sighed. "I'll just give the area another quick look-see, make sure we didn't miss anything. We need to find who did this as quickly as possible."

Nick nodded and left, surprised Avery Ames hadn't pulled in behind the chief. It would be just like Monroe to find something so he could make a grand announcement and have his picture in the paper.

He shook his head. Maybe Monroe really was just trying to figure out what happened to his friends' child.

———

Cat's hands shook as she climbed out of her car on Main Street. She took several deep breaths, trying to calm her racing heart. If she didn't get a grip, she'd hyperventilate and faint.

Now was not the time to cave in to fear. She could do this. She had to do this.

She swallowed hard as she scanned the downtown area. The mayor had recently installed a weather cam downtown, hoping it would attract more tourists to Safe Harbor. Cat was betting her life that her uncle or Garcia was monitoring the live feed.

First, though, she walked to the drugstore, where she bought a brightly colored sheet of poster board and a thick black marker. She used the hood of her car like a desk.

Then she walked back to the trunk, pulled her violin out of its case, and spent a few minutes tuning it and getting into her music mind-set. Her hands shook, so it took longer than usual, but she couldn't seem to make them stop.

She just had to play and let herself get caught up in the music. If she could focus enough to do that, she'd be OK. Otherwise, she didn't think she could do this.

After more than fourteen years of running and constantly looking over her shoulder, she was coming out of hiding in a big way. She'd avoided cameras of any kind, worn a wig and glasses, and sometimes adopted an entirely different persona. She traded cell phones regularly, left no electronic trail, and moved every couple of months.

Now she was throwing all that protection away to stand in the spotlight. On purpose.

She blew out a calming breath and glanced around, but no one was paying any attention to her.

Was this the right thing to do?

If Blaze had simply run away, was trying to figure out what happened to Teddy on her own, then Cat was bringing danger right to the marina's front door.

But if Blaze had been kidnapped, then this had to be about Cat. Whether her uncle or Garcia had Blaze, this was the only way Cat knew to get their attention. Nothing like a live-feed camera to let them know where to find her.

She couldn't hide anymore. If something happened to Blaze and she could have prevented it, she'd never be able to forgive herself. She hadn't helped Joellen, even though she knew she was in trouble. She wouldn't make that mistake again.

Her time had come to stand and fight. She'd gladly offer herself in trade, if it meant freeing Blaze and keeping her family safe.

She'd always known that, someday, it would come to this. But she'd thought they would finally catch her. Not that she'd go to them willingly.

But this was Blaze. And her family.

Her knees were knocking like a pair of old bones and she felt ill, but none of that mattered. She could do this.

She located the camera on a lamppost and positioned herself so it was trained directly on her face. She opened the violin case and set it beside her, propped the sign inside the case. It read: *A life for a life.*

Then she took a deep breath, tightened her grip on the bow, and started one of her favorite pieces, Pachelbel's Canon in D. She'd played it as Eve walked down the aisle and had always loved the beautiful, haunting melody.

It gave her courage now.

She saw people stop and turn in her direction as the sounds reached them, so she closed her eyes until she found her equilibrium. She missed a note but kept going. *Flow with the music.*

After a few minutes, she opened them again, scanned the crowd that had gathered.

Would her uncle show himself? Would Garcia?

She forced a smile and nodded, a little surprised by how many people smiled back. A few scowled, but she should have expected that. The Martinelli girls had always been labeled troublemakers in stuck-in-the-past, conventional Safe Harbor.

She launched into a second piece, then a third and fourth, and still, no one's face stood out, nobody who watched from the edges of the crowd triggered her memory.

But someone was watching. She could feel it along the back of her neck.

Come on, you coward. Show yourself.

She played for another fifteen minutes, then stopped and nodded at the applause that followed.

A flash went off, and she blinked, then saw Avery Ames lower her camera.

She took a deep breath, locked her knees when they wanted to collapse. It was done. One way or another, they'd know where she was.

Cat carefully put her violin away and climbed into her car.

She didn't see anyone follow her, but she was sure they were there. *Be strong, Blaze. I'll be there soon.*

Chapter 17

Nick pulled up in front of the Winstons' brick home and sat for a moment, studying the immaculate house and yard, the quiet street with its well-maintained homes. Teddy's father worked for a defense contractor in Ocala, which was a pretty significant commute. But it looked like he made decent money. Mrs. Winston was very involved with charity work in the community. People had nothing but good things to say about the whole family.

How did he tell them that their son had been murdered?

He climbed out of his SUV and started up the walk. The door swung open before he could knock, and he realized Mrs. Winston had been watching him through the living room window.

"Officer Stanton, please come in. Do you have news?" She wore a pretty floral dress and heels, as though she were ready to go out, but grief was evident in the lines on her face and the dark circles under her eyes.

Nick stepped over the threshold and indicated the formal living room. "Why don't we sit down."

Her husband appeared from the rear of the house.

"I'm sorry you came all the way home from work, sir," Nick said. "I could have given you an update over the phone."

Mr. Winston put a protective arm around his wife's shoulders. "I'm exactly where I need to be. Thank you for coming in person."

Nick sat down on a chair across from them. This part was almost as hard as telling them their son was dead had been. "The coroner has determined that Teddy died of a heart attack."

There was a moment of shocked silence. "But he didn't have a heart condition," Mrs. Winston cried.

"No, he didn't. There was no evidence of heart problems or any other medical condition that might have caused Teddy's death."

Mr. Winston patted his wife's shoulder as she sniffled into a handkerchief. "Then what happened? This doesn't make sense."

Before Nick could answer, a knock sounded on the front door. Mrs. Winston murmured, "Excuse me," and went to answer it.

She returned with Cat in tow.

Nick stood, studied her. "What are you doing here?" She looked tired, and wary, and the dark circles under her eyes were more pronounced. But she clearly had come with an agenda.

She glanced at him, then turned her attention to the Winstons. "Mr. and Mrs. Winston, I'm so sorry to intrude. I wanted to offer my sincere condolences on the loss of your son."

He decided to let her talk, give her a bit of leeway before he stepped in.

"I'm sorry, but why are you here? You said you were with Officer Stanton."

"I'm one of the Martinelli girls. I came home for Eve's wedding."

Recognition dawned. "You're the one who played the violin so beautifully," Mrs. Winston said.

"Thank you. Yes." She paused, and Nick saw her choose her words with care. "We are, ah, having a bit of an issue locating Blaze and wondered if perhaps you'd seen her? Or might know where she could have gone?"

"Are you saying she's run away?" Mrs. Winston looked worried. "But why? The funeral is tomorrow. I know she wouldn't miss it."

"We're not sure of anything right now," Nick added. "Just checking out all the possibilities. Any idea where she might have gone? I know she and Teddy were friends. Are there any special places they went together?"

Mr. Winston said no, but Mrs. Winston nervously twisted that handkerchief again. He met her eyes, waited. "Ma'am? Anything you can tell us might help. We just want to be sure she's OK."

She glanced at her husband, then back at Nick. "The kids like to hang out by the quarry. They think we don't know, but I did."

Her husband speared her with a glance. "Why didn't I know about that? It's dangerous."

She shrugged. "They used to go there a lot. Maybe she went out there, to be where he-he . . ." She swallowed.

Nick kept his voice low. "I was just there, and I didn't see any sign of her. No other place comes to mind?"

Mrs. Winston shook her head.

Her husband stood, propped his hands on his hips. "I'm sorry to sound unfeeling, but I want to know what happened to Teddy."

Nick cleared his throat. "Right. I had the coroner run a special test, and it confirmed that your son died from an overdose of scopolamine."

"No. Teddy would never have done something like that . . . on"— Mrs. Winston cleared her throat—"on purpose." She toyed with the lacy handkerchief, smoothing it out, over and over. "He was excited about going to college, said he had his eye on a girl here, everything was going so well for him . . ." Her voice trailed off.

"What is scopolamine?" Mr. Winston demanded. "How did he get it? Why would he have taken it?"

Nick held up a hand. "The drug is from South America and is also called Devil's Breath or the zombie drug. In small doses, it robs a person of their free will, and criminals sometimes use it to get people to hand over money, et cetera."

"But Teddy didn't have any money."

"If the dose is too large, it can cause a heart attack."

A beat of silence. Then Mr. Winston jabbed an accusing finger toward Nick. "You're saying someone poisoned our son! That he was murdered."

"I'm saying we are treating this as a suspicious death. Do you know of anyone who might have wanted to hurt Teddy?"

The parents looked at each other, both wearing identical horrified expressions. "No, he was well liked, had good friends."

"Can you run me through his last day?"

Mrs. Winston gripped the handkerchief as though to keep her hands from shaking. "It was a pretty typical Saturday. He slept until eleven and then played some video games before he reluctantly did a few chores. Then he got cleaned up—he looked so nice—to go pick up Blaze for Eve's wedding. We arrived shortly afterward. He stayed at the wedding longer than we did, but everything seemed fine when we left." She sent Nick a sad smile. "He said he was going to ask Blaze to dance." She sniffed. "That was the last time we saw him."

"Did he text you or call that night? I'm trying to set up a timeline."

"No, nothing."

Nick thanked them both and ushered Cat out the door. As soon as they were out of earshot, he turned to her, voice low. "Tell me the real reason you're here."

There went that Martinelli chin. The sisters weren't related by blood, but the same stubborn streak ran straight through all of them. "I'm looking for Blaze, like I said." Worry shone from her dark eyes. "He was really murdered with scopolamine?"

"Yes. Just like your friend." He narrowed his eyes, looking for a reaction. "Right after you arrived in town."

"You know I had nothing to do with his death!" Her eyes spit fire, but he saw something else in them, too.

He leaned in until they were nose to nose. "Then tell me who did."

As they stared each other down, Cat's cell phone rang. She stepped away, but he could still hear her part of the conversation.

"Hello? What's wrong, Sash? . . . Did he leave a name?" Nick watched as all the color drained out of her face. "OK, I'll head that way . . . No, I won't do anything stupid, geez . . . OK, I'll call you later."

She hung up. "I have to go."

When she drove away, much too fast, he hopped into his SUV and followed. Something was definitely up.

———

Cat forced herself to slow down. Now wasn't the time for another encounter with Safe Harbor's finest. She swallowed hard. Her uncle or Garcia had found her. Already. They'd even had the audacity to call the marina. Well, maybe that part wasn't too surprising. They wouldn't know her cell phone number but would assume someone at the house had it.

The man wouldn't leave a name, Sasha said, just that he'd heard they were looking for Blaze and had information for Cat. She should meet him at 416 Hammer Drive in the next thirty minutes.

Cat had plugged the address into her phone app. If she remembered right, that far out of Safe Harbor, there was nothing but scrub palm and pastureland. Why there?

She gripped the wheel tighter, heart pounding, and scanned the surrounding area when her map app said she had reached her destination. Where was it? At the last second, she spotted a rusting mailbox, half-buried under vines. She turned into the driveway. Grass and bushes scraped the sides of her car as she drove down the overgrown track. The only indication this was the right place was the flattened grass that said another car had recently passed this way.

The track opened onto a small gravel parking area in front of an abandoned cottage. The porch sagged and was missing half its boards. The windows were boarded up, and the tin roof had rusted with time.

Where was the other car? Had it left? Or pulled around back?

Cat hesitated, hand slippery on the door handle. Would whoever had called shoot her on sight? Or would they give her a chance to offer herself for Blaze? She swallowed hard. Moment of truth.

"God, help me do the right thing," she breathed, then climbed out of the car and looked around, hands on her hips, projecting a confidence she didn't feel.

"Hello? Is anyone here?" She scanned the area, braced herself, expecting the pain of a bullet, but nothing happened. Cicadas chirped and a breeze ruffled the grasses, but other than that, nothing.

Suddenly, a black SUV with tinted windows appeared in the driveway and pulled in behind her car, effectively blocking her escape.

The driver's door opened, and an impeccably dressed man stepped out. His black hair had some gray in it now, and his black suit coat still didn't cover the holster he wore under his arm, but his dark eyes never missed a thing. "This way, Miss Catharine." Phillip Chen held open the rear door, as though he'd driven her to school only yesterday.

The entire scene felt surreal. After she'd been hiding for fourteen years, her uncle had found her.

He would not have been able to get here from Miami this quickly. Which meant he had already been in town, already knew where she was. She forced her fear behind her. She couldn't let it show.

Dear Jesus, had he killed Teddy? Why?

Cat nodded and stepped toward the car, determined to play the charade out to the end. "Thank you, Phillip," she said as she climbed into the rich leather interior.

She waited for her eyes to adjust, then met Richard Wang's piercing black gaze. "Hello, Uncle."

Chapter 18

"Hello, Catharine. You look well. If a bit thin."

Like Phillip, there were subtle signs of the passing years, the gray at his temples, the ever-so-slight paunch around his middle, a bit of a sag in the smooth Asian skin.

He studied her. "Your mother would be heartbroken if she knew how you are squandering your musical gift."

Everything inside Cat stilled. Did he mean in general? Or did he know where she worked?

Cat decided it didn't matter. She needed information. Still, there were certain social mores and rules to follow. "As every good child, I endeavor to make her proud."

His eyes narrowed, no doubt searching for sarcasm. "Someone with your talent should be gracing the stage with the preeminent symphonies. It is what you were trained to do."

"And I am very grateful for the training that I was given, Uncle."

"You look more like her every day," he said, voice quiet.

Cat looked into his eyes and saw deep emotion that went far beyond that of a standard brother-in-law. "She was a beautiful, talented woman. My father loved her."

"He didn't deserve her," he bit out, then waved the words away. "You should not have run, Catharine."

She ignored his statement. She would not think about Daniel now. Not when Blaze's life hung in the balance. "Where is Blaze?"

"I do not have her."

"What do you mean? Isn't that why you called me here?"

"I'm here to protect you."

Cat almost snorted but caught herself in time. She bit the inside of her cheek to keep accusations from exploding out of her. Instead, she kept her hands folded demurely in her lap and waited for him to continue. Breaches of etiquette had never been tolerated when she'd lived with him.

"You don't believe me."

"Please, just tell me the truth, Uncle. Where is she?" Cat forced the words out. "I will happily offer myself in trade, if that's what you require."

He studied her for several moments. "Who is this Blaze that you would sacrifice your life for hers so easily?"

"She is family." The words burst out before she realized what she was saying.

Her uncle stiffened, and Cat could see him work to bring his anger under control. When he spoke, his voice was like ice. "I am your family, Catharine. I came to bring you back to Miami where you belong. To restore you to the life you were born to live."

Cat didn't believe a single word of that. Not after Daniel. "If you don't have Blaze, then where is she?"

He made a tsking sound. "Still so impatient, Catharine. Nothing good comes from rushing into things without careful thought."

Her skin itched with frustration, but she waited for him to speak, as she'd been taught. If he didn't have Blaze, then Garcia did, and Cat had to find her, fast. She'd need her uncle's help.

After what seemed like hours, he tapped his fingers on the armrest as though coming to some conclusion. "I believe Garcia is in town. Phillip has spotted some of the cretins he employs." He paused, looked her in the eye. "Daniel Habersham's family has hired another private investigator, and I hear he is looking for answers, for names to give to the police." Cat forced all emotion from her face as she waited for her uncle to continue. Her situation had just gotten a whole lot more precarious. No way would her uncle or Garcia want her talking about Daniel to anyone.

Finally he said, "I will find this Blaze and help you secure her release." Surprised, Cat started to thank him, but he interrupted. "There is one condition. You will promise to return to Miami afterward." His eyes were hard when they met hers. "You have an outstanding obligation to fulfill."

"You mean *you* have an outstanding obligation." The second the words popped out, she wanted to call them back.

Her uncle's whole body seemed to tighten with anger, but his voice was mild. "Garcia thought you were dead, all these years." He watched her, gauging her reaction.

Cat carefully schooled her features. "Why did he think that?"

"I sent him a photo of your burned corpse."

Oh, dear heaven. Did that mean someone else had died because of her? How would Garcia react now that he knew she was still alive?

His eyes flashed. "I bought you fourteen years to do as you pleased, Catharine. Now it is time to return to your family and repay your debt."

A cold chill started in her heart and spread throughout her body. Her mouth went dry at the thought of Garcia and his mean eyes, beefy hands, and twisted mind. She couldn't lose her nerve now. "I want your solemn vow that you will protect my family."

"I have always protected you, Catharine. I promised your mother. I will never go back on that promise."

Connie Mann

She clenched her fists, her expression fierce. "That's not good enough, Uncle. You'll give me your word that you'll protect the entire Martinelli family, no matter what, or there's no deal."

The silence lengthened. He studied her for a long moment, then inclined his head. "You have my word."

Would he keep it? Cat couldn't be sure, but she had no choice. She had to take the offer. She swallowed hard and nodded, sealing her fate. She had been prepared to die today. She hadn't been prepared to become Garcia's slave.

"What happens now?" she asked.

"I will find the girl. See what you can learn from the cop that keeps sniffing around but do not tell him anything. Unless you want to see him dead, you will keep him out of this."

The threat turned her insides to ice, but she kept her voice calm, almost indifferent. "Nick has a mind of his own and a nose like a bloodhound. I'll do my best, but he already knows Blaze is missing."

"Then use him. Stay close to him, get whatever information you can."

She started to climb out of the SUV.

"There is no going back." His voice was hard, implacable.

She swallowed and nodded. For Blaze, she would do whatever it took. "I won't."

Cat stepped out and waited until the big SUV disappeared before she sagged against the side of her car. Her mind spun. Her uncle was here, had been here, but, if he was telling the truth, he wasn't the one who had taken Blaze.

Which meant Garcia had her. The man's absolute indifference to Daniel's long-ago death made her shiver, despite the heat.

She rubbed her hands over her arms, tried to think. She'd make sure her uncle got Blaze released. But she had no intention of meekly turning herself over to Garcia. Not without an escape plan.

But before she could formulate one, someone grabbed her arm and spun her around. She lashed out to protect herself, but he stopped her hand before it connected with his throat.

Nick held her still, fury in every line of his body. There was a tear in his sleeve that hadn't been there before, and he had a bruise forming on his cheek and dirt on his pants.

"What happened to you?" she asked.

"Who are those men?" he demanded at the same time.

They glared at each other.

Cat waited. She didn't want to answer that question. Instead, she looked him in the eye. "Who beat you up?"

His eyes narrowed, equal parts concern and anger burning in them. "Couple of those goons didn't like me keeping an eye on you. Who are they?" he asked again.

Possible answers ran through her head, but she couldn't find one that didn't put Blaze in more danger than she was already in.

As he stared at her, Cat saw a spark of something else flash behind his frustration. Before she could raise her defenses, he yanked her into his arms and muttered, "You are making me nuts," before his mouth came down over hers.

Cat froze, stunned. This was Nick, stubborn, relentless, terrifying Nick. The heat and strength of his body made her want to melt against him.

She must have, at least a little, for he pulled her even tighter against him. In his kiss, she tasted frustration and fear, determination and strength, but there was more. He gentled his lips from demand to invitation, running his tongue along her bottom lip, seeking entrance to her mouth.

Cat opened up to him and sank into the kiss, lost in the taste of him, the safety and security within the hard strength of his arms. His hands came up and cupped her cheeks as though she were precious and something to be cherished and protected.

She'd never been kissed like this. Ever.

It was wonderful.

It scared her silly.

This was Nick. She couldn't let him get too close. Couldn't let her defenses down. Not even for a mind-numbing, toe-curling kiss.

Reality and regret slapped her in a double whammy, and she jerked away before she let her heart get tangled up. She couldn't let that happen. Never that. No ties, no entanglements. It was safer that way. For everyone.

They stared at each other, breathing hard, and Cat figured her confusion mirrored his own. He stepped away, stared off into the distance while he scrubbed a hand over the back of his neck.

After several minutes, he turned back, studied her. "You're not going to tell me, are you?"

"I'm not trying to be rude, but this doesn't concern you, Nick. Let it go."

He stepped closer until they were nose to nose again; only, this time, there was no passion, just frustration of a different sort. "Can you stand there and tell me, honestly, that whoever this was had no connection to Teddy's death or to Blaze's disappearance?"

Cat's knees wanted to buckle. She remembered her uncle's warning to keep Nick at arm's length while also pumping him for information. How on earth was she supposed to do both? The silence lengthened until she finally said, "He did not kill Teddy, and he doesn't know where Blaze is."

Please, God, let both be true.

Nick looked like he was about to explode, but finally he just shook his head. "Fine, we'll do this the hard way." He turned and walked toward the back of the cottage. Which must be where he'd left his SUV.

Cat watched him go and then climbed into her car before she succumbed to the urge to run after him and spill the whole ugly tale. She had to stay focused. Never mind that Nick tempted her like no man ever had before in her life. Strong and trustworthy, he was everything her heart had ever wanted. But his tenacity and honesty—the very things she admired most about him—could also get Blaze killed if she weren't careful.

First, before anything else, she had to find Blaze.

———

Blaze tried to keep her panic at bay. Wherever they were holding her was getting hotter by the minute, so she figured it was the middle of the day. Sweat slid down the side of her face, and she wiped it on her shoulder. She was going to suffocate in her hoodie if she didn't cool off soon. Tears tracked down her cheeks, too, and she swiped at those, irritated at the sign of weakness.

Wasn't that what her stepfather had always said about tears? Right before he pulled out his belt and gave her a chance to "practice being strong"? She shook her head to clear the memories. He was dead and gone, and good riddance. But the lessons he'd taught her still ruled her.

The strong didn't cry. They were smart, and they planned, and they struck back when the time came.

Blaze just had to wait for the right time. The two goons that had her didn't seem too smart. Otherwise, how had they grabbed the wrong person? Why had they even thought she was Cat?

She thought about that night. The clearing. Pretending to play the violin. Wearing a hoodie like Cat. No wonder they grabbed the wrong person.

Why had she been pretending to be like Cat, anyway? Cat was obviously in some kind of trouble if people were trying to kidnap her, right?

Or maybe, Cat had asked the wrong people about what had happened to Teddy. At the thought of Teddy, more unwelcome tears slipped down her cheeks, but this time, she let them fall.

Teddy had been different. He was supersmart, but he wasn't a geek. He just knew things, lots of things, was always learning, and then his eyes would light up when he told her what he'd discovered. She'd never met anyone like him, who loved to learn as much as he did.

He'd liked her. That was the part she still couldn't seem to wrap her head around. And he said he liked her just the way she was. He didn't make comments about her clothes or the way she talked or her family. He just seemed to like hanging around her, which blew her mind.

Then at Eve's wedding? She felt a blush steal over her cheeks. He'd asked her to dance, a shy smile on his face, and when he'd taken her in his arms, she'd almost tripped over the stupid dress. But he'd made her feel like one of those dorky princesses in fairy tales. He was no Prince Charming, and she was no damsel in distress, but he'd let her pretend, just for a minute, that fairy tales did come true.

He'd stolen a quick kiss, right before the song ended, and Blaze knew she'd remember it for the rest of her life. She'd never thought she'd feel anything like that, ever. Maybe she never would again.

Oh, Teddy. I'm so sorry. I wish you had told me what was going on. I would have tried to help you. You had to know that.

She pulled her knees to her chest and rested her head on them, let the tears fall. This should never have happened.

But after there were no more tears left and Blaze was drenched with sweat, she started thinking. And the more she thought, the angrier she got.

This wasn't over. She wasn't going to sit around and wait to die. She had to get out of here.

She saw a flash of light on the other side of the room. It disappeared. Then a few minutes later, it flashed again.

She rolled over and twisted until she was on her knees, her bound feet behind her. She put her bound hands down and leaned on her forearms as she inched across the small space. She was breathing hard when she finally made it to the other side. She collapsed next to the wall and tried to see behind the stack of boxes where she'd seen the flash.

There it was again. She tried to slide her hands between the boxes and the wall, but they wouldn't fit. She turned onto her backside and used her legs to push and shove the heavy boxes, until finally she'd moved them several inches. Hopefully, it was far enough.

Frustrated, she wriggled her way around again and shoved her hands down into the gap. Almost . . . almost . . . She wiggled her fingers and kept pushing at the boxes, kept trying to get just a little bit closer.

She still couldn't reach.

She pushed some more with her feet, shoved with her shoulder, and finally grasped what was back there and pulled it out.

Her cell phone.

Shock froze her in place for a moment. She'd thought for sure they had taken it from her when they'd kidnapped her. But it must have fallen out of either her pocket or one of theirs when they'd tossed her in here.

Hope bubbled up as she fumbled with the screen, saw the string of missed calls. A dozen from the marina's number. Must be Sasha. At least that many from Bryan and from an unknown number. Plus six texts from that same number. That must be Cat. A low-battery warning flashed on the screen. She didn't have much time.

Footsteps sounded outside, and she almost dropped the phone. *Not now, please not now.*

She quickly typed the word *trailer*, hit send, and tried to shove the phone into her pocket. She missed, and it slipped from her hands. *No!*

When she heard the lock click open, she kicked the phone out of sight, then scrambled back to where she'd been and slumped against the wall, pretending to be asleep.

The door squealed as it swung open, and bright sunlight speared her closed eyes.

The man climbed in and slapped her cheeks. Blaze blinked up at him, but with the sun behind him, she couldn't make out his features.

"Wake up, Sleeping Beauty, time to go." He hauled her up onto her feet, dropped some kind of fabric over her head, then tossed her over his shoulder and carted her off to a vehicle, where he dumped her into the back. The doors slammed shut, and moments later, what must be some kind of van took off. Blaze couldn't hold on, so she slammed against the metal sides, banging her head.

Nausea roiled in her stomach as the vehicle sped away. All she could think was, *Please find me. Please.*

———

Nick swung by his cottage to clean up and change clothes. He really didn't want to explain his bruised cheekbone to everyone at the station. He couldn't believe the guy had gotten the jump on him. Which proved how distracted his worry for Blaze—and OK, Cat—had made him. He'd taken pictures of the men surrounding the dark SUV and had just finished photographing the license plates and the rundown house when he'd been jumped from behind.

He'd debated pulling out his badge and hauling them all in, but then he decided against it, said he was a realtor checking the place out. Luckily, he'd hidden his official Safe Harbor police SUV several hundred yards away in the woods surrounding the house. He didn't want them to know who he was just yet.

Instead of returning to the station, he let Wanda know where he was and then pulled out his laptop and uploaded the photos he'd taken. He also did a search on the address, trying to find out if there'd been a change in ownership, but there hadn't. The same family still owned it. Last he'd heard, it had been left to a distant relative in California when the owners passed away.

He scanned the photos of the men, but none of them looked familiar. They all had Asian backgrounds, though, based on their looks, just like Cat. Two were slender, like Cat. The third, who had opened the door for Cat, had a more stocky build than the other two. Who were they? And what were they doing in Safe Harbor?

He spent several minutes typing in his passwords and credentials but finally accessed the database he wanted. He uploaded the pictures, hoping facial recognition would get a hit.

In the meantime, he read over his notes on Teddy's case again. His email chirped, and he saw a message from the toxicology lab. The water bottle he'd found at the quarry contained scopolamine.

They'd found the murder weapon.

He should have been elated at discovering another piece of the puzzle, but fury churned just below his skin. Who had dared bring that drug to Safe Harbor? And worse, used it to kill one of their own teens?

When someone knocked on his door, he walked over, gun at his side, just in case. Cat stood on his threshold, shifting impatiently while she waited. "Come on, Nick. Open the door."

He swung it open just as she raised her hand to knock again. "What brings you here—"

Her eyes were wild as she thrust a cell phone at him and hurried inside. She spun to face him. "She texted me. You have to trace it or whatever, with GPS, so we can find her. Hurry."

A quick glance at the phone showed a text message: trailer. "Are you sure it's from Blaze?"

Her expression said she wanted to smack him for asking dumb questions. "It's from her number. I tried to call her back and text her, but I didn't get a response. We have to hurry."

Nick walked over to his laptop, set the phone down. He grabbed his cell phone, called Eloise at Blue Sky Cellular. "Hi, Eloise, this is Nick Stanton from the Safe Harbor Police Department. How are you? Good. Glad to hear it. Listen, you've been such a help in the past. Right now I need a favor. Can you get me the location of a particular phone based on its GPS?"

"I'd love to help you, but I'm not authorized to give out that information, not without all the official paperwork," she answered stiffly.

He wondered briefly who was listening in. "I completely understand and wouldn't ask except that it's an emergency. I believe the person on the other end of the line is in imminent danger, and I need to locate her immediately. Can you help me?"

Nick waited while she considered. Then waited some more as he heard keys clacking in the background. Finally she said, "Please do not tell anyone where you got this information. I need my job."

"My lips are sealed," he promised.

He grabbed paper and pen and scribbled down the address that she rattled off. He thanked her profusely and then turned to Cat, who was pacing like a caged tiger. "Let's go."

He ushered her out the door and to his official police-issue Ford Explorer. He held the door as she climbed inside, then hurried around and got in. He called Wanda and asked for JD to meet them ASAP. He gave her the address, then hit the siren and lights as he sped in that direction.

Beside him, Cat twisted her hands in her lap.

"Why me, Cat? Why now?" She'd just finished telling him to mind his own business. Why the sudden change?

Cat glanced his way, then back out the window. "I'm afraid for her. I need your help."

"Which you hate asking for."

She nodded, once. "I'm used to being on my own."

No surprise there. Something else had been nagging at him. "You got a new cell phone."

He wondered if she'd respond, but then she nodded, once. Shrugged like it was no big deal. "I get a new one every so often."

Which begged the question, why? But now wasn't the time.

"You got a new one since you gave me your number," he clarified.

He saw her jaw clench. She finally looked over at him. "My experience with cops has not been what you'd call good."

He sent her a half smile. "But I'm one of the good guys."

Her answering nod was resigned. "I know. That's why I'm here."

"But you don't want to be."

That got a reaction. She half turned in her seat to face him. "I don't want anything to do with cops, no. I don't want Blaze in danger. I don't want Teddy to be dead, and I don't want to be in Safe Harbor." She blew out an angry breath. "Doesn't matter what I want. We have to find Blaze before—"

"Before what? What do you know, Cat?"

"Before whoever has her hurts her!" she shouted.

Nick let it go, for now. Getting info out of this woman was about as much fun as cleaning scallops. They were stubborn buggers, with sharp edges and slimy insides, hiding their tender center. But the effort was always worth it.

As he approached the location, he turned off both the lights and the siren and then pulled into the truck stop on the edge of town, out by the interstate.

It made sense. If you were holding someone, this was the perfect place to hide them in plain sight.

Cat was out of the SUV and running toward the restaurant almost before he came to a complete stop. He hurried after her.

Chapter 19

Cat came to a skidding halt just inside the truck stop restaurant. The noise level dropped as people stared, and she realized she must look like a crazy person, panting like she'd been chased for miles. She forced herself to take several deep breaths, to center herself even as panic clawed at her insides. If she wanted answers, she had to focus, to think.

Nick appeared behind her, and his solid presence loosened the tightness in her chest a fraction. "Do you have a picture of Blaze on your phone?" he asked.

Cat shook her head. She never took pictures, hadn't in years. It was too dangerous.

She watched as he pulled out his cell phone and started scrolling through photos. He held it up, showed her a picture of Blaze at Eve's wedding. Unbidden, Cat's eyes filled. She looked so dang beautiful.

They had to find her.

The heavyset twentysomething hostess approached, grabbed two plastic menus, a bored look on her face. "Two?"

Nick held up the phone. "Actually, we're trying to find someone. Have you seen this girl in here recently?"

The hostess peered at the photo, then shook her head and looked from one to the other. "No. Is she in trouble?"

"We hope not. We're just trying to find her."

"Sorry." She indicated the menus. "Do you want to sit?" She glanced behind them to a family that had just come in.

"We'll just ask around," Nick said and guided Cat to a table near the front of the restaurant.

Cat barely heard what he said, her eyes focused on a group of teens at a table near the back. She hurried over, checking to make sure Nick was behind her.

There were four teens at the table, two guys and two girls, obviously on a double date by the nervous glances they kept giving each other. Before anyone could protest, Cat grabbed a chair from the next table, straddled it, and eyed the four of them. "You all go to Safe Harbor High?"

They exchanged glances. "Yes, why?" said a tall boy who looked like he played football.

"Do y'all know Blaze Martinelli?"

At the blank looks, Cat turned to Nick, who held out his phone and showed it to them. One girl said, "Oh, I know her. She's in my math class. Quiet." She looked up. "Is she in trouble?"

"That's what we're trying to find out," Nick answered. He pulled a card out of his wallet. "If you happen to see her, will you give me a quick call and let me know? We just want to be sure she's OK."

The girl nodded, all of them with worried looks on their faces. Cat thanked them, and they went to the next table, and the next, but no one admitted to seeing Blaze anywhere.

They checked the bathrooms, asked the two waitresses and the busboy, and Nick used his badge to talk to the staff in the kitchen. Nothing. They went to the shower facilities and asked at the convenience store next door. Still nothing.

Once they were outside again, Cat thought she'd burst out of her skin. This was taking too long and they weren't getting anywhere. She saw the tractor trailers lined up in the parking lot and headed in that direction, Nick easily keeping pace.

"We'll find her, Cat."

She nodded but didn't slow. Every time she let her guard down the tiniest fraction, images of Joellen and Teddy and Daniel flashed through her mind. The sense that Blaze was out of time grew with every second.

Once they reached the trailers, Nick showed Blaze's picture to every driver they could find. With every negative shake of a head, Cat's hope got a little bit dimmer. She pulled out her phone and dialed Blaze's number, but with the rumble of so many diesel engines, she knew the chances of hearing it ring were slim to none, especially if Blaze had the phone on silent.

They worked their way toward the rear of the parking lot, where a row of trailers sat by themselves, no doubt waiting for a rig to come pick them up. Cat glanced at Nick, whose pace had also sped up. It was the perfect hiding place.

Here, the engine noise wasn't as loud, so Cat dialed Blaze's number again. They stood still, straining to hear it ring. "Come on, Blaze. Where are you?"

Cat waited until it went to voice mail again, still not hearing any ringing from the trailers.

Defeat had her biting her cheek.

"Let's keep walking. Call again," Nick suggested.

Cat stabbed the call button, eyes scanning every trailer they passed.

They were almost to the very last trailer in the lot when Cat froze, looking at Nick. They heard classical music. It stopped abruptly. Cat pushed the call button again. The music started once more, coming from the last trailer.

They rushed over. Cat was opening her mouth to start shouting for Blaze when Nick took her arm and tucked her behind him. "Slow and quiet. Just in case."

She looked over and saw the gun in his hand, held down low by the side of his leg, his expression full-on cop. Gone was Officer Friendly. This was Warrior Nick.

Impatience clawed at Cat's skin as they eased around to the back of the trailer, Nick scanning the area with an intensity that both calmed and terrified her.

Once they reached the padlock, Nick whispered, "Blaze? Are you in here?"

No answer. Cat dialed again, and they both heard it ring. Blaze's phone was definitely inside.

Cat reached for the lock, and it opened when she yanked on it. Surprised, she glanced at Nick, undid the hasp. He motioned her back with his gun, then slowly pulled the door open, scanning the interior.

"Police. Anyone in here? Blaze? You there?" Nick pierced her with a look. "Stay down while I check inside."

Without waiting for a reply, he hopped inside, checking behind the stack of boxes lining one side of the otherwise empty space.

As Cat watched, her heart sank. Blaze wasn't here.

He turned, a cell phone in his hand. "It's hers."

Cat sagged against the trailer in defeat while Nick stepped away and spoke to someone on his cell phone.

Several minutes later, the young cop Cat remembered from her car accident burst around the side of the trailer, leading with his gun.

"Easy, JD," Nick said when he appeared. "She's not here. But I need you to dust for prints and any other evidence you can find." He held up the phone. "She clearly was here."

JD's eyes were as big as saucers. "You think she's been kidnapped, Nick? Should we call the FBI?"

"Not yet," another voice said, and Cat spun to see Chief Monroe walk around the side of the trailer. "Let's make sure we haven't missed anything ourselves. What do we know so far, Stanton?" he said.

Cat half listened as Nick went over the timeline, her thoughts racing. Where would Garcia have taken her? She would have to find a way to call her uncle, see what he knew.

But terror grew as she paced. *Hang on, Blaze. I'll find you.*

———

Nick kept an eye on Cat as Monroe gave orders and generally took over. He let his irritation with the chief go, for now. Cat's behavior puzzled him. She was scared, yes. But there was anger there, too.

After Monroe left and JD went back to his patrol car to get his crime scene kit, Nick finally approached Cat. "Ready to go?"

With a quick nod, she marched off toward his SUV. He caught up to her, stopped her with a hand on her arm, made sure he could see her eyes when he asked, "What do you know about this, Cat?"

He saw the split second of guilt before the shutter dropped over her eyes. Her expression was fierce. "What do you mean? I know as much as you do. Someone trapped her in that hot, dark trailer, and she tried to call me for help." Now he saw anguish. "And we're too late. Whoever has her moved her, and now we have no way of finding her." She swallowed hard, and Nick reached out to pull her into his arms before he realized what he was doing.

She twitched away and kept walking, faster and faster.

Biting back his frustration, he caught up, held the door of the SUV open for her. "What aren't you telling me, Cat?"

Finally she met his eyes. "I don't know any more than you do." She swallowed. "But we have to find her, Nick. Fast."

"Agreed." He walked around to the driver's side, but his attention was caught by raised voices just behind the restaurant. He turned, surprised to see Eddie Varga and Captain Barry nose to nose. Captain Barry's face was red, and he jabbed a finger into Eddie's bony chest as he shouted. Nick eased out of sight and tried to make out what they were saying, but a truck started up nearby, and the rumble of the diesel engine drowned out their words.

Several minutes later, Eddie spun on his heel and hopped into his 1980s vintage Camaro, tires spinning on the asphalt as he sped away. Nick strode over to Captain Barry and caught up to him just as he climbed into a Cadillac of recent vintage. "Captain Barry. How's it going?"

Out of the corner of his eye, Nick caught sight of Cat slipping behind a nearby rig. He refused to look in her direction, hoping Barry wouldn't notice her.

"Afternoon, Stanton. What brings you out this way?"

"I was going to ask you the same question. What's up with you and Eddie Varga?"

"We were talking about a fishing charter. I may need him to come along as a mate on my next trip this weekend."

"That so? The conversation didn't appear overly friendly."

Barry speared him with a look, ran a hand over his balding pate. "He's an idiot, but he's a great first mate. And if he puts his mind to it, he can charm the tourists."

"What were you arguing about?"

Barry froze, then sent him a lopsided grin. "I wouldn't call it an argument, Officer. More like me stressing the importance of being nice to the tourists."

Nick studied him a moment, then nodded. "You haven't seen Blaze Martinelli today, have you?"

Nick saw a flash of fear in Barry's eyes, but it was gone so fast he thought maybe he'd imagined it. "No, sir. I haven't. Is something wrong?"

"We're just making sure she's OK. She and Teddy Winston were really good friends." Nick watched Barry's reaction.

The older man sighed. "Really a tragedy, that. He was such a nice young man. Have you figured out what he died from yet?"

"It's all part of an ongoing investigation. If you hear from Blaze, let me know, all right?"

"Sure thing. Hope you find her."

Nick nodded and turned away, and Cat fell into step beside him.

"What was he doing with Eddie Varga?" Cat demanded.

"That's a very good question. Says he wants him to first mate on a charter and charm the guests."

Cat snorted. "And I'm Queen Victoria."

Nick felt a smile curl up one corner of his mouth. Despite the situation, she made him want to laugh. He realized he hadn't had that urge in a long time.

He couldn't think about that now. He had to find Blaze, and figure out how she connected to Teddy's death. He started the SUV. "I'll drop you off at your car. I need to get back to the station."

"What? No. We need to keep looking. We have to find her, Nick."

He glanced her way, understood her panic. It hummed just under his skin, too. "If we figure out how she's connected to Teddy's death, we should be able to figure out who took her. Which brings us one step closer to figuring out *where* they took her."

He glanced over at her in time to see a flash of fear cross her face, a split second before she looked away. "Spill it, Cat. What do you know?"

Her head snapped around, her expression fierce. "I know she's missing. I know we don't have any idea where she's been taken or what her captors may do to her."

What she hadn't said clicked. "But you know who took her. Or think you do."

She tried to hide her reaction, but he saw the telltale jerk of a muscle in her cheek as she bit the inside of her mouth. She went still, arms folded over her chest. "Do you think I'd be sitting here with a cop if I could figure this out on my own?"

A good point, Nick thought, but there was more to it than that. He pulled up in front of his little house so she could get her car. "You keep checking with her friends. I'll do some digging online, see what I can find out from that end."

She was about to say something else when her phone rang. "Have you found her?"

Nick watched all the color drain out of her face.

She scrambled out of his SUV. "I'll be right there."

Nick followed her, stepped close as she climbed into her beat-up little car. "I need to go."

"Did they find Blaze?"

She looked startled by the question. "No. But I need to get home." She started the car.

"And I need your new phone number, Cat."

She began inching the car forward, forcing him to step back or get his feet run over. "Later. Gotta go."

He watched her speed away, all his instincts screaming. He didn't think she'd lied about finding Blaze. But there was a world of other things she'd left out.

Chapter 20

Cat kept her car right at the speed limit on the way to the marina, but it took a white-knuckled grip on the steering wheel to pull it off. Every instinct wanted to race to get there, but she couldn't afford another encounter with Safe Harbor's finest. Still, she had to get home fast.

Funny that the marina she'd hated as a teen now felt like home, a safe haven. This was where her family was, and they were being threatened. Because of her.

She had to do something.

They were waiting on the porch when she sped down the drive, stirring up a cloud of dust. Mama Rosa, Sasha, Jesse. Even Pop.

She hurried up the steps, leaning over to kiss Mama's cheek where she sat in her rocking chair, her knitting in her lap. "Hello, Mama."

Mama gripped her hand, eyes filled with fear. "Did you find her?"

"Not yet. But we will. Promise." She glanced over, saw the worry in Pop's eyes as he stood behind Mama's chair, a hand on her shoulder.

"What does Nicky say?" Mama asked.

Cat didn't want to talk about Nick. Couldn't think about him right now, either, the way he made her feel safe and then tempted her to say all kinds of things that must be left unsaid, for the safety of her family. "He's working on it, and he won't stop until he finds her." That part she could say with certainty. The man was a bulldog and wouldn't stop until he got the answers he needed. She shivered despite the heat.

Jesse stepped forward, made a small motion to indicate she should follow him.

"He's a good man and a good cop," Pop said, patting Mama's shoulder. "He'll find our girl."

Cat believed that, too. It was all the other secrets he might uncover along the way that terrified her.

"I got that new part for your car, Cat. It's in the workshop," Jesse said.

"Thanks. Can I see?" It was a flimsy getaway excuse, at best, but how else to escape from under Mama's and Pop's watchful eyes?

Sasha stood, too, a protective hand over her baby bump, and Cat had to look away as Sasha followed them down the porch steps. That baby would grow up safe, without a shadow of fear. Cat would figure out a way to make that happen. Or die trying.

No one said a word until they were inside the workshop with the door closed. "What's going on? Why the urgency? Did you find something?" Cat demanded.

Jesse folded his arms over his broad chest, eyes narrowed. "Who is following you, Cat? And why?"

She froze. "What are you talking about?"

"There's a guy. Showed up this morning with fishing gear he clearly doesn't know how to use, wearing clothes so stiff and new the tags might as well still be attached. He's been out at the end of the dock pretending to fish for hours. Who is he and why is he watching the marina? And what does he have to do with Blaze's disappearance?"

Cat looked from one to the other. Both Jesse and Sasha wore implacable expressions. They deserved answers, she just didn't have any to give them. Not ones that wouldn't make things worse, anyway.

"I'll go find out," she said and started for the door.

Sasha stepped forward and blocked her path. "Talk, Cat. What's this about?"

Cat looked her sister in the eyes, saw the worry there, and gave her as much of the truth as she could. "I'm not exactly sure yet, but I will find out. I promise you that."

They stared at each other for a long moment, then Sasha stepped away. But not before Cat saw the disgust in her sister's eyes. Cat had let them down. Again.

She absorbed the knowledge like a blow. Then pushed it aside. She had to know if it was one of her uncle's men or one of Garcia's outside.

The first option scared her. The second brought terror, for Blaze's sake.

———

Nick shoved his chair away from his desk, ran his hands through his hair, and massaged the back of his neck. His facial recognition search had returned results while he and Cat had been at the truck stop. And with every new bit of information he found, the more he realized Cat was involved. How far involved was the question.

He hadn't been able to see inside the black SUV to get a picture of whomever Cat had met with, but he'd gotten several good shots of the driver. Phillip Chen didn't have a record, but he'd lived in Miami for many years. It was who he worked for that had all of Nick's alarm bells clanging.

Richard Wang. He was well known to Miami's law enforcement community. His business was ostensibly import/export, but everything Nick dug up said his main product was drugs. Various kinds. And women. DEA, Miami PD, every law enforcement agency in the state had tried to get a conviction, but every time they thought they had an airtight case against the man, a key witness would disappear or die a mysterious death.

He'd also run Cat's picture through facial recognition. He got a hit, but it wasn't her. It was a woman who looked so much like Cat, he concluded she had to be her mother. A bit more digging turned up her name and the date of her death.

Once he ran her mother's name, he found out where Cat had gotten her musical talent. Her parents had been classical musicians, as she'd said. He remembered her saying they'd loved her but didn't always have time for her.

He drummed his fingers on the desk as he scrolled through more articles. He found an old picture of the three of them outside a concert hall in Cincinnati, when Cat was about ten. Then he found their names mentioned in the train crash that killed them when Cat was fourteen.

Her real name was Catharine Wang, Richard Wang's niece.

What was a major player in the drug world doing in Safe Harbor? Right after his niece showed up after a ten-year absence, and within days of a local teen dying from a drug overdose, from one of the nastiest drugs out there?

Was Cat working with her uncle? Were they trying to bring scopolamine to Safe Harbor? Though, considering Teddy's death, it was already here.

His desk phone rang, and he snatched up the receiver. "Stanton."

"Hi, Nick, this is Bev at the crime lab. We didn't find any prints on the water bottle you sent, but we did find a hair stuck under the label. We're really backed up, but I know you're trying to find answers for that boy's family, so I, ah, may have moved them to the front of the line and run the tests on my lunch hour. I'm sending the DNA results for the hair, the cigarette butt, and the prints and DNA I found on the beer bottle."

"Bev, you're amazing. Thank you. I owe you, big time."

"You don't owe me anything, Officer. Just find out who hurt that sweet young man."

"Yes, ma'am. I will. Thank you again."

He hung up and waited for his email to show incoming mail. He opened the DNA results, then went into the system and compared them to Eddie Varga's DNA, sure he'd get a match.

Except he didn't. The results weren't even close.

Frustrated, he stood up and started pacing. It wasn't Eddie Varga who gave Teddy the scopolamine. At least not that Nick could prove. So who was it?

He entered the information into CODIS and did a comparison check, not surprised when it turned up nothing. No DNA in the criminal database matched that water bottle.

He was back to square one.

———

Cat took a deep breath to corral her anger and marched onto the dock. As her footsteps pounded the weathered boards, the figure standing alone at the end of the dock glanced her way. Even with the hat, she knew.

Phillip.

"What are you doing here?" she demanded.

He glanced out at the Gulf, then back at her, voice expressionless. "My job. Just like always."

"You do realize that you stick out like a flashing beacon in your shiny new clothes and fishing gear, right? Never mind the gun in your fishing vest."

He didn't say anything. Had never had much to say, come to think of it.

"Why are you here?"

"I'm keeping an eye on things for Mr. Wang."

"And by things you mean me."

He didn't respond.

"What exactly did he ask you to do, Phillip?"

"The same as always, Miss Catharine."

"You'll watch and report back."

"Correct."

"What if someone tries to hurt my fam—the Martinellis? What are your orders then?"

"I'm here to offer protection."

Cat studied him awhile, the determined look in his eyes, and finally nodded. "Thank you, Phillip."

"My pleasure, Miss Catharine."

She started toward the house, then stopped, looked over her shoulder. "Where is Blaze?"

"We don't know. But Mr. Wang is working hard to find out."

She watched his eyes. "You think Garcia has her."

He shrugged, looked away. "It is the logical conclusion."

Yes, it was. It was also the most terrifying.

———

By the time the van slowed, Blaze hurt all over. The ride had seemed endless, though she figured they really hadn't gone all that far. Still, with her hands and feet bound, she hadn't been able to hold on, so she'd slammed against the side of the van with every sharp curve and tight corner. Even her bruises had bruises.

Her heart pounded as the vehicle finally came to a stop. Should she pretend to be asleep? What were they going to do with her?

The van doors squeaked as they opened, and someone grabbed her feet and hauled her backward toward the door. She cried out as her arms scraped the floor. She tried to hold her head up, but couldn't, and pain radiated from her skull as her head thumped the floor and she was dragged backward.

"Quit your yapping," the same voice growled as he grabbed her and tossed her over his shoulder again. The blood rushed to her head as he hurried along. Whatever they'd put over her head started to slip, and Blaze had a moment of hope that it would fall away and she could figure out where they were. Was that water she heard? She tried to sniff the air through the cloth. Her instincts said she was near the Gulf. That should help, right?

Help with what? Her cell phone was still in the trailer, so she couldn't call anyone. Even if Cat had gotten her text, provided it had actually been Cat's number she'd dialed, she hadn't gotten there in time. Now, her family had no idea where she was or how to find her.

A door opened, and she heard the man's footsteps on what sounded like concrete steps, going down into what felt like a basement or something. He tossed her onto a narrow cot, and she winced as she bounced. "Don't go anywhere." He laughed, and she heard the door click shut behind him.

Blaze rolled to her side and listened for a moment, desperate to hear something, anything, to help her figure out where she was. She'd watched enough cop shows to know that's what you should do. No train whistles, no traffic noise. But if she listened really closely, she still thought she could hear water lapping the shore.

The door opened again, and she stilled, waiting.

"*Madre de Dios*, look at your wrists." The woman had a thick accent. Blaze felt a tug, and then her wrists were freed. Another tug by her feet as the woman cut that restraint, too.

"*Un momento*, I will get you all fixed."

Blaze reached for the cloth over her head, but the woman stopped her with a surprisingly strong grip. "Leave it. It will be safer, no?"

Nodding, Blaze swallowed hard. The woman meant she was safer if she couldn't identify them. Maybe this meant they'd let her go, though, right?

The woman's hands were firm but kind as she put ointment on the cuts around Blaze's wrists where she'd tried to work her hands out of what felt like zip ties. Then came bandages.

The second the door closed behind the woman, Blaze listened, trying to make sure she was really gone. When she was sure, she eased the hood up just enough to look around. She was in some kind of storage room. The only window had a shutter on the outside, blocking most of the light. She moved closer. There had to be a way to get out.

She heard voices and froze. She hopped back on the bed and pulled the hood halfway down so she could listen.

The voice belonged to the guy who'd brought her here. "He wants us to get the other one, too, so he can take care of them at the same time."

Goose bumps broke out on her skin, and she stifled a cry. They were going after Cat. Which meant they knew who she was.

But it was his last line that made her shake. What did "take care of" mean exactly? The possibilities made her teeth start to chatter.

Maybe, just maybe, Cat could help her figure out how to stay alive until Nick came to get them out.

Chapter 21

How was she going to figure out where Garcia was holding Blaze? Cat had no idea. She paced, chewed the inside of her lip, and finally climbed into her sad-looking car and started driving.

She left the marina and headed down the two-lane road toward town. She didn't even know for sure if Garcia was in Safe Harbor.

But if a couple of hired thugs showed up around here, they'd stick out like sore thumbs. Somebody would have noticed them, and people would be talking about it. Which meant the next logical place to go was the Blue Dolphin, the best source of local news and gossip in the county.

She headed that way, hoping against hope that people would finally forgive the bratty teen she'd been and actually talk to her. But she'd deal with that when she got there.

She glanced in her rearview mirror and noticed that a white van had showed up and was closing in fast. She inched over toward the shoulder, trying to give him room to pass, but he didn't, just kept narrowing the gap. Her heart sped up as the van moved in close enough that all she could see in her rearview mirror was the front grill.

Fear and excitement churned inside her, and she kept a white-knuckled grip on the steering wheel. This had to be Garcia's men. Were they planning to run her off the road?

Almost before the thought formed, the van rammed her from behind. Cat fought to keep the car on the pavement, heart pounding. Did they intend to kill her? Or kidnap her?

She had some vague notion of allowing them to grab her, so she would be with Blaze and they could escape together, but when the van hit her again, it was hard enough that she couldn't control the car.

A strange sense of déjà vu filled her as the car rolled once, then bounced, then flipped again and landed in the culvert.

Cat felt the seat belt snap into place, her still-bruised ribs hit the steering wheel, and her head collide with something hard.

This couldn't be happening again. She struggled to catch her breath, to stay awake. She had to get to Blaze, had to protect her.

She shook her head. "Come on, stay awake, think," she muttered.

Someone yanked on the driver's side door handle, and Cat's head snapped in that direction. All she saw was dark sunglasses and a ball cap.

Her head swam, and she struggled to focus. Seconds later, the passenger door opened, and he reached in to unclick her seat belt. Before she could react or decide how to respond, hard hands grabbed her. She struggled instinctively as he dragged her up and over the gearshift and out of the car.

She yelped in pain as he lost his grip and she fell out the door. She tried to scramble backward, but he was too quick. He reached under her arms and, in one motion, tossed her over his shoulder. Cat twisted and bucked, desperate to free her legs. She'd almost succeeded when another man stepped over and pressed a gun to her temple. "Be still," he growled.

She eyed the gun and stopped struggling. She couldn't help anyone if she were dead. Between the crash and being held upside down, her stomach rebelled, and she retched. Her captor cursed long and loud when it covered his back and legs. She felt a moment's grim satisfaction and realized she was feeling better and her head had cleared.

Best not to let them know any of that, though, so she let her body go limp. Normally, she would have taken both men down without a moment's hesitation. Neither one of these goons was in top shape. But Cat was nothing if not a realist. She wasn't at her best right after yet another car crash.

Besides, getting away wouldn't be her smartest move. Not right now. She was betting her life that these men had also taken Blaze. She'd let them take her, too, bide her time, and see where Blaze was. Then she'd make her move, free them both.

The gun came out of nowhere and slammed into the side of her head before she had time to brace herself. She jerked sideways, and everything went black.

———

Nick was sitting at his desk when the call came in to the emergency number.

"Safe Harbor police, what's your emergency?" Wanda asked. "Take a deep breath, ma'am, and tell me what you saw."

Nick hurried over and stood right behind Wanda's chair so he could hear what was being said. The caller almost shouted in her agitation.

"There was a van, a white van, and I saw it ram this little car. I was going in the other direction, so I turned around and came back and when I did, I-I saw two men grab a woman out of the car."

"Were they trying to help her?"

"No, she was struggling, and the one guy tossed her over his shoulder and then headed back to the van."

"Did they see you?"

"I-I . . . oh, dear God, I have no idea."

Nick leaned closer, worry gnawing at his gut. "What did the car look like?"

"It was small, like a Toyota or something, not new, but it was all banged up. The roof was dented, even before it rolled over."

"What did the woman look like?"

"She was small, dark hair. It happened so fast, I didn't get a good look."

"That's fine," Nick said. "What direction did they go?"

"Um, I'm not good with directions, so I . . . ah . . ."

"Toward Safe Harbor or away?" Nick barked.

"Away. Definitely away."

Nick was already halfway out the door when he heard Wanda ask the woman for her name and other information.

Someone had grabbed Cat.

———

Cat woke with a burst of pain as she crashed against a wall. She forced herself to swallow her cry and, instead, tried to pull in shallow breaths and take stock of her surroundings.

She blinked and looked around. She was obviously in a van of some kind, and it was moving fast. She touched the side of her head and winced when her hand came away bloody. Geez, good thing she had a hard head. She couldn't keep doing this.

Her brain finally snapped back into focus, and the instinct to escape with it. She'd been kidnapped. By Garcia's men, no doubt.

She tried to get a good look at the driver and passenger, but both men wore dark glasses and had ball caps pulled low over their heads. They wore Hawaiian shirts over shorts and flip-flops, no doubt to try to blend in, but Cat didn't miss the holsters under their shirts.

No one in Safe Harbor would be fooled by these so-called tourists for long.

She could easily jump out of the van and escape. It shouldn't be that hard. If she leaped into the bushes alongside the road, the landing wouldn't kill her. Probably.

But she wouldn't. She'd stay right where she was. She was betting they would take her wherever they were holding Blaze, sort of a two-for-one deal.

She'd find a way to get her out, get them both out, alive.

That meant, for now, she'd stay right where she was.

I'm coming, Blaze. Hang on, girl.

———

Fury hummed under Nick's skin as he raced out of the station. No way was somebody's hired muscle going to abduct Cat. Not on Nick's watch. He sped out of the station parking lot, tires squealing, lights and sirens blaring. He only hoped he wasn't too late.

A white van heading out of town wasn't much to go on, but it was all he had right now. Wanda would relay any other information available, but Nick didn't think the caller had gotten a license plate.

Most of the cars eased over to the side to allow him to pass, but there were always a few idiots who didn't think the rule applied to them. He laid on the horn as he sped around a Cadillac with New York plates and got flipped off for his trouble. He just shook his head and sped up.

Come on, you cretins. Where are you?

It didn't take long before he spotted the van driving down the road at exactly the speed limit. They weren't total idiots. They'd made sure the van didn't have a license plate, either.

Nick filed that information away and noted the make and model as he approached. He used his microphone to say, "Pull over."

As he expected, the van sped up. "Of course," he muttered and hit the gas. He could easily catch them. His SUV could outrun the van any day, but he didn't want to get too close, didn't want to push too hard, not with Cat in there. He wouldn't risk the driver doing something stupid and rolling the van or running off the road and killing everyone inside.

He kept his hand steady on the wheel, trying to anticipate the driver's every move. The van shot down the road, and Nick's speedometer inched up to sixty, then seventy, then eighty as he kept pace. He grabbed the microphone again. "Pull over to the side of the road."

The driver glanced in his rearview mirror and sped up even more. "Where exactly do you think you're going?" There was nothing along this stretch of road except wide-open fields and cattle pasture. There was nowhere to hide.

Except there was. Sure enough, that's where the van went. Ten miles outside of Safe Harbor, the sign for Springside came into view. The nearby town boasted crystal-clear artesian springs and a river and was bordered by national forest. If they crossed the line into Springside, he'd have to notify local law enforcement.

But he didn't think they'd go that far. As Nick expected, the driver slowed as they approached the dense forest. When the trees thickened on both sides of the road, he slowed even more, Nick right on his tail. He called Wanda and told her to send JD to this location, gave a description of the van. Not for the first time, he wished Safe Harbor had a bigger department and systems that could track each officer's location via GPS.

Before the van came to a complete stop, the door opened and the driver took off running into the woods. Nick pulled in behind and was out the door, gun in hand.

A second man took off into the woods in the opposite direction. Divide and conquer. It's exactly what he would have done.

He ran to the van and yanked the door open. Inside, Cat blinked at him as she struggled to a sitting position. He climbed in and crouched beside her. "Are you OK?"

With the light behind him, it took a moment for her to focus on his face. When she did, she slugged him in the arm. "What are you doing here? Go get them before they disappear!"

"Are you OK?" he asked again.

"I'm fine, you idiot, but they're getting away." She tried to shove past him. "If you won't go, I'll track them down myself."

He blocked her path, took her chin in his hand, and wouldn't let go until he'd checked her eyes. "Stay put and wait for EMS."

He hopped out of the van and used his radio to call dispatch while he ran after the passenger, the slower of the two guys. The driver had already disappeared.

This guy clearly hadn't learned evasive maneuvers, because he crashed through the underbrush, making enough noise that Nick had no trouble following him. All the birds went quiet, but the scrub palms rattled as the guy passed by.

Mosquitos buzzed around his head as Nick ran, and sweat poured down his back, the humidity thick in the air. He stopped, breath heaving, and listened. There.

He changed course and picked up the pace.

Before long, the man came into view. He glanced over his shoulder, saw Nick, and took off with a surprising burst of speed.

"Couldn't make it easy, could you?" he muttered and sped up. He caught up to the guy and tackled him in one quick jump.

"Don't move," he warned as he pulled the guy's hands behind his back and snapped on the cuffs.

"I didn't do nothing, man. I'm just jogging through the woods."

Nick stood and hauled the idiot to his feet. He eyed the belligerent stance. He took him to be late thirties, dark skin, eyes, and hair. Built like a tank, probably played football in high school, but drank too much beer these days, so that muscle was mostly fat now. "What's your name?"

"I want a lawyer."

"OK, Mr. I Want a Lawyer, I'm taking you in for resisting arrest and failure to pull over." He marched the goon toward his SUV. "And anything else I can think of. We'll see what the woman you kidnapped has to say."

"I didn't kidnap nobody."

Given the man's belligerent stance didn't change a bit, Nick figured the guy expected his employer to come bail him out, or send a fancy lawyer to do it.

"Who do you work for? Who hired you?" He didn't think he'd get an answer, but it was worth a try.

"Lawyer."

"That's your right, of course, but this will go easier in the long run if you answer a few questions."

The guy had the gall to laugh in Nick's face.

Clearly, he wasn't the brains behind the operation. But who was he working for? Cat's uncle? Or someone else entirely?

———

Cat leaned against the side of Nick's SUV, fuming. Dang the man. Why couldn't he leave things alone? How was she going to figure out where Blaze was now?

Nick finally showed up, hauling the passenger with him. She marched over, angry that she still felt a bit unsteady on her feet. She was tired of getting beat up, especially when it didn't help find Blaze.

She poked the guy in his broad chest, demanded, "Where's Blaze?"

He glared down at her. "I don't know what you're talking about, lady."

"Where. Did. You. Take. Her?"

He turned to Nick. "You better get this loony tune some help. She's obviously crazy."

Cat gripped his shirtfront. "Tell me!"

Keeping one hand on the goon, Nick eased Cat back a step with his body. "Let go, Cat. I'll deal with him."

She opened her mouth to say more, then saw the warning in his eyes and snapped her mouth closed. She waited while Nick put the man in the back seat of his SUV and then came over to her.

"What the heck, Nick? Where's the other guy? Why aren't you getting information out of this jerk?"

Nick seemed unfazed by her panic, which only made her more furious. "Who are they, Cat?"

She fisted her hands on her hips. She had to tread carefully. "How should I know? They rammed my car and pulled me out of it."

"I know."

"How could you possibly know that?"

"A good Samaritan saw it happen and called it in."

That's how he got here so fast, drat the man. "You should have let it go," she muttered.

He stepped closer until she was flush against the SUV. His eyes were hard, every bit the cop. "I should have ignored the report that you'd just been kidnapped from your car and let them take you?" He narrowed his eyes as he studied her face. "You wanted them to take you. Are you insane?"

"No, I'm desperate," she hissed. "It was the only way I could think of to find Blaze."

"Which is a great idea, except then they'd have *both* of you! How is that a good plan?"

It had sounded much better in her head. She looked away, shrugged. "I have plenty of self-defense training. I figured once I got to wherever they were taking me, I could find Blaze and we'd escape."

"And if they killed you long before that? Then what?"

Cat's eyes snapped to his. She saw fury there, obviously, but also worry and . . . something more. The silence lengthened, and the air crackled with electricity. My, but the man looked good when he was in full warrior mode. Hard jaw, a shadow of a beard. She knew he would stand between her and danger without a moment's hesitation.

Reality slapped her upside the head. No matter how tempting, she couldn't get close to him. It was too dangerous. For everyone, especially her family.

Without thinking it through, she leaned forward and brushed her lips against his. She'd thought to distract him, but it backfired. The minute their lips met, Cat jerked as though she'd been goosed. She felt the contact all the way to her toes.

For a split second, Nick froze, then he wrapped one hand around the back of her neck and took control of the kiss. He didn't ask, he took, and she gave it all back. Cat wasn't sure if it was minutes or hours, but when he finally pulled away, she swayed slightly, and it took a second for her eyes to refocus.

His face was furious. "Don't you dare try to distract me, Cat. It won't work. Who are these men? And don't insult me by pretending you don't know."

She opened her mouth to respond, scrambling for the right answers, when JD stepped up behind Nick. "Everything OK here, boss?"

Nick stepped away, and Cat finally drew a deep breath. But he speared her with a look that clearly said, "This is not over, not by a long shot."

Cat shook off the aftereffects of the kiss. What should she tell him? Would it be better to keep bluffing? How long before the guy he'd caught started talking?

Cat still hadn't come up with a plan when the EMTs arrived and started poking and prodding. She tried to wave them away, but Nick marched over, glared, and told them to check her out—whether she wanted them to or not.

She drew the line at going to the hospital but let them bandage her minor abrasions.

Jaw set, Nick pulled a pad and pen from his pocket. "I want your cell number, Cat. Now."

She glanced at the hard lines of his face, then rattled off the number. He nodded and walked away.

But as activity swirled around her, anxiety clawed at Cat's gut. With every minute that ticked by, Blaze's situation got worse. She had to find her. Fast.

Chapter 22

Nick was bone tired by the time he returned to the station later that day. He couldn't remember the last time he'd had a good night's sleep—or much sleep at all, now that he thought about it. He'd grabbed a fresh uniform shirt from his locker, and now he picked up the coffeepot, sniffed the black sludge left in the bottom, grimaced, and poured a cup anyway.

Exhaustion dragged at his body, but his mind raced in circles like a cat chasing its tail. While his body still hummed from the effects of Cat's kiss, his mind called foul. It had been a great kiss, an amazing kiss. But it wasn't a real kiss. It was nothing more than a distraction.

He stopped, took another sip of the terrible coffee, and rolled that thought around in his head. No, that wasn't quite right. She'd pulled him close as a distraction, but the second their lips had touched, they'd both been all in. He could taste it on her tongue, in the way she made those little sounds in the back of her throat. She wasn't that good an actress.

Or maybe she was.

Frustrated, he set the mug down and studied his computer screen. The guy he'd chased down still wasn't talking, but his fingerprints told them plenty. So did a check of the guy's known associates.

Nick drummed his fingers on the desk. Hernandez had been working for Carlos Garcia for several years, since right after he got out of prison for assault.

He ran a search on Garcia's name, and the gnawing in his gut got worse. Garcia was well known among law enforcement, especially for his ability to portray himself not only as a legitimate businessman but also as a philanthropist. The list of causes he supported and donated large sums of money to every year was truly impressive. But so was the list of charges that had been brought against him over the years—most drug related, many involving sex crimes. All were either dismissed, thrown out, or otherwise abandoned due to lack of evidence. Most notably because of witnesses who died rather unexpectedly or disappeared, never to be heard from again.

There was only one reason for Garcia's enforcer to be in Safe Harbor: drugs. Either Garcia was planning to move into the area with one of his drug operations—heaven forbid he already had—or his presence was somehow connected to Teddy's death.

Nick leaped up from his chair, sending it crashing against the wall. There was no way Garcia was bringing scopolamine into Safe Harbor. Not while he was alive to prevent it.

Though by the looks of things, obviously, the zombie drug was already here.

If he set that aside just for a moment, how was Garcia connected to Cat? And where did Cat's uncle fit into any of this? Or did he?

When Cat was taken, did she know who these men were?

He checked his watch. He couldn't show up at the marina at this hour, demanding answers. Mama Rosa needed her rest.

But come morning, he and Cat were having a long, honest conversation.

———

Cat couldn't sleep. Fear of what Blaze was enduring had her pacing her upstairs bedroom until she realized that would keep Mama Rosa and Pop awake. She grabbed her violin case and a flashlight before she tiptoed down the stairs, careful of the creaky steps, then crept across the porch and out the screen door.

She walked across the wet grass, her flip-flops sliding around, and headed out into the woods to her favorite clearing. Once there, she shone the light around the area, desperate to find some clue, anything at all, that would tell her where Blaze was being held.

She still wasn't convinced her uncle wasn't holding Blaze and laughing as Cat ran in circles, trying to find her. Maybe that's why letting those goons take her hadn't seemed quite as scary as it should have.

Setting down the flashlight, she pulled out her violin and spent a few minutes tuning it before she started to play.

If Garcia had Blaze . . . Cat's fingers faltered, and she stopped, drawing a deep, shaky breath. *Oh God. Keep her safe. Help me find her.* She hadn't prayed in many years, but right now, she needed divine intervention. If not for her own sake, then for Blaze's, whose only crime was that she knew Cat.

Cat lowered her head, took a moment to steady herself, then raised the violin again. The best way to clear her mind was music. She forced every other thought out of her mind and let the music flow over her, floating on the night air, bringing a steadiness to her hands and slowing her heartbeat.

She would find Blaze.

Stronger now, Cat segued into another familiar piece and let her heart soar with the crescendo of the music, riding the swells of sound, buoyed by the melody.

Her cell phone buzzed in her pocket, breaking the spell.

She set the violin in its case and fumbled the phone from the pocket of her shorts. *Please let it be Blaze.*

It was a text from an unknown number.

Stanton has the answers you're looking for.

Cat's hard-won respite vanished and a fine trembling shook her fingers. She texted back: What do you mean?

She waited, eyes on the screen, but there was no response. Who could have sent it? Only Sasha and now Nick had this number. Well, and the EMTs, if they were listening earlier. Maybe Nick had set her number down on his desk at the station. Anyone could have seen it.

She checked the time. She couldn't just show up at Nick's house at one thirty in the morning to ask him all that.

Yes, she could. She packed up her violin, grabbed the flashlight, and hurried back to the house. Reversing her earlier steps, she grabbed her keys from her bedroom, glad now that she'd insisted on getting her car back right away. It was a miracle the little thing still ran at all, after the last few days. She climbed in and closed her door quietly before she slowly inched away from the marina, relieved when no lights turned on in the house as she left.

She never saw the black car parked along the edge of the highway, hidden in the trees.

———

Nick had finally given up trying to sort everything out and had gone home, where he'd showered and collapsed into bed at about eleven. When he heard a buzzing, he woke with a start, grabbed his cell off the bedside table. "Stanton." Nothing. "Hello? Who's there?" Still nothing.

He checked his phone. The screen was blank. No missed call, either. The sound came again. Front door.

His head cleared, and he hopped out of bed, pulled on a pair of jeans, grabbed his gun, and held it down beside his leg as he approached the door. A quick glance through the window confirmed a woman was standing there. He flipped on the porch light, and Cat threw her arm up to hide her eyes from the sudden glare.

He opened the door, glanced up and down the street, then pulled her into his house and closed the door.

As he stepped over to the sofa, he turned on a lamp on the table beside it. "What's wrong?"

Without a word, Cat shoved her phone in front of his face, and he read the text. He looked up and caught her checking out his bare chest. A lovely blush raced up her cheeks, and he couldn't help grinning. She liked what she saw, did she?

He shook his head. They didn't have time to ogle each other, though he thought she looked pretty hot in her tank top and shorts, hair mussed, like she needed a good long kiss from someone who knew how.

Get a grip, Stanton. He looked at her phone again. Unknown number. "Do you know who sent this?"

Cat took the phone, tucked it in her pocket, and crossed her arms, a motion that did nice things to her tank top. He focused on her face.

"No. But right now I'm more interested in why this person thinks you have the answers I need," she said, pacing his small living room. She looked around. "Why is it so hot in here?"

"Old house. Window air-conditioning units." He shrugged. "I keep the bedroom cool at night. No need to cool this room." He turned. "Let's sit out back."

He led her through the kitchen, across the sagging back porch, and onto a concrete pad in the middle of the yard where a couple of Adirondack chairs surrounded a fire pit. "This is nice," she commented, sliding into one of the chairs.

"It will be. Eventually. I haven't owned the place long."

"What do you know about what's going on, Nick?"

He stretched out in his chair and studied her, features barely visible by the light of the moon. "I could ask you the same question. What's this all about, Cat? And how do you tie into it?"

The silence lengthened as she studied his face, and Nick could swear she was carefully weighing different scenarios, deciding how much to tell him.

Suddenly, they heard an earsplitting bang, followed by a burst of light as an explosion rocked the sky and shook the ground.

Nick had only a split second to grab Cat's hand and run before debris started raining down on them. He dove under the hedge along the back fence, tackling Cat under him. He covered her with his body, hands over her head as the ground shook and pieces of his house landed around them. He felt a burn on the back of his leg and glanced down to see a glowing ember. He shook it off and waited. Cat started struggling beneath him. "Not yet. Stay still."

"Can't breathe," she gasped, and he raised up slightly on his elbows, giving her a bit more room, though he was loath to go even that far. He had an unbidden urge never to let go, to protect her for as long as it took. From everything and anything. He shook off the feeling and refocused. "Are you OK?"

She nodded.

Nick looked over his shoulder. The back half of his house was mostly intact, but flames shot out the front half, lighting up the night sky. He pulled his phone out of his pocket, amazed it hadn't shattered when they landed. He dialed 911, spoke to the night dispatcher. "This is Officer Stanton. There's been an explosion at my house. Twelve Oak Lane."

"You OK, Nick? Is anyone hurt?"

"I'm OK, Yvonne. Send the fire department, would you? We'll need an arson investigator, too."

There was a pause. "Ten-four. Fire rescue is en route."

"Thanks, Yvonne. Better send EMS, too, just in case."

After hanging up, he slowly crawled out of the hedge, then reached back to help Cat. He kept his hands on her arms, checking her for injury as she swayed slightly before she locked her knees and straightened.

Her eyes were wide, fierce with knowledge. "This was no accident."

"No." He blew out a breath. "Not right after you got an anonymous text and showed up at my house in the middle of the night."

Cat scanned the flames shooting into the sky, then looked at him. "I'm so sorry, Nick. I don't know what to say. I can't believe someone blew up your house."

He ignored the fire, shrugged. He'd think about that later. "Stuff can be replaced."

Cat studied his face, gaze alert. She swallowed hard. "The explosion was in the front of the house. Right where we were."

He nodded, impressed that she'd already reached the same conclusion, despite the adrenaline rush after coming so close to dying. She did not cave in a crisis, that was for sure. "The only real question is: Were you the target? Or was I? Or maybe somebody wanted to take us both out."

The sirens were getting closer. They hurried out to the street. Nick grabbed his garden hose and wet down the fence between his house and the neighbor's, wanting to be sure the fire didn't spread. Lights were flipping on in houses up and down the street, and curious neighbors were gathering to watch the spectacle. Nick went to work, establishing a perimeter, making room for the emergency vehicles.

JD raced up in his patrol car and hurried over, shirt buttoned wrong, eyes worried. He grabbed Nick's arm. "Are you OK, Nick? What happened?"

"I'm fine. The rest we still need to figure out."

More official vehicles arrived, including Monroe's. He must have gotten dressed pretty quickly, but he looked ready to hold a press conference. Avery Ames from the *Gazette* pulled in right behind him, camera in hand. Of course.

Wearing full turnout gear, Nick's friend Chad Everson raced over as the rest of the volunteer fire crew got to work putting out the flames. "What the heck happened, Nick?"

"Explosion. Front of the house."

Chad looked him over. "How'd you manage to get away?"

Nick glanced at the curb, where Cat sat in front of the neighbor's house, away from all the activity. "I wasn't in the house. I was sitting on the patio out back."

"Well you are one lucky son of a gun, then." Someone called Chad's name. "Gotta go."

Monroe appeared in front of him, Avery following closely. Nick put up a hand when the flash from her camera almost blinded him. "Not now, ma'am," Nick said and then led the chief away. Monroe frowned and followed.

"You OK, Nick? What happened?"

Nick sighed, already tired of answering the same question and realizing he'd have to do it again and again before the night was over. "Not sure yet, Chief, except that it was an explosion."

"How'd you manage to stay in one piece?"

"I wasn't inside." Nick jerked his head back. "I was out on the patio behind the house."

Monroe eyed his bare chest. "Alone?"

Glancing over toward Cat, he saw Monroe follow his eyes. "What was she doing here at this time of night?"

Nick straightened, unwilling, suddenly, to pull Cat too far into the spotlight. "It's not what you think. She got a text saying I had the answers she was looking for. She showed up to ask me what it meant."

"And you went outside." Monroe studied him. "Why?"

"It's hot inside. No central air conditioning."

Monroe looked at the house. "You went out a back door?"

"Yes. Whoever did this wouldn't have known I wasn't in the house."

"They wouldn't have known the Martinelli girl wasn't in there, either."

"Right."

Monroe clapped him on the shoulder, and Nick winced where burning embers had left their mark. He hadn't felt any of it until now, so the adrenaline must be wearing off. Which he knew from experience meant exhaustion wasn't far behind. He had a lot to do before that happened.

"We'll get to the bottom of this, Nick," Monroe said.

"No doubt. Thanks, Chief." Nick started toward Cat, eyes scanning the ever-growing crowd of onlookers. He caught a glimpse of Eddie Varga sliding behind some of his neighbors and hurried over. "Eddie. Hold up."

Eddie stopped, and people moved aside as Nick approached, then closed in around them, eager for any snippets of gossip. Nick motioned off to the side with his head. "Let's talk."

Varga's jaw clenched, and he widened his stance. "Why are you singling me out, Officer Stanton?"

Nick narrowed his eyes. He was not in the mood for Varga's attitude. "Do you really want to have this conversation in front of everyone?"

"I have nothing to hide."

Nick nodded and scanned the avid onlookers. Eddie seemed to debate for a moment, then reluctantly followed Nick just out of earshot of the crowd.

"This could be called harassment, Stanton."

"No, it couldn't. This is asking questions during an arson investigation."

"Arson? I didn't set any fires. People said the place exploded. Was anyone in there? I heard it was your house."

Nick ground his teeth at this song and dance. "Yes, it was my place. Thankfully no one was inside. How did you come to be here at this time of night?"

"I was heading home and saw the flames, came to check it out just like everyone else."

"You got here after the explosion."

"That's what I said."

Nick sighed. This wasn't getting him anywhere. "Did you see anyone coming or going, anything suspicious? Anyone acting out of character?"

Eddie seemed to consider this. "It was pretty quiet so late at night, but I did see Captain Barry heading away from here. But maybe he lives nearby, came to check it out."

Now, why would Varga throw Barry under the bus? Did it have something to do with the argument at the truck stop? He didn't know, but he intended to find out. "If you think of anything else, let me know."

"Of course, Officer," Varga said loudly, heading into the thinning crowd. "Always ready to help Safe Harbor's finest."

What game was Varga playing now? Nick stifled a yawn and headed over to where Cat still sat on the curb in front of his neighbor's house. He plopped down beside her.

Eyes filled with worry, she leaned around behind him, and he felt a featherlight touch. "Oh, Nick. You've got burns all over you."

He shrugged, sorry when she took her fingers away. "Nothing major." He ran his palm gently down her arm, checked her for injuries by the light of the flames, too. "You need to get checked out?"

Cat sent him a sad half smile. "I haven't recovered from the last time yet."

His jaw clenched. "We're going to figure out who did this, Cat. Trust me."

"Though I am truly sorry about your house, and that you got hurt, that isn't my biggest concern right now. We have to find Blaze."

"How is this connected to her, Cat? How does Carlos Garcia fit in?"

Nick watched the last of the color leave her face, until she looked like a ghost. Her eyes met his, desperate. "Was it one of his men who grabbed me?"

"Yes. You know who Garcia is." It wasn't a question.

"I know his name, know he's involved in all kinds of nasty stuff, from what it says in the papers."

Nick shook his head and stood. "How bad do things have to get before you quit lying to me, Cat?"

Her eyes widened, and then a shutter seemed to close over them. She sent him a blank stare. "I just need to find Blaze."

JD called his name, and Nick headed that way, disgusted with her and with himself for not pushing her harder. He was boxing with shadows here. Why wouldn't she tell him what she knew?

He answered JD's endless questions, his eyes still on Cat, who seemed to be studying the faces of everyone who hovered around the scene. He saw her stiffen and followed her gaze in time to see a sleek black sedan pull away from the curb.

He started in that direction, then realized he'd never get there in time to get a license plate. But he made note of the make and model. It wasn't the same vehicle he'd seen Cat get into before, but it had the same rich feel to it. Which told him the occupants weren't local.

And that Cat was still hiding things from him.

Chapter 23

The first fingers of light were edging over the horizon when Cat finally pulled into the marina parking lot. Her body was so heavy with exhaustion, it was all she could do to climb out of her car. But her brain buzzed like a swarm of angry bees, fear and unanswered questions creating a dizzying rush of sound. She still hadn't found Blaze, and every minute that went by made Cat more afraid. *Please, God, don't let it be too late.*

No. She wouldn't think like that. She would find her. She had to. The alternative didn't bear consideration.

Fishermen were already arriving, ready to head out for the day. She exited her car and waved, ignoring several disapproving glances aimed her way. Were they scowling because she'd been out all night, or because they'd heard she'd been with Nick?

She turned toward the house, still trying to come to grips with what had happened. They were the least of her worries.

Someone had blown up Nick's house.

And if he hadn't suggested they sit outside, they would have been blown up, too. What were you supposed to do with that?

The shakes started all over again, and Cat bit the inside of her cheek to keep her teeth from chattering. She wouldn't let anyone see her break down. She tiptoed upstairs with some vague notion of taking a shower and then helping Pop in the bait shop. She'd ask questions and put on a good show for the locals. But the minute she sat down on the bed, she fell backward, sound asleep, still fully clothed and smelling of smoke.

———

The practical reality of what happened didn't hit Nick until after the fire chief and all the fire and emergency vehicles pulled away and Monroe told him to go get some rest. That's when it dawned on him that he didn't have any place to go.

He stood on the sidewalk, looking at the smoldering remains of his 1930s cottage in the gray light of approaching dawn. Everything he owned had been in there. And now it was gone. Every bit of it.

He wasn't a sentimental guy, but knowing every single photo of his parents, of his whole history, was gone made him sad. He had no other family, outside of the Martinellis, no one who could send him replacement photos of the important events in his childhood. It was as if his whole past had just been erased. Every memory, every memento and sports trophy and sign of his life with his parents, had literally gone up in smoke.

He still hadn't worked through how he felt about them. He'd loved them, of course, still did, but now the lens through which he viewed his childhood had been skewed, the whole picture changed, knowing they had stolen him from the Martinellis. What kind of people did such a thing and then kept the secret all these years? The postcard his mother had sent to Rosa Martinelli years ago seemed to prove that they had known what they'd done.

Somehow, he was having a hard time forgiving them that.

And now, all his photos of them were gone.

His feelings were all muddled. It was oddly unsettling to have a murky black hole where a straightforward, clear-cut childhood should be.

He scrubbed a hand over his face. The exhaustion was getting to him. He had to think.

JD materialized at his elbow. Monroe and the reporter had long since left the scene, and he and JD were the only ones still there. "Can I give you a ride to the motel, Nick? When I called to ask if they had room, they said Chief Monroe already called and you could stay for free for a couple of nights."

Nick couldn't hide his shock. Just when he thought Monroe couldn't get any more self-centered, he did something like this. Or volunteered to help the local Little League team when they were desperate for a coach. "Thanks, JD. I'll drive myself so I don't have to bother you for a ride later."

"The chief gave you a few days off, didn't he?" JD asked.

Nick almost smiled at the eager young officer. "He did, but there's no way I'm sitting out this investigation. Besides, my bigger priority is finding out who killed Teddy Winston and where Blaze Martinelli is." He clapped JD on the back as he started for his official SUV. His personal truck had been too close to the house and had also burned, but his Safe Harbor vehicle was intact. Just the thought of all the insurance paperwork made him tired. But even now, with the smoking embers of his house in front of him, Nick's priorities were clear: find Teddy's killer and Blaze, before anyone else got hurt.

Once he arrived at the motel, Nick showered and collapsed on the bed, and didn't stir until his alarm went off several hours later.

———

It was midmorning when Cat woke. She jerked awake and sat up, the smell of smoke in her lungs, trying to figure out what was burning. When her tired brain finally worked out there was no fire—that the smell came from her—she flopped back down, heart racing, as the events of the night before came flooding back.

She and Nick had almost died.

Grabbing an afghan, she set her teeth as a shiver passed over her. He hadn't hesitated, not for one second, just grabbed her and covered her with his body, protecting her from flying debris. A woman could learn to love a man like that, a protector, who put those around him ahead of himself.

Not like her uncle. Or Garcia.

At the thought of both those men, she tossed the blanket aside and leaped from the bed. Blaze. Cat had to rescue her.

Fast. Before something terrible happened. The newspaper photo of Joellen flashed through her mind, but she pushed it away. No, that would not happen to Blaze. Not while Cat was alive and breathing. She'd find her.

Filled with new determination, Cat took a quick shower, washed her hair, twice, and marched down to the kitchen, surprised to find both Mama Rosa and Sasha waiting for her.

The minute she walked into the room, Mama levered herself up from her seat, using the table to steady herself. She pulled Cat into a bone-crushing hug, surprising since she'd otherwise been so weak from the cancer treatments.

"Oh, thank the Lord you are all right."

Cat wrapped her equally tight, careful not to squeeze too hard, and absorbed the love being poured on her. Guilt swamped her at the same time, the sure knowledge that what was happening to Blaze was her fault. Because she'd run away so long ago, Blaze was in trouble now. All because of Garcia. But she didn't say any of that because, coward that she was, she needed Mama's love like a plant needed sunshine. She'd find Blaze and she'd trade her life for hers so Blaze would be able to bask in Mama's love. She deserved that, and more. She was a sweet kid.

Gradually, Mama pulled back and studied Cat's face, palms cupping her cheeks. "I am so glad you were not in Nick's house when it burned." Her eyes were piercing, dark and determined. "Nicko, he is all right, too?"

Cat almost smiled at the new nickname and wondered what Nick would think of it. "He's fine, Mama. He's a strong man."

"You are just as strong, Catharine, and don't you ever forget it." She sank down into her chair, and Cat exchanged a look with Sasha at how easily Mama still tired. The battle wasn't over yet.

"How did the fire start?" Mama asked, and Cat went still, trying to decide on an answer.

"They aren't sure yet, Mama. Last night the priority was to put it out before it spread to the homes on either side. But I'm sure the fire department will be investigating the cause." She glanced over at Sasha, warning her not to say too much.

"What were you doing at his house?" Mama wanted to know.

Cat's mind raced, still trying to gather her wits about her. She should have expected Mama to grill her. "I needed to talk to him about something. He doesn't have central air conditioning, so we sat outside on the patio to talk. It was cooler out there. We weren't in the house when the fire started."

"Oh, thank you, Jesus," Mama breathed, patting Cat's hand.

Cat had to turn this conversation before it went in the wrong direction. No way on earth would she look Mama in the eye and tell her someone blew up Nick's house. She looked from Sasha to Mama and back. "Have you heard anything from Blaze?"

Sasha stood leaning against the counter, rubbing her hands protectively over her belly. "Not yet." Her eyes met Cat's. "I think we need to call Nick and get an Amber Alert put out, if he hasn't already done so."

"No!" The words burst from Mama, and she slapped a hand on the table with enough force to make both Cat and Sasha jump in surprise.

"Why not?" Sasha asked. "It's a great way to find her. Everyone has a cell phone these days and—"

Connie Mann

"No. Do not do that. It would make things worse." Mama speared Cat with a look. "You think you know who has her." It was not a question.

How would she guess that? Cat wondered. She chose her words with care. "I think I do, yes."

"Then we don't need this Amber Alert."

"What do you know, Mama?" Cat asked quietly.

Mama looked down, twisted a napkin in her gnarled fingers before she looked up. "Just like you, and Sasha and Eve, Blaze came to us with a past she was trying to escape. After all the time she's been here, I will not make it easy for those who wished her harm to find her so easily."

"What people? What harm?" Sasha demanded.

Mama's gaze was steady, determined. "That is not my story to tell. But I will not let anyone put her name and picture out for all the world to see." She shook her head. "No. That is too dangerous."

"But we have to find her. This would—"

Mama interrupted Sasha. "My answer is final. No Amber Alert. Nothing in the news." She turned to Cat. "You believe this is connected to your past."

Cat returned her stare. "I do."

"Then go find our girl and bring her home safe."

Cat stood and kissed Mama's cheek. "I will do everything in my power to see that happens."

Mama grabbed her hand. "You will not put yourself in danger, either."

Cat hid a smile. "I will do my best." She turned to go.

"You need breakfast," Sasha said and handed her two cold pieces of toast. When Cat quirked an eyebrow at the sad offering, Sasha shrugged. "It's been a long morning."

"Thanks. I appreciate the effort." And she did. Truly.

She walked out the door and was surprised when Sasha followed her outside.

218

Sasha stepped between Cat and her car. "Now tell me all the things you wouldn't say in there."

"I don't know any more about Blaze's past than you do, Sash. You heard Mama."

Sasha narrowed her eyes. "What really happened at Nick's house?"

"We really were outside, geez." She huffed out a breath. "Give me a little credit here."

"Diversion and misdirection might—might—work on Mama, but they darn sure won't work on me. How did his house catch fire?"

Since Cat knew that the facts would be in the next edition of the *Gazette*—if gossip hadn't spread all over town already—she saw no reason to hide it now. "Looks like a bomb of some kind. I overheard something about looking for a detonator."

Sasha paled and sagged against the car. "If you and Nick hadn't been in the backyard . . ."

Hearing the words sent a shiver over Cat's skin. She couldn't let her mind go there again, not if she wanted to keep functioning. "But we were. I'm fine, and so is Nick."

"Until the next time."

The words hit like a blow. *Oh, sweet Jesus.* Cat hadn't even considered that. Though it made perfect sense. She met Sasha's eyes head-on. "I'll be careful. We'll both be careful."

"What does this have to do with your past, Cat?"

Here it was, the moment of truth she'd spent fourteen years running from. More than anyone else in the family, Cat owed Sasha an explanation and an apology. More important, no matter how this all ended, she didn't want Sasha to carry a single ounce of guilt about their strained relationship over the years. The fault had always been Cat's alone.

She took a deep breath, looked Sasha in the eye, and gave her the facts, straight up. "My uncle, who took me in after my parents died, was not a good man, though I didn't know it right away. I suspected something wasn't right, but I had no idea how bad things were. He was in business with another man, one I learned was even worse than my uncle. I not only saw something I wasn't supposed to see, I found out I was intended as a bargaining chip. So I escaped."

Sasha studied her. "And you've been running ever since. How old were you then, Cat?"

"Fourteen."

"Does your uncle have Blaze?"

Cat marveled, again, at Sasha's quick mind. "He claims he doesn't."

She started in surprise. "He's here in Safe Harbor?"

"He was, yes. I think he still is."

"Then who has Blaze? The other man?"

"I think so."

"Who is he?"

Cat shook her head. "I can't say, Sasha."

Sasha reared back as though she'd been slapped. "Why not? After all these years, are you still holding a grudge? I'm sorry, I've always been sorry, Cat. You know that."

Cat waved that away. "It's never been about that, but about protecting all of you. It's still about that." She sighed. "I didn't leave because of the missed audition but because I thought they found me." When Sasha opened her mouth to ask more questions, Cat held up a hand. "I'm not getting into it. Please. Just know it was never about you or the audition, OK? I've always tried to keep my past away from here. I'd never be able to live with myself if something terrible happened to any of you because of me."

"If something happened? It's already happened, Cat. Blaze is missing, and from what you've just said, she's in really big trouble. How much worse can it get?"

Cat didn't say anything, just met Sasha's gaze. She watched her sister's hands go to her stomach, as though shielding the baby from hearing what was being said. Then her eyes widened, and Cat knew she'd figured it out. "This man tried to kill you. You and Nick. When he blew up Nick's house."

"I don't know that for sure, but that's my guess."

"Can't Nick arrest him? Make him talk or whatever?"

Cat sent her a rueful smile. If only it were that simple.

Sasha grimaced. "I know. You're right, but there has to be something we can do. We can't just sit around and wait for the police to do something. We have to take action."

Cat stepped closer and gripped both of Sasha's arms, held tight. "*We* are not doing anything, Sash. You have a baby to protect and a husband who loves you more than life. I'll work on getting Blaze, OK? Let me do that much. I know these people, and I know what I'm doing. Trust me to do this."

"But I—"

"Please. I need to do this."

They studied each other for a moment, and finally Sasha gave one quick nod. "Just don't do anything stupid," she warned.

"Not part of the plan," Cat quipped and climbed into her car.

Now all she had to do was come up with an actual plan.

Chapter 24

Blaze's neck and shoulders ached from straining to hear what was happening outside her prison.

She had no doubt whatsoever that Cat and Sasha were trying to find her. Nick, too. The Martinelli girls were tough, though Sasha had gotten a little softer and had an annoying tendency to cry now that she was pregnant. Bryan had told her his mom was like that. Got all weepy with every pregnancy.

Bryan's name triggered thoughts of Teddy, and tears filled Blaze's eyes. She swallowed hard and blinked them away. She still couldn't believe he was gone. He'd been her best friend, the one person she didn't have to pretend around. How could he be gone?

Even though the facts pointed to suicide, Blaze didn't believe that, not after the way he'd looked at her when they danced at Eve's wedding. Which meant someone had killed him. A few days ago, she would have considered that completely insane. Except here she was. She looked around. Whoever hurt him were probably the same people who'd trapped her in here.

Was this really all about drugs, and about him saying no? In Safe Harbor?

Her throat clogged. Was he dead because he did what she told him to and tried to get away from them?

She shook her head, disgusted with herself. Given where she'd come from, she knew it was definitely possible, but she'd been lulled into thinking she was safe from any scary stuff in a place as boring as Safe Harbor. She snorted. She knew better. But it had been so nice to pretend for a little while.

She'd scraped her fingers bloody trying to escape, but the shutters over the opening wouldn't budge.

Footsteps sounded outside, and she scooted farther away from the door, pulling the hood down over her head. She was still hoping that if she never saw anyone's face, it would help her chances of survival.

She stiffened as the door opened, never sure who or what to expect. She heard humming, so it must be the housekeeper. She'd peeked once. Short and squat, with dark hair in a bun and dark eyes, she spoke broken English, but her voice was kind whenever she spoke to Blaze.

"I brought you an early lunch, senorita. Burritos and some fruit. You eat, yes?"

"Thank you. Your food is very good."

Beyond the slightly open door, Blaze heard voices from somewhere nearby. One was harsh, demanding. The other was obviously a lesser minion getting chewed out. She couldn't make out the words, but she understood the tone. Then the second voice turned pleading, desperate, and the fear in it made the hair on Blaze's arms stand straight up.

There was a long pause.

Then the sound of a gunshot.

Blaze froze, hardly daring to breathe. The first voice called out sharply, and there was the sound of hurrying feet.

Blaze could feel the housekeeper beside her, frozen in place. Then she muttered, *"Madre de Dios,"* and hurried from the room. The door closed, and the lock clicked into place. Blaze buried her head in her raised knees, heart pounding with fear and dread, and prayed as she hadn't in a long time.

Please don't let me die. Please get me out of here.

But no one came.

———

Nick woke to a beam of sunlight coming through the gap in the curtains, spearing him in the eyes. He blinked and shifted to get his bearings in the small motel room. A quick glance at his cell phone, and he hopped out of bed, surprised to feel the stiffness in his muscles from where he'd tackled Cat. He stretched, and the scattered burns on his back protested.

He had a sudden urge to see her, to make sure she was OK. He couldn't explain his inconvenient attraction to her, couldn't seem to talk his way out of it, either. Physically, she wasn't his usual type, but that didn't seem to matter. He couldn't keep his eyes off her lean and lithe physique, and every time her hair skimmed past her jaw, he wanted to run his fingers through it, to see if it was as slippery and silky as it looked.

Which was utter madness, since he was 99 percent sure she was involved in this whole mess right up to her pretty neck, or at least she knew exactly who was. Which made him crazy. Especially since, whenever he saw her, he fought the urge to cup her cheeks, to kiss her.

Sighing, he scrubbed a hand over his stubbled jaw. How was he supposed to help if she was still keeping secrets?

He stopped by the motel office, thanked the owner for the room, and asked for some basic toiletries. After a quick shave and shower, he grimaced as he pulled on his smoky clothes from the night before. He drove over to the Stuff Mart on the edge of town and stocked up on clothes and more toiletries, changed in the restroom, then drove to the Blue Dolphin for breakfast. He'd learned early in his tenure in town that eating there offered more than just company. It was the perfect place to keep his finger on the pulse of the town, to stay abreast of what was happening, and to find out how everyone felt about it.

This morning was no exception. The moment he walked through the door, he was surrounded by townspeople asking about what happened last night, expressing concern, and telling him how glad they were that he hadn't been hurt.

Even LuAn, the owner's generally unfriendly wife, walked over, coffeepot in hand, and asked how he was doing. "Your breakfast is on the house today, Nick. We're real sorry that happened."

"Thank you, LuAn. I sure do appreciate it."

She filled his cup. "Do you know yet who blew up your house?" she asked.

That answered his first question. "Not yet. Who says it was blown up?"

She rolled her eyes. "This is Safe Harbor, Nick. Everyone is saying that, especially since it's in the paper." She walked to the counter, came back, and plopped a copy of the Safe Harbor *Gazette* on the table. A photo of his house in flames took up most of the front page. "Local cop barely escapes with his life," the headline read.

He sipped his coffee as he scanned the article. He wanted to be annoyed, but Avery Ames had stuck to the facts. Even though he'd have preferred most of those facts be kept out of the paper, at least for now.

He studied the photo, not looking at the house itself but at the people in the background who were watching it burn. He examined every face, looking for anyone who didn't belong or who seemed nervous, but it was hard to make out individual faces. He'd swing by the paper next, get copies of all the photos Avery had taken last night, see if anything—or anyone—jumped out at him.

He pulled the photo closer. He noticed Captain Barry in the background, and again, the man's presence nagged at him. He finished his breakfast, thanked LuAn, and headed outside.

The need to see Cat dug deeper, but since Barry's tire place was closer, he'd stop there first, then go by the paper.

It made perfect sense. It was logical and practical, and it annoyed him that he didn't care about any of that right now. He wanted to see Cat. Make sure she was OK and, he admitted, make sure she didn't hatch some crazy scheme and take off without him.

He'd realized that, like Eve and Sasha, the Martinelli girls acted first and thought later when it came to one of their own. He knew Cat wouldn't stop until she found Blaze, and he didn't want something else happening to her, too.

He spotted Avery Ames approaching the door of the Blue Dolphin and headed her way. "Good morning, Avery."

"Morning, Nick. Good to see you in one piece."

"Thank you." The woman wore sensible pumps and a string of pearls like she was headed to church. "I'm going to need copies of all the photos you took last night."

She eyed him as if about to argue, then nodded. "Want me to email them to you?"

"Yes, ma'am. I'd sure appreciate that. If you could do that right away, that would be even better."

"Soon as I finish here, I'll send them over."

He thanked her, mind already on the next thing. He pulled out his cell phone as he climbed into his SUV and did a search for Captain Barry's address, to pinpoint how far he lived from Nick's house. Then he headed for the tire store.

———

Captain Barry wasn't there, so Nick left his card and headed toward the marina, determined to catch up to Cat before she snuck around behind his back again. What in her past had made her distrust cops so much? And what was she so afraid of?

He had barely left the outskirts of Safe Harbor when her beat-up car came into view. She sent him a jaunty wave and a smile as she sailed past.

Oh no. She wasn't getting away that easily. Nick hit his lights and siren and whipped his SUV around to follow her. There were no good places to pull off along the two-lane road without ending up in the ditch, so he followed her until she pulled into an abandoned gas station.

He parked behind her and climbed out, curious to see how she'd play this.

Just as he'd suspected, she tried for total nonchalance as she got out of her car. "Hi, Nick. How are the burns this morning? Did you get some sleep?"

"Where are you going?" The words came out sharper than he'd intended, and he watched her automatically stiffen.

"I was unaware I had to check in with you before I left the house."

He folded his arms and waited, but he should have remembered that didn't work with her.

She folded hers and stared back. Stalemate.

Relaxing his stance, he ran a hand through his hair. "Look, Cat, I thought we were going to work together. We need to find Blaze."

"Definitely."

"I'm going to put out an Amber Alert this morning."

Cat froze. "No. Don't do that."

He stopped in surprise. "Why not? They work."

"You can't." Cat met his eyes. "Mama said no."

"Why would she do that . . ." His voice trailed off as realization dawned. "Something in Blaze's past she's worried about?"

Cat nodded. "That was the gist of it, but she wouldn't say what it was about. Said it wasn't her story to tell."

Nick didn't like it, but he understood that Mama would protect her cubs with every ounce of her strength. He eyed Cat. "How does your past figure into it? Because it does, doesn't it?"

She went very still, and it was a while before she answered, voice quiet. "You need to stop asking me that question."

"Then give me a truthful answer."

"I can't answer it, OK? You need to leave it alone."

"You know I can't. Not when Blaze's life could be in danger and you won't help me find her."

Fire spit from her eyes as she moved closer. "You don't think I'm trying to find her?"

Nick looked past what she was saying and saw the terror she couldn't completely hide. "Let me in, Cat. Let me help. It's what I'm trained to do."

"You don't know him, what he's capable of." She said the words as though she were talking to herself more than to him.

"You mean Garcia? What has he done?"

Cat spun toward her car. "I have to go."

He stopped her with a hand on her arm, his frustration like a living thing. How many more times was she going to stonewall him? "What are you planning, Cat?"

She wouldn't answer, just looked down at his hand on her arm. He released her, and his fingers found her cheeks, stroked the smooth skin there. "Don't you get that I'm worried about you?" The words came out more growl than anything. He gentled his tone. "I care about you."

She stilled, a shocked expression on her face. "Don't. Don't care about me." She tried to ease away, but he kept his eyes on hers, hands on her cheeks.

"Too late." Unsure how else to tell her, he pulled her in close and kissed her, gently at first, soft brushes of his lips over hers, to let her know what he couldn't quite say. Even though she hid from him, emotionally and with the most basic of facts, his admiration for her strength grew with every passing day, his unasked-for desire to keep her close a fight he had finally stopped fighting. She'd gotten under his skin, this slight warrior with the huge heart and deep pain. And secrets. So many secrets.

She hesitated only a moment before she relaxed against him and wrapped her arms around his waist, pulling him closer. Her lips were soft and firm, and the feel of her in his arms, rubbing her lips against his, made him growl low in his throat. Something raw and primitive woke inside him, a fierce need to claim her as his and protect her forever.

The attraction that had been simmering in the air between them suddenly burst into flame as he deepened the kiss. She opened her mouth for his tongue, and time and duty and everything else slipped away as they held tighter and the flames burned brighter. All he could think about was the way she made him feel. He ran one hand through her hair, the other stroking her back, all the while her strong fingers clutched him to her. Had any woman ever felt so right in his arms?

Except she was the wrong woman.

Reality doused him like a blast from last night's fire hose. He couldn't get involved. She was part of an ongoing investigation. Was probably withholding evidence, at the very least.

His job, his whole life, was ruled by doing the right thing, upholding the law.

If Cat didn't outright break it, she skirted right around the murky edges.

He slowly eased away and regretted it instantly. She blinked up at him, eyes wide and dazed, all her protective defenses down for that one instant. He saw his own attraction for her reflected back at him, the desire to get closer still.

He felt a pang when the shutters dropped over her eyes again and she stepped away. One step, then two. Though the real distance between them was far greater.

"I, ah, need to go." She turned and fled, and this time, he let her. He couldn't keep her, in any sense of the word. His heart couldn't get involved, and as a cop, he didn't have any evidence to hold her.

But he felt an uncommon pang of loneliness when she disappeared.

Which was ridiculous. He climbed into his SUV and slammed the door. He had to get a grip. Focus.

He had to find Blaze. And find out who killed Teddy.

Somehow, the two were connected. And right now, the only connection he could see was Cat.

———

Cat gripped the steering wheel as she drove away, heart pounding. She glanced into the rearview mirror. Just knowing Nick was behind her made her feel safe and protected.

And terrified. He could never know just how close she'd come to blurting out her whole life story. What was it about that man that made her want to tell him everything, things she'd never told another living soul?

Somehow she knew he would listen. But she also knew he would never understand. Nick lived life by the book. He was honest and straightforward and saw the world in black and white. It was part of what made him a great cop.

But her world wasn't that simple. Not when people's lives were on the line. She often lived in the gray areas, where right and wrong weren't quite so clearly defined.

Not that he wouldn't sympathize. He would. But he would never have made the decisions she had, then or now.

If he ever found out that she planned to trade her life for Blaze's, he'd try to stop her. He'd have no choice.

She couldn't risk that. Could never risk him trying to stop her.

First, she had to make very sure that her uncle wasn't lying to her about holding Blaze. In order to do that, she had to figure out where he was staying, see his face when she asked the questions.

She pulled into a parking spot up the block from the Blue Dolphin and looked around as she walked down the sidewalk. She'd been hoping Phillip was hanging out nearby. That would make it easier. But she didn't have the sense she was being watched, and that sense hadn't been wrong in fourteen years.

She walked into the diner and was surprised by the number of people who asked if she was OK and expressed concern about the explosion at Nick's place. Several others asked what she had been doing there so late at night. She ignored the wide eyes and raised eyebrows.

LuAn came over with a coffeepot in her hand. "You're the Martinelli girl who was with Nick last night, aren't you?"

Nothing like getting right to the heart of things. Cat turned her cup over, and LuAn filled it with coffee. "That was me."

LuAn cocked an eyebrow. "Lots of speculation on what you two were doing together, especially since Nick wasn't wearing a shirt."

Cat wanted to roll her eyes, but instead, she met the other woman's gaze. "We were sitting outside on his patio having a conversation. Nothing more."

"That so?"

"Yes."

"Well, folks round here are concerned, is all. Nick's a good guy, and finding out he's really Rosa and Sal's boy hit him hard. We don't want no one showing up here and causing trouble for him, understand?"

Cat understood exactly. She fervently wished she wouldn't cause him trouble, but knew she already had. And if she were honest, she knew things would probably get worse before they got better.

Cat leaned closer and spoke quietly. "Let me ask you a question, LuAn. I figure you know everything that happens in this town. If someone wanted to rent a house, a nice house, on the quiet, who would they go see?"

LuAn pursed her lips as she considered, then leaned closer and said, "Well, I heard that Avery Ames used to be in real estate before she inherited the paper and that she has connections with some big spenders."

"Interesting. Do you happen to know if she's rented any property recently to a gentleman of Asian descent?"

LuAn looked Cat over. "Friend of yours? Family?"

"Family. I think he was trying to surprise me, but not knowing is killing me. I want to spend as much time with him as I can while he's here." Which was true, as far as it went.

LuAn peered around the diner, not crowded this time of day, then back at Cat. "I did hear that Avery had rented a big place right on the Gulf. One of those mansions that were built just before the real estate market collapsed. The owners just let it sit. She's spruced it up and is trying to sell it."

"Do you know where it is?"

"Sure. Head straight out of town, then go north on US-19 for about ten miles, then west on Gulf Shore Trail. It's the only place at the end of the dirt road."

Cat thanked her, left a five on the table, and hurried in that direction, the need to find Blaze gnawing at her gut.

Please let me find her.

Chapter 25

Cat started having serious doubts about LuAn's directions as the pavement gave way to gravel, which gave way to hard sand with bone-jarring potholes. The tree canopy overhead reached down, brushing the top of her car and scraping into the open windows. She stopped, studying the narrow track ahead. It looked like cars had come in and out of here recently. Otherwise, the whole road would be overgrown, right?

She kept going, bouncing along, until she rounded one final bend and a six-foot-high wall came into view. Along with a wrought-iron gate.

She sat for a moment, debating whether to drive up to the intercom or try to find another way onto the property. From beyond, she could hear the waves lapping the shore. The mansion she glimpsed through the fence was impressive, done in an ultramodern style that suited her uncle's personality.

Before she could make up her mind, the gate swung inward. Cat glanced around, trying to find hidden cameras, but she saw nothing.

For all she knew, this might be Garcia's place, in which case things would get dicey fast.

Swallowing hard, she drove forward. *Never let them see you sweat.* The old saying from the deodorant commercial applied well to this situation.

She climbed from the car and surveyed the place as though she were just arriving for afternoon tea. Shoulders back, chin up, she walked up the wide front steps.

Phillip swung the door open before she could press the bell.

The tension in her shoulders relaxed a fraction. At least she was at the right house.

"Good afternoon, Miss Catharine," he said, wearing his usual impassive expression. "This way, please." He turned and started walking.

Cat followed him down a long tiled hallway, noting the closed doors along both sides. The hallway ended in a great room with a truly jaw-dropping view of the Gulf of Mexico. Gorgeous blue water stretched as far as the eye could see, dotted with mangrove islands in the distance and waves of saw grass lining the shore.

"Your uncle will be with you shortly," Phillip said and then quietly closed the door behind him.

For a moment, Cat simply stared out the wall of windows, her outward calm in direct conflict to her racing heartbeat. How should she play this? Would he tell her the truth?

She casually glanced around the room, trying to locate any hidden cameras. When she'd first moved into her uncle's Miami penthouse, the fact that he and Phillip always seemed to know exactly what she'd been doing had completely creeped her out. She'd been sure they were watching her, but she'd never found any surveillance equipment.

Which didn't necessarily mean he wasn't recording her then—or now.

She casually wandered over to the large sectional sofa and the square coffee table in front of it. A black leather satchel sat on top of the table, completely out of place in the otherwise immaculate room. The entire room looked like nobody ever used it, despite the desk in the corner and the bookshelves filled with novels and nonfiction covering everything from romance to biology.

"Ah, Catharine," her uncle said, sweeping into the room.

Cat turned and waited while he leaned over to kiss both her cheeks. He put his hands on her shoulders, and she fought the urge to shake him off.

"How lovely to have you stop by. What can I do for you?"

Cat folded her arms. "Where is Blaze?"

She watched his expression, looking for any signs of subterfuge. "I don't know. I take it she hasn't turned up yet?" He frowned.

"No, she hasn't. You said you would find her. Where is she? Are you holding her?"

He narrowed his eyes. "If I had information, I would have had Phillip deliver it to you. I already told you that I don't have the girl." He spread his arms. "Why would I lie?"

"Oh, I can think of any number of reasons. One of which is me."

"Ah, but I've already gotten the agreement I want from you."

Cat swallowed hard. She couldn't think about that right now. "Maybe you are keeping Blaze to be sure I follow through with my end of the bargain."

His eyes narrowed. "Is that a concern? Would you make such a promise so lightly?"

"You know I'll do what I said."

"Then I have no reason to hold the girl."

This was getting her nowhere. "Is Garcia in town?"

He nodded. "I believe so, yes."

"Where is he?"

"He is a man given to secrets. But then, so are you. But you are also a very clever girl." He checked the expensive Rolex on his arm, then glanced toward the satchel on the coffee table before he looked back at her. "I have to make a phone call. I hope you will let me know if there's anything you need." He waved a hand around the room. "Everything I have is at your disposal. If you'll excuse me."

Before Cat could formulate a response, he was gone, the door closed behind him.

She hurried over and opened it, relieved when it swung inward. For a moment, she worried he might lock her up, too.

But she couldn't leave yet. The black satchel caught her eye. Why had it been left there, and why had he looked at it before he'd walked out?

Cat stepped over to it and pulled the zipper open. Somehow, she wasn't surprised at the packets of neatly banded twenties inside. She took one out and fanned the bills, guessing there was about a thousand dollars in each packet. The bag was filled with them.

She glanced toward the doorway again, but no one burst in demanding to know what she was doing.

Rifling through the rest of the bag, she wasn't really surprised when her hand touched the cold metal of a gun. She pulled it out, then tucked it back where she'd found it. She really didn't like guns. The knives she carried gave her far more security.

She had to think. Had her uncle left the bag sitting out on purpose? For her? Otherwise, why would he have offered her anything she needed before he walked out? He never said things plainly. There were always layers of nuance, and Cat never felt she quite understood the conversation.

She glanced at the bag again. If her uncle was telling the truth and he didn't have Blaze, that meant Garcia did. What if she used the money to buy Blaze's freedom? Was that what her uncle intended?

Men like Garcia understood money, and there was a lot of it in the bag.

She zipped it closed and headed for the door. Nick's face flashed in her mind, his look disapproving. Technically, she was stealing. Maybe.

Probably. Or at least Nick would think so. Although she could argue that her uncle had left the money for her. Hadn't he?

Swallowing hard, she decided she'd think about that later. If her uncle had her arrested for taking the money, then she wouldn't have to live up to her end of the bargain. Which was good, right?

Except it wouldn't help her get Blaze. Confusion swamped her, tried to paralyze her into indecision. Now was not the time to hesitate. Blaze needed her.

She gripped the bag and hurried down the hall, relieved—and a bit suspicious—when she didn't encounter Phillip along the way.

As she approached the front door, he stepped out from a small library and held the door for her. "Have a nice afternoon, Miss Catharine."

"Thank you, Phillip," Cat said and walked to her car.

No one snatched the bag from her hand. Or shot her in the back.

She didn't draw a full breath until she was safely on the main road.

When a dark sedan showed up in her rearview mirror, she wasn't surprised. She only wished she knew if the driver worked for her uncle. Or Garcia.

———

The sound of the gunshot ricocheted in Blaze's head and conjured up all sorts of scary images. Based on the housekeeper's reaction, Blaze hadn't mistaken what she'd heard.

Someone had been shot. They'd begged and pleaded, and it hadn't done a bit of good.

Blaze squeezed her eyes shut and tried to block the images.

Oh God. She was so scared. What if they came for her next?

She'd hoped that keeping the hood on was a good thing, but what if it didn't matter? What if they were going to shoot her no matter what she did?

Panic made her heart pound and her hands shake. She wrapped them tighter around her knees and told herself to calm down. Think.

Even though she felt alone, she knew that Nick and Cat, and probably Sasha and Jesse, too, would be searching for her. She might be a total pain in the butt sometimes, but she knew they loved her.

Which, when she thought about it, was pretty dang amazing.

They'd come find her. All she had to do was stay alive until they could get her out of here.

She pulled up the hood far enough to wipe her nose on her shirt-sleeve. Then she tugged it back down and forced herself to take slow, even breaths.

She'd get a grip on herself and think. And listen, so she'd have information that could help when her family came to find her.

At the word *family*, thoughts of where she'd come from, of where she'd run from years ago, tried to sneak into her mind, but she shoved them away. As always. That part of her life was gone. She swore she'd never think about it again, and she wouldn't break that promise to herself now.

She was Blaze, not Bethany, the scared little girl. Blaze was tough. And she was a fighter.

That's what she had to remember.

She looked heavenward. "God, a little help on your end would be good, too, you know? Thanks."

She'd be smart. And she'd wait. Nick and Cat would come.

Feeling a bit steadier, finally, she climbed up onto the bed and fell asleep curled into a little ball.

———

Nick stared at the report on his computer. The fire chief had finished his investigation. He'd found pieces of a homemade bomb in Nick's living room and indicated he thought it was detonated by a cell phone. Which meant someone had been in his house while he was out.

JD had talked with all of Nick's neighbors, and no one remembered seeing anyone suspicious, but maybe the response would be different if Nick asked, instead of that "youngster."

Wanda answered a call, then looked at him over her shoulder. "For you. Line one."

"Safe Harbor police, Nick Stanton."

"Hello, Officer Stanton. This is Fred Sanders, one of your neighbors? Well, almost neighbor. I live on the next block."

Nick grabbed a pad and pen. "What can I do for you, Fred?"

"Well, now, it might be nothing, but I found the darndest thing this morning when I let Alice, that's my bulldog, out to do her thing. Alice is deaf and almost blind, but she's a fabulous companion, don't you know."

Nick curbed his impatience. "What happened when Alice went out?"

"She didn't come back right away when I called, which does happen now and again, so I went out and found her nosing around next to my neighbor's trash cans. When I got there, she was sniffing a hamburger wrapper. But there were pieces of a cell phone with it, as though someone had smashed it all to bits."

Nick stilled. "Can you give me the exact address, Fred?" Nick jotted it down. "What made the broken cell phone catch your attention?"

"Well, now, for one thing, it was lying next to the trash can, not in it, as one would expect. And if it had broken, wouldn't you put it in a plastic sack before you put it in the bin outside? This one lying in pieces gave the impression that someone had deliberately destroyed it. And that got me thinking about the explosion at your house, and how on the shows on television, the detectives always look for a cell phone detonator, so . . ." He paused to draw a breath. "I thought I should call you."

Nick grinned. "Thanks, Fred. You've been most helpful. I'll be right over to collect those pieces."

"Oh, well, ah, I'm afraid that won't be possible."

"Why not?"

"Well, Captain Barry lives there, don't you know, and when I showed it to him, he went into the house straightaway, grabbed a Stuff Mart sack, and scooped up the pieces. He put them into the bin just before the trash truck came by."

Nick squeezed his eyes shut. Of course he did. "Thanks, Fred. I appreciate you calling."

"I sure hope you catch whoever blew up your house, Officer."

"We will. Don't worry." Nick hung up and then turned to JD, who had been listening to the conversation. "The good news is that my neighbor may have found the cell phone used to detonate the bomb."

JD narrowed his eyes. "And the bad news?"

"The trash pickup just went by and grabbed it."

JD sighed. "Let me guess. You want me to chase down that dump truck."

Nick hid his grin. Trash duty was never fun. He'd done his share as a rookie cop in Tampa. "Yes. Fred said the pieces are in a separate Stuff Mart bag. If you hurry, you can catch the truck before it gets to the dump."

JD nodded and hurried from the station.

Maybe, if they were lucky, they could get fingerprints off the broken phone, or trace the number. Something. Anything.

Since the bomb had been put inside his house, he figured he was the target, that he was getting close to solving this investigation, and someone was getting very nervous. Had the bomb been thrown through the window, then either he or Cat could have been the target.

But Cat had gotten a text that said Nick had answers. Which told him someone wanted the two of them to stop asking questions. The whole two-birds-one-stone thing.

What was he missing? The nagging worry they were running out of time clawed at him. He went to the locked storage cabinet to get the box with all the evidence on Teddy's death, but it wasn't there. He rummaged around, moving other boxes, but he couldn't find it. He checked JD's desk, but it wasn't there, either.

"Wanda, did the chief take the Winston evidence for some reason?"

"Couldn't tell you. But I did see him take a box into his office earlier."

Sure enough, the box was sitting on Monroe's desk when Nick went to check. Even though the lid was on the box, leaving it out unattended was a total breach of protocol, especially since Monroe had left his office door unlocked. He'd also left his computer on, which told Nick he'd left in a hurry.

Curious, Nick went behind the desk and moved the mouse. The screen came to life with the search browser open. The chief had run several searches on scopolamine, including doses, toxicology, and anything related to death caused by the zombie drug.

Nick opened the lid of the box, then sifted through the bagged evidence to find what he was after. There it was. The button he'd found on the ground not far from Teddy's body.

He laid the plastic evidence bag on the desk, pulled out his phone, and snapped a picture before he put it back in the box. Something about that button kept nagging at him.

"What are you looking for, Stanton?"

Nick glanced up as the chief entered the room, expression bland. "Same thing you are, I expect. Trying to figure out who wanted Teddy Winston dead. And why."

"Anything new?"

"Not yet. You?"

The chief set his Stetson on the corner of the desk, then eased into the chair. "No, and it's making things that much harder for the Winstons. They need closure. They call me constantly for an update."

"We're doing everything we can—"

"I know, Stanton. That's what I keep telling them. Anything new on who blew up your house?"

"Not yet, but JD is following a lead. One of my neighbors found pieces of a cell phone by another neighbor's trash can." If Nick hadn't been watching closely, he would have missed the flash of surprise in the chief's eyes. "Captain Barry's house, to be exact."

"Were you able to get any prints from it?"

"Trash pickup just went by, so JD is trying to chase down the truck."

The chief grimaced. "That's always a good time. But he's a rookie. He'll deal with it." The chief met his eyes. "What's our opinion of him as a cop?"

Nick was surprised that the chief asked his opinion. "JD's shaping up to be a great cop. Still a little green, but he's honest and hardworking. Pays attention to the details. He'll do well."

The chief sipped at the coffee sitting on his desk. "Has the Martinelli girl turned up yet?"

The question dug deep into Nick's gut. "Not yet. But we're working on it."

"No chance she just got tired of this town and ran off? Same way she appeared a while back?"

"The family is pretty adamant that is not the case. Especially because she and Teddy were good friends. They suspect she's off trying to investigate on her own."

The chief's eyes widened. "That's foolish. We don't know who we're dealing with here."

"Right. That's why we're doing everything we can to find her."

"Why haven't you put out an Amber Alert?"

"I was ready to, but Cat says Mama Rosa is adamant that we don't. She thinks Blaze is still in town. She doesn't want her name and photo blasted all over the airwaves and Internet."

"She give a reason why?"

"Cat says it's because of what Blaze ran from to begin with."

The chief pursed his lips, considered. "Any chance Teddy died because of her past, then? Something she told him?"

Nick had considered that and dismissed it as a long shot, so he was surprised to hear the chief mention it now. Even though Monroe was clearly a politician, he couldn't forget that a smart cop lived behind all the hype. "I'll go talk to their friend Bryan again, see if we missed a connection somewhere."

Nick stood to leave, nodded at the box. "What were you looking for, Chief?"

"Answers. So far all we have are questions." Monroe shook his head.

Back at his desk, Nick noticed JD had added to the whiteboard he had put up. He studied Teddy's picture at the top and other photos taped below. His worry increased when he saw Blaze's photo. He stopped, surprised to see Cat's there, too. Plus Varga's, and a photo of Nick's destroyed home.

Nick let the questions circle in his mind. Was it possible that Blaze's past and Cat's past were all connected to Teddy's death and the scopolamine and drugs in Safe Harbor?

Or were these separate things and trying to tie them together would only complicate matters further?

Frustrated, he decided to take a walk around downtown, clear his head and talk to a few people.

If he happened to run into Cat while he was out, so much the better.

Chapter 26

The afternoon sunlight blazed through the windshield as Cat drove toward Safe Harbor. How was she going to find Garcia's place? She eyed the satchel on the seat beside her. With every mile, she told herself her uncle had wanted her to take the money. What he'd said and the way he'd left it there was tacit agreement, right?

Or would he report it stolen and have her arrested?

No, that didn't make sense. He'd never want the scrutiny of local law enforcement.

She only knew of one way to find Garcia. Cat parked downtown, near the weather cam. Just as she reached into the trunk to pull her violin out of the case, Nick stepped up beside her. She knew it was him before she saw him, as some sixth sense had started to alert her every time he was near. Maybe it was the clean sandalwood of his cologne or simply the way her heart sped up whenever he was around.

She turned, and the worry in his eyes touched something deep inside her. "Hello, Officer Stanton." She smiled, trying to lighten his expression, but he didn't return the smile. "What's wrong?"

"Let's go get some ice cream, at the new place just down the highway." He tried to lead her toward his car, but she stopped, put a hand on his chest.

"You're scaring me. Tell me what's wrong."

He let out a harsh breath. "Nothing new is wrong. I just want to talk to you."

Cat nodded, unsure what was going on. He was strung tight, like there was more humming under his skin than the worry about Blaze. She cast several glances toward him as they drove to the ice cream place, and found him eyeing her like he didn't know what to do with her.

Cat looked away. If he had any inkling of what she had planned, he'd definitely try to stop her.

———

Nick had never been at a loss for words, but as he studied Cat, he couldn't come up with a single thing to say. His feelings for her were like a wad of discarded fishing line, a twisted, mangled mess, without any rhyme or reason.

Watching her lick a double scoop of caramel sea salt ice cream wasn't helping, either. Everything inside him tightened, and he crushed the bottom of his waffle cone before he realized what he was doing.

He looked away and focused on finishing his own ice cream. When she turned toward him, those dark eyes wide and worried, he was lost.

Leaning over the console, he pulled her into his arms, and held tight. She stiffened for just a moment, then relaxed into his arms. He didn't say a word, simply stroked her hair and enjoyed the feel of her in his arms.

He shouldn't enjoy it, he knew that. Cat wasn't for him. She worked from a moral code too different from his. He was a cop, a black-and-white, right-and-wrong kind of guy. He didn't like gray. It was too wishy-washy, could too easily lead down a slippery slope straight into black. He preferred clear delineations. Sure, he knew things weren't always quite so cut and dried—he wasn't a naive rookie—but rules and boundaries kept things neat and organized. Predictable and measurable.

Cat was like a whirlwind that had blown into his life and tossed everything he knew about the world and himself into disarray. He really didn't like it.

But he liked her. Felt himself drawn to her like a stupid moth to the bright, shiny light that would kill it. Yet here he sat, wanting to hold her closer yet. Even though he knew she was somehow involved in everything going on in town.

He couldn't love a woman like that.

He stilled as the truth slammed into him. Too late. Whether he should or not, he realized he already did love her. Somehow, while he wasn't looking, he'd fallen for the petite warrior with the big, sad eyes.

But he also knew that if she didn't leave soon, he'd probably end up arresting her. How could he live with that?

———

Cat held perfectly still, afraid to move a single muscle and break the spell. She'd never felt so safe in her whole life. Not even when her parents were still alive. They'd loved her, sure, but it was more of an obligatory love, not a spontaneous affection stemming from who she was. It was more a cultural expectation. Parents loved their children because they were supposed to, not because they wanted to. Nick, on the other hand, had every reason in the world to avoid her like a stinging insect. Yet here he was, offering comfort and protection. She knew it wouldn't last. It couldn't. She planned to offer her life for Blaze's. And if that didn't work, she'd still be gone, drawn into Garcia's sick and twisted world.

An involuntary shudder passed through her, and Nick stiffened, the connection broken. Unexpected tears filled her eyes, but she wouldn't let them fall. Still, she allowed herself this moment to grieve, to wish for what could never be and to imagine, for just an instant, what it would have been like if things were different, if they were two regular people falling in love.

She did love him, she realized. How could she not? He was everything a man should be: strong and protective, honorable, a guy who kept his word. All the things that made him the wrong man for someone like her, a woman who did whatever needed doing, never mind where it fell in the rule books.

Would he grieve when she either died or disappeared?

He pulled back, and she saw the sorrow in his eyes. He was grieving already. She reached out a hand and cupped his cheek. "I'm sorry," she whispered.

Searching her eyes for a moment, he reached out and tucked her hair behind her ears. Then he tugged her closer and gave her the sweetest, most tender kiss she'd ever experienced. He touched her as though she was spun glass and he didn't want to break her.

Her heart broke into thousands of sharp, jagged pieces as she leaned closer for one final kiss. He didn't hesitate but cradled her head as his lips met hers again.

For an instant, Cat let down all the walls she'd kept around her heart and poured everything she felt for Nick into the kiss. The longing, the wishes, the regret. As the kiss deepened, she tried to convey all the things she knew she could never say, should never say, for both their sakes. Nick could never be happy with someone like her. He'd spend forever trying to justify the things she said and did and trying to reconcile them to his world and his moral code. She would never ask that of him.

And truthfully, she knew she would never escape from Garcia and her uncle. She was never sure exactly what her uncle wanted from her. But with Garcia, she knew—had known it from the time she was a scared teenager. The lustful, possessive look in his eyes still made her want to throw up. She had to get Blaze out of Garcia's grasp, now. No one should have to spend their life on the run the way she had, either.

If she could spare Blaze that, she would. Even if she had to offer herself in trade.

It would require every ounce of strength she possessed.

Equally hard, she had to let Nick go. Now. Before they hurt each other any more.

She put her hands over his strong ones where they cradled the back of her head and slowly inched away, already missing the taste and feel of him.

She took a deep breath. "As soon as we find Blaze, I'll get out of your hair. I have another gig I need to get to." Which was true, as Walt Simms had said she could come back anytime. She didn't want to. But she would never tell Nick that. Best to leave certain things unsaid.

The dazed look in his eyes said the kiss had affected him as much as it had her, but then the fog cleared and he snapped back into warrior cop mode.

He sat back, cleared his throat. "Right."

Cat looked at him and couldn't hide her terror. "She's out there, Nick. All alone. She's just a kid."

"I know. And we're going to find her. If we're right and either Wang or Garcia has her, they're holding her for a reason, so I don't think they'll hurt her."

"Garcia has her. And it's me he wants."

"We don't know that for sure."

Cat looked away. "Yes, we do."

Nick tipped her face up, forced her to meet his eyes. "What are you saying, Cat? What haven't you told me?"

The questions whirled around in Cat's head as she looked at Nick, tried to decide how much to say. Could she trust him with the whole sordid story? And if she did, would he try to stop her from doing what she had to do? She almost snorted. Of course he would. He was a protector, and he'd want to save her. But he'd also do everything in his power to save Blaze.

That was what mattered. Blaze. She had to make sure Blaze was OK.

Her heart pounded and her hands wanted to shake, but she ignored all of that. She laced her fingers together and glanced at him from the corner of her eyes. "It's kind of a long story."

Something in her voice must have alerted him. He turned so that they were facing each other, knees almost touching. "I've got time. Start at the beginning."

His gentle tone gave her the courage she needed to begin. She told him about her parents. About the hours and hours of practice every day, the isolation from other children, and her parents' attitude of superiority over the rest of their little Indiana town.

Once she started, the words just kept coming. She told him how she always felt like the outsider in her parents' relationship, of how her ability to play the violin seemed the only redeeming quality they thought she had.

"And then they died in the train wreck, traveling from one concert venue to another."

"You were with them."

Nodding, she squeezed her eyes shut against the memories. The sights, the sounds. She'd never forget them. She cleared her throat. "My uncle—my father's brother—showed up. I guess the orchestra contacted him, and I was whisked away to his penthouse in Miami. Suddenly, I was surrounded by people. He had a huge staff, and people came and went at all hours, but I was just as lonely as before. Nobody talked to me. It was a really hard time. And if I thought my parents were strict about my music practice, that was nothing compared to my uncle. I spent hours and hours with my violin, and he expected me to play for him every night. Phillip drove me to and from school and made sure I never went anywhere else. I had no friends, no one to talk to. Except one person."

She stopped, dug deep for the strength to tell him everything. Nick gave her an encouraging nod and took her hand.

"I met Daniel Habersham several months after I arrived. I knew he came from a wealthy family, but he was the kindest, gentlest person I'd ever met. He seemed to care for me, not as a violinist, but just as Catharine. He called me Cathy, something my uncle would never allow."

"Daniel wanted to take me to the spring dance, but I knew my uncle would never allow that, either. I'd asked to go, and he'd already said no. But Daniel said he wanted to do things properly and insisted on coming home with me after school one day to speak to my uncle himself."

Nick nodded his approval. "Sounds like he was raised right."

"I knew it wouldn't go well, but Daniel wouldn't be dissuaded. When we got there, Garcia was also at the penthouse, and there was tension in the air. We chatted for a bit, and then my uncle told me to go to my room while the three of them talked. I didn't want to, but I left. I snuck back downstairs to the library, next door to my uncle's study. I'd learned that if I stood under the air-conditioning vent, I could hear what was happening in his study."

She looked up, met Nick's eyes. Here's where it got tricky. How much should she tell him? She decided to say as much as she could. "I couldn't see, but all of a sudden, I heard Daniel make a horrible choking sound. My uncle sounded angry, demanding to know how much of the drug Garcia had given him."

Her hands shook, and she tucked them under her thighs, so Nick wouldn't see. "When I heard them say he was dead, I raced back up to my room and threw up. I was terrified." She squeezed her eyes shut against the memories. "My uncle knocked on my bedroom door a little while later and said Daniel had to leave unexpectedly."

The silence lengthened. Then Nick asked, "Why did they drug him? Do you know?"

"It sounded like they wanted information from him." She couldn't bring herself to explain Garcia's questions about her virginity.

Nick's eyes narrowed. "What did they give him?"

"Devil's Breath. Scopolamine."

Nick's jaw clenched. "So that's why you recognized it."

She swallowed hard. "Yes. Seeing Teddy that night brought it all back."

"Is that when you ran away?"

Cat looked up, saw nothing but compassion in his eyes. "Yes. I was terrified. I tried to call Daniel, hoping I'd misunderstood, but he didn't answer. I took my mother's violin and climbed out the window at my violin teacher's house. I've kept moving ever since."

She could almost see the wheels turning in Nick's head as he fit the pieces together. She'd left one out, but she couldn't tell him about what Garcia wanted from her. Maybe he'd figure it out on his own.

"You think Garcia knows you overheard? Or at least suspects?"

She shrugged. "How could he not? I was in the house when it happened, and then Daniel was gone. It was all over the news, since his family was pretty prominent."

"Did they recover his body?"

"Yes. I saw it in the paper. I had stayed in Florida, trying to find him, still naively hoping he might be alive, but I never found a single trace. He was found in the Everglades, the victim of an apparent alligator attack." She shook her head. She wouldn't let those metal images in. Couldn't.

"Why did you run? Didn't you think your uncle could, or would, protect you?"

"I had overheard enough to know that the two of them were in business together. I didn't want to be a bargaining chip."

Nick stared at her for a long time, searching for more, but that was all she could say. "You were what? Thirteen?"

"Fourteen."

"You are one tough cookie, Cat. The fact that you survived and stayed under the radar all these years is pretty amazing."

She shrugged, uncomfortable with his praise. She hadn't done anything praiseworthy. She'd merely survived. And done some sketchy things along the way to help other young girls get home safe. "I just kept moving."

"From what Walt said, you've done more than that. You've been helping other runaways and women in trouble." He paused. "And now you're trying to help Blaze."

She met his gaze. "She reminds me of me."

"You think Garcia wants you and is holding her as bait."

"That's my guess. Yes."

"I can't let you do it, Cat."

She scrambled out of the SUV, scowled at him over her shoulder. "I knew I shouldn't have trusted you. You don't get to make decisions for me. I've been making them on my own for a long time, as you just said. You do your cop thing, and I'll do what I need to in order to protect my family. And make no mistake. Blaze is family."

He hurried around the SUV, stopped her with a hand on her arm. He cupped her shoulders, his expression fierce. "We are going to get Blaze out of there. I promise. But I don't want to lose you in the process. Don't try to do this without me, Cat." He shook her lightly. "Promise me."

Cat looked into his eyes, heart racing, indecision warring with common sense. He was a cop. He had resources she didn't have. But he'd also do everything by the book, and Garcia had his own twisted code that was light-years from Nick's.

The silence stretched. "I can't. I'm sorry."

He studied her for several minutes, and Cat wondered if he'd try to arrest her or something. But finally he simply nodded and said, "I'll take you back to your car."

Neither said a word until he'd pulled up next to her beat-up car. He walked around to her side, opened the door, and hauled her into his arms for a kiss that left her shaken to her core.

Then he climbed into his SUV and drove away.

The regret she'd seen in his eyes would haunt her forever. But she'd think about that later.

Right now, she had to find Garcia, and there was only one way she knew to do that.

As before, she pulled out her violin and stood before the camera trained on the street and started playing, trying to ignore the trembling in her hands. *Come on, come on.* She kept her eyes on the people coming and going, especially the cars along the square. She'd played most of *Panis Angelicus* before she spotted the car she was looking for. At least she hoped it was the one.

Without giving herself time to change her mind, she clutched her violin and sprinted across the street, nearly getting hit by a pickup for her trouble. She didn't stop until she reached the dark sedan with tinted windows. She knocked on the driver's side window.

When it slid down about two inches, Cat asked, "Do you work for Mr. Garcia?"

The top of the head nodded.

"I need to speak with him. Will you tell me how to get to his place?"

"One moment." The window glided all the way up, and Cat felt ridiculous standing in the street beside a parked car.

Sixty seconds later, the window eased partway down, and dark hair and eyes appeared in the opening. "Follow me."

Cat pointed over her shoulder. "Let me get my car." She took off running, quickly put her violin in the trunk, and then sped after the other car. She wouldn't risk them disappearing.

With every mile, she wondered if she'd made the biggest mistake of her life. Then she'd think of Blaze and renew her determination.

Whatever it took.

———

Blaze couldn't stop thinking about Teddy. She woke up from her nap and realized she'd been dreaming about him yet again. In the dream, he'd been trying to tell her something, but the words didn't make sense. She kept trying to get to him, but he kept moving farther and farther away.

She swiped at her cheeks, annoyed at the tears sliding down her face. Something had clearly been bugging him the last few days before he died. He'd been acting so weird. No, not weird. Scared.

She remembered the day he'd shown up to biology class late, which wasn't like him. He was always early and always prepared. Said it made him feel more in control that way. But that day, he'd raced in, earning a raised eyebrow from the teacher, and slipped into a seat at the back of the room. Not his usual spot at all.

When Blaze asked him about it after class, he tried to brush it off, but she wasn't buying it. "Where were you?"

"I had to drop something off at the police station for my dad. His company sponsors the Little League team Chief Monroe coaches."

"Okaaay? So why are you pale and your hands shaking?"

He shoved them in his pockets and wouldn't meet her eyes. "It's all good. I'm fine."

"You don't look fine, Teddy."

He turned on her. "Just leave it alone for once, OK, Blaze? Stop badgering me."

Blaze held up both hands, palms out. "Whoa. I was just asking because you look freaked out. Sorry for caring." She stormed off, hurt.

He caught up with her halfway down the hall. "I'm sorry. I'm being a jerk. Just a lot on my mind."

Blaze studied him. "Did you finally tell him no?"

Teddy swallowed hard. "Not yet, but I will."

Blaze had heard that before. Every day for a week. "When exactly?"

They stared each other down. Finally Teddy looked away and muttered, "Today."

"I'm going to hold you to it."

He smiled then, that beautiful smile that melted her insides. "I know you will. See you later."

Thinking about that day, Blaze swiped at more tears, scanning her prison from underneath the edge of the awful hood. She thought of Teddy's smile, but more than that, she tried to figure out what had shaken him up so badly. If he hadn't told Varga no already, then what was he so afraid of?

It made no sense. But it definitely meant something. She just had to figure out what.

———

Cat followed the sleek black car south for about thirty minutes, trying to keep from hyperventilating by studying the landscape. Just as by her uncle's place, this area sported mangroves, seagrass, marshland, and rivers that dumped into the Gulf. Farther south, the shoreline changed to the stereotypical beachfront that attracted tourists by the planeload.

They left the two-lane highway heading west, and Cat tried to figure out what she'd say to Garcia after fourteen years. Nothing came to mind except shaking her fist and shouting, "Let Blaze go!" the way Charlton Heston had shouted, "Let my people go," in the classic movie *The Ten Commandments*.

Though that was the crux of the matter, she probably shouldn't lead with that. Smarter to see what information she could get out of him. Maybe even find out who killed Teddy. She snorted at her own wishful thinking.

She had to stay focused. There was only one goal: to get Blaze away from Garcia.

Despite her fear, her eyes widened as they approached the coastal mansion, this one twice the size of her uncle's. Built in a Mediterranean style, it sported warm colors and a red barrel-tile roof, the grounds surrounded by an imposing wrought-iron gate meant to intimidate.

Cat gripped the steering wheel as the gates swung open. No turning back now. She followed the black car around to the side of the house where the driver indicated she should pull into the detached garage.

Her heart pounded faster. No one would be able to see her car. But it didn't matter. Now wasn't the time to wimp out. This is what she'd planned all along. She'd get Blaze out of here. No matter what.

She grabbed the satchel of money and followed the man to a side door of the mansion. Beyond her, the Gulf sparkled in the sunlight, and closer in, the water of an infinity pool stood like a shimmering beacon. Whoever had built this place hadn't spared any expense.

Garcia's henchman pointed for her to precede him. He was built like a tank, and didn't even try to hide the shoulder holster he wore beneath his black suit. His eyes held no emotion, and his black hair was slicked back from a broad forehead.

She felt an odd sense of déjà vu as she was led down a long hallway. Unlike her uncle's place, though, most of the doors here stood open, showcasing stunning views and heavily carved furniture.

The man opened a door, waited until Cat stepped through, then closed it and leaned against it, hands clasped in front of him. She assumed he'd been told to make sure she didn't try to make a break for it or something.

As at her uncle's, Cat wandered to the wall of windows, checking to see if there were neighbors close by. If there were, she couldn't tell, what with all the tropical landscaping. Beyond the house, an impressive yacht was tied to the dock. Satchel in hand, she circled the room, trying to act casual as she searched for hidden cameras. Her hands wanted to tremble, but she refused to press them to her churning stomach. *Never let them see you sweat.*

Cat's tension was wound tighter than her violin strings by the time a side door opened and Carlos Garcia strode through the door. Cat turned, mouth dry as she came face-to-face with the man who had killed Daniel all those years ago.

She was sure sparks shot from her eyes, but she didn't care. This man was a murderer. Anger boiled inside her, searching for release. Knowing she'd never be able to get justice for Daniel, not the way he deserved, made her want to scream and kick and pound this monster to a pulp—right before Nick dragged him away in handcuffs. But none of that was going to happen. Garcia's smug expression said he knew it, too.

Cat forced the anger down deep. She couldn't help Daniel right now, but she could help Blaze. She could not lose sight of that. Freeing Blaze—at whatever the cost—was why she'd come.

He crossed to stand in front of her, tried to kiss her cheek, but she pulled away. He simply raised an eyebrow in response. "Hello, Catharine. It has been a long time since I've seen your lovely face."

As he looked her over in the same slimy way he had fourteen years ago, Cat's skin crawled. He'd clearly wanted to do more than look back then. And now, the way his eyes lingered on her breasts said he still did. She folded her arms over her chest to block his view, and his eyes eventually returned to her face. His smile chilled her to the bone.

He sat behind a desk the size of a barge and waved her into a seat across from him while he studied her like a painting on display. The possessive look in his dark eyes was pure evil. She tucked her hands under her thighs so he wouldn't see them shake. This was the man her uncle expected her to meekly give herself to?

No. Not if there was another way to free Blaze.

She took a deep breath. *Help me, Jesus.*

"What brings you here, Catharine? Have you come to fulfill your part of the bargain?"

Had her uncle told Garcia of the deal she'd made? That didn't make sense. Everything she knew and had read said they were business rivals. They worked together but didn't like each other. "I don't know what you're talking about. What bargain?"

He threw his head back and laughed, his meaty jowls shaking. "Your sense of humor is delightful. We are going to have such fun together, you and I."

Cat swallowed the bile that rose in her throat and bit the inside of her cheek to keep the vehement denials inside. She had to play this smart. Narrowing her eyes, she let a small smile play around her mouth and wagged a finger at him. "Have you and my uncle been talking about me again?"

His smile vanished. "Your uncle has an outstanding debt to me, and make no mistake, it will be paid."

Cat kept up her innocent act. "You will have to take that up with him, then. It has nothing to do with me."

"It has everything to do with you," he snapped.

Cat waited, unsure what to say next. She watched Garcia visibly calm himself, then he said, "To what do I owe the pleasure of your visit this afternoon, Catharine?"

Cat kept her voice smooth and calm. "I have a proposition for you."

He arched a brow, smiling. "Oh? I am all ears."

After grabbing the bag from beside her chair, she lifted it, then set it back down. "I believe you are holding Blaze."

"Who is this Blaze?"

"Please. You know exactly who she is. She's the Martinellis' newest foster child. I'd like you to release her."

"Assuming I had her, which I don't, why are you so interested in her? What's she to you?"

Cat chose her words carefully. She shrugged. "She's just a kid, but Rosa Martinelli wants her back. Knowing she lost a child already, I thought I could help."

"And what's in it for me?"

"Fifty thousand dollars."

Garcia whistled through his teeth. "That's a lot of money. Where would a girl like you get such a sum?"

"That would be my business, wouldn't it?"

Garcia narrowed his eyes, then sat back and laughed. "You are delightful, Catharine. I admire your spirit, even though you are very foolish."

He paused, studied her.

Her heart pounded in her chest. *Please, just take the money.*

He glanced over her shoulder to where his henchman waited by the door and nodded. Then he looked back at her.

"Wang should not have sent you to try to buy me off, certainly not with so paltry a sum. His debt is greater than that, especially after his deception in pretending you were dead all these years."

Cat's stomach dropped. She had to get this conversation back on track. Fast. She squared her shoulders. "My uncle didn't send me. This is between you and me."

"Do not insult my intelligence. Where else would you have gotten that much money?" He leaned closer, eyes flashing. "Did he think I wouldn't know there is a tracking device in the bag?"

Oh God. I should have thought of that. She jumped up. "No. He has nothing to do with this. He doesn't even know I'm here."

"If that is true, then you are even more foolish than I thought." He motioned to the man. "Manuel, take her away."

"What? No!"

She whirled around, just in time to see Manuel make a grab for her. Dodging his hand, she spun out with a kick that clipped his chin and knocked him backward. He stumbled, then righted himself and came at her again.

"Stay away from me," she hissed, whirling, using her legs to keep him away. All those years of capoeira had not been in vain. She kicked and spun, knocking him back, again and again, every time he got close. Eventually, he started tiring, but she didn't let up.

"Enough," Garcia said, and Cat looked over to see a gun aimed at her chest. "You will calm yourself, or you'll die where you stand."

"Wouldn't be the first time, would it?" Cat snarled.

He smiled. "I do like a spitfire in my bed."

Revulsion swirled in her stomach, and she clenched her teeth so she wouldn't throw up. She took a deep breath, then held up both palms in surrender. "You have no reason to hold Blaze. Let her go, take the money." She swallowed. "And I'll stay."

He studied her, then chuckled. "You foolish girl. You still think you have a say, or any measure of control here. I make the rules."

Manuel grabbed her from behind, and Cat felt the bite of a zip tie around her wrists.

Garcia lowered the gun. "I'll consider the money a down payment from your uncle. Blaze will stay here." He indicated the door. "And I'll look forward to enjoying your fire—and hers—in my bedroom."

"No! Let her go, please. She has no part in this." Cat wasn't afraid to beg, if that's what it took.

"My men grabbed her by mistake, but their stupidity worked in my favor, since it brought you here, too. The fact that her ultimate death will cause pain for your family is simply a nice bonus."

Cat froze at his words. *Oh, sweet Jesus, no.*

Garcia nodded toward Manuel. "Take her away."

"No! Don't do this! Let her go!"

Manuel lifted her by the arms as though she weighed nothing. Cat struggled for all she was worth, desperate to break free. She kicked and writhed and bit his arm, which earned her a hard slap across the face. Shocked, she stilled for a moment, and suddenly his gun was pressed against her temple.

"Stop struggling."

Cat glanced across the room to where Garcia sat at his desk, checking his phone, as though what was happening had nothing to do with him. He made a shooing motion with his hand. Manuel slung Cat over his shoulder and marched from the room, one beefy hand around her ankles, the other holding the gun.

She looked back and saw the bag still sitting on the floor by Garcia's desk.

Was there really a tracking device in it? Would her uncle help her?

Garcia was right about one thing: she was foolish. Her heart sank. Her uncle wouldn't save her. He would say his debt was finally repaid and move on to other things.

But Blaze . . . she had to get Blaze out of here.

Manuel walked down the hallway and carried her out a side door. Nausea threatened when she realized he was taking her aboard the yacht. As he marched through a fancy living room and then down more stairs and into a stateroom, she swallowed the bile in her throat.

He finally dropped her in the middle of a huge bed. Gun in one hand, he secured her bound hands to the headboard. He patted her down, and she glared when he lingered far too long on her breasts. He smirked and kept going, pulling the knife from the sheath at her back, then running his hands along her legs. She almost shouted in frustration when he also found the one strapped to her ankle. He removed it, made a tsking sound, and put both knives in his pocket. Slipping off her tennis shoes, he tucked them neatly under the bed before stepping back and shooting her a lecherous smile. "Don't go anywhere."

He left, the lock clicking into place behind him.

Cat tried to still the panic building in her chest. Was this Garcia's room? *Oh God.* She shook her head as the terror tried to close over her mind. No, she wouldn't think about what he had planned. She had to formulate her own plan. And that included being long gone before Garcia showed up to collect on his so-called debt.

Her stomach did a slow roll. She hated boats. They made her seasick, something she'd learned when she hid on a boat after she first escaped Miami. But if she could get to her shoes, she could escape.

All she needed was the knife hidden in the left sole.

She hadn't stayed alive this long without being prepared.

Chapter 27

Nick had stared at the whiteboard for so long his eyes burned and his shoulders ached from sitting in the ancient desk chair. But he still didn't have any answers. When his cell phone rang, his heart rate picked up at seeing Sasha's number. So far, the only time he heard from her was when one of the Martinellis was in trouble.

"Hey, Sasha, what's up?"

"I think Cat's done something stupid," Sasha burst out. "I told her and told her to be smart, but she never listens to me. She never did. And now she's done it again."

Nick interrupted her stream of words. "Slow down and tell me what's going on."

He heard her take a deep breath. "Jesse just got back. He tried to call, but I didn't hear it—"

"Hear what?"

"Sorry. OK, so Jesse was in town a little while ago, and he saw Cat do the same stupid thing again. She stood right there on Main Street in front of the mayor's weather cam and started playing her violin. Before Jesse could get to her, she spotted a black sedan and took off after it in her car."

"Did he get the plate number?"

"No, there was a delivery truck blocking the road by the Blue Dolphin, and by the time he got past, both cars were gone."

"Which way were they headed?"

"West, out of town."

"Why didn't he call me right away?"

There was a pause.

Nick sighed. "You still think she'd involved in something illegal, don't you?"

"No!" Sasha burst out. "Not illegal, but maybe . . . gray."

"She won't tell you what's really happening?"

"No. And believe me, I've tried to get it out of her."

Nick almost smiled. They thought they were all so different, but he knew firsthand that stubbornness ran deep in all three—if he included Blaze, make that four—of the Martinelli girls. No blood relatives had ever protected each other more fiercely.

"Can you describe the car?" he asked.

"Jesse was too far away to get a great look, but he said it was a newer make, luxury black sedan. The windows were tinted, so he wasn't able to get a look at the driver."

"If you were guessing, what's she up to?" Nick asked.

Another pause. "You know about her uncle, right?"

Nick did, but he was surprised Sasha knew. "I do. From what I've dug up, he has his fingers in a lot of illegal pies, including drugs."

"That doesn't mean Cat is involved in any of that!"

"I didn't say she was."

"I think she's trying to figure out if her uncle has Blaze and will try to get him to let her go."

Nick was thinking the same thing. "Did Cat give any indication where her uncle is?"

Sasha snorted. "No. She barely said much at all about the man, telling me that the less we knew, the better. I don't understand why she won't let us help her!"

Nick almost laughed. "Don't you? Didn't you want to solve your own problem when you first got back to town, Sasha? To protect your family? And now you're pregnant. Is it really surprising she'd try to protect you?"

"You sound just like Jesse," she muttered. "But we can help."

His estimation of the man went up another notch. "You are helping, by calling me."

"You'll find her?"

"I won't stop until I do. Let me know if you hear from Cat."

"You do the same," Sasha said. "Find them both, Nick."

"That's the plan."

But as he hurried to his SUV, he acknowledged he needed more than that. He had to know where to start looking.

———

Blaze pulled the hood down over her face when she heard footsteps. The scent of Mexican food reached her seconds before the door opened.

"Eat, senorita," the female voice said. "You must keep up your strength."

Blaze knew she was right but was having a hard time choking food down, some crazy corner of her mind afraid it was poisoned and she'd end up just like Teddy.

"Why you no eat your breakfast? I make good food for you."

"I'm sorry," she mumbled through the hood. Her stomach rumbled in response to the smells, and she pressed a hand to her belly.

"Eat. Please." Then the door closed behind her.

Blaze pulled up the hood and slid closer to the tray. The tacos and refried beans did look good. And they smelled like heaven.

She carefully took a bite but didn't notice any weird taste or smell, so she took another. And another. Before she knew it, she'd scraped the plate clean.

When the room started spinning, she realized she'd been duped. The food had been poisoned.

She threw up, then slid toward the floor as her mind shut down and she fell unconscious.

———

Hope bloomed in Cat's chest as she eyed her tennis shoes. If she could just get to them, she could cut these blasted zip ties and escape.

Easing off the bed, she moved as far away from the bedpost as she could, then stretched out her legs, trying to pull the shoes toward her.

She couldn't reach.

She strained toward that left shoe, muscles screaming. She crept her toes forward, lost her balance, and the shoe slid farther under the bed. *No!*

She tried again. Sweat dripped down her back as she struggled, the zip ties biting into her wrists, but she ignored the pain. All her focus was on that shoe.

Where was it? It had slid too far under the bed for her to see, so she was feeling around blind, afraid she'd push it farther away without realizing it.

Come on, come on. Arms burning from the effort, she forced herself to keep tugging, keep reaching with her foot. She had to get it.

Footsteps sounded in the hallway.

Cat climbed back onto the bed, pulled her knees to her chin, and glared as the door opened.

There was no way she was going down without a fight.

———

Nick itched to race off in search of Cat, but first he needed a destination. So, he did what everyone in Safe Harbor did when they needed information. He went to the Blue Dolphin.

Within minutes of his arrival, LuAn told him that Cat had been asking the same questions. And Avery Ames gave him the address of a property she had rented to an Asian man.

He arrived at the wrought-iron gate within minutes. When it swung open before he'd come to a complete stop, he realized there were cameras positioned outside the estate, too. Good to know.

He drove through and parked in the circular drive, tempted to whistle at the size of the place. Mansions like this required seriously deep pockets.

The black SUV he'd seen at the old farmhouse sat in front of the six-car garage at the side of the house.

The massive front door opened, and he recognized Phillip Chen, Wang's driver. He was at the right place.

"May I help you?"

"Nick Stanton to see Richard Wang."

"Please come inside. He's been expecting you."

Nick followed him inside, not sure how he felt about that.

The place was even more impressive from the inside. Whoever built it had spared no expense. Nick made note of all the closed doors along the corridor, mentally calculating an escape route, should one become necessary.

At the end of the hallway, Phillip opened a door and stepped aside for Nick to enter. Richard Wang sat behind a massive desk. "Thank you, Phillip," he said and then waved Nick to a chair in front of the desk.

Nick sat down and studied Cat's uncle. Well dressed, still in good shape, he had an unmistakable air of control. Nick could clearly see the family resemblance in the high cheekbones and dark eyes. There was no mistaking that these two were related.

But was Cat connected to his business?

"What can I do for you, Officer Stanton?" Wang sat back in his chair and folded his arms over his chest, showing his impatience. The whole house was cold, the air conditioning set at a temperature that accommodated the other man's dark suit. Expertly tailored, it probably cost more than Nick made in a month.

"Where is Cat?" Nick tossed the question out and watched Wang's eyes, looking for a reaction. Either the man didn't care, had anticipated the question, or was a master at schooling his emotions, because Nick saw no reaction whatsoever.

"What makes you think I have the answer to your question?"

"She's your niece, correct?"

"Correct."

"You arrived in Safe Harbor just after she did." It was not a question. Avery had told him exactly when she rented Wang the house.

Wang nodded. "But that does not mean I have knowledge of her whereabouts."

"Oh, I think you have more than knowledge. I think you're holding her. But I don't know why."

Wang shook his head as though disappointed. "You have not done your homework. I thought you had." He spread his hands wide. "Why would I hold Catharine? Are you implying I kidnapped my own niece? To what end?"

"Maybe to keep her from talking about your involvement in Teddy Winston's death?"

This time, he got a reaction, though Nick wasn't sure if it was fake or not. "That young man's death was a tragedy. His parents have my sympathy. But that had nothing to do with me. I know that you are investigating his death, but tossing out unfounded accusations is not the way to go about it."

Interesting. Nick sat back and folded his arms, mirroring the other man's posture. "So how would you go about it, then?"

Wang looked impatient. "I expect you have already questioned the local individuals rumored to have drug connections, like Eddie Varga and Captain Barry."

Nick hid his surprise. For a guy who'd just arrived, he was well versed in the local players. Or did the man have local spies? Like Cat? He pushed that last thought away. "I've spoken to both of them. What do you know about scopolamine?"

Wang shook his head. "That is a powerful drug that should be carefully controlled. That it was somehow given to a local teenager is a rather frightening scenario."

On that, at least, they agreed. Nick tried another tack. "If Cat's not here, you won't mind me taking a look around the place, then."

Wang almost smiled. "I may be sympathetic to your investigation, but without a warrant, that won't happen." He paused. "As you well know. Tell me, Officer, how much is Catharine worth to you?"

Nick hid his shock. "Are you offering me a bribe?" Richard Wang wasn't stupid, not by a long shot, so what was he up to?

The silence lengthened. "I haven't offered anything. I only asked a question."

He wasn't sure how to answer. He didn't want Wang to think he'd take a bribe, not under any circumstances, so he simply said, "Cat matters to me." He could have added any number of things, like the confusing mix of emotions she stirred in him, but that was none of Wang's business.

"If I said I am fairly certain I know where she's being held? How would you respond?"

Nick stood and pulled out his cell phone. "Give me the address."

"Not so fast, Officer. There is something I want from you in return."

Nick leaned over the desk, palms flat in front of him. He didn't have time for this nonsense. "Where is she?"

Wang simply shook his head and gave Nick a smug smile that made him want to grab the man by the neck of his fancy tailored shirt and shake the truth out of him.

Nick stiffened as Wang simply continued to stare at him. "I don't have time for your mind games. What is it you want?"

"Only a small favor, really. I quite like Safe Harbor, especially if Catharine decides to make her home here. I want you to make sure that local law enforcement doesn't waste their valuable time watching me and my interests."

Nick laughed. He couldn't help it. The man had gall. He'd give him that. "You really think I'm going to turn a blind eye to whatever illegal activities you decide to set up here—and get everyone else to do the same?"

"You will if you want to know where Catharine is."

He should have expected this, would have, under normal circumstances. But somehow, Cat had messed with his internal radar. She made him question everything he knew. From the moment he'd met her, he'd been following her into gray areas, where the truth got fuzzy and lines blurred. He didn't like it. Until this moment, Nick had never had the slightest problem with moral decisions. Things were either right or wrong. Black or white. And he had no trouble whatsoever choosing what was right.

But this was Cat. He knew he was out of time. Every cop instinct he possessed was screaming that if he didn't find her, fast, he'd never see her beautiful wide eyes mocking him again. Could he risk her life over his moral convictions? He'd never be able to live with himself if she died because of him.

"Do we have a deal, Officer?" Wang pressed.

The temptation to agree to whatever the man wanted for Cat's sake yawned like the open mouth of hell itself. In his mind's eye, Wang turned into the devil, tempting Jesus on the mountaintop with everything He wanted. Everything that was already His.

"I don't make deals, Wang. I'll find Cat." He pierced the older man with a look. "But if I find out you had anything to do with her disappearance, there won't be a hole deep enough to hide from me." He turned to go.

"She stole from me."

Halfway to the door, he stopped, looked over his shoulder. "What are you talking about?"

"Catharine. She stole fifty thousand dollars from me."

He narrowed his eyes. "When?"

"Earlier today. If you agree to leave me and my associates free from legal entanglements, I won't press charges."

Nick snorted and kept walking. Once outside the mansion, he hurried to his SUV and left.

Had she really taken money from her uncle? If she thought she needed it to save Blaze, he didn't doubt it for a minute. He'd have to deal with that later.

First, he had to find her.

As he drove, a little voice asked if maybe she took the money because she was working with the drug dealers in Safe Harbor.

He ignored it and hit the gas.

Chapter 28

Cat's stomach continued to churn from the motion of the yacht, and she clenched her jaw to keep from throwing up. Closing her eyes didn't help. That just seemed to make things worse.

She braced herself when the footsteps stopped right outside the door. Was this it? Was Garcia going to kill her outright or . . . She swallowed, refusing to picture the alternatives.

She didn't move a muscle as she waited. After several minutes, the footsteps moved on again, and Cat allowed herself a deep, careful breath. She swallowed bile and redoubled her efforts to get to her shoes. If she could just reach her knife, she'd have a chance of getting out of here and finding Blaze before it was too late.

She stretched out again, as far as the zip ties would allow. Her shoulders strained against the position she was in, but she didn't stop reaching. Her years of capoeira made her more flexible than most, but no matter how far she stretched, she still couldn't quite reach her shoes.

She was panting and covered in sweat when the door suddenly swung open. She froze, leg outstretched. Manuel stood in the doorway. He eyed her position, then sent her an evil grin.

He set a tray on the shelf bolted into the wall beside the bed. He reached down and scooped up her tennis shoes, then tossed them out into the hallway. "I'll just get these out of the way since you won't be needing them." He reached into a sheath at his side and pulled out a wicked-looking knife.

All the saliva in Cat's mouth disappeared. Was this it? Was he going to stab her right here? She met his eyes defiantly. She wouldn't give him the satisfaction of cowering. She'd go out with dignity.

Before she could say anything, he leaned over and slit the zip ties binding her wrists with one quick motion. Her arms dropped, and she gasped as the circulation rushed back into her hands. She rubbed them, her eyes locked on the man.

He stepped away from the bed, nodded to the tray he'd left. "Mr. Garcia says to drink up and consider what your foolishness has cost."

He disappeared, and Cat's eyes went to the tray. A liter bottle of tequila sat beside a photo. Her hand shook as she reached for the picture. She squeezed her eyes shut, then slowly opened them again. The picture didn't change. It was Blaze, lying on a concrete floor.

Her skin had a bluish tinge, there was blood on the back of her head, and she looked like she was dead.

The boat kept up its gentle rocking, and Cat wrapped her arms around her middle. *Please God, no. Please don't let her be dead. Please.*

She leaned over and threw up on the fancy carpet, panic clawing at her chest. She had to get out of here. She had to save Blaze.

She fell back against the headboard as defeat swamped her. If the picture was real, then she was too late. Blaze was already dead. She couldn't save her.

This was all her fault, just like Garcia had said. If she'd only agreed to whatever he wanted, hadn't tried to bribe him with money—what an idiotic idea!—then Blaze would still be alive.

Defeat hit her like a rogue wave, and she curled into a ball as bitter tears of regret ran down her cheeks. Despite everything she'd tried to do, Blaze was dead. It was all her fault.

She'd let someone else she cared about die. She hadn't done enough. She hadn't been fast enough or smart enough.

She'd been a coward. And because of it, smart, tough, spunky, wonderful Blaze was dead.

Her eyes went to the bottle of tequila. Temptation flashed in front of her eyes, even when she squeezed them shut, taunting her, calling her name. Just a few sips, and she could take the edge off the self-loathing. Maybe a few more, and the pain wouldn't be so bad it hurt to breathe.

No. She wouldn't give in. She swiped at the tears, forced the nausea down.

She picked up the picture again and cursed herself for the arrogant fool she'd been. When Blaze had asked for help, she'd said no. She'd left her to fend for herself because of some selfish, misguided belief that it would help her family.

Only it hadn't. And now Blaze was gone.

Her hand trembled as she reached for the bottle. What did it matter if she drank herself into oblivion? No matter what she did, the people she cared about died. Because of her.

She fumbled with the top and finally wrestled the bottle open.

I'm sorry, Blaze. I'm so very sorry.

———

As Nick hurried away from Richard Wang's mansion, he prioritized his next steps. He'd bet his police pension that Cat had gone after Garcia. Whether she had ties to him or not, he couldn't worry about that right now. The only thing he knew for sure was that she wouldn't quit until she found Blaze.

Wang and Garcia had a history and, from what he'd read, a long-standing rivalry. That they were both in Safe Harbor right after a teen died of scopolamine poisoning could mean he had a drug turf war on his hands. With Blaze and Cat caught in the middle.

He hurried back to the station and logged in to his computer, searching local property records. He didn't think Garcia would buy or rent a place under his own name, but he didn't want to miss the obvious. There was nothing. He called Avery Ames, but the call went right to voice mail.

"Avery, this is Nick Stanton. Call me as soon as you get this, no matter what time it is. Thanks."

Then he hung up and went back to his computer, running every check and search he could think of to figure out where Garcia was hiding out.

Chapter 29

Cat felt like she'd been turned inside out. She couldn't remember ever hurting this bad. Outside the porthole, the night was dark and quiet, adding to her sense of isolation. She rubbed her chest, feeling like she'd swallowed shards of glass. Blaze had gotten under her skin in ways that surprised her. Maybe it was because the teen reminded her of herself at that age. Tough and with a huge chip on her shoulder, trying to keep anyone from getting close enough to hurt her.

Blaze had crossed those barriers and had asked for help. A huge thing. And like the idiot she was, Cat had said no. Somehow thinking that would protect her.

She'd failed. Again.

And someone she cared about had died. Again.

She picked up the bottle of tequila and studied it. Saliva pooled in her mouth just thinking of how it would taste. She brought the bottle closer, inhaled the sweet scent of oblivion.

She squeezed her eyes shut, fighting the urge to gulp it down with everything in her.

Blaze's picture mocked her.

Hand shaking, she brought the bottle to her lips. She paused, temptation like a coiled snake, and then, before she could give in, she threw the bottle against the wall, where it shattered and filled the room with the smell of regret.

Cat pulled her knees to her chest and watched the tequila run down the wall while she gulped in air, fighting tears.

She leaned her head back and cursed herself for being a fool.

Her eyes suddenly popped open.

She studied the shattered glass, then scrambled to her feet and hurried over to inspect the pile. She picked up and discarded several shards before she found one that would make a suitable weapon.

She wouldn't put it past Garcia for one nanosecond to have drugged Blaze or doctored the photo. Until she knew for sure—and she gulped at what that meant—she'd go on believing that Blaze was still alive and waiting for Cat to come help her.

Blaze hadn't had a lot of people in her life show up for her. Cat swore she'd be the one who came through.

Or die trying.

When Cat heard footsteps coming toward her stateroom, she grabbed a piece of glass in each hand and stood beside the door, ready to pounce.

The door opened, and she leaped at the guy who opened the door, jabbing the glass straight into his center mass. He was built like a mountain, and Cat's strike hit him just below the collarbone. He yelled as he jerked away and yanked out the glass. The tray he'd been holding clattered to the floor as Cat tried to rush past him and into the hallway. He grabbed his chest where blood poured from the wound and then swung his other arm out to stop her forward momentum.

Cat bounced off his beefy arm and immediately tried to jab him again, but he was quicker than he looked. Before she could reach him, he sidestepped and whipped a gun from his shoulder holster.

She spun around and knocked the gun from his hand with her leg. He cursed and reached for her again, but she twisted out of his reach and lunged for the door.

She'd almost made it when he grabbed the back of her shirt and yanked her backward against his chest. His other arm came around her neck, and the gun bumped her temple. "Quit it," he muttered, but she ignored him.

She kicked backward, twisted and turned like a whirling dervish to try to free herself, but he simply tightened his hold. She refused to give in. She reached around with the shard of glass she held in her left hand and stabbed the arm he had wrapped around her neck.

Shock made him let go, and she ducked under his arm and flew down the short hall with him right on her heels. She ran up the stairs and didn't slow down even when another black-suited goon on the upper deck turned at the sound of her footsteps.

Without thought, she raced along the narrow outside hallway, ignoring the wire railing that was all that separated her from the water below. When Manuel appeared in front of her, she knew she was out of options.

She glanced over her shoulder at the bleeding hulk closing in, then sent Manuel another quick glance. For a big guy, he moved fast.

Cat looked down, way down, where the water lapped the sides of the boat. She hated the water.

She sent Manuel a smile and jumped. She didn't know how deep it was but figured the big boat, yacht, whatever, needed deep water, right?

The water closed over her head, and she fought the usual panic. She started flailing her arms, eventually finding her rhythm as she made her way to the surface. The moment her face cleared the water, she gulped in air. But in the next second, bullets hit the water far too close to her head for comfort.

Right. Guns. On the boat.

She dove under the water. She swam parallel to the boat, popping up like an otter every few yards to catch her breath and check Manuel and the others' location. They kept pace, firing every time she popped up. Drat the moonlight.

She sucked in air and dove down again, trying to stay far enough below the surface that she wouldn't get shot.

Once she reached the back end of the boat—the stern?—she glanced right and left, trying to decide which way to go. Off to her right were two more docks farther away, no boats near them, so no place to hide.

To her left was another big mansion, with another dock and another big boat. If she could get behind that, she'd be able to get to shore without being seen. She spun in that direction, gulped air, and dove again, kicking with all her might to get as far toward the next boat as she could before they realized what she intended.

She swam through the dark water, salt stinging her eyes, and hoped she was closing in on the dock. Her lungs were desperate for air, and her legs and arms were exhausted, but she kept pushing forward. Just a little farther.

When her lungs felt about to burst, she quietly eased her head up and tried to take a breath without making a sound. She looked up, relieved to be in the shadow of a boat that looked even bigger than the one she'd just leaped off. She swam around it to the other side, out of view of the goons who were after her.

It seemed to take forever, and her legs and arms felt like wet noodles, but finally, finally, she found herself in sight of the seawall. She kept swimming and almost wept with relief when she spotted a ladder attached to one of the dock pilings.

She climbed up as fast as her tired legs would go. She couldn't seem to catch her breath, but she didn't slow down. It wouldn't take them long to figure out where she'd gone.

Staying behind the boat, she ran up the dock. She peeked around the front of the boat, didn't see anyone running toward her, so she hurried up the dock and onto the paved walkway, then veered sharply to the right and ran around the stucco fence that ended at the water, desperate for a place to hide.

Nick snatched up the phone when it finally rang. "Avery. Thanks for calling me back. Have you rented any other big properties near Safe Harbor recently? Especially on the Gulf?"

"Was the address I gave you not the place you were looking for?"

"It was. Thank you. Did Cat ask about any others?"

"Is this part of an official investigation? Otherwise, I don't know how I feel about sharing that information."

Nick snorted. Avery Ames prided herself on reporting only facts in her newspaper, but she didn't hesitate to hint and speculate when she was talking to the locals. She liked having knowledge others didn't. "Now is not the time, Avery. Tell me what you know. And yes, it's part of an investigation."

"And you'll give me an exclusive interview?"

"I'm sure the chief will do that. Afterward."

There was a long pause. "OK. Here's the other address. It was rented by a corporation named GDH Enterprises. It's right on the Gulf."

He scribbled it down on a scrap of paper. "Thank you, Avery. Do you know if they rented a boat, too?"

"The place came with a nice-size yacht on deep water."

He thanked her and hung up. Just as he did, the door to the station opened, and Wally, who owned the Gas-N-Go, walked in. Nick glanced at the clock, surprised the man was here so late.

"Hey, Nick. I got those tapes you wanted," Wally said, holding up several videotapes.

Nick glanced up from the GPS bird's-eye view of the property Avery had just given him, his mind already on how he was going to get to Cat without alerting Garcia or his goons.

"Thanks, Wally. You brought the ones from Saturday night up until now?"

"Just like you asked." He paused, rocked back on his heels. "I had to buy a couple more blank ones, though, since I'm giving you these."

Nick resisted the urge to roll his eyes. The guy made regular tight-wads look like big spenders. "Bring me a receipt, and I'll make sure you get reimbursed."

Wally thanked him and left. Nick stuck the tapes into his desk drawer and hurried out. Once he found Cat and Blaze, he'd focus on finding Teddy's murderer.

Turning on his lights but leaving the siren off, he headed out of town. No sense waking everyone as he went by.

He hadn't gone ten miles when he came around a bend in the road and slammed on his brakes. A tractor trailer lay on its side across the road, another car halfway under it. It must have just happened, as there were no emergency vehicles on the scene yet.

He pulled off the road and called dispatch as he ran, shouting instructions.

———

Once out of sight, Cat crashed through the woods, desperate to get to the road. She knew she shouldn't make any noise, but somehow, moving fast to get out of sight felt like the wiser choice. If she remembered right, the gravel road was only about a mile long before it connected with the paved two-lane road. Another few miles on that one, and she'd hit the convenience store at the intersection of US-19. Which sounded so easy and quick if you had a car.

She stopped, leaned against a pine tree, and panted, trying to catch her breath and shore up her strength to keep going. In a perfect world, she would grab her car, but she didn't think Garcia's men had conveniently put her keys in the ignition on the off chance she'd come by to get it.

She didn't think she'd find her violin lying out in the open, either, even if she risked going back for it. Pain sliced her heart at the idea of leaving her one real link to her parents behind forever, but she couldn't think about that now.

When she heard a car coming down the road, she ducked behind some scrub palms, wincing when the thorny spines scratched her skin. She waited, thighs aching from her crouch, and peeked through the fronds, trying to see if it was Garcia's men.

Sure enough, one of his black SUVs came into view from the direction of the mansion. She couldn't see the driver, but the man in the passenger seat looked like Captain Barry. Was he involved with Garcia, too?

She ducked down, gritting her teeth against the swarming bugs until the car was no longer visible. Once the SUV passed, Cat worked her way back toward the road, each step agony on her battered feet.

Exhausted and unsteady, she stumbled, and suddenly the ground fell away. She fell headlong into a black hole and landed with a thud.

Her eyes blinked open for a moment and then slid closed.

Blaze was her last thought.

Chapter 30

The sun was barely over the horizon when Nick pulled up to Garcia's mansion. He'd been at the accident scene most of the night. As soon as he'd finished there, he'd grabbed a shower and more coffee and headed this way. He wasn't surprised when the big, imposing gate swung open the moment he gave the disembodied voice his name.

He let out a low whistle as he climbed out of his official SUV. While Richard Wang's place bespoke casual elegance, this Mediterranean-style monstrosity simply screamed money. Pots of it.

A black-suited man built like a linebacker answered the door and, without saying a word, led him down a long hallway to a large room overlooking the Gulf. A beauty of a yacht, easily fifty feet long, lolled at the dock. The whole setup was pretty darn impressive, which was no doubt part of the reason Garcia had rented it.

Nick walked over to the wall of windows to investigate, checking out the neighboring docks and yachts, trying to figure out where Garcia was holding Cat.

He glanced over his shoulder as Garcia entered the room. "Nice place."

Garcia smiled and stepped behind the massive desk set off to one side, angled to take advantage of the views. He indicated a chair in front for Nick, like a genial host. "It'll do while I'm here." What was it with these guys and suits, especially in this heat? Like Wang, Garcia kept the air conditioning set cold enough for frostbite.

"How long are you planning to stay in Safe Harbor?"

Garcia's smile didn't reach his eyes. "I haven't decided yet. Though I do like this provincial little town."

Nick refused to take the bait. "What brought you here?"

"Business." He folded his hands over his expansive stomach as he leaned back in the chair.

"What kind of business exactly?"

"Mainly import and export, but I'm guessing you already know that, Officer."

"And drugs." Nick kept his eyes on Garcia's, but there was no reaction whatsoever. No widening of pupils or any other tell. He hadn't really expected one, but he'd hoped.

"I'm a busy man, Officer. So please let me know what brings you to my home this early in the morning."

"Where is Cat Martinelli?"

"You are assuming I know who that is, I imagine. You'll have to enlighten me, Officer."

Nick's patience strained its leash, but he knew how these games were played. He smiled, all teeth. "You know, Cat, aka Catharine Wang, aka the niece of your business rival Richard Wang."

"Oh, Catharine. She was a lovely girl. How old is she now?" He considered. "Probably late twenties. Tell me, is she still as beautiful as she was as an unspoiled young teenager?"

Fury knotted the back of Nick's neck, and he clenched his jaw. If he found out Garcia had put his hands on Cat when she was young . . . But he shoved that thought away. For now. First, he had to find her. "I have it on good authority that Cat came to see you yesterday. She didn't come home, and her family is worried about her." He shrugged. "The Martinellis' daughter Blaze is missing, too. They're worried."

"And you think they came here?" He spread his hands. "Why would you think such a thing? I don't understand."

Nick studied the man, weighing his next move. Unlike chess, the stakes here were much, much higher.

"Blaze has been trying to find out what happened to her friend Theodore Winston, the young man who died recently."

"That was a terrible tragedy. Have you figured out what he died of yet?"

"Scopolamine."

At that, Garcia's eyes widened, though the reaction could have been feigned. He shook his head. "I have heard that is a very dangerous drug. How did it come to be here in Safe Harbor?"

Nick hid his frustration. "I'm still trying to figure that out. What do you know about it?"

Garcia had the gall to laugh. "You are quite amusing, Officer Stanton, with your obvious fishing expedition. If you are worried about a dangerous drug in Safe Harbor, I suggest you look much closer to home. I am merely a businessman renting a vacation retreat."

Nick was done with the game. "Where is Cat?"

"I do not know. She is certainly not here."

"Prove it."

"I don't have to prove a thing."

"True. But if I have to come back with a search warrant, there's no telling what will turn up."

Garcia's eyes narrowed, voice quiet. "Are you threatening me?"

"No, sir. Wouldn't dream of it. Just asking for your cooperation."

Garcia drummed his fingers on the desk, then seemed to come to a decision. He waved a hand at the man still standing guard by the door. "Ramon will go with you. Feel free to look wherever you'd like in my home. But you won't find anything, because Catharine isn't here. But if you want to waste your time looking, be my guest." He waved Nick away and pulled out a cell phone.

He'd been dismissed.

Nick reined in his frustration. Garcia wouldn't have made the offer if Cat were here, which meant he'd moved her somewhere else and this was nothing but a way to waste his time. Time he didn't have. Time he needed to find Cat.

Still, he dutifully followed Ramon from room to room, checking every closet and under every bed. They checked the grounds and garden sheds, and after that, Nick searched every square inch of the yacht. There was no sign of her, or of any illegal activity, but Nick knew she'd been here recently.

In one of the staterooms, he stopped, sniffed. He crouched down near the wall. The carpet was damp, and the stench of tequila hadn't quite been masked by disinfectant. He must have been holding her here.

He turned to Ramon. "Please thank Mr. Garcia for his cooperation."

Ramon nodded. "I'll walk you out."

Nick scanned the estate as he walked out to his car. Where was Cat now? And was Blaze with her?

———

Cat woke slowly, every muscle in her body aching. Sunlight filtered down, and she realized she was lying in what looked like a sinkhole. Thankfully, it wasn't very deep, and she managed to climb out. She slowly ventured back toward the side of the road. The soles of her feet were raw from all the debris she'd stumbled over, and every step was agony. At least, alongside the road, there was a bit of sand and grass mixed with the gravel, which made the walk a bit easier.

She limped along, sweating in the humidity, trying to stay focused on her goal. What had taken her only a few minutes by car seemed to take ten years now. But she could do this, doggone it. For Blaze. She was in good shape. This should be a piece of cake, right? Except she hadn't had anything to eat or drink in . . . she couldn't remember how long. Her throat felt parched, and her hands were starting to shake.

She heard the sound of a vehicle coming down the road. Was it coming toward her or away from Garcia's? She wasn't sure. The humidity was starting to make her dizzy. She needed water.

It was safe to assume these were Garcia's men out looking for her, however, so she stumbled into the woods lining the road, out of sight.

She was trying to be quiet but knew she was doing a terrible job of it. She took another step and fell, scraping her palms as she hit the ground. Lying there, panting, cheeks stinging, she waited until the sounds of the car faded in the distance.

Then she levered herself up and gingerly kept going.

She hadn't taken twenty steps when a click sounded behind her. Cat froze, then slowly turned toward the two men with guns aimed her way.

"Not so fast, girly. Mr. Garcia ain't done with you yet."

Cat hid her desperation as they shoved her into the SUV, heart pounding. She had to stay positive. With any luck, they'd take her where they were holding Blaze. Then Cat could figure out a way to get them out of there, together.

And if she was really lucky, she'd find a way to get justice for Daniel at the same time.

———

Nick's SUV churned up clouds of dust as he hurried away from Garcia's mansion. That comment about looking closer to home echoed in Nick's mind. Was Garcia trying to deflect attention? Of course. But just maybe, Nick could put some pressure on Varga to get him to finally spill what he knew.

It didn't take long to reach Varga's place on the other side of Safe Harbor. The minute he pulled up to the rusting mobile home, he knew it was empty. But just in case he was wrong, he climbed onto the rickety steps and banged on the door.

"Varga. It's Nick Stanton. Open up."

He listened, but there were no sounds from inside. He walked around the mobile home, knocked on the back door, too. Still nothing.

As he was coming back around, he stopped at a small fire pit ringed by a haphazard circle of rocks. Beer cans and various rusted lawn chairs proclaimed this a gathering spot.

Nick moved closer, noticed that three of the heavy wooden kitchen chairs had been knocked over, while the lightweight aluminum chairs were still standing. The broken bottles confirmed there'd been a fight of some kind. But whether it had any relevance to what was going on was anybody's guess. It could just be normal, everyday behavior for Varga and his friends.

He turned his back on the scene and studied the surrounding woods, unable to shake the feeling he was being watched. Was Varga hiding out, hoping he'd leave?

Before he climbed into his SUV, he called, "Eddie? If you're out here, come talk to me. It'll be better all around if you do."

There was no response, but he hadn't really expected one. Lowlifes like Varga survived by being quick and sneaky.

After one last check of the area, he left.

———

"Have you looked at those tapes Wally dropped off yet?" Wanda asked as Nick walked into the station. "He's already called to see if you found anything helpful on them."

Nick snorted. "Angling for gossip, is he?"

Wanda chuckled. "Isn't everyone?"

Desperate for anything helpful, Nick pulled the tapes from his desk drawer and then went to the small conference/break room in the back of the station. He knew he was still missing something important.

The aging television, plus a DVD player and VCR, sat on a console against the wall. He turned on the television, pushed the tape in, and rewound until he got to the time stamp for the night of Teddy's murder. There wasn't a lot of activity late in the evening, so he fast-forwarded until anyone entered the store, played it at normal speed, then fast-forwarded again.

He watched for several more minutes, but there was nothing suspicious and no one who looked out of place.

He was just about to stop the tape when two men came into view. He rewound the tape and played it again.

"What are you looking for?" JD asked as he walked into the room.

Nick hit pause and went over to the television for a closer look. He reached for his cell phone and took a picture, then went forward several more frames, stopped, and took another one.

JD stepped up beside him. "That's Captain Barry and Chief Monroe. They were both at the wedding, right? What are you looking at?"

"Captain Barry is missing a button on his jacket cuff." Nick had stopped the tape again, checked, just in case. Nope, Chief Monroe's cuffs weren't visible, so that didn't help. Though it was highly unlikely that both men would be missing a button and that those buttons would be identical. He turned everything off and led the way back to his desk, where he pulled up the picture of the button found at the quarry and compared the two.

They matched. Which meant that Captain Barry had likely been out there the night Teddy Winston died, unless the man regularly went out wearing his Sunday suit. Which Nick doubted.

But was he involved in Teddy's murder? Did the chief figure into this, too?

He turned to JD, grabbed his keys. "I'm going to check out Captain Barry's place." If he was involved in Teddy's murder, some pressure from Nick might net the location where Cat and Blaze were being held.

———

Sweat dripped down Blaze's cheeks and mingled with a rogue tear. She'd been so sure Cat or Nick would come barreling through the door, guns blazing, and get her away from these crazy people.

But no one had come. She'd prayed, too, and told God she was sorry for all the crappy things she'd done, but He hadn't sent help, either.

She figured Mama Rosa would cry at her funeral, if they didn't hide her body in a swamp somewhere. So would Pop. Probably. No, he would.

But what about her real parents? Would they care, even if they knew?

She doubted it, and somehow that just made her sadder. Defeat pulled at her, and she curled into a little ball, lonelier than she'd ever been in her life. She kept trying to do the right thing, but it never worked out for her. Nobody loved her.

Sasha and Jesse do, a little voice said.

Yeah, maybe, but they didn't have room in their lives for her. They had a baby on the way and their dog, Bella, to take care of. They didn't need her hanging around.

What about Eve? She's a major pain, but she and Cole have definitely tried to be there.

Blaze couldn't really argue that.

Cat and Nick love you, too.

Her heart hitched. Maybe. Or maybe they just tolerated her. They were both busy. No, if she was going to survive this nightmare, she would have to find a way out by herself. Just like always.

She sat up and wiped her cheeks. Enough sniveling. She'd have to be tough.

And smart. Eventually, someone would come to the door.

When they did, she'd be ready.

She'd just climbed to her feet when she heard footsteps outside. Before she could formulate any kind of plan, keys rattled and the door burst open.

Somebody came in and grabbed her by the arm. "Let's go. The boss wants you."

He yanked off her hood and exchanged a look with the man with him, who laughed in a way that made Blaze's skin crawl.

By the time they had shoved her up the short gangplank onto a yacht, Blaze was even more scared than before. She could identify them. Which meant they didn't plan to let her go. She bit her lip to keep it from trembling.

Once onboard, they led her through a fancy living room that made Blaze's eyes widen. This scary creep must have buckets of money. The yacht looked like the kind you saw on television.

The burly guy pushed her into a bedroom and pulled the door closed behind her. The men's laughter receded as they walked away.

Another man sat on the bed and patted the space beside him. She didn't like the way he ran his eyes over her. His clothes were expensive, but the evil in his dark eyes made her insides quiver. "Have a seat."

She folded her arms over her chest. "No, thanks. I'm good. Who are you?"

He laughed. "They told me you were feisty. I like that."

Blaze almost threw up.

"You are very much like Catharine. Spirited beauties." His expression darkened. "She owes a debt." He looked her over like she was a prize heifer at the state fair. "I do believe I'll keep you both. I might quite enjoy that."

He stood, and Blaze moved around the bed, well out of reach. "I really expected someone would try to rescue you. Apparently, you're not that important." He smiled then, and goose bumps popped up on Blaze's arms. "Don't worry. I'll take good care of you."

Still smiling, he walked out the door and left, locking it behind him.

Blaze waited until his footsteps faded away before she sank to the floor, shaking like a leaf.

After a while, she stood and prowled the room, looking for a way out, a weapon, something.

She wasn't sure what he'd been talking about in terms of a debt, but she wouldn't let him get to her. Nick and Cat would come. She had to believe that. And when they did, Blaze would be ready.

Chapter 31

Nick arrived at Captain Barry Brown's house, not far from where his own used to be. The house was a Craftsman style, with a deep front porch and columns at either end. It was well kept, with flowerpots all around. Since Captain Barry spent most of his time at his tire store or the marina, he guessed the white wicker furniture on the porch was his wife's doing.

Nick reached up to knock on the front door, and it swung inward. He slowly pushed it open, then pulled his gun out and held it next to his leg. "Captain Barry? Mrs. Brown? It's Nick Stanton, Safe Harbor police. Anyone home?"

He walked all through the downstairs, but there was no sign of either of them. Nothing seemed out of place in the upstairs bedrooms, either.

As Nick came back out onto the porch, a little convertible sports car zipped into the driveway, and the captain's wife climbed out. She hurried up the walk, stiletto heels clicking, eyes wide. "Is everything OK? What's going on?"

Nick looked up and down the street, noticed curtains twitching behind several windows. He indicated the open front door. "Why don't we step inside?" Once away from prying eyes, he asked, "Mrs. Brown, do you know where your husband is?"

"No. I haven't seen him. I went by the shop, and they said he left just after he opened this morning, but he hasn't come back." Her eyes were worried. "Sasha says he hasn't been at the marina today, either. Why do you want to talk to him?"

"You've called his cell phone?" Nick asked.

"Of course. Half a dozen times. This isn't like him. We had an, ah, errand to run today."

"Did you and your husband attend Eve and Cole's wedding on Saturday night?"

She glanced away. "We weren't there long. We had another engagement that night."

Nick walked over to a small table by the front door where a baseball cap lay. He picked it up, then turned to Mrs. Brown. "This your husband's? Do you mind if I take it with me?"

She narrowed her eyes. "Why?"

"It's part of the ongoing investigation into Teddy Winston's murder."

"What does that have to do with Barry?"

"Maybe nothing. Process of elimination."

"Don't you need a warrant or something?"

"Not if you give it to me."

"Sure, fine, whatever." She waved a hand, then turned to Nick. "Has something happened to him?"

"I don't know." He pulled out his card. "But please let me know if you hear from him, OK?"

———

Nick clenched his jaw as he drove. Varga and Captain Barry were conveniently missing, and there was no sign of Cat and Blaze at Garcia's.

The smell of tequila suggested she'd been on the yacht, but a smell was not enough for a search warrant, especially since Garcia had already let him look around.

Where were they? Nick was out of time and out of options.

Halfway back to the station, Wanda called. "Hey, Nick, I just got a call from a fisherman out by Gull Point who says he thinks he found a body."

"Did you tell him to stay put and not touch anything?"

"Of course. He's from Chicago, here for a few days after a convention in Tampa, and is totally freaked out. I said you'd be right there."

"I'm heading there now."

"By the way, I called the chief, but he didn't pick up his cell phone and hasn't responded to my message yet. JD is on his way."

Interesting. The chief was usually all about high-profile calls and would be eager for the press coverage. "Thanks, Wanda. Try to keep Avery away for now, would you?"

"I'll do what I can."

Nick flipped on his lights and sirens and headed toward the two-lane road that led out to Gull Point. The pier was popular with the tourists, as it was easy to get to.

A small crowd had already gathered by the time he arrived, and Nick sighed when he spotted several fishermen talking on cell phones and videotaping the area.

He walked over to a twentysomething guy and snatched the phone from his hand. "I'll get it back to you when I'm done with it."

The man started to argue, but one look at Nick's face, and he simply nodded.

He turned to the assembled crowd. "This is part of an investigation. No pictures. No video. Step away, please, and wait over there. I'll want to talk with each of you." He pointed to a shady spot several yards away.

Then he approached the fisherman who'd called the body in. He looked pale and shaken, and based on the smell and the stain on his shirt, the man had tossed his cookies more than once. Nick looked over the railing and saw a fishing line attached to a body that was half-covered in the marshy grass. "I'm Officer Nick Stanton with the Safe Harbor Police Department. You made the call?"

"Yes. I was going to climb down to see if he was still alive, but then I was afraid I'd disturb the evidence or something."

"Thanks for calling us right away." Nick had been out here before and knew the water wasn't that deep, not with the tide out. He climbed over the railing and waded over to the body. The victim was facedown in the water, covered with blood and evidence of what appeared to be a recent beating. Just in case, he checked for a pulse, but given the severity of the injuries and the angle of the neck, he didn't expect to find one. He was right.

JD arrived and waded over to him. He paled when he saw the body. Nick glanced over at him. "You OK?"

He swallowed hard. "Yeah." Then he straightened his shoulders. "What would you like me to do?"

"You're doing fine, JD. Doing fine. Why don't you start interviewing that crowd over there, get their statements while we wait for the coroner. Check their phones, too, for any pictures we can use. I'll talk to him." He nodded to the fisherman leaning heavily on the railing.

Doc Henry arrived and examined the victim. He turned to Nick. "Someone went to great lengths to make sure we can't identify the body, not immediately, anyway. His fingers are mangled so badly, I'm not sure I'll be able to get any prints. He hasn't been dead all that long, but it was a painful way to go. I'll know more after I get him on the table."

"Thanks, Doc." Nick paused. "Do you mind if I get a strand of hair? I may have a way to confirm identity."

The man studied him. "Not usual protocol, but go ahead."

Nick took the sample and bagged it, then continued processing the crime scene.

Though Avery Ames arrived with her camera, there was still no sign of the chief. According to Wanda, his wife had called the station three times because she was worried. She was out of town visiting family and couldn't reach her husband.

Nick tried Monroe's cell phone again, but it went right to voice mail.

———

It was hours later before he and JD finished processing the scene. Nick felt exhaustion seeping through him and rolled his shoulders and shook his head to try to stay alert. As he drove, he got a call from his insurance adjuster, who said they were sending a check to help cover his living expenses while they settled the claim on his house.

Nick hung up and almost laughed. He'd been so focused on finding Blaze and Cat, as well as Teddy's murderer, he'd momentarily forgotten he was homeless. On impulse, he swung past what was left of his house on the way back to the station. He sat in the driveway for a moment, looking at the charred remains.

His past was gone, along with all the tangled emotions and mementos of his parents that went with it. He let out a deep breath and made a decision. He'd have the lot cleared, sell it to a young family that wanted to build a house. He'd find another place. It would be good to start fresh, make new memories.

Cat's face popped into his mind and brought him sharply back to the task at hand. He started the car and backed out of the driveway. He had to find her.

JD pulled up behind him at the station, and they walked in together. Wanda looked tired, too, her desk littered with messages, while the phone continued to ring.

Between calls, Nick asked, "You doing OK?"

She nodded. "Everyone in town is calling to tell me who they think the body is and to pump me for my guess." She held up a hand. "Don't worry. I'm not speculating." She met his eyes, hers worried. "Still no word from the chief?"

"No. And Captain Barry's wife has called several more times asking if we've found him yet."

A somber silence settled over the room.

"Has anyone said anything about Eddie Varga?" Nick asked.

Wanda looked surprised. "No. Want me to call the Gas-n-Go and see if he's been there today?"

"Please."

Wanda picked up the phone. "We have gotten a number of calls mentioning a 'suspicious-looking Asian man' and also several black SUVs in town that apparently looked like 'them government types drive.'"

"Thank you, Wanda." Nick hurried into the chief's office and looked around, surprised to see his official Safe Harbor police Stetson hanging on the coatrack in the corner. That wasn't like the chief at all. He did love that hat. Nick checked the band, saw two strands of hair, and hoped there was a root attached so the lab could get DNA.

He bagged the hat, then found a box in the storage room and put the hat, the evidence from the body, and Captain Barry's baseball cap inside. He walked back out front. "JD, I need you to run this box over to the crime lab. I'll let them know you're coming."

JD looked at the Stetson, then back at Nick, and swallowed hard. Nick made sure all the necessary information was entered in the log, completely by the book. He wanted to ensure there wouldn't be a problem with chain of custody down the road.

Once JD left, Wanda glanced at him, obviously fighting tears.

"Why don't you head home and get some rest. It's late and there's nothing more we can do tonight."

"You'll get some rest, too?" she asked.

"I'm getting ready to head out."

Satisfied, she said, "Good night," and then left.

Sleep wasn't on Nick's agenda, however. He had to find Cat and Blaze. Fast. Earlier, JD had searched the farmhouse where Cat had first met with Richard Wang to see if there was any sign of either of them, but there was nothing. If Wang was telling the truth—and Nick believed he was—then Garcia had them. So where was he holding them? Even though he'd searched Garcia's mansion, it would have been easy enough for Garcia to move both women while he was there. Or even gag them so they'd be quiet.

How could he make Garcia show his hand?

He drove back to his motel, mind spinning. There had to be a way.

Doggone stupid, misguided woman had used herself as bait. He muttered a string of curses. He knew exactly why she'd done it. He just couldn't agree with it.

He sat at the small table in his hotel room and pulled out his laptop. He searched for Daniel Habersham and found article after article about his disappearance and the subsequent search fourteen years ago. Daniel's face appeared on the screen, and Nick could understand why Cat had fallen for him. He looked like a nice kid—had been, by all accounts. He saw a brief mention by a reporter that he'd last been seen with Catharine Wang, the niece of Richard Wang. When he googled Garcia's name along with Wang, he found several mentions of a bitter rivalry between the two men. Cat had alluded to that, too.

He dug deeper into Garcia's background, and the more he read, the angrier he got. The man was into all kinds of sick, twisted stuff. His stomach turned when he read a police report about a woman whose body had been found. She'd last been seen in Garcia's company.

He read article after article until the words blurred and his stomach churned. He didn't remember falling asleep, but one minute he was thinking about Cat, and the next a buzzing woke him.

He sat up and grabbed his phone off the table. "Stanton."

"Hi, Nick. It's JD. Have you heard from the chief? His wife just called again. She's on her way back to Safe Harbor because she's so worried. She still can't reach him."

Unease slithered down Nick's spine. He glanced around, realized it was daylight. "I'll swing by his place on my way in. I'll let you know."

Five minutes later, hair still wet, Nick headed to Monroe's fancy house on the outskirts of town. It sat back from the road and somehow screamed, "Look at me." Or maybe he was confusing that with Monroe and his wife, who both loved the spotlight. He parked in the circular drive and climbed out, his unease growing. A quick peek in the two-car garage showed it was empty. He used the ornate brass knocker and waited but didn't really expect a response.

He knocked again. Still nothing. He called the house and heard the phone ringing from inside, but nobody answered. Just as he turned to check the back door, a minivan came down the drive. A young woman climbed out with a bucket of cleaning supplies in one hand and a little girl of about four holding her other.

"Good morning."

"Hi, I'm Nick Stanton." He held out his hand as he walked toward her.

She shook it. "I'm Carrie Sanders. This is my daughter, Callie."

"I'm looking for Chief Monroe."

She checked her watch. "He's usually left for the Blue Dolphin by the time I get here to clean."

"Do you come every day?"

She laughed. "I wish. No, Mrs. Monroe just has me come once a week. Is something wrong?"

"You have a key to the house, right?"

"Yes, of course. Why?"

"Mrs. Monroe hasn't been able to reach the chief. I'm just making sure he isn't ill or something."

"Oh, my goodness. Why didn't you say something?" She hurried toward the door, jabbed her key in the lock.

"Wait out here," Nick said.

He stepped into the foyer, and when he was out of sight of the little girl, he pulled out his weapon, just in case. There was no sign of the chief anywhere on the first floor, so he went up the sweeping staircase and checked the second, too. Thankfully, there was no sign of a break-in, either.

He went back downstairs and let Carrie and her daughter in, then called JD. "He's not here, JD. But there's no sign of foul play, either. So maybe he just decided to escape for a day or two." Which was entirely possible, since his wife was out of town, but the chief prided himself on always knowing what was going on in Safe Harbor. His not being connected, at least by phone, was out of character and made Nick's radar twitch.

"Mommy, look what I found!"

The little girl went running by him, a toy clutched in her hand. Nick saw the bright-red paint, and a flash of memory slammed into him.

He followed Callie into the kitchen, where her mother crouched down and said, "Oh, honey, where did you get that?" She eased it from her daughter's grip. "We can't take things that don't belong to us, sweetie."

The little girl's chin quivered. "I just wanted to play with it."

Nick stepped forward. "May I see it?" Carrie handed him the hand-carved wooden boat, and the minute he touched it, he felt like he'd been catapulted back in time. He was three again, and Sal Martinelli was holding him on his lap and handing him this wooden boat, saying he'd carved it for him. Nick shook his head and looked at the little girl. "Will you show me where you got this?"

She looked from him to her mother, who nodded and held out her hand. "Why don't we all go?"

They followed Callie into a room at the end of the hall that had to be the chief's study. A big mahogany desk, floor-to-ceiling bookshelves, and leather furniture filled the room. Callie's eyes were wide and worried as she pointed to an open desk drawer.

Her mother's expression went stern. "Did you open that drawer, Callie? You know better than that."

Their voices faded into the background as Nick pulled a pair of gloves out of his pocket and snapped them on. He opened the drawer all the way, reached in, and shock rippled through him as he pulled out his baby blanket. The blue one Mama Rosa had knitted for him. He'd seen it in pictures.

He stood stock still, frozen between past and present, absorbing the implications. Here was proof that Chief Monroe had been involved in his kidnapping. Or, at the very least, had knowledge of what happened. Why hadn't he said anything? He knew Nick had been searching for answers.

Nick fingered the blanket as his mind spun. This just raised more questions. Why had Monroe kept these things? Was he blackmailing Sal in some way, after all this time?

He had to find out. First, he snapped pictures of both items with his phone. Then he went to his SUV and grabbed more evidence bags, mind racing. Once he'd bagged both items, he found Carrie in the kitchen, a subdued Callie coloring at the table.

"I'm so sorry, Officer Stanton. She knows better than to go snooping."

Nick glanced at the little girl, who ducked her head and wouldn't look at him. "Mind your mama, now." He sent Callie a quick smile. "I'll see myself out."

Once in his SUV, he got the search warrant for Monroe's place in motion, then glanced at the bagged items on the seat beside him. Was it possible he'd just identified who was behind his kidnapping? Why would the chief have been involved? Or was he protecting someone?

Did this mean Garcia was holding the chief, too? Were the two connected?

The stakes kept getting higher.

He had to find Cat and Blaze. Now.

Chapter 32

Cat had spent a miserable night trying to figure out how she was going to get Blaze out of here. Her arms ached from being held above her head and tied to the bedpost again.

As much as she didn't want Nick involved, part of her hoped he would figure it out and come charging in, guns blazing, to free them both. She especially worried about Garcia getting his filthy hands on Blaze. That thought made her shudder. She should have taken the time to teach Blaze some basic capoeira moves the minute she arrived in Safe Harbor. Over the years, she'd taught dozens of young women how to protect themselves from evil men like Garcia. She just wished more of them had listened. Women like Joellen. The newspaper image of the girl flashed through her mind, but she shoved it away. She couldn't think about Joellen now. She had to get Blaze out of here.

She turned herself around far enough that her feet could touch the wall behind the bed and then started kicking. The pain in her bruised feet brought tears to her eyes, but she didn't stop. She kept it up until someone wrenched the door open.

"Cut it out!" Manuel hissed. "You do not want to wake the boss."

"Don't I?" Cat asked. She smiled.

Manuel muttered and started toward her.

"I want my violin."

He laughed. "And I want a million bucks. Doesn't mean I'll get it."

"Mr. Garcia likes it when I play my violin."

That gave him pause.

"I can't play for him if my shoulders are pulled out of joint."

He eyed the restraints, then glared at her before he walked out and locked the door behind him.

She nodded as he left. Now all she had to do was wait. And hope it worked.

———

Nick's mind spun as he drove to the station, trying to figure out if all this was connected somehow.

What was Monroe doing with those things? Why would he have held on to them for so long? If the chief had been involved in his long-ago kidnapping, why hang on to proof? Arrogance? Guilt? Or was the chief holding said proof over someone else's head?

None of that mattered right then.

Just as he sat down at his desk, his phone chirped with an email. He glanced down, surprised it was from Bev at the crime lab. That was fast. He opened it and froze.

With Captain Barry and the chief both missing, Nick had asked her to compare their DNA samples to the body found yesterday. She wrote that she knew there was a rush, so she'd gone ahead and run all the tests and compared all the results. She'd obviously worked through the night.

Based on DNA, the body was that of Captain Barry. He stopped, let that sink in for a few minutes. Why would someone kill Barry? None of it made sense.

He went back to his email. Bev had also run a DNA test on the water bottle filled with scopolamine found near Teddy's body.

What he read made him shake his head and squint, to be sure he had read it right. What was Chief Monroe's DNA doing on the water bottle? Had he somehow contaminated the evidence? Or had he killed Teddy? And if so, why? Nick shoved to his feet, paced. Monroe? That didn't make a lick of sense, either. What motive would he have for killing that young man?

Did Teddy's death have something to do with the things he'd found at Monroe's house? That seemed like a real long shot, but he couldn't ignore any possible connections, no matter how unlikely.

Still, none of this got him any closer to freeing Blaze and Cat.

He had to get them to safety. Now. He'd been a fool to let himself get so sidetracked.

He'd have to go onto Garcia's property without a warrant, since there was no way a judge would issue one based on Nick's hunch. It would probably cost him his badge, but that was cheaper than Cat or Blaze paying with their lives.

He tugged on his Kevlar vest, grabbed an extra rifle and ammo. He turned to JD. "I'm going back to Garcia's place. I think he's holding Cat and Blaze on his property somewhere."

JD stood, uncertain. "Did you get a warrant?"

"No time. But I want you to stay here."

JD grabbed his own vest, put it on. "I'm coming with you."

"No. You have a great future in law enforcement, kid. I don't want you to blow it today."

Nick's cell phone rang just as JD opened his mouth to argue. He scooped it up, noted the out-of-state area code. "Stanton."

"Good morning, Officer. This is Richard Wang. I've just received a call from Garcia. He says I should be on a small skiff, ready to leave my dock by eleven a.m. He will call with GPS coordinates."

"I'm sure he told you not to contact the police, so why are you calling me, Wang?"

"He did say that, yes. As I expected him to. But I also believe he plans to kill both Catharine and Blaze. I would like to prevent that."

Nick's blood chilled at the man's matter-of-fact tone. "You and me both, Wang." He paused. "You do know getting me involved means I'll arrest you at some point?"

Wang had the gall to laugh. "You can try, Officer. Others have. But right now, my greater concern is Catharine's safety. Will you help?"

Nick grabbed more ammo, running logistics through his mind. "Of course. Get the skiff ready. Are you going alone?"

"No, I told Garcia that Phillip would be at the tiller of the boat."

"OK, when he gives you the coordinates, call me immediately. I'll be on a boat standing by. We'll free them. Just follow my lead. We'll sort the rest out later."

"Consider it done."

Nick turned to see JD standing at his elbow, rifle in hand. "You sure?"

"I'm sure. What's the plan, boss?"

Nick looked him up and down, glanced at his watch. "How do you look in a dress?"

"What? I don't, ah . . ."

Nick couldn't help grinning at the expression on his face, then he sobered. "Garcia is setting up a meeting with Wang, out in the Gulf. We need to intercept them. We'll be a couple of clueless tourists. Go find a dress, hat, sunglasses, wig. Whatever it takes to turn you into a woman. You have forty-five minutes."

For a moment, JD simply stared, then he burst into motion. "Right. Got it, boss."

Wanda turned to JD. "Let me make a call. I can get you set up ASAP."

Nick looked from one to the other. "Let's do this."

Chapter 33

When the yacht's engines started, Blaze's heartbeat sped up. Where were they taking them? Were they going way out into deep water and then, like, planning to throw her and Cat overboard? Could Cat swim?

Blaze had gone fishing with Sal a time or two and had enjoyed the quiet, the peace out on the water. She could swim, a little. Probably enough not to drown. But if she were dumped in the middle of nowhere, she wasn't sure how long she would last.

Stop it. She couldn't think like that. She had to be smart. Cat was here, on the boat! She'd really come! Blaze felt a pang of guilt for doubting that she would, but then she pushed it away to deal with later.

Cat was keeping their captors off balance, no doubt planning something. Blaze had heard her yelling, and then she'd heard banging and angry words a little while ago.

She had to help, too. But how? What could she do? It wasn't like she had mad ninja warrior skills. She didn't have any skills, really, unless being a dork counted. She was good at that.

She looked around the stateroom. Considered. She was good with technology, and if she could get her hands on a phone, she could call Nick. He'd be able to lock into the GPS on the phone and find them.

Shouldn't be too hard. Except the "get a phone" part. She'd never been a particularly good pickpocket. Hadn't lifted a single thing since she arrived at the Martinellis' marina. But could she use that now to get help?

The boat picked up speed, and her stomach pitched slightly, then settled back down. At least she didn't get seasick.

She waited, heart pounding. How long before someone came to check on her?

It seemed like hours before one of them did. He walked in, glanced her way before setting a tray of food on the built-in dresser across the room. This was it. Her one chance. She almost sighed with relief. He'd made it easy for her. His cell phone was in a holder on his belt.

Without giving herself time to change her mind, Blaze leaped up from the bed and rammed the guy from behind, knocking him and the tray off balance. As they crashed to the floor, she swiped the phone from the holster and shoved it down the back of her jeans.

"What the—!" He scrambled to his feet and grabbed her by the arms. "What are you doing?" He glanced at the scattered contents of the tray. "Go hungry, then. See if I care."

He slammed the door on his way out.

Blaze fumbled the phone out and swiped to open it. "Please no password, please no password, please no—yes!" He hadn't used a password.

Heart pounding and eyes on the door, she quickly hit the location button to turn on the GPS, then typed in Nick's cell phone number.

"Stanton."

"It's Blaze. I'm on some scary guy's boat. It's moving. Cat is here, too."

"Good to hear from you, kiddo. How'd you get a phone? Does it belong to the scary guy?"

"Not his. One of his minions. I turned the GPS on."

"Good girl. Are you, ah, hurt?"

"No. I think Cat's OK, too. She was making a racket a while back." She listened. "Someone's coming."

"I'll be there soon. Stay tough, Blaze."

She didn't want to hang up, to lose the connection. But she wasn't stupid. She couldn't let them find the phone. She clicked end, stuffed it under the mattress, and hopped on the bed.

The door swung open, and she scrambled back against the headboard.

"Where's my phone?"

"What? What are you talking about?"

"You took my phone."

"Why would I do that? You must have dropped it somewhere."

He ignored her as he scanned the room and poked through the contents of the tray that littered the floor. He checked all the drawers but didn't find anything. As he came closer and closer to the bed, Blaze tried to keep her expression blank.

He searched both bedside tables and under the bed.

He reached over to frisk her, and she stiffened at the look on his face. But a shout from above had him rushing from the room. She didn't let out a breath until the door clicked shut behind him.

———

The minute Blaze hung up, Nick called Eloise at Blue Sky Cellular again and asked her to find the location of the number Blaze had given him.

"I'm sorry, Officer Stanton, but I cannot continue to do this."

Her stiff tone startled Nick. Someone must be listening. "No, ma'am. I wouldn't expect you to. But I'm trying to locate a missing teenager, and she just called from this number. I need to find her. I believe her life is in grave danger."

A pause. "Well, then. Just one moment." Nick heard her fingers flying over the keyboard. "Here is the current location. Though it seems to be moving west-northwest."

"Thanks so much, Eloise. I definitely owe you. I need to go rescue this young lady."

"Let me know she's all right, would you?"

He smiled. "You bet."

Behind him, JD hurried out of the men's room, a woman's beach cover-up flowing to the floor. Nick hid a smile at JD's red cheeks, especially when Wanda took one look at him and declared him "beautiful."

"Cut it out, Wanda. I feel ridiculous."

Nick studied the blonde wig, baseball cap, and dark sunglasses. "That'll work. The hat will keep the wig from flying off. You have your weapon?" He nodded to the straw tote bag slung over JD's shoulder.

JD nodded, suddenly serious. "Yes. And an extra clip. Plus a spare gun in an ankle holster."

"Then let's go." Nick led the way, wearing a Hawaiian shirt, plaid shorts, a fisherman's hat that covered most of his face, and a cheap pair of sunglasses. It wasn't much of a disguise. But he hoped it would be enough to get them close to Garcia's boat.

———

Cat didn't have to wait long to see if her plan worked. Several minutes later, Manuel opened the door, her violin case in one hand and a bunch of clothes in the other. "Let's go." He indicated the door.

She froze. "Go where?"

"Mr. Garcia wants you to take a shower, then put that dress on and play for him." He nodded toward the clothes he'd dumped on the bed, then grabbed her arm and marched her down the interior hallway.

"I'm not showering. Not with you there." She made sure her voice was loud, in case Blaze could hear her.

"Too bad. Orders are orders." He stopped at another stateroom and walked her through to the bathroom. "You can do it yourself or I can do it for you." He leered at her. "Your choice."

Cat decided not to bait him. She nodded and walked into the room.

"Just so you know. There's no way out of there, except past me."

Cat nodded and closed the door in his face, relieved when it locked. She took the world's fastest shower, not wanting to be caught in such a vulnerable position. She quickly dried off and put her stinky clothes back on, then let the goon lead her back toward her stateroom.

"Don't worry, Blaze! We're going to get out of here!" she yelled and got backhanded across her cheek for her trouble.

"Shut up," Manuel muttered, shoving her into the room. He slammed the door, and Cat leaned against it, heart pounding, cheek throbbing, until she heard his footsteps retreat.

She grabbed the clothing that had been left, scowling at the scanty underwear and slinky red dress, but put them on anyway. Now was not the time to show weakness.

As soon as she had the outfit on, she combed her hair and used the hair products and makeup.

Taking a deep breath, she pulled her violin out of the case and walked over to the porthole. Then, with apologies to her late mother, she started playing one of her favorite pieces, Charlie Daniels's "The Devil Went Down to Georgia."

Not only did the lively piece give her courage, but she figured Blaze would hear it, too. And since Garcia wanted her to play for him, hearing it might get her out of this room sooner. But most important, when Nick arrived—and she had no doubt he would—it would be easier for him to find them.

Chapter 34

When they reached the Safe Harbor Marina, Sal had a skiff gassed up and waiting for them. He glanced at JD's disguise and Nick's shirt, eyebrows raised. "You think this is going to work?"

"We think so, yes."

"Bring my girls home, Nick." Sal's expression showed his fear.

Nick understood. He was battling his own. "I plan to." He glanced at the house. "You keep Mama Rosa from worrying, OK?"

Nick's cell phone rang. Wang. "You get those coordinates yet?"

Wang rattled them off. "I'm heading there now. Do you have a plan?"

"I do. You'll have to trust me."

"Get her out of there, Stanton."

Nick didn't answer, just hung up and turned to JD. "Ready, Sally?"

He grinned, batted his eyelashes. "Ready, darling."

Nick burst out laughing, as did JD, dispelling some of the tension. "Let's get out there, then. It's showtime."

———

Blaze had her ear pressed to the wall, listening. Things were starting to happen, she could feel it. Cat had been yelling, and it sounded like she got slapped. Blaze hoped she wasn't hurt badly.

The door to her room suddenly opened, and the same guy walked in and dumped some clothes on the bed.

"Get dressed. Mr. Garcia wants you on deck in five minutes."

He closed the door, and Blaze picked up the clothes, wincing at what she saw. The whole outfit looked like it was bought at Hookers-R-Us. A thong, a teeny bra, and a blue slinky dress with a slit that would come almost to her hip. There was also a bag with makeup, deodorant, and a bunch of hair products.

She slipped into the dress, pretty sure Cat was going to be wearing something similar. Good thing there wasn't a full-length mirror. She really didn't want to know what she looked like. She decided not to think about what Garcia had planned, either, because that made her want to throw up. She had to stay focused and positive, ready to help Cat when the time came for them to escape. She didn't figure leaping off a yacht would be a good idea, but she was game, if that's what it took.

Nick would be here soon, too. She was counting on that. They just had to stay alive until then.

She struggled for calm as she paced the small room. This would all be over soon. *Please, God.*

———

Anxiety gnawed at Nick's gut. He was sitting at the stern, hand on the tiller, as they raced across the choppy waters of the Gulf. JD sat on the wooden bench in front of him, wincing as they bounced along. "Sorry, JD. It's windy today."

Nick kept his head down, hat pulled low, chin strap in place so it wouldn't blow off his head, gun at the ready. "Wang's boat is still on course, right?"

"Yes. They're approaching from the south. Going about the same speed we are. The yacht is still heading west-northwest."

Nick and JD had left the marina and caught up to the yacht in the channel, staying a nice, unobtrusive distance behind them. Now, they were almost past the end of the channel, where the water was deeper. That's where they'd make their move to intercept the yacht.

"Good. Once Wang is close enough to the port side, we'll swing in from starboard. But first, we need to do a little acting. You ready?"

JD nodded, his back ramrod stiff, one hand holding the brim of the ball cap against the wind.

"I'm going to zip around the yacht like we're going to pass, but then I'll collapse. Ready?"

Keeping his back to Nick, JD trained his eyes on Wang's boat. "They're almost there. Closing fast. And . . . go."

Nick made a show of clutching his chest and collapsing, just in case someone on the yacht was watching through binoculars. JD turned and grabbed the tiller, slowing the boat, then made a show of trying to do CPR on Nick.

After several minutes, Nick muttered, "Now," and JD took the tiller and raced over to the yacht. Once he got close to it, he started waving his arms, calling for help in a terrible falsetto. Nick winced, hoping the wind would distort it enough so this would work.

Nick heard a Charlie Daniels tune and let out a breath he hadn't realized he'd been holding. Cat was alive and playing her violin.

Fully in character, JD guided the skiff around to the starboard side where a boarding ladder was secured, and kept calling, "Help! My husband has collapsed, help me! Please!"

One of Garcia's men peeked over the side of the boat. "Go away."

JD brought the skiff closer yet and grabbed the bottom of the ladder. "My husband. Please, we need help."

"We don't have a doctor. Go back to the mainland. We can't help you."

"He'll die before then. Doesn't anyone know CPR?"

The music stopped. "I know CPR. I can help." Cat's voice was loud and confident, and it turned Nick's insides to ice. What was she doing?

He suddenly realized that she was trying to get them aboard. He moaned and clutched his heart, playing his part.

Before long, one of Garcia's men climbed down the ladder and hopped into the boat. He slung Nick over his shoulder as though he weighed nothing and climbed back up.

Once he was on board, the man dumped him onto the teak deck. Nick's moan was real this time. His eyes opened to the sound of two rifles, each chambering rounds.

Garcia stood over him, holding a cigar, smiling. "Welcome aboard, Officer Stanton." He watched as JD was dumped on the ground beside him. "Who is your lady friend?"

One of Garcia's men whipped off JD's hat and wig. He heard a muffled gasp and glanced up to see Cat and Blaze huddled together, wearing dresses more suited to ladies of the night.

"Get their weapons," Garcia said.

One of the men took Nick's gun and the knife on his belt, and then took the secondary piece he had strapped to his ankle. Beside him, they did the same to JD. "Gentleman, please join us." Garcia motioned toward the sectional sofa, where Wang already sat holding a drink, as though this were a social gathering.

Nick met Cat's eyes. *Are you OK?*

She nodded.

He inclined his head at Blaze.

Cat nodded again. They were both fine.

There was a commotion near the boarding ladder, and suddenly Chief Monroe strode into the middle of the group, gun in each hand. "Police. Drop your weapons."

Garcia laughed, and his men raised their rifles into position. Blaze moved closer to Cat, who whispered something in her ear.

Nick glanced over at Wang just in time to see a look pass between him and Chief Monroe. In that moment, one of his questions was answered. The two men were definitely working together.

Nick and JD exchanged a look, and Nick realized JD had seen it, too.

"You're not listening, Garcia. Tell your men to stand down," Monroe said.

As all eyes turned to Garcia, Nick and JD leaped up from the ground and lunged for Garcia's men.

Chapter 35

Cat had been watching Nick. The second he started moving, she pulled Blaze behind her, grabbed her hand, and prepared to make a run for it. She had to get the girl belowdecks and out of sight.

A gun fired and Cat took off, Blaze right on her heels. She didn't get far before Garcia lunged for her from out of nowhere. He grabbed her arm and yanked her back against him. Before Cat could react, he had his arm around her neck, a gun at her temple.

"Run, Blaze!"

Footsteps pounded on the teak flooring behind her, and she saw Blaze disappear down the aft stairs. *Good girl.*

"You'll not escape me this time, Catharine," Garcia muttered.

"That's what you think." She elbowed Garcia's midsection with all her might, then spun hard to break his hold. While he gasped for air, she jumped out of reach and turned, kicking his gun from his hand and sending it clattering across the deck. She ran after it but glanced up just in time to see her uncle fire his weapon at Garcia.

At the same time, Cat saw red bloom on her uncle's white shirt, the stain spreading as if in slow motion. She scooped up the gun and hurried over, saw him slump to the ground.

She heard another gunshot and glanced over her shoulder as Garcia collapsed on the ground.

Before she could figure out what to do next, Nick came flying at her and tackled her, shoving them both in the corner and covering her with his body.

Around them, more shots were fired, until finally everything went still.

Nick raised his head, gun in hand, and scanned the deck. "You OK?" he asked, but he didn't look at her, just kept scanning the scene in front of them.

Her heart pounded, her breath coming in short gasps. "Yes. But we've got to stop meeting like this."

He glanced down then, and that quick smile shot straight into her heart. "Don't move. I mean it."

He stood and slowly made his way to the first sprawled body, one of Garcia's men. He carefully moved the weapon out of reach. Did the same for the second man.

"JD? You and Blaze OK?" His voice was quiet.

"We're good."

Cat let out the breath she'd been holding and eased to her feet.

Though he glared when he saw her get up, he didn't say anything as he worked his way around the deck.

Cat hurried over to where her uncle lay on the white sofa and gasped at all the blood. She crouched down, checked his neck for a pulse, and sucked in a surprised breath when his eyes opened.

She looked around for a towel, saw one behind the bar, grabbed it, and pressed it to the wound in his chest. Behind her, she heard Nick talking to Florida Fish and Wildlife.

"I am not that easy to kill, Catharine," he said, smiling.

"Shh, don't talk. Help is on the way."

She glanced over her shoulder, saw that Nick was trying to stop the bleeding in Chief Monroe's chest, too. Garcia appeared to be dead, along with both of his men. She couldn't find it in her heart to feel bad about that.

As far from the carnage as possible, JD had both arms around Blaze, keeping her back to the scene on deck. She had to admire the protective way he held her.

"I would not have let Garcia have you, Catharine."

She snapped her eyes back to his, snorted. "Really? Because that's not what you've been saying."

"It was a test of your loyalty."

Cat couldn't believe her ears. This was some kind of crazy test? To what end? Before she could find words, he kept talking.

"I asked Nick to come rescue you. He is a good man, worthy. You are a daughter to me. You should have been mine. Be happy, Catharine." His eyes slid closed, and for a moment, Cat thought he'd died. But his chest continued to move up and down.

Cat's mind spun, trying to make sense of it all. Had he been in love with her mother? She couldn't begin to process that right now.

After what seemed like hours, but was probably only minutes, two Fish and Wildlife boats raced over. Two of the officers loaded Monroe and Wang into a boat and took off, while Nick and JD talked with the other FWC officers and the shaken captain and first mate, who had heard the gunshots but had not seen anything.

After Cat and Blaze had answered question upon question, Nick and JD finally took them back to the marina. The other bodies had been secured on the yacht as it headed for shore. The Fish and Wildlife vessel followed the yacht, which would be held as evidence.

Cat felt like she was watching everything happen from a distance. The only thing that seemed real was Nick's hand holding tight to hers the whole ride to the marina.

When they arrived, Sal and Jesse were waiting on the dock, and she and Blaze found themselves hugged until they couldn't breathe. Seeing tears run down Pop's cheeks as he embraced them would stay with her for a long time.

As they walked up to the house, Cat slung an arm around Blaze's shoulders. "You OK, kiddo?"

Blaze glanced back at JD, who gave her a shy smile as he lounged against Nick's police SUV. She turned toward Cat, who raised an eyebrow. "What? He's a nice guy."

"He's too old for you." Cat heard the words and almost laughed at herself. When had she become parental sounding?

Blaze rolled her eyes, then said, "Thanks for coming to get me." She looked over her shoulder at Nick, walking behind them. "Both of you. I knew you would."

Something in Cat's heart shifted, clicked into place. What if she'd left? But she hadn't. Today, she'd come through for the people she loved. That had to count for something. She pulled Blaze close for a hug, and for once, the teen didn't pull away.

More tears and hugs from Mama Rosa and Sasha for all three of them. Finally Nick turned to Cat. "Walk me out?"

She nodded and followed him across the porch, aware that the whole family was watching. They walked halfway to his truck before he stopped and pulled her into his arms, kissing her with a desperation that fueled her own. She'd almost lost him today. Had almost lost Blaze, too. Might have, if not for him.

"You were a complete idiot going after Garcia on your own. But I love you," he muttered.

She grinned against his lips and poured her love for him into the kiss. She loved him, too, without doubt or hesitation. But before she could work up the courage to tell him so, JD called, "Nick. We have to go."

He pulled back. Slowly. Reluctantly. Then he tucked her hair behind her ears, and his eyes cruised over the skimpy red dress she wore, lingering on all the interesting places. "You are beautiful, and you were amazing today. Would you—"

"Nick. Hospital. Now," JD said again.

"Hold that thought." He leaned in for a quick, hard kiss, and then he was gone.

Chapter 36

The Following Week

"Come on, Blaze. You can do better than that. Hit me like you mean it," Cat taunted. She and Blaze were facing each other, sparring in their favorite clearing, where Mama Rosa couldn't see them and get upset. Sweat dripped into their eyes, and Cat's muscles ached, but Blaze wasn't ready to stop yet, so Cat wouldn't, either. Blaze had asked Cat to teach her some basic capoeira moves, and Cat was making sure she kept her promise.

"You ready to call it a day?" Cat asked again a while later.

Blaze stopped, grinned. "Why, do you have a hot date?"

Cat smiled, raised an eyebrow. "As a matter of fact, I do, smarty-pants."

"Where is Nick taking you?"

"He didn't say." She looked down at herself. "But I'm thinking I should look a little better than this."

Blaze fisted her hands on her hips, tossed her hair. "Fine. Quit. See if I care."

Without warning, Cat swept Blaze's legs out from under her, and the teen landed on her butt in the sand. Blaze looked up at her, shocked, as Cat reached a hand down to help her up. "Don't ever get too confident, grasshopper."

"Sneaky," Blaze accused.

"Smart," Cat countered.

Grinning, they walked to the house, surprised to see Nick already there, talking with Mama Rosa on the porch. He was wearing jeans and a polo shirt, hair still wet from the shower. Her mouth went dry just looking at him.

"I'll, ah, just go get ready," she mumbled.

The look he sent her could have melted paint.

After one of the fastest showers ever, she hurried downstairs, wearing jeans, cowboy boots, and a cute little blouse she wasn't sure about until Nick caught sight of her and his eyes widened and his grin spread over his face like a slow southern drawl.

They were all on the porch now, Sasha and Mama Rosa in the rocking chairs, Pop, Jesse, Blaze, and Nick in the wicker furniture scattered here and there. Eve and Cole stood in the corner, arms around each other. They had just returned from their honeymoon, and their happiness glowed like an aura.

Nick looked over at the two of them. "I got a call today you'll both find interesting. A sheriff from a few counties north called to say they'd arrested a guy named Eddie Varga. Seems he was transporting a tractor trailer full of stolen cattle. Apparently, it wasn't the first time he's done it, either."

Cole straightened. "You mean he's the one who stole my cattle?"

"Not sure yet. But it's a possibly. I'll keep you posted."

Then Nick stood and turned to Sasha, cleared his throat. "So, ah, Sasha. I thought you might like to have these. For the little one." He reached behind his chair and placed a plastic sack in her lap. "I probably should have wrapped them, but . . ."

His voice trailed off and he looked so uncertain, Cat came up next to him and slipped her hand into his. He glanced her way, but all his focus was on Sasha and what she was pulling out of the bag.

Mama Rosa gasped, and her eyes flew to Nick's. "How did you find it?"

Nick hesitated.

Blaze looked from one to the other, confused. "What's the deal? It looks like an old blanket."

Nick turned to her with a smile. "It is an old blanket. Mine. One Mama Rosa knitted for me when I was a baby. I thought Sasha and Jesse might want it for the new arrival."

Cat met his eyes and smiled while Sasha swiped at her cheeks, then stood and hugged him. "Oh, Nick. Thank you. It's perfect."

"There's something else in there," he said.

Reaching into the bag, Sasha pulled out what looked like a hand-carved wooden boat.

Cat watched Nick, whose focus was on Pop. Nick smiled. "I remember the day you gave this to me. I thought we should keep it in the family." All the color drained from Pop's face, and he seemed to turn into himself. He didn't say a word, just slipped off the porch and headed toward his workshop by the marina.

They all fell silent for a moment. Pop would have to deal with his guilt in his own time, his own way. Chief Monroe had died in the hospital before Nick could get any more information out of him about his kidnapping.

Cat whispered, "It was the right thing to do. Hard but right. There are good memories inside the bad ones." She tugged on his hand, raised an eyebrow, and smiled, trying to lighten the mood. "Don't we have somewhere to be?"

He nodded, sent her a grateful smile. "We do. If you all will excuse us." Turning, he saw a box of stuff by the door leading from the porch, an empty tequila bottle on top. "What's this?"

Cat held up two of her wigs, several pairs of glasses. "The theater department at the high school said they'd love to have all these costumes."

They shared a look. He grinned as they walked out the door and to his truck.

After they'd gone a few miles and Nick still hadn't said anything, Cat asked, "Are you OK, Nick?"

"It's all a lot to process, you know?"

"Yeah, I know."

His eyes were sad. "I talked to Teddy's family. They're glad to finally have some closure. It's hard for them to come to terms with the fact that the police chief killed their son."

Cat shivered. "I still can't believe Monroe killed Teddy because he saw him shank Demetri. From what Blaze said, Teddy just stopped by the station that day to deliver some Little League forms for his dad."

"I know. But the chief couldn't let Demetri testify against him. Without Blaze remembering that conversation with Teddy and the security tape from the police station, we'd never have figured it out."

"What about Captain Barry?" She shuddered. "Do you know yet why he was killed?"

"From what we pieced together, he saw Monroe blow up my house and then tried to blackmail the chief. Not sure if there was more to it than that, but we found some threatening texts to Monroe on his phone."

"So Monroe killed him, too? That's crazy. I can't believe he got away with so much evil over the years."

"People often see what they want to see, especially in small towns." He paused, uncertain.

"What?"

"Your uncle . . . ," he began.

Cat's heart skipped a beat. She didn't really want to think about him. She'd gone by the hospital to see him, but when she'd gotten there, she hadn't known what to say, so she left. He'd covered up Daniel's death. But he was family. How was she supposed to reconcile that? She held her breath. "What about him?"

"He's gone."

She sucked in a breath. "What do you mean, gone? You mean he died?"

"No. He disappeared."

"From the hospital. Where he was chained to the bed and under guard?"

Nick scrubbed the back of his neck. "Right."

"You wouldn't know anything about that, would you?"

Nick glanced at her, eyebrow raised. "I told him I planned to arrest him."

Cat smiled. "Of course you did." Then she sobered, swallowed hard. "He and Garcia got away with Daniel's death. I should have found a way to make them pay. I'll regret that until the day I die."

Nick took her hand. "No regrets, Cat. You saved Blaze. And from what Walt said, you saved lots of other girls over the years. Daniel would be proud of you. He'd want you to stop doing penance and live. Do the things he never got to do."

Cat absorbed his words, letting them sink in as tears slid down her face. Nick was right. It was time to let her friend go. *Oh, Daniel. I wish you'd gotten to grow up. What a wonderful man you would have been.*

She brushed the tears from her face and glanced around, realizing they were in a quiet neighborhood on the outskirts of Safe Harbor. Nick pulled up to a small white 1940s cottage that fit right into the neighborhood. "Why are we here?"

"I'm considering buying this place, and I want to know what you think."

Cat looked at him, but his expression was unreadable. He came around and opened her door, then led her up the brick walkway and into the house. The white walls were freshly painted, the polished wood floors gleamed. Multiple windows filled it with light. "It's beautiful, Nick."

He led her through the kitchen and dining room, then down the hallway, past two bedrooms and a bath. At the end of the hall, he opened another door.

She walked into another bedroom and stopped short. Like the rest of the house, this room was completely empty—except for the music stand in the middle of the floor.

She looked over her shoulder at him.

Shrugging, he seemed endearingly uncertain. "I thought maybe this would be a good place for you to practice."

Sasha had contacted everyone she knew and a few she didn't, and now Cat had an audition with the Orlando Philharmonic Orchestra in two weeks, an opportunity she was almost afraid to hope for. "I don't know if I'll get in."

"I know you will. But even if you don't, you'll need a place to practice."

They moved closer. "What are you asking, Nick?"

He took both her hands, tugged her closer, his eyes filled with emotion. "I love you, Cat. Marry me. Build a life here. With me."

Temptation crooked its finger and beckoned. Could she stay here, in this little town? Where everyone knew everyone? She smiled so wide her cheeks hurt. How could she not, when she had this man's love and the love of her family?

After all the years of running, Cat Martinelli was home.

She cupped his cheeks, blinked back a tear. "I love you, too. Yes, I'll stay. And yes, I'll marry you."

He let out a whoop and pulled her into his arms, spun her around in circles before lowering her to her feet.

She sighed. "I guess I'll have to go back to the DMV, get my license redone yet again."

At his puzzled expression, she pulled out her new driver's license and handed it to him. It listed her name as Catharine Wang.

He laughed, and their lips met in the most delightful of kisses.

As he pulled her close, and her love for him filled her senses, Cat could have sworn she heard Daniel laugh and her mother playing the violin in the background.

ACKNOWLEDGMENTS

I am ever grateful for the wonderful team of people who work so hard to bring my stories to life.

Amanda Leuck, encourager, savvy businesswoman, and agent extraordinaire—thank you for employing your mad skills on my behalf.

Sheryl Zajechowski, Erin Mooney, Gabby Trull, and the entire Waterfall team—you all are such a pleasure to work with, and I so appreciate everything you do.

Leslie Santamaria, critique partner and amazing friend—thanks, always, for riding this crazy roller coaster called life with me.

Thanks to writer friends Jan Jackson and Lena Diaz for all the encouragement, and to Debi Maerz, artist and dear friend, for pushing me to make Cat's story the best it can be. My thanks to Scott Mitchell for the information about scopolamine and Doris Neumann for always being willing to listen.

I couldn't do this without Harry, awesome husband and encourager, who gamely picks up my slack and eats way too much insta-food when I'm on deadline. Or without my children, who always cheer me on.

My heart is humbled that the Great Creator gives us the gift of stories.

And I am thankful for you, dear readers, who invite my stories into your life. Thank you all.

ABOUT THE AUTHOR

Photo © 2015 Michele Klopfenstein

Connie Mann is a licensed boat captain and author of the romantic suspense novels *Hidden Threat* and *Tangled Lies* in the Safe Harbor series, as well as *Angel Falls*, *Trapped!*, and various works of short fiction. She has lived in seven different states but has happily called warm, sunny Florida home for more than twenty years. When she's not dreaming up plotlines, you'll find "Captain Connie" on Central Florida's waterways, introducing boats full of schoolchildren to their first alligator. She is also passionate about helping women and children in developing countries break the poverty cycle. She and her hubby love traveling and spending time on the water with their grown children and extended family. (Hubby says they are good at fishing but lousy at catching.) Visit Connie online at www.conniemann.com.